DON'T FORGET ME

EDEN EMORY

NOTE

This is a work of fiction. Names, characters, business, events and incidents are the products of the author's imagination. Any resemblance to actual persons, living or dead, or actual events is purely coincidental.

Before moving forward, please note that the themes in this book can be dark and trigger some people. The themes can include but are not limited to; BDSM, stalking, flogging, knife play, abandonment, murder, gore, PTSD, severed limbs, voyeurism, blindfolding, handcuffs, branding, dubious consent, "watching you while you sleep", mutual masturbation, degradation, and self harm/unhealthy coping mechanisms through sex and pain.

If you need help, please reach out to the resources below.

National Suicide Prevention Lifeline
1-800-273-8255
https://suicidepreventionlifeline.org/

National Domestic Violence Hotline
1-800-799-7233
https://www.thehotline.org/

BEFORE YOU CONTINUE

This is not an accurate portrayal of the BDSM community, if you are curious and what to learn more please conduct your own research and do not rely on what you find in this book as accurate knowledge of the BDSM community, their etiquette, and their ways. Things in this book have been dramatized and are not an accurate reflection of reality or my personal thoughts and opinions on these matters.

ALSO BY EDEN EMORY

EDEN EMORY

ELLE MAE

Winterfell Series Box Set

Short and Smutty:

The Sweetest Sacrifice: An Erotic Demon Romance

Nevermore: A Deal with a Demon

PATREON ONLY

Wicked corruption: An FF Mafia Romance

Watch Me

Tales of the Stolen Demon Brides

For person in my IG dms who suggested teacher x student. This probably is not what you had in mind, but I had a blast and I hope you will too.

WILLOW

I hated when things were outside my control. It was painful at times. Especially when it was my own emotions that I couldn't control.

It reminded me too much of how my life felt before the crash. The fear, anxiety, and phantom pain from my scar swirled around my body until it was too much to ignore. I tried not to think of it too much, but the memories of it were like ghosts constantly looking over my shoulder.

The crash materialized in my life in the weirdest ways.

Some of the trauma was woven into my paintings. Others needed a more... *thorough* handling.

The paintings were obviously the healthiest way to deal with the emotions swirling inside of me, but sometimes it wasn't enough. Sometimes if left untreated, the emotions would eat me up at night until the early morning sunrise peeked through my curtains.

It had been years since I had my first encounter with someone with an affliction for pain.

Sometimes I held on to those memories with all my might, hoping they could bring me out of the spiral of emotions, but since then, I had found it hard to trust anyone for fear of what they would do with it once they had it.

After all, I wasn't asking for some quick fling. I was looking to fall into complete submission. To let them play me like an instrument. To force all the violent emotions to come bursting forth.

For a while, I had found solace in my career. It was something to focus on other than whatever hid in the darkness, but then that, too, started to make me feel things.

Sex helped sometimes. Made the big feelings feel all that less daunting. Sometimes, if the orgasm was good enough, it would guarantee days of sleep. But other times, like *that* night, it did nothing to satiate me.

The first night I visited Club Pétale marked a year of sleepless nights with a vibrator in hand while listening to audio erotica. It was only a few weeks later when I decided to take a plunge and sign up for their matching services.

I was chasing the memories of the only person who had helped me realize what I truly needed.

Pain.

Logically, I knew I should do something else. Seek help, maybe. But the voice in the back of my head was louder than any of the rational thoughts were.

Too quickly after visiting, the fantasies started. I had fantasized about being fucked into oblivion, being at the mercy of whoever it was, all while they flogged my ass or choked me out. I imagined how it would feel to be in total submission to them. To finally be able to let go of everything inside me.

... and most importantly, to be taken care of while I was in that state.

These were fantasies that I had never dared act out with anyone else. Even in my little experience with pain, my fantasies had never veered this far. I had been worried about Club Pétale being able to accommodate them, but from the first showing, I knew that I had come to the right place.

On the night of my match, I had signed up to visit their newest club in Norwich, one that I hadn't visited before, but it was closer to the place I had been renting. It wasn't far from the border between New Jersey and New York, so I didn't mind the trip.

It had taken me all day to psych myself up enough to even get the taxi to the club. A part of me was giddy with excitement, but the other part was worried that I would be met with the disgusted looks of whoever I was matched with.

Club Pétale matches would always see who they were paired with before it was made, so they should have known what I wanted, but it didn't stop me from overthinking everything.

I was surprised when we pulled up. The other club was placed in a neighborhood among other big houses and if you didn't know about it, you probably wouldn't have known there was a club there to begin with. But with this one, there was no hiding what it was.

The entire place had been gated off and there were cars lining the road it took to get up to the property. I had asked the driver to drop me off at the end of the winding drive and walked up to the call box at the gate.

My legs shook as I made my way up the hill and while I should have been chilled, I was so nervous that my body was uncomfortably warm. I clutched my small bag to my side. There was nothing in it but a mask and my cell phone, but it was the only thing weighing me down to the earth.

I didn't even have to press the button before the gates opened.

"Mask on," the crackly voice from the other side of the intercom demanded.

I jumped at the sudden noise and put on my mask with shaky hands.

The mask was new but cheap. I bought it from the place that normally sold my sex toys after being accepted into the club.

It was one of their rules, apparently.

A stupid one given that my hair would probably be recognizable from miles away.

The deep-auburn hair that had been passed down from my grandmother had been a blessing and a curse my entire life.

But it's not like it's an issue if anyone knew you came here.

Or at least that's what I tried to tell myself. Though admittedly, I'm sure Princeton would be rather peeved that a professor of theirs would have a double life. One that involved getting fucked until they couldn't move a muscle. Though there were many other things swirling around my mind that they would be appalled to learn of.

But this was before I even officially started my position. Before this, I had been working my ass off to get a professor spot and had been assisting for most of my time there.

I couldn't get in trouble before I officially started... could I?

With that thought, I rolled my shoulders and straightened my skintight dress. The lingerie underneath was suddenly uncomfortably tight. I took a deep breath before walking straight into the club with my head held high.

The club itself was a masterpiece.

Every wall was decorated with beautiful erotic photographs that caused a low buzz to run through my body.

The people here were kind and helped me out with a tour of the place before they showed me to my room.

On the outside, the place looked like a mansion, but on the inside, it was even more breathtaking. Golds, blacks, and whites were splashed around the interior. People were dressed in nice, expensive-looking clothing and while there were a few people getting it on in the corners, many people were just there mingling.

I caught sight of the various showrooms and exhibition halls, but I didn't linger on them too long. Maybe it was the presence of the girl who was showing me around that caused the sudden bout of shyness, but I didn't like her calculating stare when she watched me take in the people on display.

By the time she had shown me up to the halls where I would

meet my match, there was a low and uncomfortable heat that settled in my belly.

I had never been a voyeur, but this club was making me rethink things about myself.

The girl left me in front of the door with a cheerful, "have fun!" and I was alone again.

Though for the first time that night, I thought that maybe I had chosen the right place when I sought out what I wanted. Even through my nervousness, I could tell that the club was clean, welcoming, and had their shit together.

I didn't know what I expected when I walked into the room, but it sure as hell wasn't seeing an already half-naked woman tying ropes to the dark hardwood headboard. It had been designed with closed hooks sticking out of them, sturdy ones by the looks of it.

The room itself was dim and a bit lackluster. There was a large bed in the middle of the room with dark satin sheets. There was a trunk in front of the bed that was open and showing me all the delicious toys that were inside.

There was a room off to the side, which I guessed was the bathroom. A soft red carpet was placed under the bed but didn't reach the entrance, so the clacking of my heels against the hardwood sounded throughout the room. The windows behind the bed had been shuttered off and allowed for the utmost privacy.

In other words, it was perfect for what we were about to do.

The woman turned to me and all the fake confidence I had mustered melted right off of me and seeped into the floor.

Jesus Christ, she's hot.

She had dirty-blonde hair that fell around her face in light waves and striking blue eyes. The soft yet cocky smile she wore caused a jolt of heat to go through me. She didn't bother with a shirt, but I had to mute my shock when I saw the mastectomy scars that ran across where her breasts should have been. She didn't bother with getting her nipples grafted on again. There was a tattoo on her chest, but her sudden movement caused my eyes to jerk back up to her face.

"Eva, right?" she said with a tone so warm it caused my cheeks to heat. She stopped what she was doing and began to cross the room. The action snapped me out of my daze and I closed and locked the door behind me without taking my eyes off her.

The fake name was also a must, one that I didn't particularly enjoy. It was right behind the "confiscating cell phones" on my list of things I didn't like about the club.

But after seeing *her*, the list of things I liked was growing longer by the second.

"Yes," I said with a forced smile. "I didn't know you could take off the masks in the rooms."

She stopped in front of me and held out her hand. An oddly formal gesture for someone who was about to rail me into an inch of my life. I took that moment to take all of her in.

She stood tall with her chin up and kept the smile on her lips. I was careful not to look her directly in the eyes. There was a cockiness to her, but her shoulders were relaxed and her body slightly slouched.

She wasn't the least bit nervous.

I hesitantly grabbed her hand. It was rough on contact, something I liked far too much. When our eyes met, the tension in the room became so hot I froze to the spot.

Her eyes narrowed, and her lips dropped slightly. The cockiness was still there, but there was something else lingering under that darkening gaze of hers. Something like... desire with a hint of danger.

She looked like she was about to eat me alive, and I desperately wanted nothing more

I blinked quickly and forced my eyes to her chest, trying to get ahold of the nervousness that started to flutter up inside me. I realized then that the words scrawled over her heart were not a tattoo at all but a branding.

Images of her gritted teeth, skin slick with sweat, all while her hands were being held behind her back as she was branded, filled my mind. I heard people did something like this in the BDSM scene, but this was my first time witnessing it in person.

"I technically work here, at least for a bit longer and employees are not required to wear them." She leaned forward, brushing her lips across the shell of my ear. "I won't tell anyone if you take off yours either."

The sultriness of her words caused shivers to run through my body. We had been in the room together mere minutes, she barely touched me, and I was more affected by her than I had been by anyone in my life.

It caused an uneasy feeling to rise in my chest and that was *not* what I came here for.

"Balloon," I blurted.

She froze and pulled back. I looked back up at her, and my face became unbearably hot. She raised a single brow.

"The safe word," I clarified. "It's balloon. Or three taps on whatever body part of yours I can reach if I am unable to speak."

Her eyes lit up, and a slow, almost feral smile spread across her face.

"Your profile said you were into breath play," she said. "I like to save that for last though, so maybe a gag?"

Her fingers hovered over my lips before pausing. I realized quickly that she was asking for consent to continue.

"We can start now," I said and kicked off my uncomfortable heels. The hardwood floor was cold against my nylon stockings. "Gags are okay. You can touch me anywhere though I would like to take it slow on anal for tonight. Other than that, I don't want you to go easy on me tonight." I paused when I tried to reach behind me to pull the zipper on my dress, but it was just out of reach. I met her hooded gaze and without me having to signal, her rough hands were on my back, helping me with the zipper.

"Impatient," she said as if annoyed, but the smile on her face told a completely different story. It caused my heart to skip a beat.

All the dark thoughts and emotions that had been plaguing me the last few nights disappeared, and I was left with a low buzz of excitement traveling throughout my body. The heat from her body sank into me and caused goose bumps to break out across my skin.

"To the point," I countered with a smile of my own. I kept her gaze as she pushed my dress off my shoulders, causing it to fall into a heap on the floor. "And horny."

"I love that in a woman," she breathed and wrapped her arms around me. "I can't wait to break you."

"You can try," I countered again with a smirk.

Before I could blink, her lips were on mine, and she was hoisting me to the bed.

"Is that all you can manage?" Avery said breathlessly as her hand tightened in my hair. "You're going to have to work harder than that if you want to earn your orgasm."

I let out a pained whimper as I licked the length of her cunt.

My hands were tied behind my back and I was forced into a position between her legs. There was an egg-like vibrator on its lowest setting inside me that had a thin hook-like arm that sent vibrations straight to my clit. Avery had the controller and would speed up or decrease it depending on how well I obeyed her.

Though in the little time I had spent with Avery, she had proven to have a malicious streak and had yet to let me come even once the entire time we had spent together. I hated it as much as I loved it.

I latched myself to her clit and sucked hard, pulling a moan from her. Like me, Avery seemed to have an affinity for pain, so I made sure to suck and nibble on the sensitive flesh until she was writhing under me.

She had come three times already, but I worked just as hard for the next one as I did the first. Seeing her come was intoxicating. She would ride my face, chasing her orgasm with little to no regard for me. And took what she wanted with an ironclad fist. Even in the throes of pleasure, she didn't allow her control to slip for even one second.

"Fuck yes, just like that," she moaned, pulling at my hair so hard it sent spikes of pain. "Good girl. I'm so close."

She upped the speed of the vibrator, but I couldn't let it distract me, not even when it caused my pussy to clench so hard around it that I was sure I'd come on the spot.

"Don't you dare come," she warned when a groan spilled from my mouth. She had learned my cues so quickly I almost cursed myself for being so easy to read.

Her naked thighs clenched around my face and before I knew it, she was coming with a low groan. I couldn't stop myself from licking every drip of her orgasm from her folds. She could have told me to stay between her legs the entire night and afterward, I would have thanked her. Her taste was delicious on my tongue.

That and I loved just how easy it was to get me to bend for her. With others, I could always sense a bit of hesitancy when they tried to order me around in the bedroom and it was a straight turnoff. But her? It was like she was made for this role.

She oozed confidence and knew exactly what she wanted.

The hand that was buried in my hair forced me back abruptly, only for her to crash her lips to mine. She pushed us to the side of the bed with urgency.

"Over my knee," she growled against my lips.

I scrambled to get situated as she sat on the edge of the bed. The position was familiar to me after so many times now.

I sucked in a harsh breath as she massaged my already sore ass.

"I think I'll let you come soon," she murmured and turned the vibrator up to the highest speed. The sound of toys rustling behind us caused my entire body to freeze. "Ready to try the one with weights?"

I nodded and was delivered a swift but stinging slap to my ass by her hand.

"Words."

"Yes!" I cried. "Please!"

"Good," she muttered. "Let's see how long it takes you to come. Given the last time, I'm guessing three times. Let's test that, shall we?"

I didn't have time to speak as she used the flogger to smack the meaty parts of my upper thighs. This one had leather strips with the lightest of weights on the end. It was a powerful hit, but unlike the ones with strips alone, it felt like more of a hard thumping rather than sharp slices of pain.

The pain and pleasure mixed so violently that when I opened my mouth to scream, no sounds came out. I had been denied an orgasm over and over again, but all of those lost ones seemed to be creeping up on me at a dizzying pace.

I was so wet that the next hit from the flogger stung far more. I arched into her, crying out as the wave of my first orgasm started to rise in me. She gave me no reprieve and instead of pulling away and letting me ride it out, she continued to flog me.

Each smack of it against my ass stole my breath from me. I was gasping for air by the time the orgasm had subsided, but just like she promised, she was nowhere near done. Quickly she undid my hands and pushed me back against the bed.

Toys were scattered on the bed around me and with ease, she pulled out the still-on vibrator and threw it across the room.

"Three taps," she reminded.

Her flushed yet excited face covered my line of sight. She reached past me to grab the wand with a bulbous head and forced it against my clit.

"Avery. Please, I need to—"

Her hand closed around my throat and cut off all air to my lungs.

"You're so perfect," she cooed. "Every *single* part of you. I could easily get addicted to the way you feel around me."

My body was shaking from the violent vibrations of the toy and I knew I was going to come far faster than I ever had in my life. As a stranger, her words shouldn't have had such an effect on me, but the praise caused a burst of satisfaction to flow through me and only aided in pushing me violently over the edge.

"We won't be done here until I have fucked you so thoroughly that I'll ruin you for everyone else," she murmured. "You'll never think of anyone else. Every time your hands wander between your legs, you'll remember the feeling of me between them. The taste of me on your tongue. You won't be able to get enough."

And true to her words, she did ruin me.

But after multiple orgasms and the best sex of my life, this would be the last time I would visit her.

AVERY

There was something cathartic about walking in the middle of the night with bloodstained hands and the smell of gunpowder still stuck to your clothing.

The air had a chill in it, but I barely felt it. The heat from the adrenaline and exertion of my body as I cornered those two FBI agents were still carousing through my veins.

A smile tugged at the corner of my lips and a sort of crazed giggle pierced the night air.

Those fuckers had no idea what they were getting themselves into.

They tried to snoop around my house, not knowing that I had put time and money into getting a security system that would alert me to their every move. I would have to have words with whoever had given them a key in the first place, but that was over now.

This place was supposed to be a new start. A new home while I hid away from my father's influence. But now that I killed the two agents and set the house ablaze, I seriously doubt they would let up anytime soon.

But that was okay.

Once Father found out, he would send men to find me as well and when they undoubtedly ran into whoever was following me, a bloodbath would ensue. It would give me just enough time to escape and hopefully not run face-to-face into my father's men.

He was still pissed that I hacked into his bank account and siphoned over thirty million dollars for a Manhattan penthouse. To anyone else, that may have been a blow, but because of his work, he didn't even notice until I had already vacated the premises for my newest obsession.

A thrill ran through me when I weaved through the dark trees. The houses here were spread out much farther than in the city and allowed me to hide in the shadows of the greenery. The warm-yellow light of the house just beyond the line of trees was inviting, but I made sure to stay out of its reach.

Peering from behind a tree, I could make out the back bay window that gave me an unobstructed view into the kitchen. I had lost count of the times that I had stood out in the cold and peered into this house.

Even before stepping foot into the surrounding area, I had pulled up all the information I needed about it. Owned by an elderly lady that was currently retiring with her husband in Florida while she rented out the place to students.

Princeton University was not far... if you had a car at least. The cheap rent had made this place a hub for multiple students to get together and rent out all three of the rooms, but that had changed earlier this year when a single resident took over the place.

Willow Evens, granddaughter to the owner, had moved in after trying—and failing—to find an apartment in her price range that was also conveniently located next to the university.

But if the stack of boxes on the countertops held any indication of her future, she was about to move out.

My breath caught in my throat as a familiar flash of deep-auburn hair showed just beyond the door that led out of the kitchen and to the rest of the house.

Willow.

She was wearing a threadbare tank top that showed her midriff and gray sweatpants that hung low on her hips. The single silver locket that she wore nonstop shone in the dim light and complemented her tanned skin.

Her eyebrows were pulled tight as she looked over the mess of boxes in her kitchen. Her full lips formed a pout. The urge inside me to brush my fingers across them was enough to cause my head to spin.

I reached for the closest tree next to me, my fingers digging into the bark. A powerful wave of need burst through me. With all the adrenaline and anger running through me from the earlier fight, I had trouble staying in my carefully picked hiding spot.

I watched her pack with a burning impatience.

By the upcoming weekend, she would have fully moved out of this house and to an apartment that was less than half its size, but it was closer to the university and she would no longer have to drive.

It hadn't taken me long to realize that she enjoyed walking. I was not sure about her aversion to driving, but I was sure I could find it without much hassle.

After all, I had found out everything else in a matter of hours. But I couldn't bring myself to care about finding this tidbit of information.

Or maybe it was that it would be more thrilling to find out in person. After all, I would be joining her soon.

Willow paused when she noticed the note I had left earlier this morning when I had stopped by. I hadn't planned to be here when she opened it, but when her face shifted to one of terror and then quickly to a type of morbid curiosity, I was glad those fuckers made their way into my house.

She looked out into the darkness, her eyes rolling over where I was hidden. Even though I knew she couldn't see me, it didn't stop the pounding of my heart in my chest.

She reached for the note and when she opened it, I caught the sickening excitement flashing across her eyes.

It had been the same one I saw when I had her bound and gagged at Club Pétale as I forced her to beg me for an orgasm after denying her one for hours on end. I knew deep inside she wanted to be controlled. That's why she requested me.

And ever since then, I had been unable to get her out of my mind.

It couldn't have come at a better time.

I had written the note by hand and picked the lock to the back door to slip it in. It was almost laughable how easy it was. I wanted so desperately to know what she was thinking, but I knew already I had let myself grow too comfortable.

I turned back and started the long walk to the university, where a dorm was waiting for me under a fake name.

I couldn't help the excitement that ran through me because in just a few days' time, I would see her again.

I've missed you, Professor Evens.
Hope you haven't forgotten about me just yet.

WILLOW

Rough hands caressed my body, pulling violent shivers from me. Pain and pleasure mixed, leaving me gasping as Avery pulled away from me.

I let out a whine when she grabbed my face roughly and forced me to look her in the eyes.

"Don't tell me you're already giving in?" she teased.

She forced her fingers into my mouth, pulling it open before leaning forward and—

Books being slammed onto the desk I was sitting at caused me to jump in my seat. I clasped my hand over my mouth to stop the shriek from spilling out.

I looked up to catch a smirking Daniel. His green eyes were lit up and his brown hair tousled around his head, making it look like he had just come from a make-out session.

His button-up shirt and deep-navy vest were slightly undone and untucked from his pants. Giving me the impression that maybe he *was* in the closet with one of the teachers.

I took a deep breath to slow my racing heart.

It had been months since I had last visited the sex club, but still, Avery had taken over my mind. Just like she had promised, just that single time with her had been enough to ruin me. I couldn't stop thinking about it. When I could sleep, I couldn't stop dreaming. And daydreaming as well, evidently enough.

I was supposed to be preparing the syllabus for my upcoming class that started in just a few days. It was already done, but my anxiety caused me to look over it again. I had been in my office for hours, and I hadn't gotten any further than the first few paragraphs because images of our time together kept flashing through my mind. I had tried watching porn. Tried all the toys I could find, but nothing had given me the rush of being with her. And nothing chased away the thoughts, either.

"Did I interrupt something?" he asked, his voice oozing with insinuation.

My body wanted to flush and embarrassment rose in me so quick I almost lost my mask. I kept my face straight and let an easy smile spread across my lips.

"Looks like maybe I interrupted something," I teased back while making a show of trailing my eyes down his form. "You don't have to pick me up, you know. If you want to get laid instead, you can do that."

"Who said I didn't?" he countered.

I couldn't help a laugh. Daniel was someone I met during my time assisting at Princeton. I knew he was older than me, though I never made a point to ask.

He had been a teacher here for a long time—or at least that's what the students said—and had been the one to recommend me for this position.

Without him, I probably wouldn't have gotten it, especially with such little experience and a shit résumé.

I was drawn to him instantly. He was carefree and easygoing, something I couldn't relate to. But he had a really bad habit of making his way through the faculty and teachers here. On more than one occasion, I had walked into his office to see him with someone either on top or under his desk.

I was envious of how easily he picked up women.

"Well, it could have lasted at least..." I made a show of looking at my nonexistent watch. "Five extra minutes. Given that's about the time it takes you to walk me to my new apartment." I gave him a look. "You don't have to keep doing that, y'know? It made sense when I lived at the bigger house, but they moved me *two weeks* ago."

His smile fell for just a moment. It was so fast I almost didn't catch it.

"Maybe I just want to spend more time with you," he said, though we both knew it was a lie. Because the last time I was there, I forced him to help me move out everything as soon as I spotted a carefully folded note in my kitchen.

It was the first and last so far. The notes seemed innocent, and at first, I had to admit it kind of intrigued me, but then the anxiety started kicking in. The worry that no matter how much I locked up or took precautions that someone could get into the house started to overwhelm me... so I called him for help.

The next day we were moving boxes into his car and to the apartments next to the university.

I quickly gathered my papers, my purse, and my jacket, then stood.

"Sure you're not going to join me tonight?" I asked.

"You know I don't fuck with galleries," he said with an almost exasperated tone. I had lost count of how many times I asked him, but I made it a point to ask every time there was a chance. I didn't have many friends and I would have liked to share this with him. "I couldn't care less about all of that. No offense to you."

I rolled my eyes at him. Daniel was a computer engineer. Had the brains and the looks to back up his overconfident personality. I guess it was part of his appeal, but he had an obvious lack of respect for the arts, and at times, it would grate on my nerves.

He and my previous professor, the one that whose position I was taking over, were friends. Though I had no idea how. My previous professor was really stuck up and thought that there was a single way in which a gallery was curated. For someone in the arts, he proved to be really stuffy and I was almost glad that the opportunity for me to take over for him showed up so suddenly.

"You couldn't offend me if you tried," I said with a smile. "Now let's go. I plan to pregame before I show up."

"Oh, so it's *that* kind of party," he said with a chuckle and swung his arm over my shoulders as we walked out of the office. "Maybe I will join."

I leaned into him, enjoying the warmth, but even after his teasing, he wouldn't take me up on the offer to go to the gallery.

The gallery was near the border of New Jersey and New York and was one of the newer ones with up-and-coming artists from all different genres and walks of life.

Even though I taught art history and exhibition design, this will be the first time in real life that I would actually be able to contribute to an exhibit... and even that only happened because of connections I knew deep down that I was riding on a constant wave of luck. For the most part, there weren't many things that I was good at, but for this moment, I allowed myself to be excited about what I'd done.

I wasn't able to design a big part of the gallery, but I was working with an artist for a specific exhibition that took over the back few corners of the gallery. It was nothing crazy. The person was new. But it was a start. And it was something that I could show my students that I hoped they would be proud of.

And hopefully, it made them realize that maybe I wasn't such an impostor.

Though it all hinged on if anyone purchased the artwork tonight. Half of the work was done by the artist, the other by the gallerist. If her photographs were too far in the back, in some dim corner somewhere, it was unlikely that they would sell. I had done my best to work with the other gallerists here, but because of the types of photos we were showing... people were less than willing to work with us.

Though when I was younger, I wished for my paintings to be shown in a gallery like this. But I knew deep inside that no one would ever want *my* art in a place like this.

So I would have to settle for second best.

"Willow!" a familiar voice yelled through the gallery. It had a light, almost singsong tone to it that would have caused even the grumpiest of people to smile.

The place was more packed than I thought it would be, with couples dressed up in fancy clothing and a few people that looked like they probably were famous in the scene with how people flocked to them. I had caught a glimpse of the artist list, but none of the people on it were familiar to me. Maybe it was a sign that I needed to learn more about the space, especially with people like *this* here.

If we were lucky, maybe one of them would see something in Lillian's art.

Their murmurs filled the space with a low buzz, but the yell of my name caused them to quiet just enough to make me uncomfortable. I may not have been good at much, but I knew that I was good at bullshitting. So I quickly fixed my face, turned around with a smile bigger than I could realistically manage and met my friend head-on.

Lillian. Her curly hair bounced with each step and she strutted up with a confidence that I only wish I had. She had her camera in hand and wore a dress that fitted her curves.

Lillian and I met through the gallery owner. He and his wife had apparently been opening up a bunch of them across New York and New Jersey and were looking for some new talent to bring along with them.

I guess you could say this was my trial run.

But they would have never given me a chance if it wasn't for how cozy they had become with my previous professor. I had been riding off of his name for what seemed like years now and it left a bitter taste in my mouth.

Even after meeting with them multiple times, I had no idea what they did outside of these galleries... until I met Lillian. She was also new in the scene and hadn't had her work shown in many galleries. Of course, I asked why, not being able to keep my curiosity to myself. The three of them looked at me with a kind of sheepish expression and explained that it was because Lillian mainly dabbled in erotic photography in the queer BDSM scene specifically.

I don't want to admit how excited that made me when I first heard about it, but I overall thought it would be tame until I saw her pictures. I expected some tasteful nudes, maybe some chains and collars close up, a hand on a throat, or in a mouth. But Lillian had an eye to capture people in their most vulnerable and pleasure-filled moments that took my breath away. And as beautiful and as sensual as they were... I understood exactly why no other galleries in the area would want to take her.

"You're not here to work," I said as she came up to me and I pulled her into a small hug.

When she pulled away, she looked down at her camera and gave me a light smile before nudging me. We both turned to look at the art that was hung up on the wall, basking in the moment.

"I wanted to capture this moment," she said with a smile, then pushed me forward. "Go stand there."

I tried to stand in the middle of the various pieces, but she moved me until I was standing right in front of the middle photo. When I tried to turn and look at her, she snapped at me, causing a light giggle to rise in me. I turned my attention back to the piece I had seen about a hundred times before.

This one was not as vulgar as some of the other ones I'd seen, but it was sensual enough that it made my skin heat. It was two girls, one leaning against the other's back with her hand around her throat. Both of their faces were cut off, and the picture was zoomed in on her hand. The girl's breasts were in the picture, but they were covered by thin, flimsy lace that showed her hardened nipples.

There was something in her mouth though we couldn't see much of it and her drool had fallen down her chin and to her chest.

I didn't even think to pose when Lilian took the first picture, as I was too wrapped up in the artwork.

"You should be proud of yourself," I said as she came up to me. She showed me the image. It was of my back to her. You could see just a bit of my face. Enough to know that I was transfixed by the art.

I hated to admit that it was good.

"I am," she said with a smile. "But you've seen the ones in Club Pétale. Those are the ones I liked the most, and seeing them there feels an awful lot more satisfying. I always thought my end goal was a place like this... but maybe that has changed now."

"Let me take one of you," I said, trying to grab her camera. She quickly pulled it away from my reach and shook her head.

"No one touches my camera," she said quickly. "I only allow one person, and I'm sorry, but that's not you."

Even though her tone wasn't harsh, it was panicked, and she sent me a sheepish smile afterward as if to tell me she was sorry. I wasn't offended in the slightest. I knew what it meant to want to keep the work in progress close to the heart. And honestly, I would die before I let anyone see what I had locked up in my closet.

It didn't take long for us to move on to the other exhibits that were around. Though we realized very quickly that we were suited for a place more like Club Pétale than here.

They were serving drinks at one small corner, so she took me to get a glass of white wine for both of us.

I knew the question was coming before it was even out of her mouth, but it still shocked me when she pulled us to the far corner and whispered, "So, how was your match?"

I swallowed a large gulp of my wine before I had the courage to speak up. I never told her about that night, even though it happened a few weeks ago. We had both been pretty busy, and I was so panicked about my stalker situation that I didn't even think to debrief her on what happened.

She was the one that got me in there in the first place. And I had to admit I was glad because that had been the best sex of my life.

"It was good," I said, feeling my cheeks heat. "*Really* good."

"Who did you get?" she asked. "I mean, I was thinking of asking Sloan to tell me. But I wanted you to tell me and I wouldn't ask her to break that confidentiality, no matter how curious I was."

Sloan, Lillian's fiancée or wife, I guess. I didn't pry too much into their relationship, but the dermal piercing on her left hand told me all I needed to know. She talked about her often but never gave too much information about her away. All I knew was that she somehow worked with the club, so the idea of Sloan being able to see who I matched with and tell Lillian caused me to panic inside.

I let out a forced laugh. If I could, there was no fucking way I would tell her.

"I don't kiss and tell," I said, trying to keep my voice light and not at all like my mind was screaming at me to run.

Lillian probably saw more than her fair share of people at the club, but having to sit face-to-face with someone that I thought was becoming my friend... how could I look at her and tell her I needed pain to get off?

"So it was that bad, huh?"

Panic seized my chest.

"It was *not*," I said quickly. "It was really, *really* good, and I mean that."

"Then why haven't you been back?" she asked and then added, "I've been looking for you whenever I am there. I thought maybe we scared you off."

Scared me off?

I almost wanted to laugh.

It's her that should be scared of whatever the fuck I was doing with that girl in that room.

I was a completely different person as soon as I stepped in there. That's why I was there in the first place. So I could explore this part of myself that I would never allow to be shown in the light of day.

But it wasn't something that I was ready to talk about.

"No, you didn't scare me," I said. "I've just been... preoccupied. School starts soon."

She nodded.

"I understand," she said, her eyes looking out at the guests. A smile spread across her face. "Then, before that, we should celebrate!"

"Celebrate what?" I asked with a small laugh.

"Everything," she sang. "Your exhibition, the start of the new school year, your first job as a professor."

I let her drag me back to the front and outside with little complaint. Lillian was hard to say no to, and she was even harder to keep secrets from. With a few simple questions, she knew almost everything about me.

But no matter how much she tried, I would not be telling her about what happened between Avery and me.

Nor would I tell her about the stalker.

AVERY

I had promised myself that I wouldn't get closer than I needed, but staying outside of her house at night or leaving her little notes wasn't cutting it anymore. I had been good since the night I stayed outside of her grandmother's house.

I blamed that time on the high of killing those annoying fucking agents, but now I had no excuse. Now I was just spiraling.

She had been like an itch that I couldn't get rid of.

This had happened once before with a woman. I had a tendency to get obsessed, but usually, the sex would help me get over it and I would walk off into the sunset, never to see them again. It was better than that, safer for me and everyone involved.

I had spent my life running and the longer I was in one place and the more people I knew, the more dangerous it became.

Yet somehow, Willow had managed to burrow herself inside my mind like some sickening parasite and knock me straight off of the safe path I had built for myself.

I didn't understand it fully. The sex had been on the tamer side, and yes, we fit well together... but what else was it that caused me to fall so deeply for this little redhead? My mind was clear now, but it still couldn't make sense of it all.

I hadn't planned to follow her to the gallery, nor had I intended to stick around, especially when I saw her with Lillian.

My ex-boss's soon-to-be wife.

I loved my work at the club. Or at least I did when it lasted. Because of my father and the involvement of the FBI, Sloan thought it safest to let me go, but not before warning me. It was honestly more than I deserved and no matter how bad it felt to lose a place that was becoming my own, I couldn't help the warm feeling in my chest when I realized how much of a risk she took warning me about the impending investigation.

Seeing Lillian here with Willow was just another reminder of what happened then and that because of the family I was born into, there would never be a time in my life when I *wouldn't* be running from something.

With that thought, I realized that maybe it was a little deserving that little Willow burrowed herself so deeply in my mind that I had no choice but to follow her. Maybe it was a blessing in disguise and Willow herself could be my very own gift from God.

Or maybe Lucifer himself.

It was easy to hide myself in the bar Lillian had chosen for them. It was dark, and the music was so loud it threatened to blow my eardrums. They didn't notice me in the corner, though Willow's gaze did dart around as if looking for something.

Maybe she felt me here.

The thought caused more giddiness to run through me than I expected.

She leaned against the bar with a colorful drink in her hand while Lillian was explaining something with a sweet smile and light gestures. My eyes washed over Willow's face, taking in the slightly upturned nose, flushed, high cheekbones, and skin that seemed to glow even in the dim lighting of the bar.

I had all but memorized her face and the feeling of it under my fingers by then. My thoughts had often veered toward this dangerous type of territory regarding Willow. Something I didn't quite understand or like. But no matter how hard I tried, I couldn't stop thinking of her. I longed to touch her again, though if Lillian had anything to say about it, the object of my obsession would be stuck here for at least another hour.

Her fingers gripped the glass in her hand with too much force and her lips were pulled into a straight line. She didn't like it here, I realized.

Maybe we aren't so different after all.

I tried to clamp down on the excitement running through me. I had to watch a few times as men came up to talk to her. I didn't like how they looked at her, their eyes lingering on her chest. Some even had the audacity to reach out to her.

I bit my tongue and sank farther against the wall as she allowed the newest visitor to buy her a drink. The look that lit up his face when she sent him a smile caused jealousy to burn in my gut.

It should be me buying her that drink.

I knew I shouldn't have followed her. There was nothing I could have achieved by coming here.

But somehow, I still couldn't bring myself to leave.

There was something about watching her that caused a pleasant heat to rise in me. I liked seeing how she interacted with the world around her.

She was so different than she was in the room. On the outside, she was all smiles and sweet words. But I knew that I was the only one that saw how heated and messy she got when she gave up total control.

No one else knew just how sassy she could be or how intoxicating she looked when she was begging me.

That image of her was for me and me alone. So it didn't sit right with me when the men attempted to pull the same image out of her. Did they really think buying her drinks was the way to get her to open her legs for them?

Even if she did, I wouldn't let them get any closer than they had been.

When her eyes drifted over to my corner, I quickly looked down, the bill of my hat covering my face. I had hoped my outfit of jeans and a hoodie with a hat would look casual and inconspicuous, but in that moment, I thought maybe it made me look more like a stalker than anything else.

Isn't that what you are though? A little voice in my head asked. *After all, digging up her information from the club's database and inviting yourself to a gallery showing she was a part of is not normal behavior.*

I ignored the voice and blamed my actions on curiosity.

When I looked back up, Lillian was at the bar alone.

Panic ran through me, and I pushed myself off the wall to look around the club for her. Anger rose through me when I caught her next. She was trying to leave the bathroom, but the man that had bought her a drink had been waiting right outside for her. She tried to step around him but his hand shot out to grab her wrist.

I pushed through the crowds. Panic turned to rage. Red coated my vision when he tried to pull her closer. Her face was obviously telling him no, but he didn't get the hint.

When I was close enough, I paused when her voice hit my ears.

"Touch me again and I'll ensure you never have kids in this lifetime," she growled, her voice just loud enough to be heard over the music.

"Hey bitch, I don't just buy drinks for free—"

She used her free hand to smack him across the cheek. The action shocked him enough that his grip on her wrist let up and she was able to pull herself free. But she didn't just storm away. *No.* Willow reared her foot back and delivered a hard kick to his shin.

The man crumpled to the ground, and she used that chance to stand above him with a slow smile crossing her face. I wasn't even sure that she realized it was there.

Her final blow was spitting on the man before turning and walking back into the bar. She walked past me without even looking up. I turned to see her find her place back to Lillian like the encounter had never happened. She gave her a sweet smile, and they were sipping on their drinks once more.

The man on the ground let out a huff and pushed himself off

the dirty ground. By the unsteady way he stood, I guessed he had one too many drinks.

"Fucking bitch."

Anger boiled through me and before I even registered what I was doing, I pushed the man into the girls' bathroom. I didn't even register the area around us or check if there was another person in there with us.

The anger had a mind of its own. It had me in a vise grip and had taken over all rational thought.

"Hey, what are you—"

One hand threaded through his greasy hair and the other on the back of his jacket, allowing me the leverage I needed to slam his face into the sticky bathroom wall. The sound of the bones in his face cracking filled the space.

His body slumped to the ground, and his snore echoed through the bathroom.

I let myself revel in the moment. Let myself feel the heart-pounding excitement that ran through me. I took a sick satisfaction in hurting him, even more so than I did with any of my father's men.

Even a dumbass could realize that it was because he had touched Willow.

I quickly straightened myself and exited.

So much for keeping it low key.

For weeks I had been planning on the best way to sneak into Willow's life, none of tonight was in that plan and if I wasn't careful, shit like this would cause my plan to go up in flames.

I looked around the bathroom, noting how grimy it was. Though I was relieved to see that no one was in here with me to see what I had just done.

I rolled my shoulders and let out a long sigh while looking up to the ceiling above. The flickering fluorescents caused a dull ache to start behind my eyes.

Get it together, Avery.

I allowed myself another moment to calm down before I pushed myself out of the bathroom and back into the club. There were still just as many people here from before, none of them even looking my way as I pushed through them. I made my way to the bar and signaled to the bartender. She held up her hand, motioning for me to wait a second while she took care of the two girls at the counter.

After one of them pushed a wad of cash into her hands, she all but ran to my end of the bar. When she reached me, I gave her a sheepish smile.

"I think a man is passed out in the ladies' room," I said. "Maybe get him to go help?" I jerked my thumb toward the bouncer near the door.

The girl's eyes widened, and she nodded and waved for the bouncer. As soon as he left his position, the girl moved down the bar to go talk to him.

With a sigh, I looked away from her and back toward Willow. My heart stopped when I met her gaze. There was a second between us where I froze and all the thoughts I had left my mind. For the first time in forever, I had no idea what to do.

Would she recognize me? If she did, should I go up to her? But then that would ruin the plans I had set in place. Damn. Maybe I can pretend—

Then as quickly as it happened, she looked away.

I prayed to God that it was dark enough in here that she didn't recognize me.

When she and Lillian turned to leave, I had about five minutes where I was successful in not following her. I tried everything. I looked at the people dancing. Stared at the back wall while trying to think of anything *but* her. I even tried to read off all the labels on the rows and rows of alcohol behind me.

But, of course, the urge to keep her in sight was much more powerful than any of the thoughts in my mind telling me not to follow her.

I tried to stifle my disappointment when she and Lillian got into separate taxis. I wanted to see more of Willow out in the world. I wanted to see what she looked like when she knew she was being watched by the strangers of the city and then, when she was home alone, compare it to the real her that awaited me there. The promise of seeing her like that alone was enough to shove my disappointment aside and replace it with a rush of excitement.

It was the same promise that caused me to grab a taxi of my own even when I knew I should have stayed in the cold night air and let my anger subside. As long as I was in this state of mind, I would do anything.

"Princeton University," I told the driver.

He let out a huff before pulling onto the road and following Willow's taxi.

I gave him the exact address of my dorm, but I knew that it was unlikely that I would be going home tonight. Not after seeing the way Willow looked down on that man.

There was a power in her as she stared down at him. And seeing the sureness in her moves combined with the slight tilt of her lips, I knew this wasn't a first for her. Inside, I wondered if she, too, had a dark side that she wasn't showing to the world.

I caught a glimpse of it when we were together... but what else was she hiding?

I threw my pocket change at the taxi and exited the car before he could complain. The night was still young when I walked the campus and caught more than a few students still out.

Classes hadn't officially started yet, but there were many students that lived on campus and had just moved in to prepare for the semester. Many of them were laughing and joking with their friends as they explored. There was maybe a time when I envied their carefree attitudes, but now they just annoyed me.

I ignored them as I made my way to Willow's apartment. It was an older building with an electronic lock at all exits. More than one time, I had snuck in, but tonight, I decided I needed to try something a bit different.

The obsession was beginning to become too much and the voices in my head that told me to stick with the plan were getting quieter with each step.

Like normal, I waited near the exit. I leaned against the sharp bricks and dug my pack of cigarettes out of my pocket.

There were only a few times I allowed myself to indulge in the disgusting little sticks, an addiction I picked up while in high school. I tried to kick them fully, but never had the willpower. At least this time, they provided a sufficient enough excuse to be standing outside of an apartment building.

Like clockwork, it was only about six minutes before someone came out of the building. They barely even acknowledged me when they exited and I quickly slipped into the opening. Humans were such trusting creatures. Whether it was the entrance to the dorm, a bank, and sometimes even their own hearts, they gladly held the door open for even the most dangerous strangers.

I threw my cigarette to the moldy carpeted floor, stomping it out before going to Willow's apartment. I was disgusted by just how shabby the place was. *Wasn't this supposed to be one of the best universities in the country? Yet they somehow couldn't even give enough shits to keep up the place?*

The path to her apartment was ingrained into my mind and the key I made burned a hole in my pocket. It had been easy to sneak into the property manager's office and steal her key to make a mold for myself.

I told myself it was just supposed to be for emergencies. That I shouldn't use it for personal reasons. Nor had I planned to use it so soon. Not at least until I had the cameras ready.

But as soon as I came across her door, my body had a mind of its own.

The walls were thin, so it was easy to listen and see if she was moving around in her apartment. I waited a few minutes to be sure before opening her door.

It was a gamble, breaking in already, but the need to see her was driving me insane.

The door creaked as I entered her dark apartment. I made sure to close it behind me softly and pause in case she heard me. When silence greeted me, I walked in. The carpet muted my footsteps, but my heart was pounding so hard in my chest I was sure she would hear it.

When I caught sight of her curled up on the couch, my entire body froze.

Stupid idiot. You couldn't just wait a few days until she was—

Her light snore broke through my rambling, and a violent relief passed over me. Luck was on my side tonight. I tiptoed to her side. She was spread out on the couch, barely covered with the fuzzy white blanket she had haphazardly thrown over herself. The room was dark save for the small bit of moonlight that peeked through the window and lit up her face.

Dark red hair splayed across her face, and those perfectly kissable lips were slightly open. Unlike in the bar, she looked so relaxed here. In the bar, she had been watching the people move around them and her nervousness was almost palpable. But then she was fast asleep and totally unaware that I was there.

The locket that she kept on her at all times lay on her chest. It was like a beacon, testing my resolve. My fingers itched to open it and see exactly what Willow kept close to her heart, but I stopped myself. In this position, something like reaching for her necklace may pull her out of her sleep and ruin my plans.

My eyes fell to her open hands. They were both hanging over the side of the couch and below them was a fallen notebook and pen.

Against my better judgment, I reached for it. When I grasped a hold of it, my heart stopped in my chest, and blood froze in my veins.

Both pages were covered in dark scribbles that, clumped together, made horrifying images. Images of soulless eyes. Images of demons preying on humans. Tearing them apart. Images of blood splatter and missing limbs.

A flush of warmth traveled through my body, and as I flipped through the pages, my head spun. Willow had a darkness inside her that even *I* had never experienced before. Each page was filled with things only someone would see in their nightmares.

Until the most recent pictures.

My breath whooshed from me like I was punched straight in the gut.

The last few images were all of the same person. Light hair, a feral smile, mostly naked, and in all of them, she looked positively demonic.

My fingers traced the scars on the chest.

She had gotten my mastectomy scars exactly right. I was so taken aback by seeing me in her notebook that it took me a few moments for my brain to start again. Then a euphoric sensation washed through me.

She, too, couldn't get our time together out of her mind.

Thinking back to it, this was the single moment where any type of hesitation I had when it came to pressuring Willow became nonexistent. After this, I realized that the woman I had been pursuing had been placed in my path because she and I were more perfect for each other than we ever realized.

I let my hand push the hair out of her face and I let out a sigh. She was so beautiful, even in the darkness and with her makeup staining her face. She was more beautiful than I could have ever hoped for.

She's perfect.

Willow had a darkness in her. I could feel it calling out to mine in that moment. Similar to when we were together that night. It wanted me here. Needed me just like I needed her.

I leaned forward and brushed my lips across her forehead.

"We'll figure out a way to let your darkness out, lovely," I whispered. "Maybe you just need a little push."

The next time she left, cameras would be installed. I was done trying to rationalize this.

WILLOW

I held my breath as I ran the brush across the canvas.

A bead of sweat fell down my face, and I didn't even bother to wipe it away before it fell down onto the painting.

My back ached from my position on the floor, and my neck was begging to be stretched. Phantom pains from the scar stemming from the base of my neck to my midback racked my body, but they were more of a push to keep going rather than stopping me in my tracks.

The sun had set long ago and I hadn't bothered to turn on the lights in my apartment save for the single kitchen one right overhead. It was awful for my vision, but I didn't care enough to try and fix it.

I had lost track of time. It could have been thirty minutes or three hours and I wouldn't have been able to tell the difference. It always happened like this when my mind was fixated on an image.

Though this one was different.

Instead of glassy eyes and the gaping mouth of my nightmares, for the first time, an image came to me that was not from the darkness of my mind. Renditions of corpses were nowhere to be seen and for once, some may even call it... ethereal.

It had taken some work to sand down and paint over the

previous painting, but once my hands were grasping the paintbrush, I couldn't stop myself. My body moved by itself, carving at the image in my mind.

I had sketched this image in my notebook over a thousand times during the night. The woman in the picture had the same elongated neck with a playful smile on her lips. By then, I had committed the curves of her face to memory and it became easy for my brush to block out the shapes of her sharp jaw and hooded eyes.

Golden hair haloed her head and at first, she looked very much like an angel from heaven. But as always, my mind took a different turn.

The blue eyes turned sharp. The playful smile became feral. The white sheet that covered her turned gray and slowly started to dissolve into the background. There was so much I wanted to bake into this painting. I wanted to show that at a glance, she was an angel sent from above... but beneath her surface, there was so much more. Something dangerous.

The sound of an alarm blaring caused me to jolt and pulled me out of my trance.

I sat up and looked around wildly for my phone. I had forgotten that I forced myself into my small kitchen in order to paint. The world tilted around me. The sudden change in position caused the world to spin.

I grasped the counter to steady myself. When the world came to a halt, I pulled myself up with what little strength I had and grabbed the discarded phone on the counter. I quickly quieted the annoying alarm.

At least I had enough foresight to set an alarm for two a.m.

I hadn't realized that I had been at it for that long. Or that I would have enough built up inside me to keep going. My heart was pounding from the sudden interruption and I was keenly aware of the sheen of sweat that covered my body.

Painting like this felt like a full-body excursion, even though most of it was mental work, at least in my case.

I grasped the locket that hung around my neck, trying to use it to ground me so that I could break out of the spiral. The coldness of it felt good in my heated palm. The image of my dad and I were not as clear in my mind, but just the thought of him being in there was enough to calm my heart.

I looked back down at the mess I had made on my kitchen floor. A few of my paints had tipped over and leaked onto the cheap tiled flooring. The canvas itself was a mess, and now that I had been torn out of it, I realized just how shitty of a job I had done trying to clean it before this.

I didn't use many colors in my paintings, but there was a dark green that lingered over from the previous work and caused the corner of the painting to look a bit muddy.

I didn't think of myself as a professional when it came to painting, but it was definitely not a hobby.

Just like sex, it was a release. Something I needed in order to deal with the feelings swirling inside of me. And it was one of the few things that called to me. Some people did boxing, went for runs, or journaled... but the act of using my entire body to paint out the images that had been haunting me just felt so right. And being able to see all the anger, panic, fear, and despair come into this world and take physical form was much more satisfying.

Maybe at one point, I thought I would have a career in this field, and while I wasn't too far off, my work was nothing to be proud of.

Many times, it was dark and nightmarish and lacking in the techniques I had seen employed by the artists I helped in the galleries. And if I was being honest, the types of feelings I poured into any art were exactly the things that I wanted to hide from the world.

With a sigh, I walked toward my fridge before pulling out a fizzy alcoholic drink. I didn't even look at the label when I bought it. All I saw was that it had alcohol in it and it was in my cart.

I opened it and took a swig before wincing. The lemon taste that exploded across my tongue was almost too strong for my liking. But alcohol was alcohol and it would take the edge off.

I had one last day to myself until the start of the term and my very first class alone. The nerves had been eating at me for the last few days, so I decided to indulge myself tonight. I took a break from abusing my poor sketchbook and allowed myself another try at the canvas.

I looked down at it with a heavy feeling in my chest. It was different from the monsters I normally painted.

This one looked just as demonic, but it was no monster, at least not in the literal sense.

It was Avery.

She had been invading my dreams more often lately, and I swore when I was in my drunken haze the other night, that I saw her in the bar with me. I knew it was unlikely to see her in public again. Or that I would ever see her again, period.

But that didn't mean that the memory of us would let up anytime soon.

The vibrator waited for me in my drawer, but I didn't want to use it, not yet, at least. I wanted to pour all these feelings into something more permanent as opposed to a small release that would only make me feel better for a few hours before disappearing again.

Though looking at how horribly I portrayed her on this canvas, I wished for the orgasm instead.

I let myself fall into the memories of us. Into the way the heavy flogger felt against my thighs. Let myself get carried away in the feeling of her lips ghosting across my shoulder.

I leaned against the counter with a heavy sigh, looking up at the ceiling. It had been one night.

A single night that I fixated on an unreasonable number of times. Even as the rational thoughts about how obsessed I was swirled around my mind, they did nothing to bat away the heat that was pooling in my belly. Or did anything to stop the descent of my hand past the waistband of my pants and into my underwear.

My eyelids fluttered closed as my fingers trailed my swollen clit. Heat burst through me at the single movement and the image of Avery in the bar hit me like a truck.

I couldn't stop the fantasy from appearing. Even though I knew

I should snap out of it, my mind went further and my hand worked myself faster.

I imagined her there, watching me. I imagined her coming up to me after the man tried to harass me. She would push me into the bathroom. We wouldn't need to say anything. In my fantasy, both of us would feel the tension, feel the electricity burning between us.

She would push me against the wall. We would stare at each other until one made a move. After, I wouldn't have been able to tell who, but in an instant, our lips would be fused together and her hands would be undressing me.

"So needy." She would say when her hand slipped into my pants.

I inserted two fingers inside of me while using my heel to grind my clit. Low pants spilled from my mouth and an orgasm rose in me so fast I could barely keep up.

Until *"Avery."* Spilled from my mouth.

Like ice-cold water splashed to a flame, I was brought back to my reality, the fire I was stroking inside me gone.

I blinked a few times, chasing away the blurriness in my eyes. My bland, dark kitchen looked even worse after the letdown.

I yanked my hand from my pants and looked down to the painting on the ground.

This is... insane.

This behavior wasn't normal. Neither were the thoughts surrounding a person I fucked once. Imagining her in place of strangers so I could fuck her in my fantasies was too much for me to excuse.

I swallowed thickly. Shame and embarrassment filled me.

I need to get out. Date maybe.

But as soon as the thought of dating someone that *wasn't* Avery entered my mind, a bitter taste spread across my tongue.

I let out a sigh. *Get over it.*

With one last look at the mess, I debated whether or not to clean it up but decided that it would be the next day's issue instead and left my unfinished drink in the kitchen in favor of my warm bed.

AVERY

The apartment... was a mess. Blood was splattered all over the walls and glass littered the floor.

I had less than a half hour to get in and out before the FBI flooded the area... *again*. They knew there were things in here that could lead them to my father's demise and unluckily enough for them, my father knew that too.

It was sad to see my once beloved Manhattan apartment become a battleground between the two superpowers, but I had bigger things to worry about. And if I played my cards right, I could get an even better one. One with Willow in it.

Hopefully, next time I wouldn't need Father's money to fund it.

I liked it because I was able to look over the city in a way not many could. I could take in the sights, the people and still feel like I was on top of the world... and that's because I was. Not just in the metaphorical sense but the physical too.

I walked through the apartment in silence, pausing at a particular pool of blood that no doubt had a body in it mere minutes ago.

I had been watching from afar as my father's men and the plainclothes FBI agents that broke in went at it. There were only two agents, so my father's men overpowered them, but they made sure to take the bodies with them as they hightailed it out of there.

They were overambitious when it came to catching me, but they had years of experience to back them up, so I could count on them taking out the trash for me while I waited for the opportune moment to sneak in.

No doubt people called the cops with the ruckus, and they and the FBI agents would be here any moment. And every moment I stayed here staring at the remains of my old life only made it that much more likely that I wouldn't make it back in time to see Willow.

I pulled my hoodie tighter around my face, making sure that I was not caught on any cameras they may have placed here. I guessed that my father's men probably staked the place and had taken everything of value before the FBI came, and if they hadn't, the feds would.

I walked up the stairs, looking over the destruction. Windows were broken. Chunks of wood were taken out of the tables and chairs. The granite had been chipped and stained with blood.

Such a pity.

When I got up to the third floor, I passed my bedroom and headed straight to one of the many guest rooms. I kept them well furnished and cleaned often.

But I never had guests.

In the first room, there was a bed, a dresser, and a bookshelf, but I went straight to the dresser first. There was a false bottom on the second drawer to the right and I was pleasantly surprised to see that my computer, a cell phone, and cash were still there.

This was only one of the computers that I kept, but it was the most important. It was the one I used for my father's financials and offshore accounts. Without it, I would be forced to find a way to get into his bank accounts without being flagged by his security team... *again.*

There was another one around here with documents that I could use at a later date, but I would need to find it first. The money was good for my own living, but blackmail was pertinent to keeping me safe.

I put the cash in my backpack with the computer and turned the phone on before slipping it into my pocket.

Next, I went to the bookshelf and rummaged through some of the books. Many of them were from the thrift store and I didn't think twice when I dumped them in the cart. Some romance books, some nonfiction, and a few textbooks. I never attempted to read them, and I assumed no one else would either. But the older and more worn they looked, the better. When my fingers trailed the length of an old textbook, a smile spread across my face. I pulled it out of the shelf, the weight of it causing a burst of satisfaction to run through me.

"Dumbasses," I muttered with a laugh. Though, who could fault them for not wanting to learn quantum physics?

I pried it open. The inside had been hollowed out, and I had stashed a passport, ID, and a handful of cards connected to various different accounts. Of course, this was also all from my father's account as well.

For someone who mostly dealt in information, my father had proven to be one of the dumbest ones out there.

As if he had been summoned, my phone started vibrating in my pocket. I knew that as soon as I turned it on, he would be able to find me, but I hadn't expected it so quick.

I placed it on the shelf and put it on speaker while I filled my backpack.

"Why were the FBI at your house?" My father's gravelly voice filtered through the speaker. It was hard not to get lost in the memories that slapped me in the face when I heard his voice.

On the outside, it looked like I lived a comfy life. But no one knew what it really was like on the inside. My mother married my father, no doubt because of his money, but that made it so that whatever I needed growing up, I had.

Of course, except for love and affection, but *money...* we had more than enough of that.

"Who knows?" I asked as I zipped up my backpack. "Maybe it

had something to do with the fact that my father's name has been caught on a falsified report of water toxin leve—"

"You shut your mouth," he growled. "You know nothing about what I do."

I let out a laugh and left the room.

"You and I both know that isn't true," I sang. My voice echoed throughout the hallway. "I learned from the best, remember?"

He was silent for a few moments and I used it to go through the next guest room. This one had another computer and a few guns taped to the underside of dressers.

"I didn't mean to snap," he said in a low voice. "I was just worried. Come home, Avery. We have things to discuss."

I bit my tongue. I wanted to cuss him out for his words and call him out on the faux father attitude. He had groomed me from a young age to take over his business when I got older. When I was younger, I didn't think much of what he did and there were even times that I was excited to get involved.

That, on top of the money and easy access to anything I wanted, should have made me the perfect complacent child.

But he had fucked up and made me a bit too much like him. Unlike him, though, there was no way I would stoop as low as him.

He may have dealt mostly with extortion, but there were some of his other dealings that I wouldn't touch with a ten-foot pole. I had standards at least.

"I don't want any part of what you do," I said as I placed the computer and extra gun into my bag. I threw the phone on the ground and made sure that he heard the sound of me loading the gun.

"Don't lie to yourself, Avery," he grunted from the other side. "You and I both know how much you love the money. The power. If you come home, you never have to get your hands dirty again. You can relax. You can stop running."

I let out a laugh and pointed the gun toward the phone.

"That's where you and I are different," I said. "My favorite part is the dirty work. Send in your men and I'll kill them."

Without another word, I fired a single round at the phone. My father would find me again at some point, it was only a matter of time, but there was no fucking way it would be tonight.

I stopped by one more room for some ammo before going back down the stairs.

When shots rang out, I cursed and threw myself back into the hallway. I had felt the air of the bullet whooshing past me. They weren't aiming to kill, but my father was serious about taking me back.

He had to have learned by now that no matter how much he had tried to make me like those perfect heirs I went to school with, I was nothing like them.

Inside, they were disgusting. They didn't care about the people beneath them and only looked out for ways to make them richer. Many of them grew up in abusive environments, but they would not give up any of it because they knew without it, they could not function.

They went to the best private schools. Had nannies and tutors and servants doting on them at all hours, leaving them with no life skills whatsoever.

But not me.

I knew from the moment I entered middle school and from the first time that my mother admitted to me that she never wanted me, that there was no way that I was staying in that house.

So I had to improvise.

When the shots paused, I peeked around the corner. Two men were downstairs, both wearing all black and holding handguns.

A smile played on my lips.

Father should have at least upgraded their weapons.

I was by no means a professional, but after fighting with the guards all my life and putting myself into dangerous circles, I picked up a few skills here and there.

I delivered one shot straight to the first man's head. The other jumped and began shooting at me. I hid back in the hallway. When the thundering sounds of his feet against the stairs echoed throughout the house, I slipped into the main bedroom. It was completely dark, thanks to the blackout curtains. I perched myself behind the door. I made quick work of grabbing one of the bullets from the extra casings I had in my backpack before standing as still as I could against the wall.

His footsteps were slow and hesitant as he walked the third floor. When he was just peeking into my room, I threw the bullet toward the opposite end of the room. His gaze snapped toward it.

Idiot.

He took another step inside with his gun raised. He didn't even have a chance to turn around when I pushed the door back and aimed the gun toward his head.

A smile spread across my face when I pulled the trigger.

His body fell to the floor with a thud. I reached to turn on the light, but only so I could take a good look at the guard he sent. I let out a disappointed sigh when I realized I didn't recognize him.

Must be new.

I searched his person for anything I could take. Of course, I pocketed his phone and anything else of value, but besides his gun and phone, he didn't have much.

I took a picture of his face before standing to leave.

My eyes lingered over the violin that I had placed in the corner of my room. It, unfortunately, was close enough that it, too, was splattered with the guard's blood. I wanted nothing more than to take it with me, but I was in a time crunch and nothing would call more attention to myself than a blood-splattered violin.

And that wouldn't do... because, after all, I had a date.

A thrill of excitement ran through me when Willow Evens's pleasure-filled face flashed through my mind. That one encounter in the club wasn't supposed to mean much. It was supposed to be a way to ease my frustration. A last hurrah for my time at Club Pétale, but it turned into so much more.

And seeing my picture in her notebook only solidified the fact that I needed her.

I took a picture of the other guard and pocketed his valuables as well before taking his picture and sending them both to my father with a warning.

Don't try again.

I took one more look at the place around me. Even through the adrenaline and giddiness from killing these guards, I couldn't help but feel sad.

Because at the club, I had found a place I loved. It's a BDSM club, something many people may not think is important, but for the first time in my life, I was accepted there for who I was. No one asked me to change who I was or try to fit the mold that the world was asking of me. And that meant more than anything had in a very long time.

Until, of course, I met Willow.

I let out a sigh and turned my back on the place, more than ready to meet the person that awaited me.

I may have some obsessive tenancies, but I'm not delusional.

I had no problem stalking Willow, but I didn't do it under the pretense that it would make her love me. It was a wish, not an expectation. From the start, I knew that the only way to get myself into her life would be through careful planning.

First, I needed to carefully manipulate a meeting and then curate an environment in which she could fall in love with me. But given what happened at the club and the added knowledge that lovely Willow was just as fucked up as I was, I didn't think it would be hard.

Getting into Princeton was the first step, and that had come and gone. I had graduated college years ago, or at least I attended some

classes and forged some documents so that I could graduate early...
but it was the same thing. I wasn't too happy about being back,
given the risks it posed, but as long as I didn't have to actually learn
anything, I wouldn't mind it so much. Being near Willow was an
extra perk.

Whatever I want to learn or do... I could do it by myself. I didn't
need to pay a fancy tuition or get a diploma from a preppy school.
As long as I had the internet and the resources, I could learn whatever I wanted to do.

It helped that while in between my high school years and
working at the club, I had some unsavory ties with people that
needed someone who was good with computers. I wouldn't call it
hacking, but I was able to easily break into systems and put information where there otherwise wasn't
, like adding my name to the student roster or auto-enrolling in
all of Professor Evens's classes.

It was even easier to assign myself a dorm room, one of the last
single ones open and it was a mere block away from Willows'
apartment.

But all of that was child's play. Now what I really needed to do
was to implement something that would get her to notice me.

Even before making the move to Princeton, I had been watching
her from afar. And just like most people, she was a creature of habit.

Before school started, Professor Evens would visit the campus
almost every day, except for when she was invited to a gallery or
when she had her cycling classes on Tuesday mornings. She'd come
into her office, stay there for a few hours, and then walk the campus.
There were many times when a male teacher would walk her home,
but during the middle of the day, she was all alone. And it seemed
that she didn't like to be cooped up in one place for too long.

Something that I could relate to.

I could also relate to her loneliness.

Since watching her, I had not seen a single friend visit her apartment besides the male teacher that would walk her home. He had
never been inside, *thank God*, because if he had, I wouldn't be able

to hold myself back. But just like me, she was on her own here. She had no one to reach out to, no one to talk to.

All my ties had to be cut because I was constantly trying to get away from my father's scrutiny. He would use anything or anyone to get what he wanted, so a solitary life was my only option. Even if I so much as had my name and social submitted into a hospital database, he would find me. There was nothing that man wouldn't do.

But overall, the solitary life perfectly suited me.

I grasped the stolen violin in my hands, enjoying its weight. It was a nice one, sturdy. I took it straight from one of the music halls. I'm sure the students here had their own, but this was an extra they had left behind and I doubt they would miss it.

I was even tempted to keep it after what happened to my last one.

I notched it under my chin, readying my stance and took a deep breath. I could easily learn a lot of things, but there's little joy in many of them. True joy came when I was alone with music. The first strum of my bow against the cords was already enough to help me lose myself in the notes. I didn't have a specific song in mind, but I played like there was an audience.

I played like I was back on stage. Played like there were people coming to see *me*. It had been one of the times in my life when I was the happiest and in that moment, I allowed myself to miss it.

I had found a corner in one of the old outside hallways that had a perfect arch to it that amplified the sound outward and across the empty quad. The music floated around me and caressed my skin. Warmth radiated out from my chest and I hoped those touched by the sound of my music could feel it too.

There were many students walking around. I could hear the shuffling of their feet and their whispers. There were some that paused to hear my music, but many of them just moved on. I doubted music students practicing was something uncommon in these halls. And it wasn't their attention that I was looking to get.

Professor Evens would take her afternoon walk anytime now and that walk was usually the same one every single day and she would be passing by this exact hall in a mere moment. I imagined her walking down the stone-laid road. Imagined the music floating around her, beckoning her to follow it.

Her curiosity would get the better of her, that much I knew. I saw it in the way her eyes would sometimes linger on a person or object when she was passing by. She would debate going up to it, and sometimes, if the curiosity was enough, I would catch her staring up at one of the various art pieces that littered the campus.

This would be the exact thing to lead her to me. Call it a hunch.

I swayed along with the music, letting my body relax as I played.

I imagined her peeking around the building in search of music. Maybe she would shed her mask and approach me, or maybe she would stay behind and watch me like I had been watching her.

A thrill went through me when I thought of her sneaking by unknowingly.

Would she like what she saw? What would she think when—

Her gasp was all the signal I needed. I hadn't realized that I had closed my eyes, but I let myself linger in my state for a few moments longer, getting her to take me in like I had her so many times. The weight of her gaze was probably all in my head, but I swore I could feel it traveling the length of my body.

I didn't want to rush it, so I allowed her a few moments until the need to see her was gnawing at me. I couldn't wait to see how she would react to seeing *me* here. For her to see that the space she had cultivated for herself was no longer hers alone.

Slowly, without stopping playing, I opened my eyes and there she was at the end of the hallway.

Her dark auburn hair was pulled into a high ponytail and she wore brown slacks with a white button-up blouse. If she paired it with a vest, she would look very much like a stereotypical professor.

She was just as beautiful as when I snuck into her house that night, but this time she had deep dark circles under her eyes. She wore minimal makeup, so that made her lack of sleep that much more apparent.

I wondered what kept her up at night, though I hoped selfishly it was me. And if the notebook filled with drawings of my face had anything to say about it, I would say the chances of me taking over her dreams were high.

Her hands came to grasp the silver locket hanging on her neck and her brown eyes grew wider by the second. I couldn't help the smile that spread across my face. Her plump lips were open slightly, giving me just a taste of the pink tongue within.

I remembered the feeling of it between my legs. Remembered how those brown eyes looked as they were begging me to let her come. I also remembered just how delicious her ass looked after I flogged it.

God. Even just her standing in front of me was enough to drive me insane. *How on earth was I going to fucking sit in her class when all the thoughts I could manage revolved around fucking her again?*

Before I could stop playing, she was gone. She turned and high-tailed it out of the hallway. My instinct was to run after her, force her to the ground, and make her submit. I made no move to give in to that instinct, allowing myself to relish in the panic that flashed across her face. There would be many more times for her to panic, this was just a small taste of what was to come and I couldn't wait to see how she reacted when she realized just how close we would be.

Meeting number one down.

WILLOW

I slammed the door to my apartment behind me.

My breathing was heavy and my heart was pounding so hard in my chest that it began to ache.

I had fucking called her into existence, hadn't I?

I was not done with everything I needed to get done that day, but the moment I saw Avery's face, my entire world stopped and memories of us slapped me in the face. There was no way after seeing her that I would be able to focus on anything but those memories.

I hadn't expected to see her here or ever again if I was being honest. I couldn't help but think that I manifested this into existence. My dreams of her, my drawings, all of the things that I used to try and get her *out* of my system, only seemed to call her to me.

How the fuck did she get to Princeton? Why, out of all places, would she be here?

I was on my usual afternoon walk when I heard the sounds of a sweet melody being played on the violin. The hall she was playing in had caused it to reach out toward the building over where I was roaming. It was so light and beautiful that I couldn't help but pause and listen.

She wasn't the first student that had taken advantage of the arches within the halls to play, but she was by far the most talented. Even to the untrained ear, there was something so magical about the way she played.

I became entranced by the music, the notes that swirled around me and hugged me in a way that made it impossible not to follow. I hadn't even realized that my feet had guided me to the sound until I caught sight of her.

And it was a *magnificent* sight. I had seen many beautiful things as someone who worked in the arts. I saw pictures and paintings of the most beautiful people and creatures that people could dream of.

But there was something otherworldly about seeing her there.

The light had leaked into the hallway and caused a sort of halo effect around her. Her dirty-blonde hair had lightened and was almost golden. She held her violin with a sturdy yet graceful hand. Her eyes had been closed and she had been swaying lightly with the music. It wasn't even that she was totally in tune with the music, it was like she *became* the music.

She wore jeans and a short-sleeve shirt that had the chest open. It wasn't open enough so I could see her mastectomy scars, but I knew they were there. I knew her body all too well. The presence that she commanded just by standing there, playing the violin, was enough to cause me to lose all rational thought.

I thought Avery was beautiful when she was leaning over me and making me see stars, but it was nothing compared to the image that I saw in that hallway.

It was a stark contrast to how I saw her in my dreams and how that then translated to my scribbles in the notebook. In the hallway, she was akin to something like a god. Like she had come down from heaven in order to mesmerize the humans with her presence. The issue was that it worked. And the angelic image had fit her so well.

But in my dreams and memories, she was the exact opposite.

And then when her eyes opened and met mine, I caught the sight of the devil that haunted my dreams. The image outside was carefully curated and used to reel in unsuspecting humans, but the inside was a predator waiting for the curious to get too close. In that moment, all the images in my notebook flashed through my mind and in moments, the facade was snapped in half.

So I ran.

I ran because I had no idea what to do. I didn't know how to speak to her.

What would I even say to her? Hey, I can't get the night we had out of my head, and slowly, you've taken over my dreams?

I stood up straight and hit my head against the door.

She probably didn't even recognize you, you dumbass.

I was wearing a mask the entire time. Maybe it was only *I* who recognized her. And a night like that was probably normal for her. She worked there, for fuck's sake. To her, I was probably just another notch on the headboard.

At least that's what I hoped because there was no way, knowing she was here now, that I would be able to act like a normal human being.

With a shaky breath, I opened my eyes and looked out at my empty apartment.

I'm overreacting.

I knew I was. I had to be.

The campus was huge, so there was little chance that I would ever run into her again. So there was even a chance that this may have been the last time we ran into each other.

A thought that both comforted me and caused me to panic all the same.

Part of me wanted to run into her again, though. The part that didn't understand why I was freaking out so much about seeing her here.

But no matter what the devilish voices in the back of my head told me, there was no way I would seek her out again.

I walked farther into the apartment and froze when the sight of the painting I left on the kitchen floor was revealed to me. In the light, it looked even worse than it had last night. But the image of Avery was unmistakable.

And as if the painting had been some sort of hint to what

happened today, the figure in the painting wore the same expression Avery had when she saw me.

The figure, to the naked eye, looked angelic with a halo of gold around her head. She had smooth skin and a delicate pose. But when you looked closer, the smile turned into something more sinister. The narrowing of the eyes looked dangerous. And the sheet that had been covering her body had started to rot.

Panic exploded inside me and I launched forward to grab the painting.

I wanted nothing more than to slam it down onto the floor and be done with it, but I couldn't bring myself to ruin it so violently.

Instead, I ran to my room, opened the closet, and threw it in. The image landed against the back wall, causing it to look like Avery's smile was mocking me.

With a high-pitched, angry huff, I slammed the closet door shut.

Right where it was supposed to be.

All of those dreams, those depraved thoughts, all of them deserved to be locked in the dark, just like the painting had.

It was best this way because, in less than twenty-four hours, I was supposed to face the students as their newest professor.

I didn't have time to be distracted by these issues. By *her.*

The campus was big enough anyway, I would probably never see her again.

I should have felt that something was wrong from the moment I woke up. There was a lingering shadow looming over me, warning me that as bad as I thought it was, it would be even worse when I woke up.

But the morning went on as if it was any other term.

I had been an assistant for some time, so becoming the professor didn't change my routine. Still, I found myself getting up at six a.m. to start getting ready for class that didn't even start until eleven.

I needed that extra time to mentally prepare to stand in front of those students. The night before, I barely slept, not only because my anxiety was deteriorating every morsel of fake confidence I had but because I couldn't get the fact that I had seen Avery out of my mind. Normally, the dreams I had of her were something I relished. In those dreams, I could lose myself to the feeling of her. It was like reliving that night over and over again. It was much better than the nightmares that had plagued me for years. But this time, when I met her in my dream, I couldn't help but feel ashamed.

What would she think of me? Now that she knew that I was a professor at a school that was supposed to be one of the best in the world? One that liked being choked out by her?

I didn't dwell on the thoughts for too long because the anxiety of having all of those eyes on me started to overwhelm me and if it went on for too long, I would find myself crippled by it.

I imagined them staring up at me with smirks of amusement. They had to have known me from around the campus and already realized that I was in no place to teach. Many of them had probably signed up for this class, thinking that it would be my mentor in my place and would be disappointed that it was *me* who stood at the front of the room.

Worse, what if no one showed up at all?

My thoughts ran rampant as I got ready and by the time the clock hit seven, I had showered and finished my makeup before I realized what I was doing. I was just going through the motions, letting the thoughts consume me from within.

My hands twitched when the image of Avery flashed through my mind again. I wanted nothing more than to draw her, but I had left my computer bag in my office after hastily leaving yesterday.

With a sigh, I focused back on the mirror.

The entire bathroom had been filled with steam from the shower, but I guess that I had been standing there for so long that it began to dissipate.

I flinched when I saw just how bad my dark circles were under my eyes. My face was puffy, eyes red and irritated, and my hair a tangled mess on top of my head. The silver locket sat on my chest and for the first time, I felt the need to yank it off and lock it in my bedside table.

Not once since after the accident did I ever have the thought to take it off. But shame and panic swirled inside me at the thought.

What would he think of me? Would he be ashamed? Would he be angry?

No, but looking at the disheveled version of myself in the mirror, he would definitely be disappointed that I let myself become like this.

"You're literally fine," I spat at myself. I gripped the counter hard, my nails digging into the counter.

During times like these, I wished I had a friend I could call, but who was I kidding? How on earth could I even begin to explain what was happening to me? Lillian was an option, but I didn't want to drag her into this. Not to mention I wouldn't even be able to meet her eyes when she realized what I was into.

It's not the end of the world. Focus on actually getting through your day.

Though the words did nothing to help me mentally, the flash of pain that came from me gripping the counter was enough to pull me out of my dazed state.

I let my wet hair dry naturally but made sure to pile on extra leave-in conditioner and oil so that I could look somewhat presentable today. When it was done and thoroughly brushed, I went out of the bathroom into my small connecting room and froze when I saw a delicately folded letter on the bed and a wrapped black package topped with a peach bow.

An odd choice for a ribbon color but also my favorite color, coincidentally enough.

Fear clogged my throat and rooted me to my place. I couldn't have been in the shower for more than thirty minutes and then it took me maybe another twenty for my makeup and hair. I should have heard someone come in and I knew just by looking at the letter that it was the same stalker that had visited me back at my grandmother's house.

But how do they even know I am here?

I never gave anyone this information besides Daniel. He was the only one that knew where I lived.

I looked toward the opening of my room and into the small living room and kitchen, but there was no sign of anyone.

I tiptoed to the open door, peeking out just to make sure that there was no one hiding from sight. My windows were still shut and so was my door. I squinted to look at the lock, and even that was still where it should have been.

"Show yourself," I said in a voice that I tried to make loud and intimidating, but it cracked toward the very end.

I waited a few moments, but no one showed up. I didn't let that calm me though.

Instead, I went out and looked in every place a human could hide. After thoroughly searching the kitchen, I came back to the room and only then did I peek in the closet. No one was in there and the painting was still in the same spot, looking at me with that mocking smile.

I then checked under the bed and any other place they could hide, but whoever was there was long gone.

Carefully, I stood still, clutching my towel and looking at the present. With shaky hands, I grabbed the letter. My mouth dried when I opened it and caught the first few words of the familiar delicate script that had been burned into my brain.

Happy first day. I got you a present.
No need to thank me. Just think of me when
you use it.
See you soon, Professor Evens.

My eyes darted toward the present and carefully. The rational part of my brain told me to leave it where I found it. But I had never been known to listen to those voices.

I pulled on one end of the ribbon, undoing the intricate bow entirely.

A part of me was scared that there was some type of poison in there, but with the present and letter, I don't think what they wanted was to hurt me.

At least I prayed that they didn't.

When I opened the box, my heart stopped in my chest as I made out the image of a blue vibrator. It wasn't just any vibrator though, it was one of the ones you put in your panties while your partner controlled the speed.

There's another note inside.

> If you're seeing this, it means you opened the box. I can't tell you how pleased I am that you did that instead of throwing it away.
>
> But I know now that you're a creature of curiosity.
>
> Wear this sometime. I hope you will do it while you're teaching. Or maybe, if you're too shy, you can wear it to sleep and I'll wake you up with it.

Horror ran through me and a shiver ran up my spine.

I threw the letter back into the box and took a shaky step back.

This can't be happening. Not again. I thought I left the stalker when I moved.

But this present was so much more than what they had done up until then. Up until the present, they had just been leaving me notes. Watching me. I could feel their gaze at times, especially when I found a new letter.

But never had they given me something like this. They were baiting me. They knew I would be dying inside until I opened the present, then again until I tried the toy. But there was a promise there.

The promise that they would be watching me.

The thought of them coming in here when I was just feet away caused my entire body to stiffen. But there was also a warmth that shot through me causing an ache between my legs at the thought of using the present.

The image of a shadowy figure hiding outside of my windows and peering in while I was writhing on my bed because of the toy flashed through my mind.

Disgusting.

It was disgusting that I was even turned on by this.

WILLOW

I *definitely manifested something.*
    As it would turn out, I had been disillusioned to think that the universe decided to give me a break these last few months.

It's like the world had been gearing up for this exact moment before delivering the final blow and had allowed me to fall into a sort of lull. Minus the fear of the stalker, of course.

I got the job I wanted. Worked with an incredible photographer that led me to Club Pétale. Had the best sex of my life. Got an apartment that was close to the school.

Everything was looking up. And that should have been my first warning.

I made it into my room a full fifteen minutes before class started. I rushed to my office beforehand and made sure to grab all of my stuff.

There were a few students waiting outside, so I let them in. They were the studious type, the same ones sitting in the halls with their notebooks ready. No doubt, either studying the syllabus for another class or catching up on coursework.

Because mine was art, I doubt that they would ever have to do that for one of my classes. But I appreciated these types of students, nonetheless. A few smiled and introduced themselves. I did the same and told them to pick whatever seat suited them.

I made sure to test the projector and hook up my computer while students filed in. A majority of the ones that had been waiting outside picked front-row seats, with only a few in the back. It sent a small burst of confidence through me and I couldn't help the genuine smile that spread across my face.

As the other student started to trickle in, more of the rows started to fill. I expected them to take me out of my previous mentor's classroom due to the fact that we never had many students in this beginner course, but surprisingly, they allowed me to keep the amphitheater.

It was old and probably hadn't been updated since the seventies, but it would work. Even if the heat didn't.

But the size of it only made me more nervous because when lecturing, I would no doubt home in on those empty seats. I shook those thoughts off as I continued to set up.

I pulled up the presentation that I had prepared for the syllabus and projected it onto the wall behind me. It took a few moments for it to start to work, but when it did, I let out a sigh of relief and turned to the class with a smile. But when I looked back up at the room, my heart skipped a beat.

I hadn't heard all the students come in, but I was shocked when I saw that there were many more than I thought would be there. I had been helping with my professor's class for the better part of a year and I had never seen so many seats filled. To be honest, no one came to this school for arts, really, nor this *specific* beginner's art history class.

When the clock hit eleven, I stood up with a smile and walked around my desk to lean on it with my arms crossed over my chest.

"Welcome to art and visual culture," I said, smiling warmly at them. I tried to look over each and every student, starting from the left to the right. "This course, among others you are probably taking, is an easy prerequisite for many of the arts degrees that we have here. I know that you have a handful of choices to make about these courses, so I'm honored that you chose my class. I hope that this class can help you—"

My voice cut off when I met a familiar blue-eyed gaze. My heart stopped in my chest.

Avery.

The blonde-haired, blue-eyed devil that refused to stop haunting my every thought was now sitting far too comfortably in my classroom. She had a laptop in front of her, but it was closed and her gaze was targeted straight at me.

What are the chances that she's a student in my class?

This was a beginner class. There's no way that she was a first-year. She had to be at least in her early thirties.

I cleared my throat.

"Can help you shift your thinking when it comes to the arts." I grabbed the clicker that was on my desk and started going through my slides. If the students noticed my nerves, no one made any outward signs of it. "We will meet on Mondays and Wednesdays. I will only take attendance on Mondays though. *Don't* tell the rest of the faculty that."

There were a few laughs here and there and it allowed me to regain control of my wildly beating heart.

"Seriously, though, if you need any help or if you can't get an assignment to me on time, please just let me know. I know that as college students, you have a lot on your plate and the last thing I want is a *beginner's* art history class to be the thing keeping you from graduating."

A hand shot up toward the middle section. I motioned for her to speak.

I tried to keep my eyes trained on the girl, but I could feel Avery's gaze burning into the side of my face.

"I saw that before this, Mr. Bergamot was the one to teach this subject, for many years actually. Is there any reason why it's you now?" Someone laughed off to the side and the girl flushed. "Oh no, I don't mean it like—"

"It's okay," I said quickly and finished with a smile. "Mr. Bergamot retired early and suddenly. I had been his assistant before this in this specific class and others and I will be taking over from now on."

I let the class sit in the silence and then nodded before moving on.

"These are my office hours," I said, motioning to the screen. "If you need to talk about anything during this *specific* time, please come find me in room 305 in the Bar building. It's not far from here. But seriously, these are the only hours I am available. If I'm gone too long, my cat will miss me." I didn't have a cat, but it did cause a few students to smile. "Now, before I get into the nitty-gritty of the syllabus, any questions?"

I was relieved when there were none. The rest of the class went by in a blur and I ended up letting them out fifteen minutes early. There was one more beginner class after them, so as soon as they left, I made sure to clean up my desk and presentation materials and tried not to watch the students as they left.

More particularly, tried not to watch *Avery* as she left.

When I looked up, I noticed that she was getting up as well, but instead of following the other students out, she moved closer to the front and sat down.

She gave me a smile.

My mind went into overdrive and panic caused my blood to rush to my head, and for a moment, I stopped breathing.

Realistically, if I was any other student, I would ask them what they needed... but I couldn't get our time in the room out of my mind. Even just staring at her across the room, I could feel the phantom roughness of her hands squeezing my neck.

I cleared my throat.

"Can I help you with something?" I asked with a forced smile.

A smirk spread across her full lips, almost like she was goading me. I tried not to let my overactive imagination tell me that she recognized me without my mask. But in that moment, I felt for sure that she had recognized me and not only that, but that she had placed herself right here in my safe space to fluster me on purpose.

"I'm just waiting for the next class," she said. Her voice carried across the room and settled deep in my chest. Shivers ran up my spine.

God, this was so inappropriate. It didn't matter that she looked to be well above the age of everyone else here. She was still a student.

"My class is next," I said, and I looked at my watch. "In fifteen minutes, to be exact. And it is the same one."

She leaned back in her chair like she was getting comfortable.

"I know," she said. "Check the roster. I should be on there. Last name Maddox."

Avery Maddox. That fit her too well.

I opened my mouth to speak again but was interrupted by students flooding into the class. Their laughter cut through the tenseness of the room.

I sent them a smile.

"Please sit down. We'll begin shortly."

I cast one last glance to Avery, but she was already watching me.

By the time I made it back to my apartment, I was exhausted. *Drained*. It felt like every ounce of my energy had been siphoned out of me, and it wasn't even because of the teaching.

The students were easy. Today was just supposed to be an introductory class. We weren't even doing real work until Wednesday.

It was because of Avery.

I only had two classes, but she was in both, *and* she just sat there watching me as I taught. And it wasn't the same type of *watching* as the other students. Her eyes were heated as they watched me like she, too, had been letting her mind run through our time together. I was fully clothed, but the entire time I felt so exposed I might as well have been naked.

Who the fuck enrolls in two of the same classes?

I'm not even sure how the administration had let her successfully do that. I debated tipping them off about it, but then that would mean that they would talk to Avery about it and force her to pick another class and she would know that it was I who tipped them off.

And Avery didn't seem like a person that would let that slide under the rug. *No.* She would talk to me about it and that was something I knew I couldn't handle just yet.

I was relieved when she didn't try to talk to me after class. I had been dreading it, and the whole last class, I'd been wondering what she was going to do. But as soon as it ended, and I told people that they could leave, she slowly grabbed her computer, stood and then left with the rest of the students.

What was even worse was the sight of her in my classroom had given me all sorts of inappropriate thoughts.

When we were separated, it was easy just to keep these thoughts in my mind and to break out the vibrator when I needed to. But by the time I had gotten to my apartment, my entire body was buzzing with need.

I don't know how many times I had fantasized about her finding me and fucking me over the desk in my classroom, but I couldn't keep it inside anymore.

I dumped all my stuff near the door and walked straight into my bedroom. I didn't even hesitate. I shifted through my dresser drawer and got my favorite vibrator. The Satisfyer Pro, the one with a bulbous head that, when placed straight on your clit, made you see stars.

I was big on clitoral stimulation, and so this one was exactly what I needed to get me off. And fast.

And tonight, I had a feeling that I wouldn't be satisfied with one or two orgasms. I needed to fuck myself like Avery would in my fantasies.

Stripping down, I lay on top of my bed.

I had a moment where I thought that *maybe I should stop this* or *maybe I shouldn't have some fucked-up fantasy about a student that I accidentally slept with,* but then I decided that I deserved to be a little selfish. Even just for this moment.

So I looked up at the ceiling, spread my legs, and placed the vibrator right on my clit. I wasn't even that wet yet, but it did not dull the sharp bursts of pleasure that stemmed from it. I let out a low moan and closed my eyes.

It was far too easy to sink into the fantasies I had while I was teaching.

The fantasy of Avery coming behind me after class while I was on my computer and forcing me over it. In a world where I didn't care if she broke my stuff, her throwing everything to the ground to make room for me only heightened my arousal.

I imagined her rough hands pulling up my skirt, even though I so rarely wore one so that I was bared to her. Of course, in this fantasy, I wasn't wearing any panties, and with ease, she ran two fingers from my clit to my entrance.

My legs fell open even farther and I pushed the vibrator harder against my clit and upped the intensity. My entire body was hot and the need to come right then and there was overpowering me.

"*Fuck.*" Avery's name was on my lips, but I didn't let it fall.

It took no time at all for my orgasm to rise. I had been so worked up that all I needed was a little push—my entire body froze when I heard a vibration coming from the drawer.

Normally, I wouldn't have paid attention to it, thinking it was my phone... but I had left that in the kitchen.

With a gasp, I sat up and looked around my room. There was no sign of anyone and even though I practically ran in there, I noticed nothing out of place. Quickly I stood up and looked in the bathroom.

It was empty

When I looked back at the drawer, the vibrating ceased for just a moment and then started up again. I lunged toward the cabinet and opened the drawer.

The vibrator that had been given to me as a present from my stalker was whirring to life. I swallowed thickly.

I had reached forward to touch it, but I pulled back quickly.

What the fuck was I doing? I am not thinking of getting off by that thing right now... am I?

I let out a groan. *I totally am.*

If there was any time to do it, it would be right now. When I was so horny and incapable of rational thought that the stalker controlling my vibrator wasn't something that scared me but turned me on instead.

I had been so close to coming and all of that had passed now, but there was an ache between my legs and I was obscenely wet.

Without another moment to waste, I grabbed it and it turned off.

With shaky limbs, I lay back on the bed and hesitantly put it on my legs.

It started again almost immediately. I had no idea if they were watching or if they could hear me. But I let out a moan and pushed it hard to my clit.

"You better get me off with this thing, or I'll go right back to fucking myself," I threatened.

No sign anyone had heard me until the vibrator upped its speed.

Fuck.

Just that small gesture caused a flood of heat to fill me. They were watching right now. I imagined them standing at the end of the bed, looking down on me. I didn't have a visual of what they looked like but knowing some random stranger was doing this to me only made it that much more erotic.

In my mind, images of Avery's smirking face took the place of the stalker and I was too far gone to try and stop it. The fear of knowing that someone was here and now toying with me only caused me to get wetter.

I let out a cry as my pussy spasmed. I hadn't even realized how close I was to coming until I was already writhing in the bed. I had half a mind to take it off me and throw it across the room, but instead, I cried out, "*Again.*"

AVERY

Magnificent.

She was absolutely breathtaking.

I had thought I knew everything there was to know about Willow, but she still somehow was able to surprise me.

After seeing how she reacted to me in class, I thought that it would be a long time until I saw *this* side of her, if at all. She had a tendency to run and hide from the things that scared her, but I was beginning to see that maybe, *inside*, she craved a bit of the danger she was so afraid of.

I sat back with a sigh as her moans filtered through the speakers. The soft glow of the camera on the monitor lit up my face and desk.

It would be a lie if I said it was because I was worried about her.

This was just another way to feed my obsession with her. And I would relish every single moment.

One of my hands trailed down my front and to my already unbuttoned jeans, the other holding my phone with the toy's app open.

I let out a hiss as my fingers came to run lazy horizontal strokes on my clit. There was a pleasant hum of warmth running through my entire body as I watched her squirm on the bed. The cameras gave me a perfect look at her dripping cunt. Enough so that it caused my mouth to water.

I wanted nothing more than to break back into the house with the key I had made for myself, but I restrained myself.

No matter how much I wanted her in the moment, I *needed* to act carefully.

I hadn't felt like this for anyone before. There were times when my emotions got the better of me and I found myself lusting over someone, but never like this. Never so much so that it invaded my entire being and set my body alight.

After being with her, nothing else mattered.

Her back arched and her mouth opened into a silent cry. Quickly, I lowered the intensity on the app.

She let out a long whine.

"Oh, you fucking ass, I was so close—"

When I turned it on again, she let out a throaty groan. She widened her legs, giving me a better look at her impossibly wet cunt. Her hips were bucking wildly as she chased the waning orgasm. It took far longer than I liked for her to get close to another. I decided in that moment that I would be ordering her another, a stronger one.

There was a certain satisfaction in seeing her struggle for an orgasm, but I'd enjoy it much more if it was a constant pull from one extreme to the other, one that would make it so she wouldn't get the chance to up and leave. I had sensed her getting annoyed with my pacing, but even so, I lowered the intensity once more.

I upped the pressure on my own clit, letting out a groan as Willow used her free hand to pinch her nipples. My goal for myself wasn't to come, but if she kept touching herself like that, I was going to, whether I liked it or not.

As a reward, I upped the intensity by a single level.

"Oh, you like that, huh?" she asked in a hoarse voice. She made a show of trailing her hand down her body before slipping her hand between her legs and spreading her pussy lips.

For me. She was doing that for me.

Satisfaction unfurled in my chest and my pussy fluttered around nothing.

I upped the intensity of the toy by one more level. When two lithe fingers slipped into her entrance, I upped it one last time.

She began to fuck herself along with the toy.

"This is so sick," she groaned. "But fuck does it feel good. Can you see me? See how wet my pussy is?"

I cursed under my breath and slipped two fingers into my wet cunt. I was going to come faster than I ever had before. Normally I needed more. Needed to feel her against me. Needed to hear her begging... but seeing her like this, knowing that I was behind the camera watching her and she *liked* it.

She came with a cry and my entire body went taut. I couldn't contain my groans as I came. My release flooded my underwear, but I couldn't bring myself to care. Not when Willow's pants filled my room.

I turned off the vibrator and watched to see what she would do next, but to my surprise, she didn't move. When I switched to a different camera, I realized that she had fallen asleep.

Without letting another moment pass, I stood and beelined for the door, grabbing her apartment key before I left.

Watching Willow sleep was my second favorite hobby.

Besides fucking her, of course.

I held my breath as she shifted in her sleep and rolled over to face me fully. Her hair was wildly spread out around her pillow. Her plump lips opened, her face relaxed. Her hands were tangled in the sheets and she pulled them tight to her chest.

Normally, I would have just kneeled down in front of her and watched as she slept, but after our moment together, I couldn't help but give in to the urge to crawl into bed next to her.

The sheets were not the ones from her grandma's and they were cheap and itchy against the skin. I made a note to get her new ones when this game was over.

I reached out to let my fingers lightly brush across her lips.

She's so, so beautiful.

I wondered what she would do when she realized that I was going to be in every class with her.

Would she get angry? Would she confront me?

I hoped so.

She let out a small whimper in her sleep and I had to hold myself back from pulling her into my arms. I leaned as close as possible and placed a light kiss on her lips.

The thought of my hand clamping around her neck and waking her up with my lips and tongue on her body flashed through my mind. I imagined her naked under these blankets. I imagined myself being able to peel them back while she was asleep and pull her nipple into my mouth. She would wake with a moan before I fucked her back from dreamland.

It took everything I had to pull myself away from her, but not without letting my tongue brush across her lips.

The taste of her was so familiar, yet still so intoxicating.

Carefully, I left the bed and straightened the pillow and sheets. I had to pause every time she shifted, but Willow was so deep asleep it would take much more to wake her up.

I was about to leave her room, but the slightly ajar closet door caught my attention. Casting one glance back at Willow, I carefully pried the closet open.

I had to cover my mouth with my hand to stop the crazed giggle from spilling out of my lips.

Apparently, the lovely Willow didn't stop at just sketching me.

There, hidden toward the back of the closet, was a full painting of me. It was just as twisted as her sketches, but seeing it in this medium held a different type of satisfaction.

She painted me like an angel. A fallen one.

On my face, she captured the perfect expression. The true one that only I had seen that night.

I inhaled deeply and steadied myself against the threshold of the closet.

I'm invading her mind. Our first meeting was mere days ago, but here is a completely dry painting of me.

A burst of heat ran through me. Willow was just as obsessed as I was. She had to be. Why else would I fill her sketchbook? Why else would she paint me?

Did she dream of me too?

I turned back to look at her form in the bed.

The vilest thoughts entered my mind in that moment. The urge to throw away my plan and wake her up with my tongue on her was stronger than ever before.

She likes me. She still thinks of me.

Knowing that felt similar to a high. My head was in the clouds and a giddiness rose in me.

I bit my lips hard in order to contain my excitement.

Calm down. You have a plan.

With shaky hands, I leaned down and grabbed the painting. I wanted so badly to take it home with me. Hang it for all to see. To show everyone how much Willow thought of me.

It was like my own personal sign that we were perfect.

With a heavy heart, I placed it on the outside of her closet and turned to leave because if I didn't, I knew damn well that in a few moments, I would be between her legs.

WILLOW

Fig, sandalwood, and a light hint of the sea.

That was the scent I woke up to and it followed me my entire day.

I didn't recognize it at first, too taken aback by my actions the night before.

I woke up wrapped in blankets with the vibrator thrown somewhere in my sheets. My thighs were caked with my own dried release, making it impossible to forget what I had done.

Against my shame, I shot up from the bed and ran to the shower to try and get rid of as much evidence as I could. The cold water was enough to shock me back to reality.

But if that wasn't enough, seeing that the painting I did of Avery somehow made it out of the closet sure as hell was. That fucking picture was haunted. It had to be.

I debated throwing it away, but instead, I forced it back into the closet and made sure to cover it with some of my clothes before I slammed the closet shut.

After getting dressed, I grabbed the vibrator and sheets and threw them straight into the dumpster on my way out. I didn't want to think about how much it would set me back to buy new sheets, but that was future me's issue.

I—*unfortunately*—had a class at ten a.m., so I couldn't linger on the fact that I had a real-life stalker, one that helped me orgasm until I almost passed out. One that was still probably watching every single one of my moves.

Just the thought of it caused every hair on my body to stand pin straight. Even though I knew the school like the back of my hand, I found myself peering back over my shoulder, feeling like I was all of a sudden in an unfamiliar environment.

The looming buildings with cracked blocks and a musky scent to them had once brought me comfort, but now every time I looked into the shadows, I imagined someone standing in there, watching me.

What did a stalker even want with me?

I was a boring professor with literally zero social life. But in the back of my mind, I knew *exactly* what they wanted. The gift and last night made that perfectly clear.

I navigated through the school, careful not to go into any of the many long corridors that could lead to a possible ambush. I allowed myself a few minutes on my phone to place an order for new sheets but barely got through it without pausing every five minutes to look back up to where I was going.

The walk to my office felt like it was taking three times as long as it usually did.

I let out a sigh when my building came into view. At least there, I was surrounded by my students and other faculty.

A firm hand on my shoulder caused me to jump and let out a shrill, choked scream. I whipped around to view the perpetrator.

Daniel's worried green eyes filled my vision and all the tension that had coiled in my body released. That was until I saw the person behind him.

A man with cropped short blond hair feathered with gray, light-blue eyes and wearing a flannel with jeans. *Professor James Lynch.* He scored major points with his students on a regular basis, many of them liked his laid-back style. Like me, he didn't care much for attendance or turning in assignments on time. Though unlike me, he taught history and had been friends with my previous professor. I had gotten to know him through the years as a student here and even more so since it was announced that I would take over for my old mentor.

But what the students and other faculty *didn't* know is that Professor Lynch was a slimy bastard that would corner the young female faculty on multiple occasions and force them into silence when they so much as rejected him.

I knew because he had done the same to me when I was still an aide for my professor.

His eyes roamed over my frame, and suddenly, I wished I had put on a sweatshirt and joggers instead of the silk button-down and jeans. I felt far too seen by him in that moment.

"I was calling you for like five minutes," Daniel said with a small frown. "Are you okay? You look..."

I held my book bag close to my body and quickly tried to comb through my hair.

"Is it bad?" I said, dropping my voice in a whisper. "I didn't pay much attention to getting ready this morning."

Acting like Professor Lynch wasn't standing directly behind my friend was easier said than done, especially when it was obvious how much he wanted to butt into the conversation.

"No," Daniel said quickly and stepped forward to help me comb through the back of my hair. His movements were gentle and a comforting warmth radiated from him. It made me want to lean into him. We were nothing more than friends, but the comfort he had brought me the last few months had been immeasurable. "There, beautiful as always. Though you could roll out of bed and I'm sure you would look just as good."

I gave him a forced smile.

"First-year nerves?" Professor Lynch asked from behind him.

Instead of turning to look at him, I simply muttered, "Something like that," and turned back to the building to go to my classroom.

"You have a class soon, right?" Daniel said and stepped up so that we were side by side. I took it as my cue that he was going to walk me all the way there. Something I couldn't tell if I should feel grateful for or annoyed by because as soon as he took my left side, Professor Lynch took my right.

"Yes," I said and leaned toward Daniel.

"I'm surprised the board kept the classes. I bet since Richard left, there has been a decline in enrollments. After all, many of them came for him," Professor Lynch said. While his tone was light, the jab in there was so obvious even Daniel paused.

But I continued on.

"Actually, enrollment is up," I said, puffing my chest. I didn't like his insinuation, even if my own thoughts told me the same. "I even have a waiting list for this next class." I turned to look at him with a fake smile that I hoped would forever be burned into his mind. "Though I heard your course on the Ottoman Empire had been taken off the course catalog this year, pity. That one was in the four hundreds, wasn't it? Having such a high-level class taken off the roster must hurt."

His eyes narrowed at me and he lifted his chin as if to try and save some face by sneering down at me. Guess he didn't like being called useless either. He had grown a big head after being in the school for so long. A little bit of leveling would do him some good.

It also caused a burst of satisfaction to explode in my chest.

The clock tower chimed in the distance, cutting off our conversation. I stepped away from the two, a smile spreading across my face.

"No need to walk me, fellas. I'll be good from here," I said and turned on my heels. Regardless of everything that happened in the last few days, my heart felt lighter as I walked into my exhibition design class.

"Did we go viral on social media or something?" I asked with a small laugh. "Or maybe there is a sudden influx of art majors in Princeton?"

I leaned back against my desk, looking out at the almost full room. There were over twenty people waiting toward the back, hoping that they could get a spot.

There were a few laughs and whispers among the crowd, but no one answered.

I shrugged. I wouldn't knock the fact that this was the most packed this class had been since I got here. If anything, it would look better to the board. I could handle all these students in my first year.

"Crash the class you want and leave your name with me after class," I said with a wave. "I don't have that many people I will be able to add, but I will try my best."

I grabbed the clicker to the projector from my desk and started my presentation.

"Today will be an introduction to the course, we can expect to finish in about forty minutes and then I will let you out early, that is, if there are not many questions." I clicked to the next screen, showing a picture of me with my most recent exhibition.

Even though it was a small wall with photos that others may believe were too vulgar, I was still proud of them.

"My name is Willow Evens and this class is exhibition design. Or, in other words, the art class for people who can't draw." There were a few laughs around the room. It was enough of a signal to release some of the nerves that had coiled tight in my body. "In this class, we will learn how to curate a showcase of art that not only takes into consideration the artists' vision that we are working with but the rules and guidelines of the place showcasing the art, whether that be a museum, gallery, retail spaces, trade show—"

The door opened in the back, calling the attention of myself and multiple students.

My entire body froze when familiar wavy dirty-blonde hair and striking blue eyes came into view. Avery wore half her hair up in a bun, leaving the rest of the short strands to curl around her neck.

She wore an oversized black hoodie and loose black jeans. She gave those who looked at her a seemingly sheepish smile, but when her sharp eyes traveled toward mine, I couldn't help but think she had come late on purpose.

I needed to talk to someone about getting her schedule fixed before it killed me.

Instead of just slipping into a seat in the back, she walked all the way down the steps, crossed the floor, and then took a seat right in the front.

Whatever gods were out there were really having fun with this season of my life.

"Glad to have you join," I said after realizing how long I had paused.

"Wouldn't miss it for the world, Professor Evens," she said. Her voice was far too sultry to be appropriate.

"As I was saying," I said and cleared my throat. "Half of this class will be taken here at the university. There are times when we will be at the studio on the first floor of this building. We will work with the physical art classes and learn how to build these exhibits. Other times, we will partner with outside art galleries and work with them to create the exhibitions. Though there will be limitations on how many people can work on the exhibits outside this class as we are at the whim of the galleries that wish to employ us. Understood?"

There were a few nods here and there.

"How are we chosen to work on them?"

Of course it was Avery that asked.

"That depends on how well you do in class. Our job is to make both the artists and gallery money, so we have to be selective about who we bring in," I said and went to the next slide. "Now, let's move on to the syllabus. I don't know about you, but I strongly wish to end this early so I can get a coffee."

A few students cracked smiles, but otherwise, they remained silent.

Tough crowd.

I made it a point not to look at Avery for the rest of the class, but when it ended, not only did those on the waiting list stay after class, but she did as well. As it would turn out, just like the day before, Avery had enrolled in every single class I had that day. It was only two, but it was enough to cause alarm bells to ring in my head.

By the time the last class had ended, I had stood back and watched the students leave. When Avery was about to stand up, I cleared my throat. Her gaze shot toward mine and what was originally a slightly shocked expression turned into a smug one.

"Stay back, please," I said. "Do you prefer Ms. Or...?"

"Yes," she answered with a smirk. "And she/her for the pronouns."

I nodded.

"I'm meeting with the administration later, Ms. Maddox," I lied. "I am not sure how you got into all my classes, but you only need to be in one each."

Her smile slowly dropped.

"And if I wanted to be in all of them?"

The shutting of the door caused me to still. Every other student had left. The air was sucked out of the room and suddenly, my lungs were not cooperating.

"That's not how that works," I said, then pressed my lips into a tight line.

She stood straight and gave me a long, lingering look.

I hated when she did this. It made all the memories of *that* night come back like a tidal wave. It didn't help that I was already exhausted after last night. There were far too many things to deal with and coming face-to-face with the girl I slept with, who was now coincidentally my student, was too much to bear.

"I think it can work however we want, Professor Evens," she said and took a step forward.

I leaned back into my desk, gripping the edge with everything I had.

Her eyes trailed from my face to the locket on my neck and back up.

I'd like to think I was a brave person. That I wouldn't sit around and let anyone give me shit.

But there was something about the way that Avery carried herself that made me want to fold in on myself.

There was an aura of confidence that oozed from around her. Her stare was commanding and that smirk that spread across her face was one that told me she knew exactly what she was making me feel.

But in that moment, there was something serious about her. Something that made me almost... wary of rubbing her the wrong way.

Later that night, I would spend hours trying to re-create the same look in my sketchbook.

She took another step closer. This time, she was so dangerously close to invading my space that my breath caught. She leaned her hands on either side of my desk. With one deep breath, our chests would be touching.

Heat spread throughout my body and pooled in my belly. I imagined her pushing against me. Forcing me back onto my desk and slipping her hands beneath—

The buzzing of her phone caused me to jump. The movement broke the stare-down between us and she was forced to take a few steps back. When her gaze finally left mine, I took a deep gasp of air. My heart was pounding in my chest and my entire body felt hot. I hadn't even realized that she had not taken just a single step forward but was about halfway to me when the phone interrupted us.

She dug the phone out of her pocket, her eyes widening when she caught sight of the caller ID. With a curse, she declined the call and gave me one last look before exiting the classroom.

When the door closed behind her, I maneuvered around my desk to flop down on my chair.

Who did I kill in my last life to deserve this?

WILLOW

"You don't understand, someone has been—"

"Did you change the locks?" The gruff voice of the landlord of my apartment came through the other end of the receiver.

I had been on the phone with this man for the better part of half an hour. The first half, I was explaining to him how someone had been in my house. The rest of the time, he was trying to poke holes in my story while simultaneously trying to gaslight me into thinking that I didn't even live in the apartment I was calling about.

"Does the university know how incompetent you are?" I growled. "I have told you multiple times that they got into a locked building that requires an access car—"

A knock on the door of my office caused me to jump. I expected to see Daniel here for my regular pickup, but it was Professor Lynch that was peeking through the door.

My heart dropped to my stomach.

"When I call you back, I expect a better answer," I said and slammed the office phone down on the receiver.

"Bad day?" he asked.

"How can I help you, James?" I asked, my tone curt. I was not in the mood for whatever games he wanted to play.

"Daniel expressed concern that you haven't been yourself lately and asked that I walk you to your apartment," he said. "He was... held up in his office."

Held up. I almost snorted aloud. He was hooking up with someone and dumped me onto Professor Lynch. I would have words with Daniel after this. It didn't matter if no one else saw how much of a creep James Lynch was, I didn't want to be around him.

And it was time for me to stop relying on Daniel so much. Maybe his sending the professor was just a way for him to tell me that he was sick and tired of always having to walk me to and from my office.

"That's kind of him to think of me, but I do not need it," I said and stood up. I squared my shoulders and raised my chin.

Men like him prey on your weakness. Don't let him see through it.

"I would like to," he said. "You have been... off lately."

"Off lately," meaning that over the last week, I'd had to juggle all my classes, trying to get my landlord to care about the break-in and working up the courage to call the administration to get Avery out of my classes.

I hadn't had the time to call about Avery just yet, but tomorrow was the deadline I made for myself. Friday, so hopefully, by Monday, I wouldn't see her in more than two classes. This week I had her in eight classes, with a total of ten hours in the same class together.

She hadn't tried talking to me again. Though, to be fair, I never gave her a chance, not after what happened last time. I was a mere brush of her hand against my thigh away from folding for her. If there was any indication that she may have stayed behind, I would grab my stuff and leave before she could corner me. She hadn't started to follow me out yet, but by the narrowed look she gave me, I knew it was just a matter of time before she tried to talk to me again.

"Regardless," I said with a huff. "I am fine."

I quickly shoved my computer and papers into my bag before walking around my desk and toward the doorway. He didn't move as I came close, as if the space he occupied belonged to him and him alone. His eyes narrowed on my face and ran down my body.

I tried to hold in the shiver of disgust.

We were alone now, so there was no need for him to try and hide his leering.

"Just let me help a little, Willow," he said, lowering his voice and softening it like he was trying to lull me into a false sense of security. "No matter what happened between us before—"

"You feeling up my ass?" I interrupted him.

It happened one day when I was helping my previous professor grade papers. I was alone in his office and didn't hear the door opening behind me. I had been standing because my back started to ache, and I was fully focused on my task.

Before I knew it, I felt the harsh grip of his hand against my ass cheek. When I turned around to confront him, he was almost surprised that I would even have the audacity to do so.

That was when I figured that there were many more before me and there would be many more after.

He shot a look behind him and into the hallway.

"Can you not—"

"Anyway, I am not going home," I lied and used his shock to push past him.

My panic rose when I started walking down the hall and he followed. The sound of his shoes against the linoleum echoed through the hallways.

"Then let's just talk before you go to wherever you are going," he said. "I want to clear the air."

His voice was panicked now. As strong as I was acting, his panic scared me more than his anger.

A wild animal backed into a corner only had one way out and I wasn't willing to stand around and become a casualty in this situation. Professor Lynch had never shown me that he would be dangerous in *that* way, but I would rather be safe than sorry.

"No need, Professor," I said with a sickly sweet tone and sent him the fakest smile I could manage.

Luckily, my office was on the first floor, so it was mere moments before we were out of the building and in a public space. Though to my dismay, it was much later than I realized and there were barely any students out.

It was no different than being stuck in that room with him.

His hand shot out to grab my wrist and force me to look at him. I let out a shocked gasp when I met his eyes. They were wild and showed exactly what I was afraid of.

I shouldn't have mentioned anything. I should have just let him walk me home and shut my fucking mouth.

"You know nothing like that happened," he said in a low voice. His grip on my wrist was becoming painful.

I tried to pull my arm from his grip, but he only held it tighter.

I looked him over. He was older and I had seen just how tired he got after walking around campus all day. I could easily deliver a kick to his balls that would render him useless.

...but here?

Even though there weren't many students out here, I didn't want to chance them seeing their able-bodied professor absolutely wailing on the older one. He had way more of a reputation here with both the students and faculty. There wouldn't have been many people that would be on my side if I had made a scene.

"Let me go, Professor," I spat.

I was proud that my voice came out as strong as it did but cursed myself for my stupidity when his expression hardened.

"I can't have you going around saying shit like that, Willow," he said in a low tone. "Do you realize what could happen if anyone overhears you?"

I looked around. Still, no one was in the vicinity to help.

"You're hurting me," I forced out, raising my voice as I did.

"Tell me you understand," he growled. He tried to pull me closer, but I jerked myself back.

"Fuck you—"

"I swear to God, Willow. If you don—"

A warm arm looped around the front of my neck and shoulders, pulling me back into a soft body. Warmth spread throughout my body on contact and I was tempted to just sink into it instead of forcing my way out like a rational person.

Fig, sandalwood, and a light hint of the sea.

Startled, I looked up to see Avery's stone-cold face glaring at Professor Lynch. I hadn't seen her like this before, except in my dreams. Throughout all our encounters, she'd held a somewhat amused mask and only a few times had it dropped to allow me to see what she was feeling underneath.

This was different.

She wasn't trying to hide her anger at all. She was visibly threatening him with this look. A type of cold aura filled the space between us and the professor.

His grip slackened before he flung my hand away and took a step back.

"Who the hell—"

"Assaulting a professor in public is mighty ballsy of you, James," Avery drawled. A satisfied smile spread across her face. It caused my heart to skip in my chest. I looked toward Professor Lynch to catch his face paling.

"Assault?" He scoffed. "We were just talking—"

"Save the excuses for someone who hasn't seen your criminal record," she said.

I should push her away.

But I couldn't move. The warmth from her body was too comforting. My eyes began to sting. In any other situation, I would have wailed on the assailant at a moment's notice... but I had been so concerned with thinking about what the others would think that I froze.

This wasn't my first time dealing with a man who couldn't keep his hands to himself. Just the other night, something similar happened in the bar and I did just fine. But somehow, having Avery here to take care of it made me feel that much worse about it.

"What are you talking about? I don't have a—"

"Money doesn't hide *everything,* Professor," she said, her tone patronizing.

He opened his mouth to speak, but Avery let out a loud sigh.

"Leave it," she said. "Willow and I have a previous arrangement, so I will be taking over from here. Make yourself scarce before I decide to change my mind."

As angry as Professor Lynch was, he didn't fight her. His chest puffed and his face turned red, but he thought better of responding and stormed away.

I tried to step out of Avery's grasp, but she only held me tighter.

From one awful situation to another.

Though if I had to choose, I would pick Avery over James Lynch any day of the week.

"I should have known that there would be some slimy people hanging around you," she said. "I can't blame them. With a face like that, who could resist?"

My face heated. I pushed her away and turned to send her a glare.

"You didn't need to—"

"Did you miss my arms around you, Eva?" she asked.

My heart stopped in my chest, and the world around us stilled. The creeping dread that had settled in the back of my mind subsided somewhat when she didn't recognize me at first, but it came back in full force.

"I don't know what—"

Avery tsked.

"You're better than *that,* Willow," she said, stepping forward. She was much taller than me, so she had to lean down to meet me straight on.

The action unleashed a storm of butterflies in my stomach.

"Whatever you are playing, you need to stop," I warned.

"You haven't had me removed from your classes yet," she said in a voice barely above a whisper. "Maybe you don't want me to stop."

I didn't want to admit how right she was.

"I haven't had time," I said quickly.

That goddamn smirk spread across her lips again.

"Or maybe you just miss me as much as I have missed you," she breathed.

I couldn't answer her. Not a single thought flashed across my mind. Not when her eyes trailed to my lips. And especially not when her tongue darted out to swipe across her lips.

I swallowed thickly.

How inappropriate would it be if I admitted how hot and bothered she had me when we were just standing here? Or worse, how much I wanted her to wrap her arms around me again?

"You're my student," I choked.

She tilted her head.

"Come on now," she said in an amused tone. "Do I look like I need a degree?"

"There are many people who go back to school," I muttered.

"Admit it, Willow," she all but purred. "Me being in your classes hasn't dampened what you feel for me. If anything, it only makes the fantasy more desirable, doesn't it?"

Yes. But I slammed my mouth shut. I was toeing a dangerous line. This was only my first week and I wasn't ready to throw it all away yet.

When I didn't answer her, she stood to her full height. Her smile had dropped a bit.

"Run along," she said. "You've had a long week. Relax a bit at home, maybe treat yourself to some banana split ice cream and binge that crime show of yours. I'll see you soon."

Without waiting for my response, she turned and walked away.

What the actual fuck?

AVERY

I hadn't planned to corner her like that but when that bastard—
Anger burst through me, boiling the blood in my veins.

I took a deep sigh and screwed my eyes shut. I couldn't lose myself to the anger. *Not now.*

Not when I had a job to do. The plan was ruined, but I would just have to figure out how to work around it.

I should have been watching her closer. If I hadn't been so distracted in the last few days, I would have gotten to him before he even got close enough to hurt her.

Her pain-stricken face flashed through my mind, sending another fresh wave of anger through me.

It's all because of that stupid call.

I shouldn't let *him* fool me. I was losing my touch. The memory of the call was a hard reminder of just how much I had messed up.

I pushed out of the classroom with my heart pounding and an uncomfortable feeling in my chest.

Mother's caller ID flashed across my screen again. I quickly navigated the halls until I found an empty classroom. It was on the smaller side, with just a few tables and a chalkboard at the end, but it would suffice for my purpose. The lights are off, but I preferred the darkness for this conversation. I leaned against the door and listened for footsteps. As soon as I was sure there was no one around, I answered her call before it went to voice mail.

"Mother?" I asked in a low whisper. "Are you safe? Do you need me to—"

"I'm embarrassed that it took me this long to find a way to get in contact with you." Father's voice came from the other line. I pushed off the door and froze. He shouldn't have been able to get this number. The last one I planted was specifically for him to find and use when I needed it, but this one should have been safe. "You always did try to win your mother's love in the most unusual ways."

My mind was whirling.

Was he trying to locate me already? If so, he would probably already have my location. My name was splashed all over the Princeton admission records. I thought he would overlook them, given it was unlike me to go to school.

Or maybe there was still hope he hadn't found me yet? It was like him to try and use my mother to corner me. Maybe he was trying to track me as we spoke.

"What do you want?" I growled.

"You're lucky I haven't sent more people after you for the money you cost me." There was a rustle of papers or clothing from the other line and I swore I heard people talking in the background. "Not only did the FBI take the penthouse, but you killed two of my best men. Men with families who I now have to pay."

I closed my eyes and took a steadying breath.

"Your time would be better spent tracking down those agents instead of me," I said. "Wouldn't want your only heir to end up in their clutches. Who knows what kind of infor—"

"Remember your place," he warned. "I am calling to tell you that if you do not come back home. I will—"

"What?" I asked. "Blackmail me? It's too late for that. Kill my mother? We both know you don't have the balls. She's too prominent in society. They would smell the cover-up a mile away. There is nothing you can do to get me back. Just come to terms with it already."

I used to hate what my mom had done to get in with my father. Shackle him with his only heir so she can live the rest of her life in luxury.

"No, I don't suspect that would be enough to call you back to me," he said with a hum. "You're not invisible, Avery. I will find a way to bring you back to me, to the company. It's time. No more of this running game. I have been bending over backward, trying to clean up after you. I can't promise that I will continue—"

"Yes, you will," I said and opened my eyes to take in the empty class. If there was one thing I knew, it was my father. "You will continue to cover up for me. To clean up. To let me take the money. Because my reputation is yours, Father. Don't think I don't realize that."

"Avery, you—"

"Goodbye, Father," I said. "Send people for me again and I will kill them and deliver them to the steps of your home along with the paparazzi."

Without another word, I hung up.

Since then, I had been looking over my shoulder and, unfortunately, staying away from Willow. Father would send more people, that's just how he worked. So instead of following Willow home and continuing what I wanted to since the first night, I was forced to keep my distance. To be safe, I also added my name to the roster of a few classes I never planned on attending.

He would be smart enough to see that all the classes I took were by one teacher.

Staying in class was a safe bet because there was no way they would make themselves known so easily, but as soon as I was outside of those doors, there was no saying what they would do.

It was by chance that I had run into Willow and that old fart. But at least now, I had something to take my anger out on.

James Lynch lived in a small one-story house only fifteen minutes away from the school by car. There was zero security system and the back sliding glass door that led to a brown lawn had a broken latch.

He had grown complacent in his old age. Assuming that no one in the area would break in, or at least if they did, they would just take whatever was the most expensive and leave. It was his laptop. Though it was almost five years old and would sell for nothing more than a few hundred dollars.

The pictures he kept in there, on the other hand, were another story.

I made myself at home on the single recliner, not bothering to turn on the lights. I lit up a cigarette and inhaled deeply. The nicotine flushed through my system and caused my entire body to relax into the smelly chair. I could picture the professor here, every night of the week, eating a stale microwave dinner and watching the news on repeat.

When looking into him, I was surprised to see how many of the students loved him. He was obviously a sick bastard. You could see it in his eyes. There was something twisted behind them. Especially when he looked at Willow.

He thought she was an easy target. Young, and probably wouldn't report him. He was wrong, though I wouldn't give him a chance to find that out.

The rest of the house was furnished with hand-me-downs. A stained couch. An old refrigerator sounded throughout the place. There were a few rugs and pictures of family and possibly nieces and nephews on the walls, but no other sign of life in there. I doubted his family even visited anymore. Probably all of them were too creeped out by him and tried to keep their children away just to be safe.

Almost made me feel bad for him.

Almost.

The sound of the lock on the front door caused my heart to race. I stayed in my seat, my eyes darting to the hallway that led to the living room.

He was almost silent as he closed and locked the door behind him. He let out a light groan and there was a cracking of his joints as he walked down the hallway.

He paused right before he walked past the opening of the room I was in. He sniffed lightly before darting backward and looking straight to where I was sitting.

"I knew you were a lonely bastard before this, but this place is just sad," I said.

His entire face flushed red.

"How the fuck did you get in here? I'm calling the police—"

I took another drag of the cigarette, drowning him out. The man was spiraling now. I exhaled slowly, savoring the rare cigarette that I only allowed myself in these cases.

"I wonder what they would say about the laptop full of your students' nudes on it."

His shaking fingers were trying desperately to unlock his phone, but he froze when I spoke. All the color drained from his face, and finally, it looked like the situation was dawning on him.

"Willow was appealing as an aide, wasn't she?" I asked. "Not quite the student you normally go after but young enough to look it. You're lucky I didn't find her picture on there."

"What do you want?" he asked. "Please, just leave. I don't want any trouble."

I stood slowly and took one last drag. I looked at the burning stick with a small smile before exhaling the smoke.

"These will kill you," I said. "Which is why I only allow them on special occasions. Though those seem to be on the rise. This is my fifth in the last three months."

"Please, I don't know why you—*Stop*!"

I sent him a smile as he met my gaze with one of horror as I flicked the cigarette toward the corner where a particularly flamma-ble-looking rug was.

Just as planned, he tried to dart toward it, but I was faster. As soon as he got close, I threaded my hand through his hair and forced his head back. He let out a guttural scream as I forced him to his knees. I grabbed the pocketknife from my back pocket and held it to his throat, forcing him to watch as the corner of his room went up in flames.

"Feel stupid for not getting your sprinklers maintained now, huh?" I asked and leaned closer to him. "Must feel even more stupid for touching Willow the way you did."

"Is this about her?!" His voice was desperate. "She's nothing! She is lying to you, don't you see? Let me go and I can explain everything, please! Don't believe that cunt's words—"

His pleas were cut off by the knife sinking into his throat. I was careful to not cut the artery. I didn't want an easy death for him.

The smoke was getting heavy, so I quickly dragged him toward the open sliding glass door and out to the backyard. He was struggling to breathe and was wildly trying to stop the bleeding, so he didn't even fight back as I climbed on top of him.

"Say your prayers," I said, a laugh bubbling from my chest. He opened his mouth, trying to speak, but I lifted my arms and brought the knife straight to his chest. "Oh, oops, I guess your gods won't be able to hear you now."

I pushed the knife as deep as it could go before looking up to the starry sky. It was a particularly beautiful night. No clouds in the sky and bright stars filled the sky for as far as the eye could see. The moon was almost full and shone brightly on us. I let out a sigh, imagining Willow's face. Would she be smiling down on me as I took revenge for her? Would she be happy?

Would she be proud?

Warmth spread across my chest as the man under me squirmed and tried desperately to breathe. Each breath must have felt like a thousand sharp needles embedding themselves into his lungs, which were now filling with blood.

Images of his grubby hands grabbing her caused a fresh wave of anger to go through me and without even thinking of it, I pulled the knife out of his chest before embedding it right where his heart should have been.

"Ah, damn," I murmured as his struggle subsided. His eyes were fading and his breathing had all but stopped. "I wanted this to last a bit longer."

But even if he didn't suffer as much as I wanted, it was all the same. He would never get the chance to touch what was mine. Not *ever* again.

WILLOW

D aniel placed the hot cappuccino down on the rocky table
with an expectant look.

I signaled for him to hold on for just a moment. We
had chosen a quiet café about a five-minute walk from the campus
to talk about our first week. After all, I didn't have anything to grade
and I'd much rather spend my Friday off *far away* from my
apartment.

Even last night, I had trouble sleeping just thinking about the
look that Professor Lynch had given me. But Avery wasn't too far
away from my mind either.

"Right," I confirmed. "Avery Maddox."

The clacking of the keyboard on the other side of the line was
starting to grate on my nerves.

I grabbed the cappuccino to take a sip, only to end up burning
my tongue.

"Slow your roll, Will," Daniel said with a soft smile before
pulling the cup from my hands.

I sent him a grateful smile.

"Are you sure that's their name?" the girl from the other line
asked. "I don't see them in my system."

"Positive," I said. "And it's on my roster, so how is it that it is not showing on your end?"

"Maybe it's outdated?" she offered.

I couldn't help but roll my eyes. I knew she was just trying to help, but we had been going around in circles for fifteen minutes. Thirty, if you count the time it took for them to even find my class while I was on hold.

"She's coming to every class," I growled. And I needed her *not* to. Especially when she just came out and confirmed my greatest suspicions.

"Send her to our office the next time," she said. "We may have to deal with this in person."

I barely concealed my groan. If we went that route, then I would need to actually talk to her. Something I wasn't all that happy to do.

"Got it," I said with a sigh. "Thank you for your help."

"You are welcome, sweetie. Sorry about this."

"It's okay," I muttered and hung up the phone.

Daniel was looking at me with his brow raised.

"Trouble already?" he asked, a slight teasing to his tone.

I shrugged and grabbed my coffee before taking a sip. It was slightly cooler this time.

"Nothing big," I muttered.

"Is someone bothering you?" he asked, still prying. "If you need me—"

"I don't need handouts, Daniel," I snapped.

Heat flashed across my skin when I realized what I had done.

"Sorry," I said quickly and shifted in my seat.

"It's okay," he said and reached over to grab my hand in his. "Has... *it* started again?"

It meaning the stalking and notes. I couldn't help but freeze. Slowly, I nodded.

"We are getting you out of that place," he said. "You're moving in with me."

"And stay on your couch?" I asked, feeling uncomfortable at his proposition. I liked him, but this was going a bit too far and the last thing I wanted was to commandeer his space. "It's okay. I am going to change the locks anyway."

"But they know where you—"

"If you feel so bad, maybe you can drive me?" I asked, cutting him off. His brows furrowed and his bottom lip jutted outward in a pout.

"Don't try to distract me," he said.

"If you want to help, this is how you can do it," I said and pulled my hand from his grasp.

He held my gaze before sighing and leaning back in his chair.

"We can go after this," he muttered. "But if you so much as get a whiff that anything is off, I am taking you out of there immediately."

I nodded and sent him a strained smile.

"I already talked to the property manager about it."

He nodded, seemingly satisfied with my answer. My skin was still warm, just thinking about the lines I had already crossed. How I had used the toy they sent me. How I had begged them to make me come over and over again.

Every night I swept my apartment looking for anything resembling a camera or mic, but I found nothing. Meaning that whatever I *thought* was happening while they got me off was probably not. I was on the third floor with no balcony. They wouldn't be able to see or hear me.

At least I hoped that to be the case.

Daniel didn't push me too much after that and we fell into an easy conversation about our current classes and students. It was what I liked about him. He had the uncanny ability to make even the most stressful of situations seem much less in his presence.

By the time we had finished our coffees, picked up his car, and shopped around for locks, it felt almost as if Avery or the stalker had never existed.

Daniel was able to change the locks without the help of a locksmith. I was sure I could too, after watching him, but having him in the apartment was a nice change. Then when he stood to leave, my heart dropped and all the memories of what happened the last few days came back like a tidal wave.

I somehow, in my panic, convinced him to visit the school cafeteria with me for a light dinner, but by the time seven o'clock rolled around, he had to leave.

Then, I was forced to go back to my apartment alone. Though this time, as I walked the campus, I felt no different than I had a few months ago before the first note showed up. For the first time, I was able to enjoy the cool air. I even smiled at some of my students that passed.

I made a point of sitting under one of the magnolia trees. It was not in season to bloom just yet, but I had often sat on the bench below it, watching as people passed. The aging wooden bench creaked under my weight, breaking the silence of the area.

I tried not to think of Avery, but when I caught a glimpse of dirty-blonde hair walking past me, my heart sped up. I froze trying to see if it was her, but when the person moved to look out at the building behind me, I was almost disappointed to see that it wasn't her.

How am I disappointed over someone I barely know? A student, no less?

There were so many things off with the situation with Avery. *Why is she here, anyway?*

I was able to kill another thirty minutes under that tree until the chill forced me inside.

When I finally pushed myself into my toasty apartment, I should have noticed something off right away. I had left a few lights on, one in my bedroom and one in the bathroom, but the rest of the main room was dark save for the moon shining lightly through my windows.

The first sign was that the heater had been turned up. I hadn't turned it on before I left, but in that moment, I had been so happy to get out of the cold that I didn't realize it right away.

The second was the faint smell of cologne. One that I should have recognized the moment I stepped through the door.

But instead, I kicked my shoes off and threw my coat on the small couch I had taken from my last place. I placed my purse on the cushion as well and bounded for my bedroom.

My blood froze when I saw a perfectly placed white letter on the top of my comforter. I hadn't made the bed before I left, but it was made when I got back and there were rose petals thrown all over the room. And right at the foot of the bed was another large box in the same packaging as the first "present."

I knew I shouldn't have approached, but my legs had a mind of their own and carried me to the bed. The curiosity of seeing what was in that box would be the death of me. Maybe not literally, but it would be enough to make me wish I was dead.

I grabbed the note first. With shaky hands, I unfolded it.

I had another present planned, one I think you might have liked better... but you've upset me.

I looked toward the foot of the bed and reached for the present. The ribbon was silky smooth under my fingertips and the box was heavy. My heart was pounding in my chest and blood was rushing in my ears so loud it drowned out even my thoughts.

Opening the box, I was greeted with deep-blue silk lining the bottom and on top was an elegant pair of leather handcuffs. The leather was black and the inside was light with soft padded suede.

Gloved hands circled my body. One clamping down on my mouth, the other around my waist. A warm body pressed against my back and a hot breath wafted across my face as the person leaned forward.

"I had really exciting plans for you." The voice was deep, feminine, and so familiar it made my knees buckle. She caught me from falling with the arm around my waist. "A new vibrator. A night tied up and at my mercy. Then I saw you bringing *him* in here?"

I sucked in a sharp breath through my nose. There was no doubt who this was now.

I tried to speak, but my words were muffled by her hand.

"You want to tell me what you are doing inviting that man into this place?" she asked. "I've seen how he looks at you."

I didn't know whether to scream or moan when her hand slipped under my shirt. Nor did I understand if the heat rising in me was because of panic or because the realization of Avery being the one watching me had unlocked a fantasy I didn't know I had.

Her hand slipped from my mouth to my throat.

"Well?" she prompted.

"Why are you—"

Her hand squeezed my throat hard enough to stop the words from my mouth.

She clicked her tongue.

"I should kill him," she whispered.

Panic exploded through me and my blood ran cold. For some reason, I believed her. It was in the way she held herself, in the way her eyes narrowed in on Professor Lynch. I knew not only that she was capable of murder but that she probably would.

"Don't," I croaked.

"You fighting for him won't make me feel any better."

"Please, it's not like that with him—"

"I changed my mind. I don't have patience for this tonight," she said with a chuckle, then before I could say anything, her hands left my body. I tried to turn to face her, but she forced a silk blindfold over my eyes, tying it tight around my head.

In an instant, she'd pushed me onto the bed and forced my hands behind my back.

"Was this what you always wanted?" I asked before I could stop myself. "Is that why you accepted me that night? So you could find a new target? Is this some type of sick game you play with people you fuck?"

She paused, letting out a chuckle from behind me. The sound caused a shiver to run up my spine.

"Talkative tonight," she teased. "Maybe I'll find another use for your mouth."

Against everything in my mind, my mouth watered. I imagined her riding my face. Taking total control of me until she came all over my mouth.

"Safe word is the same and three taps if your mouth is occupied. Remember it," she commanded. "Say it and all this stops."

The melding of the person in that room and the one that had been watching me this entire time caused my head to spin.

"The notes, the gifts—it was all you, wasn't it?" I asked.

She didn't answer. Instead, she just looped her hand under me and started to pull my pants down.

"Tell me you want this," she murmured against me. There was something in her voice that caused my heart to skip a beat in my chest.

I more than wanted it. I was mere seconds away from begging her to take me. And I knew that once we started, I wouldn't be able to stop. Even the multiple orgasms from the toy with her watching did nothing to satiate me. I needed *her* until I couldn't possibly think of anything other than how she felt about me.

"I want this." My voice was breathless as I spoke and had a bit of a shake to it.

"Are you scared?" she asked. Her voice low and almost teasing.

It caused another shot of heat to radiate through me. I was unbearably wet by then.

"Yes," I whispered. It was the truth... but a part of me craved this. Craved the fear. Craved the darkness she pulled out of me.

I didn't want it to stop.

"You should be," she said with a chuckle.

She was pulling my pants down oh so slowly, her touch lingering on my skin and leaving waves of heat in their wake.

"Please, Avery," I begged, my entire body shaking from the anticipation.

"Safe word and this stops," she reminded as she got my pants down to my thighs. She paused, running her hand down my bare ass before squeezing it. Her movements were rough, uncaring... and I loved it. I wanted it to hurt. I wanted to remember it for days afterward and have her marks be proof that we existed in this room together. "But I would be lying if I told you I didn't have this fantasy of me coming behind you and fucking you when you least expected it."

I whined as her hand dipped between my legs. She used a single finger to swipe up the wetness that had gathered on my cunt. Everything was heightened with the blindfold. Her breaths, her smell, even just that single movement was enough to cause my entire body to go up in flames.

"Maybe I'd sneak in here when you were sleeping, having you wake up in handcuffs and on the verge of an orgasm. Would you like that? Waking up to my strap-on deep in your pussy?"

"Yes," I breathed. She rewarded me by slipping a single finger into my wet cunt. I shifted against her and spread my legs. I needed *more*.

"In my office too," I said. "In the classroom. I want you to push me over the desk and fuc—"

A sharp, stinging pain radiated from my right ass cheek. The added wetness from my own pussy caused it to sting more, but I found myself pushing back for another.

"Dirty, dirty slut," she said with a breathy chuckle. "I should have known when you let your own stalker make you come. You liked being watched, didn't you? You liked imagining I was there. That it was my fingers fucking you instead of your own. Maybe that's why you looked like you did when you saw me in that room. With your face flushed and looking like a cat in heat. I could practically see how ready you were for me to bend you over that desk and make you mine."

The sound of her zipper being undone caused a thrill to go through me. I expected her to turn me around and force me to eat her out like she did back then, but instead I felt the pressure of a dildo at my entrance. *She came prepared.* The realization sent a flare of heat through me.

Even with just the tip, I could feel how big it was and I knew it would hurt. It didn't matter that I was getting wetter by the second. It was bigger than I had taken before.

She teased me with it. Sliding it from my cunt to clit, then back up again.

"You look so sweet bent over with your ass up to be fucked by a stranger," she cooed. "I was going to make you come so many times you saw stars, but I am a woman of my word."

I opened my mouth to say something, but in one harsh movement, she thrust inside me, burying the dildo to the hilt. A high-pitched whine escaped from my lips as the sting from the pain radiated throughout.

"Again," I command, my voice hoarse.

"You're not the one in control here," she reminded then grabbed my hands and forced them behind my back. She leaned over and grabbed the cuffs from the box. "Keep up that delusion and you won't get a single orgasm from me."

I didn't struggle as she fastened them onto my wrists. In my mind, I was begging for more. Begging for her to hurt me like how she did when we were in the room together.

She slowly pulled out before slamming back into me. A deep groan spilled from my lips. The stretch still stung, but when her hand slipped under me to rub my clit, I forgot all about it.

"I'll be good," I promised breathlessly. "*So good.*"

She let out a laugh. She wasn't any bit more gentle when she began pumping in and out of me. The pain from the stretch slowly subsided, but a part of me wished the pain would linger. The stretch was enough to cause my head to spin and my breath to catch.

Her movements quickened with each thrust and she dropped the gentle act. She was driving into me so hard I couldn't even catch my breath.

The sound of the fake cock moving through my wet cunt filled the room, a disgusting reminder of just how turned on I was by this whole situation.

She rubbed lazy circles on my clit and let out a satisfied hum.

"You're mine. You realize that, right?" Her voice was so sure and words slipped from her as easily as discussing the weather and not as if she was fucking the life out of me.

I let out a whimper and pushed back onto the dildo, trying desperately to match her pace. Even with the pace on my clit, heat was coiling in my belly. For the first time, I wouldn't need that much attention on my clit to come. The eroticism of what was happening was enough to send me spiraling.

"So. *Fucking*. Needy." With each word, she drove the fake cock into me harder than before. I would feel it tomorrow, that was for sure. But I couldn't help but think that was her point. That she wanted me to ache as I stood in front of the class—*in front of her*—and tried to act like I hadn't been railed within an inch of my life.

"Fuck, Avery. I'm gonna—"

"Say it," she growled. "Say you're mine and I'll let you come."

I probably shouldn't have entertained her, but I couldn't help myself. Not when my pussy had the dildo in a vise grip.

"I'm yours," I moaned. "Every part of me. Please, please let me—"

I couldn't finish my babbling as I came so hard my body froze and not a sound left my mouth. The orgasm rocked my entire being and with each rhythmic pulse around the toy, muffled sobs began spilling out of my mouth.

"You're fucking dripping," she said with a laugh. Even after my orgasm, she hadn't stopped fucking me with the toy. "*God*, what would everyone think of you if they knew you'd been fucked by your student? That you begged me for an orgasm? Do you have no shame?"

Her words twisted something inside of me, but again, I couldn't bring myself to fight her.

"Again," I moaned and tried to spread my legs even wider.

She let out a mock gasp of realization.

"You like it. Don't you, Professor Evens? You like when I treat you like the little needy whore you are."

I didn't want to like it, but *god*, did her words start a fire in me.

"*Your* needy whore," I corrected.

She cursed under her breath before pulling the dildo out of me. In an instant, the feeling of her hot breath against my folds caused a violent shudder to go through me.

Her fingers were still strumming my clit as she licked the length of my slit before dipping her tongue inside me. I felt the flash of heat between my legs before I realized what was happening. Tingles started in my core and expanded outward. I couldn't hold it back.

"Wait, don't—"

She slipped two fingers inside of me before curling them. Heat exploded inside of me and wetness leaked down my legs.

Her tongue trailed up my inner thighs, drinking every last bit of it. I buried my face in the bed as embarrassment racked my body. But it wasn't just that. I was so close to coming again that I was afraid if I said anything, she would stop.

A high-pitched whine came from my throat as I felt my pussy contract around her fingers. Then without warning, Avery was standing again and her hands were untying the cuff.

"Avery, please—"

"Stay there."

The command caused my pussy to contract around nothing.

I waited in that position no matter how much my pussy ached because I knew that Avery would take care of me. At least, that was what I thought.

And then her footsteps sounded as she walked away from me. I assumed she was getting another toy.

Not until the sound of my door slamming did I realize what had happened.

"Fucking asshole!"

WILLOW

A very did not come to the next class. Or to the one after that. She had been absent for a total of three days and with each one that passed, I found my sanity deteriorating more and more with each passing hour.

The absence of her was even more nerve-racking than seeing her. I began looking over my shoulder far too often. I spent hours trying to lock up my place while searching for microphones or cameras.

I had half a mind to throw away the gifts... but each time I held them over the trash can, I found myself unable to move. I was controlled by a mix of fear and an unreasonable attachment to the only gifts I had received since the crash.

It was Thursday when it happened. I had taken my first class over to the showroom used for our physical art students. It was refreshing to see just how excited they were, but my mind was preoccupied. Usually, when I went down to see the physical art students, I couldn't help but feel jealous of their work. They had the ability to create the most beautiful things while my mind was filled with rot.

But that day, comparing myself to them was the least of my worries.

Not just because of Avery but because Daniel had pulled me away as soon as I dismissed the class with a pinched look on his face. "Professor Lynch?" I paused in my hurried steps to turn to look at Daniel. We were in the middle of walking back to my classroom to meet the next batch of students. I was in a hurry and had less than five minutes before students gathered outside of my class, but the mention of Professor Lynch caused my heart to skip a beat.

I could still feel the pressure of his hand around my wrist. And the weight of Avery's arm around my neck when she pulled me away from him.

"He's missing." Daniel's brows were pulled together, and for the first time, the mask of confidence and cool fell. For the first time that day I looked at him critically. Wrinkles were spread across his forehead from the furrowing of his brows. His hair was greasy, and he had dark circles.

I hadn't realized they were that close. The thought of them being buddies was enough to cause me to hesitate. But still, he was my friend too, right?

I reached out to him on instinct but pulled back as Avery's words flashed through my mind.

I should kill him.

"I didn't know. We saw him just the other week, no? He's been missing since?" I asked. Daniel shook his head.

Fear and panic laced my veins and caused a shiver to crawl up my spine. There was a lingering weight on my neck, and I had to ball my hand into a fist to stop from reaching for it.

I didn't know if it made me a bad person to not feel anything at all at the news. If anything, I was hoping that he would stay away for longer so I would have a chance to get a break from his pestering.

"His house was burned to a crisp, but no one has been able to find him," he explained. His gaze fell to the floor. "His body wasn't found in the ruins. The police are being very tight lipped about it."

My heart sank to my stomach. And my hand absentmindedly came up to grip my locket.

"You think he's still...?"

I couldn't finish my sentence.

"There is always hope, isn't there?" he said with a sad smile.

I swallowed the bitter feeling inside me and nodded.

"Sure there is," I turned to look back toward the hall where my class was held. "Listen, I have a class, but let's meet after—"

"Sorry," he said quickly. "I forget. Let's talk later."

His words were quick and forced. I had never seen Daniel like this before. My heart went out to him, but there was another nagging feeling in my gut that kept me in place.

I nodded but let my gaze linger as he turned to walk down the hall. When he rounded the corner, I turned with a heavy feeling in my chest and marched straight to my classroom. I tried to keep the thoughts of the last time I saw Professor Lynch out of my mind, but with each step, the nagging in my mind got louder and louder.

She couldn't have... right?

When I finally got to my classroom, I expected the students to be lingering outside as I locked the door before the last class, but when I got there, the door was already wide open.

Maybe I thought I locked it and then just forgot?

I poked my head in and took a look at the students who were sitting and chatting.

"Hey guys, we are actually going to take a look at the gallery design for the physical art students..."

My voice trailed off when I spied a large box on top of my desk. It was all black and shimmered in the light. Worst of all, it was topped with a peach bow.

"Who put that there?" I asked.

A few students shook their heads or shrugged.

"It was there when we came in," one girl toward the right side of the room popped up.

"An admirer," another student joked.

I didn't have the energy to muster a smile on my face.

With shaky legs, I descended the steps.

"Pack up your stuff," I said in an unsteady voice. "We'll be leaving soon."

My mind told me that I should have just left it on the desk and gone about my day, but there was a sort of pull to it. The shuffling of the students' stuff only caused my nerves to heighten.

I knew Avery was the one who left it, but she wasn't sitting in her normal seat. Suddenly, I was scared.

I had another present for you... but you made me upset. Was this the present she meant? But why make it so public?

When I reached my desk, I spied a carefully folded note with the words "Professor Evens" on top.

I grabbed it with a shaky hand and opened it.

He will never touch you again.

My breath was stolen from me and my heart began pounding so rapidly that it rattled my chest.

The students were talking around me, but all of their voices were like low buzzes running through my mind.

Don't open it, my mind chanted. I needed to turn back and leave that very moment. But I couldn't.

My hand had a mind of its own as it reached forward and started to open the box. The first thing I noticed was a chemical-like smell that spilled from the opening. The second was the appendages that were still oozing thick, dark blood.

The scream that ripped from my throat was one like I'd never released before.

I clutched the blanket close to me as I took a shaky breath.

The cold concrete steps of my building dug into my numb ass. The entire area had been roped off by yellow tape, and there were about twenty cops directing people. There were even more in the building behind me, coming and going. Many of them held bags with evidence in them, but they had yet to bring out the hands.

Even just the thought of the hands caused my stomach to lurch.

It had been three hours since I had found the hands. After my bloodcurdling scream echoed throughout the classroom, the students all scrambled to see what had happened. A few called 911 but a majority pushed me out of the way to get a look.

The look of shock and disgust was something I would remember for my entire teaching career.

It was easy to forget that many of them were just barely growing into their young adult life. Just a few years ago, months for some, many were still in high school. They weren't ready for something as traumatic as what they had seen.

Some threw up, some started to cry.

When I got my bearings, I forced them away from the box and attempted to cover it while yelling at them to get out.

School police were raiding my room in minutes and I tried my best to herd the students out of the classroom. Some of them too inconsolable to even move.

Many of them were questioned by police, but most of them were dismissed less than an hour after it happened. The dean and various other admins had stopped by to talk to me, but many were shooed away by the police.

I was the only one that they kept here for hours. They hammered me with the same questions. As if my thoughts called them, two officers in suits stood on the steps in front of me. One was a woman with a grim expression, her hair pulled back into a long ponytail. The other was a man that was balding and looked like he had far better things to do than be here. I hoped for them to move around me, but alas, they stared at me in silence until I lifted a brow at them.

"We have a few questions we need to ask you—"

I cut off the woman with a wave of my hand.

"The other officers already asked me everything," I said with a huff. The nerves and anger mixed together and even though I knew

I should shut my mouth, the words came out anyway. "My ass is so numb it feels like it's gonna fall off. When can I leave?"

The woman looked toward the man, who let out a heavy sigh.

"You answered questions from the campus police—"

"And the NJPD." My annoyance was clear in my tone.

"We are a special division," the woman said and gave me an attempted smile. It was the type that was supposed to calm the victims. I knew what she was playing, but I wouldn't fall for it.

I had already answered the other officers' questions as best as I could without giving anything away about Avery. I didn't know how much of this questioning I could take without breaking down.

I don't know why I felt the sudden need to keep her a secret even though I now knew exactly what she had done.

I was afraid of her... but that's not why I didn't tell the police. Some part of me knew that no matter what, I wasn't about to end up with the same fate as Professor Lynch. Because, after all, she did this as some sort of sick way of *protecting* me.

The crumpled-up note felt like it would burn a hole through my pants pocket.

"Make it quick," I muttered.

"How did you know the victim?" the man asked.

Aren't you supposed to give me your names first? The question was on the tip of my tongue, but I swallowed the words instead.

"I met him when I was an assistant," I said. "I guess you could say we are—*were*—coworkers."

The woman was busy scribbling notes while the man's eyes narrowed on me.

"*Were*? You think he's dead?"

I bit my tongue.

"His hands were chopped off and delivered to my classroom," I spat. "Excuse my assumption, but that's not an injury you just *live* with."

"We're not the enemy here, Ms. Evens." The woman gave me another forced smile though she didn't pause her scribblings.

"I didn't say you were."

"Did you notice anything off with him lately? Or did he tell you he was troubled by anything?"

"We weren't close," I said slowly, taking in the man before me.

What is his angle?

"Multiple people report seeing you and him speaking on various occasions around campus," the woman said. "I would assume that you were more than just coworkers if that was the case?"

Red filled my vision.

"I was being cordial," I said with a bit too much venom. "When a coworker comes up to you, it's rude to ignore them."

"But you didn't notice anything off?" the man interjected.

"*No.*"

"Are you sure he didn't tell you anything?" the woman asked.

I closed my eyes and took a deep breath before answering them.

"We were not close."

"Then why did he enter your office building late at night just a week ago?"

There it is. The puzzle pieces were slowly falling into place.

"To offer to walk me home," I said truthfully, though if I was being honest, their line of questioning was starting to make me panic.

They were getting far too close to exactly the thing I was trying to hide from them.

"His badge says it was almost eight o'clock at night," the woman said with a hum. "Is that a normal time for someone to be visiting you in your office, Professor Evens?"

So it's professor now?

"Daniel asked him to check in on me," I said. "Sometimes I get scared at night. You know, being a woman roaming around a dark campus isn't always the safest choice."

My voice was calm on the outside, but inside I was panicking.

"Still, it's odd that he would stay so late—"

"What are you insinuating?" I snapped, my eyes narrowing on the man. He straightened his suit and allowed his eyes to roam behind me. The sound of footsteps descending the stairs filled the silence.

"I wasn't fucking him," I said. "And frankly, I'm tired of your questioning."

"Are you and Daniel close?" she asked. "I guess you are, given he walks you home sometimes, you said?"

"I guess you can say we are friends."

"Any romantic feelings between you two?" the man asked.

"No."

Rage was boiling under my skin. The woman was scribbling on her pad like there was no tomorrow.

"What I don't understand is why the hands were left on *your* desk," the man said with a hum. "That's an oddly... intimate gesture. One could say maybe rooted in jealousy. Are you sure you have no idea—"

"You should let the man take his own notes," I spat, my anger rising so fast my head felt light. The scribbling of her pen against the paper grated my nerves. I sat up straight when the woman gave me a shocked look. "Sorry. Look, it's been a long day. I've been here for hours—"

"It's okay, Ms. Evens," the man said with a forced smile of his own. "We will be in touch."

The man motioned for the woman to follow him and I was left there with lead filling my belly.

It would be another twenty minutes before a policeman would dismiss me. The entire time I was thinking about just how much I had fucked up. I shouldn't have been short with them. If anything, it made the whole situation look even more suspicious.

... but a sick part of me was relieved that they were focusing on Daniel and *not* Avery.

I let my hand travel to the back of my neck, scratching the skin there. The weight of the many gazes in the courtyard was becoming too much.

Worst of all, I swore I could single out the one from the devil herself.

AVERY

*S*he *protected me.*

A blazing warmth expanded in my chest as I watched Willow on my phone. I had connected it long ago to the cameras around her house and even though my mind should have been elsewhere, I couldn't help but take a quick peek at her.

I had watched all day as the police questioned her. I had expected her to hand over my note and tell them everything I had done up until now... but she stayed quiet.

She stayed quiet because she knew that there was no one else in this world like me for her. She protected me because she felt the same pull that tied us together.

Even if she wanted to pretend otherwise, she *liked* my attention. The thought caused the heat in my chest to expand outward. I would give her all the attention she craved and more. She didn't even have to ask for it.

The clearing of a throat caused my gaze to waver from Willow to the person sitting across from me.

The seedy bar was dim and I had chosen the booth farthest from the handful of working lights, so it was difficult to make out the facial features of the person sitting in front of me, but I already knew who she was.

She wore a hood and face mask, leaving only her almond-shaped eyes visible. Though I couldn't make out the color, I could see the distinct broken pupils she was known for. If I was any less of a woman, those piercing, cold eyes may have caused me to squirm. I think, in her world, they called her a demon or something. I couldn't help but think the nickname suited her.

She wore human clothing and looked like one, but those eyes told a different story, and not just because of the broken pupils. It was more so how dead the blue had become.

She sat across from me, not moving an inch as I assessed her. She was doing the same to me.

"I have someplace to be," she said, her voice in a low whisper. "Make this quick."

A smile spread across my face.

"Oh yeah, with that secret service agent, right?" I asked, my voice far too loud. "What was her name again? Tiff—"

She lunged forward, her hand wrapping around my throat and stopping the words from my mouth. Her stare was heated and even through the mask, I could sense her bared teeth. Her fingers were strong, her skin calloused.

This was a woman who did this for a living. To her, I was but an amateur.

The sound of a heavy glass hitting the table caused her to slowly sit back in her seat, but not before giving my throat a final warning squeeze.

I flashed a smile to the server, who had just set down a pint of beer and waved her away. She gave my friend a lingering look before disappearing. I was sure she had caught glimpses of similar happenings in this place, so a little hand-on-the-throat action shouldn't have fazed her.

I let my eyes wander over the patrons and noticed none looked our way. Still, I waited for a few moments before I lifted my phone, showing it to her. Without a second of hesitation, I dropped it into the beer, causing the liquid to spill over the top and onto the table.

"Russell Maddox. He has a pistachio allergy."

She kept her face stone cold. Seconds ticked by before she let out a sigh.

"I am not one who likes to owe debts," she said. "But there is even a line I won't cross."

Even as anger licked at my veins, I forced the smirk to stay on my face. I knew she wouldn't have been jumping at the opportunity to kill Father. As much as I hated him, I had to admit that the black-mail he had raised me to collect would come in handy on more than one occasion.

"You owe me," I reminded. "And if you refuse to pay up, I may just leak that Henry's death was not an accident. Maybe the school can even get back the settlement money they—"

"Stop," she said quickly, her eyes widening and darting around us.

A jolt of excitement ran through me.

This wasn't the first time Quinn and I were meeting. Or at least I think that was the name she was going by now. It was hard to keep track with all the jobs she took on throughout the years.

I had been lucky to come across her. It wasn't every day that a person was able to get a contract killer indebted to them, but I had been at the right place at the right time, and my family had a reputation for being in the right place at the right time.

We went to school together. Henry and I. I was going to get close to him, use him for information on the other students and maybe even the royal body behind him... but instead of meeting him in our secret spot, I found something much more interesting.

"Are you always this sloppy?" I asked as I leaned against the cool concrete.

She let the body of the young boy flop to the ground, her eyes narrowed on me.

She didn't answer at first. Both of us took the other in. I wondered just how much the little assassin knew about the Maddox family. Father made sure to clamp down on all information about my existence until he was ready to introduce me to the world, so I wouldn't be surprised if she knew nothing.

"Avery Maddox." I offered but made no movement.

She may have been messy, but I was in no position to take on a professional.

"I don't care."

I tilted my head to the side. So maybe she didn't know much.

"You gonna kill me now?" I asked.

"Yes," she huffed and stalked toward me.

I held a hand out to stop her.

"What if I told you I could make this look like an accident?"

She paused in her steps before casting her eyes back to the body.

"It is not supposed to loo—"

"I am sure your employer will pay you handsomely if there is less fallout," I said and leaned to the side to catch her gaze. "Let me guess, this is your first job?"

I couldn't help the smile that spread across my face when she froze.

"What do you want?" she asked.

"A favor," I said. "And a way to contact you to cash it in."

She let out a sigh, then nodded.

"Fine, but it goes both ways," she said. "If there is ever a time I need to—"

"We can discuss specifics later," I said and stepped forward before placing a hand on her shoulder. "Pick him up. It's a long trek to the lake and I have to get my hands on more of those little pills he likes."

I had almost forgotten about her. Until her profile landed across my desk when I worked at Club Pétale. She had gotten in contact with me right before she applied. I wasn't the one that owed her the favor, but I wouldn't let go of the chance to get another one out of her.

I tried my best to warn Sloan about her without saying outright that she was a literal assassin for hire, but she ended up slipping right past them.

"Listen, it's not that I am ungrateful for back then," she said. "But Maddox is out of my reach."

"You also wouldn't be with your little toy if I squealed," I reminded.

Anger flared to life in her eyes. *A woman after my own heart.* It seemed like she, too, had someone she was protective of.

"I said no," she growled. "Anything else, but not this."

I sat back against the sticky booth with a sigh. I knew there was a chance this would blow up in my face, but I at least had a bit of hope that she would help.

"Fine," I said and dug in my pocket for an envelope. "Give this to Special Agent Jonson. Tell him it's from me."

"You want to get me killed?" she asked. "The FBI, really?"

"Something else you can't do?" I teased and tilted my head to the side. "Don't you have a reputation or something? I guess the rumors aren't true."

She looked at it for a long moment before taking it from me.

"There better not be anthrax in here," she grumbled.

"Rincon, actually."

She dropped the letter like it burned her.

I let out a laugh. Maybe after this, we could be best friends.

"Kidding," I sang and slipped out of the booth. "A little humor would do you good, y'know."

She sent me a glare.

"Get that to him and we are even," I said. "For Henry. You still owe me for entry."

She grumbled something under her breath, but I ignored it. I was already so focused on seeing Willow again that her attitude did nothing to dampen my own.

WILLOW

School was released for a week before I found myself back in my office and preparing for another week.

Avery hadn't visited me once since that night and I was starting to get worried.

I almost scoffed aloud when I first realized that I was *worried* and not relieved like I should have been. Even the fear of her watching my every move had been somewhat muted compared to it.

There was also this loneliness that settled in my chest. I didn't want to admit just how much her presence and gifts had changed my life. Before this, I was mostly on my own.

I didn't have friends or much family. I didn't go out or really have plans for my future.

All I did was study, work, come home, and do it all over again the next day. Then I went to that BDSM club and everything changed.

I had thought to maybe go back there, but now that the term had started and everything with Professor Lynch... I didn't have much desire to go back.

So that's why I found myself on a Sunday night, held up in my office and prepping for the next week. I also didn't want to admit how it felt to sleep in my bed, not knowing if Avery would show up.

The issue was not that I was scared that she would... it's that I was almost *excited* about it. I would stay up for hours, listening to every creak of the floorboards or voices from the apartments next to me. It would be early in the morning when I would be able to fall asleep again, so I decided that instead of lying in my bed awake for hours, I would get some work done.

When my back started to ache, I stood and stretched my arms and neck. I cast my gaze down to my phone to notice that it was already almost eleven o'clock. With a sigh, I began to gather my stuff but paused when I heard the door swing open.

When I looked up, I was met with Avery's hungry gaze and a small smirk. She was dressed in a simple hoodie and jeans and leaned against the doorframe. So normal looking.

Seeing her was like a complete shock to my system.

My heart skipped a beat. My palms became sweaty. All the coherent thoughts left my brain.

"Are you going to scream again?" she teased. She took a few steps forward so she could close the door before locking it behind her.

The sound was akin to a gunshot in the silence between us. My heart was beating against my rib cage. Adrenaline pushed through my blood, but it had nowhere to go. I froze.

"Maybe," I said weakly.

Her smile only widened.

"Good," she purred. "It turns me on."

I made a sort of choked noise, not expecting her answer. Though honestly, I wasn't all that surprised.

"You're sick." My words came out harsher than I meant, but they were more of a reminder to myself than to attack her.

I stepped back, my legs bumping against my chair. She was silent as she stalked forward.

The room was dim enough that she melted into the shadows, but her face and the way the light twinkled in her eyes were hard to miss.

"You like it," she said with a small laugh.

"Please," I breathed.

Panic rose in me. I was the only person left in this building. If she wanted to do anything to me, now would be the time.

She had cut off Professor Lynch's hands, for god's sake. But... she wouldn't do that to me, right? What she was looking for was...

Panic and fear were mixing together inside me and quickly, there was another more potent feeling rising. One that caused the hairs on the back of my neck to rise while also heating my body.

"God," she moaned. "Screaming *and* begging? I'll be on my knees in no time."

She walked forward until she reached my desk and placed both her hands on it. It was so much like that day in the classroom, but the situations were completely different now. At that time, it was more innocent than this and the desk behind us was the only thing protecting me from her. At that time, I only had an inkling of what she was capable of as if it was my own subconscious warning me. But no, there was no hiding it.

She leaned forward, looking up at me with an expression that made me shiver.

"You didn't tell the police about me."

I swallowed thickly.

"I should have."

She let out a small huff of a laugh.

"You should have," she said. "But you didn't."

"Why are you watching me?" I asked.

"Don't change the subject," she warned.

"You were there," I said quickly. "Watching me with the police. Was it to make sure I wouldn't give you up?"

I was going out on a limb to even think that she would answer these questions, but the longer she was here and not driving a knife into my back, the more sure I was that she wasn't here to hurt me.

"Is that what you think of me?" she asked. "That my interest in watching you is solely to cover my own hide?"

No. But I didn't speak it aloud.

"How would I know?" I asked.

She straightened slowly and moved as if she was afraid she would scare me off. Her footsteps were silent as she walked around the desk and slid into the space between me and it. Her knees brushed against my thighs as she did so and caused me to inhale a sharp breath.

She leaned against the desk and when I wouldn't meet her gaze, she leaned forward until she was so close her breath wafted across my face.

I was forced to look at her then.

"Because if I were the way you are implying, I would have slit your throat the other night instead of fucking you," she said.

Her words were so blunt they caused me to physically recoil. Her hand shot out to grab my shirt and pull me to her. I brought my arms in front of me in order to stop myself from crashing into her, but all it did was put my hands right on her chest. I knew that under her hoodie were mastectomy scars, but the act of putting my hands in a place so intimate was still enough to fluster me.

I tried to pull back, but her other arm wrapped around my waist and kept me planted. She was tall enough that even with her sitting against the desk, I had to look up slightly to meet her gaze.

"I'm..." I paused, looking for the right words. "Curious."

The words held not an ounce of power to them.

Her lips twitched.

"You don't lie to the police for curiosity," she murmured. The hand that had been gripping my shirt brushed against my elbow, then trailed the length of my forearm with a featherlight touch. The softest, most gentle touch I had received from her to date.

It caused something in me to ache.

When her hand stopped its ascent to grab mine, I had stopped breathing altogether. The warmth of it spread through my body and I found myself wanting to lean into her.

It was such a simple gesture, but it was enough to hypnotize me.

"Tell me, lovely." Her voice was silky smooth as the pet name rolled off her tongue.

My throat was closing in on itself. The words I wanted to say were heavy on my tongue and just waiting to be let out, but the fear of what I was about to admit kept my lips sewn shut.

The other hand around my waist loosened enough for her warm hand to spread across my lower back. She pushed me lightly into her, bringing our faces awfully close.

In my mind, I knew I shouldn't have been swayed by such tricks and that the person in front of me was an unhinged, dangerous killer... but none of those thoughts could cut through the haze of having her attention focused on me.

She leaned closer to me, her lips parting as if she was ready to kiss me, but she stopped a few centimeters away. A teasing gesture that caused my knees to weaken.

"I know you want to," she whispered and grabbed hold of my hand to ever so slowly place it around her neck. The action caused my breasts to brush across her chest. Her other hand trailed around my back and to my hip before trailing it up my side, around the sensitive swell of my breast, and to my neck.

Heat shot through me and pooled in my core. She squeezed my throat lightly with just enough pressure to give me flashbacks of our time in the room together.

A light moan slipped past my lips.

"I can see it," she said. "The truth is fighting so hard to break free. You try so hard to put on this image for others. To act like the perfect professor, colleague, even friend... but I have seen the *real* you. The dirty, selfish, cruel *you*. You don't have to hide from me."

I swallowed thickly, but it felt all the more intense when her hand squeezed the column of my throat.

"I... like it," I whispered.

"*Ah.*" It's like a sigh of relief mixed with her breathy chuckle. It caused a tingly feeling to expand in my chest.

"I like the attention," I confessed. "I like when I can feel you watching me because I know that in that moment, I am your sole focus." I paused, watching as her smile dropped. "At first, it made me feel scared."

"And now?" she asked. "Are you not scared I will bring you more severed hands?"

A smile tugged at my lips.

"Why did you do that?" I asked, tilting my head.

"You know why."

Her hand tightened around my neck. My face flushed when a small whimper escaped my mouth. I wanted so badly to kiss her in that moment.

"Tell me," I breathed.

"He touched you. *Hurt* you," she explained.

"And if others... hurt me?" I asked. Her eyes trailed to my lips and back up to my eyes.

"I will kill them." Her tone was dark, but instead of it causing a chill to run through the room, a shiver of excitement ran through me and the warm sensation in my chest expanded outward.

"But not me?"

"*Never* you," she growled. My eyes widened at the declaration. It was so sure, so *angry*. Like she was offended I would even insinuate it.

Her hand squeezed tighter then, cutting off my air supply.

"It makes you feel scared when I say those things."

"No," I forced out. I wrapped my arm tighter around her neck. If she had not been so firm in how she held my throat, we would have kissed. "It makes me feel *powerful*. Tell me, Avery... you'd do just about anything for me, wouldn't you?"

Lips connected with mine in a hot, frenzied kiss. Though it wasn't much of a kiss really. It was too violent. Too hurried. Our teeth and tongues clashed together like we were animals fighting against each other to establish dominance.

Her hand left my throat in an instant so that both her hands could hike my thighs around her before she turned us and dropped me unceremoniously onto the desk.

The kiss was unlike anything I had experienced before. It caused my entire body to melt against her, and suddenly, I couldn't take my clothes off fast enough.

I broke our kiss when I pulled my shirt over my head.

As soon as it was thrown to the side, I was wrapping my arms around her again and fisting my hands into her hair.

"Take your pants off," she forced out against my lips before trailing her lips across my jaw, then down my neck.

I quickly kicked off my shoes and did as she asked while she undid my bra. In seconds I was completely naked on the desk.

She stood back and took in my panting and sweaty body. The room had been chilly the entire day, but as soon as she stepped into the room, the temperature rose quickly. She looked at me with a hungry gaze. Her eyes were hooded and her tongue darted out to lick her lips.

She let out an appreciative hum before grabbing my chair from behind her and sitting down on it.

The vulnerability of the situation caused my chest to feel tight, but instead of giving in to the feeling, I raised my chin and spread my legs, giving her a front-row seat to my already wet cunt.

With a single hand, she flicked the button of her jeans open. She put one elbow on the arm of my chair and the other hand unzipped her zipper. The action caused a bolt to go through me and before I could comprehend what I was doing, my fingers found my clit.

"Is this what you do when you watch me?" My voice was husky as I spoke. Seductive even. I started to rub light horizontal strokes against the bundle of nerves. I had been so wound up through the last few weeks that I knew I wouldn't last long.

Especially when she looked at me like that.

Her lips formed a confident smile that caused my motions to pause.

"Fuck myself, you mean?" Her voice was even, but the opening of her mouth, an almost hidden sigh, let me know how she was feeling about it. I watched, mesmerized, as her hand slipped into her pants and I could just make out her fingers rubbing circles on her clit under her black underwear.

"Yes," I breathed and picked up the motions on my clit. I

wanted so badly for her to touch me, but I also wanted the eroticism of her watching me like this.

She let out a low moan and spread her legs as her fingers picked up the pace.

"You don't know how many times I imagined taking you every time I see you in class," she said. "I've shown great restraint."

"But not anymore?"

"No," she groaned. "I think we are both past that."

I placed one leg up on the desk and teased my entrance with my fingers before holding them out to her.

Her movements were slow and she leaned forward and pulled them into her mouth. The feeling of her tongue running across the sensitive pads of my fingers caused me to shiver. When she had finished cleaning all of my wetness off of them, I brought them back to my pussy.

"No," she growled. She removed her hand from her pants and fell to her knees in front of me.

Seeing her kneeling before me with her head just inches away from my pussy was enough to send my mind into a frenzy. Again, the power surge ran through me. I tangled my hand in her hair and forced her closer to my folds.

"How long?" I asked.

"Since I've been watching you?" she asked, then gave me a long lick from my entrance to clit.

I shuddered.

"Yes."

"I tried not to give in to my desires." One hand trailed up my inner thigh. "But that didn't last long. I started with researching you, then after three days, the first time I tried to go see you."

I let out a moan when her fingers came to rub hard circles on my clit.

"Why?" I gasped.

"You talk too much."

She ended the conversation by leaning forward and devouring

my cunt. Her sudden change caught me off guard and the pleasure that curled in my core caused me to lose all coherent thoughts.

It was uncanny how well she could control my body. I should have been scared. Afraid that she was here and had been watching me. But instead...

"There's nothing wrong with wanting to know more about you."

She stood up, almost knocking me back, before her hand tangled in my hair and jerked my head back. Her wet lips were at my ear in seconds.

"I'm not going to hurt you," she said. Confusion ran through me. She plunged two of her fingers into me before pulling them out and thrusting them back in again. Her motions were hard, unforgiving, and I was so turned on that the sound of her hitting my wet cunt filled the air.

"What do you—"

"I thought I told you that you didn't need to lie to me." Her teeth grazed my ear and pulled a shocked gasp from me.

I clenched down on her so hard I was afraid I'd come right then and there.

I couldn't respond. Not when my orgasm was so close. The promise of it caused my body to heat and my limbs to tingle.

"Come for me, lovely. You know you want to."

Her words were my undoing. I opened my mouth in a silent scream as the orgasm racked my body. Her thumb was on my clit, pushing me through wave after wave of it. She pulled back to look me in the eyes. There was a triumphant smile on her face.

When I had finally caught my breath, I gripped her hoodie and looked into her eyes.

"I want to know more about you, Avery," I said. "It's not a lie. You know far more about me than I do you."

Her lips pulled into a scowl.

"That's not how it's—"

She cut herself off, but I could hear the ending of the sentence floating around us.

That's not how it's supposed to be.

I slipped my hand into her pants and moaned when my fingers came into contact with her wet cunt. I expected her to stop me, but she just held my gaze and I slipped two fingers inside of her.

"We compromise then," I said, pumping my fingers in and out of her. Her eyes dropped and a low groan came from her chest. Her pussy clenched around me, and I used that signal to add a third finger into her.

She let out a shaky breath.

"If I can't get to know you, then we can't do this," I said.

She leaned forward and rested her forehead on mine.

"You're not in charge here," she grumbled.

"But you would do anything for me... wouldn't you?" I asked, lowering my voice and curling my fingers inside of her. She let out a whine and spread her legs wider for me.

"That shouldn't even be a question," she growled. She shimmied her pants down farther, allowing me more movement.

"No more murders. No... cameras. For me."

The last part may have just been my own paranoia speaking, but I couldn't help but try.

I forced my other hand into her pants to rub her clit. Her pants were getting louder and her pussy was gripping my fingers.

God, she's so fucking hot.

Her face was contorted with pleasure. Her eyes were fluttering closed. Her hand gripped my wrist, forcing me to keep my pace. Her skin was starting to shine in the dim light with sweat and a sick part of me wanted to lean forward and taste it.

"Cameras stay," she forced out.

The ice-cold shock was almost enough to cause me to stop, but I pushed forward.

"I need to know more about you," I said. "We can't just—"

Her mouth covered mine and she let out a loud moan as her pussy clamped down on me. I worked her cunt faster, focusing on her clit. She shuddered against me as her orgasm took over.

"Don't push," she huffed and pulled away from me. She looked down at me with an expression that caused my blood to freeze.

Avery *did not* like being told what to do. A part of me was afraid that this would make her pull away from me. Maybe even make her lose interest. But I couldn't stop myself.

"I kept your secret," I said hastily. "The least you could do is give me somethi—"

Her eyes flared, and her hand shot out to grasp my cheeks. The sudden movement pulled a gasp from me and my heart started beating erratically.

"Resorting to blackmail?" she asked in a low tone, a smile spreading across her face. "It should make me angry, but instead, it just turns me on."

She used her other hand to push two fingers into my mouth and pushed down, forcing it open even wider. They were in so deep they were threatening to cause me to gag.

"I can't wait until I can have my way with you," she said with a sigh.

I pushed my brows together as if to say, *If this is not you having your way, then what is?*

"Ever since I saw that painting you did of me, I couldn't help but imagine what I could do to make you view me like that again," she whispered, her eyes narrowing. "Did you paint it because I made you see God? Or maybe even became your god?"

Her voice sent shivers up my spine. She spoke with an excited but hushed tone. Slowly, she pulled her fingers from my mouth.

"It's because I saw the devil inside you," I whispered, holding her gaze.

Her eyes widened. But it didn't seem like she was surprised by my confession but more... satisfied with my answer. She nodded with a hum before quickly starting to pull up her pants.

She grabbed me by the neck and pulled me into a burning kiss before she pulled back with a smile. She sent me a wink before walking around the desk.

"Hey, wait—"

"I'll see you soon, Willow," she called behind her. When she opened the door, she gave me one last glance and I swore the devil in my picture materialized right in front of my eyes. "And don't forget to lock your door."

Without another word, she was gone and I was frozen in my office, exposed.

Avery

I couldn't stay away. Not that I wanted to anymore. I tried to give her at least a few days to digest what was happening between us, but I didn't even have that in me anymore.

With each day, I felt the pull to Willow grow stronger and stronger. Seeing her through the camera wasn't enough anymore.

On top of that, I had been worried about my father's men finding us, though it had been suspiciously quiet over the last few days.

I didn't get any phone calls. My cards were still active. And my dorm was untouched.

Now I was just waiting. I didn't do well with waiting. Never had.

I never needed to. Whatever I needed was at my fingertips in seconds.

Money, women, houses, cars.

Willow was my first encounter with something I had to wait for. The second being my little message to Jonson.

I leaned against the cold wall of Willow's apartment with a sigh. The room was basked in darkness and I could barely make out her figure under the comforter. Willow was curled impossibly tight into her covers which would make it all that much harder to move her without waking up.

Her small snores filled the apartment and I took the time to relish in the moment where it was just us two. The darkness would hide us from each other. Hide us from having to face what the other was thinking.

I wanted to see her as she woke in shock. Wanted to see her wide-eyed expression as I licked that sweet cunt of hers.

I wondered briefly if she was going to scream for me again.

The other part of me was glad that she didn't have to see my expression. Maybe she wouldn't see how hopelessly obsessed I was with her now. She said before she wanted to get to know me. I don't think she understood the panic it caused inside me.

I was conflicted. I wanted to spill everything. Spill how beautiful I thought she was. Tell her all about the club. I wanted to take her out on the town. I wanted to whisper secrets in her ear as we looked down on the people that were just like my father.

But most importantly, I wanted to be right here with her.

She saw the devil in me, as she put it, and she wanted to know more. She wanted to see *me*. Know *me*.

It excited me as much as it scared me.

I pushed off the wall slowly and went to stand at the foot of her bed. The handcuffs I had given her as a present weighed down my right hand and my other was left in a tight fist.

I had never been at the whim of my obsession quite like this before.

I unclenched the fist and stretched out my sore fingers before grabbing hold of her blanket and yanking it off of her. A part of me wanted to wake her up with my head buried between her thighs, but I wanted to give her at least a few moments to call the safe word.

Maybe when we trusted each other a bit more, we could venture into that territory.

She stirred almost immediately as the blanket had been clutched in her hand and caused it to be yanked toward the end of the bed.

She let out a groan before I could just make out the blinking of her eyes. But it wasn't enough for me. I couldn't make out her facial expression as much as I wanted to.

With quiet steps, I walked toward her curtain-covered window and pulled one side of it open enough that the moonlight shining from the lights outside filtered into the room.

The beam of light hit her bare torso and just enough of the bottom half of her face for me to catch the slightly open-mouthed expression she gave me. She was wearing an oversized T-shirt that had ridden up her belly and just a pair of lace panties.

She pushed herself up on her elbows shakily, Turning to face me as she did. Her eyes were trained on me, yet there were no words coming out of her mouth. Her eyes trailed my face, pausing at the face mask that canceled the bottom half of my face. My hood was still pulled over my head and I wondered if she even recognized me.

"Come to finish me off?" she asked with a slight shake to her voice, though there was a small, almost playful smile pulling at her lips.

"If I were, I would have drugged you first," I admitted.

This caused her breathing to stutter.

"Do you like when your women are unresponsive?" she asks.

I pulled my hood off, then my mask, before walking closer to the side of the bed. She didn't move at first, just watching me with those wide eyes as I moved in closer. I licked my lips and couldn't help but notice she did the same. Her action caused them to shine in the moonlight and it gave me the most devious ideas.

I threw the handcuffs onto the bed and leaned forward to place my hand on the mattress. When she didn't move, I used one of my hands to grab an ankle and pull her legs apart so I could place myself between them.

When I walked my hands across the mattress, dipping my head to hers, she started to push herself back toward the headboard.

I couldn't help but smile at her actions. I followed her movements and by the time her back hit the headboard, my knees were between her legs, my hands were on either side of her hips, and my lips mere centimeters from hers.

When her eyes shifted down toward the mattress, I gripped her chin gently and put just enough force on her to look up at me.

"I don't like my *woman* unresponsive," I said, putting emphasis on the singular use of the word. There were no women anymore. Not since her, and I am starting to think that if she keeps looking at me with those wide eyes that there will never be another. "Submissive. Though the snark you give sometimes is cute."

"Am I not submissive enough?" she asked, her legs spreading wider for me.

God. The movement, plus the playful lilt in her voice, caused heat to flash through me.

"You're perfect," I murmured and swiped my thumb across her full bottom lip. It was still wet from when she ran her tongue over it. She opened her mouth wider without me even having to ask.

I slipped my thumb inside and pushed the pad down on her tongue. She stuck her tongue out farther for me.

"Is it the darkness inside you? The thing that makes you crave someone like me? Someone who can come in and unleash the darkness from its cage?"

Her eyes widened, but she said nothing.

"I've thought long and hard about that picture, about being your devil. I don't think you know what you've gotten yourself into. I would do anything for you. More accurately, I would do anything to keep you."

I removed my thumb from her mouth.

"I'll take everything you give me," she vowed. "You're right, I crave you. I crave how you make me feel. You once said you would ruin me for everyone else... and you're right. I'm ruined. *You* ruined me."

Another wave of heat ran through me and without hesitation, I gathered the spit in my mouth and let it drip down into her open mouth. Her hand shot out to grab the hand on her chin and force it between her legs. Her pussy was warm against the thin fabric of her panties and the wetness seeping through it was unmistakable.

She kept her mouth open as I teased her pussy lightly. I gathered what wetness I could from the fabric and shoved the fingers back into her mouth.

She gagged on them this time.

I wasn't going to be gentle with her. No matter how submissive she was trying to be. I was going to fuck her just like I did before. I was going to hurt her just the same as well.

She let out a whine before she started to suck on my fingers. Her tongue swirled around them as she did and it caused a groan to spill from my throat.

When I pulled my fingers from her mouth, I wiped the excess spit across her mouth, enjoying the way it glistened in the moonlight.

"Can I kiss you?" she asked.

A sort of satisfaction whirled in my chest.

"No," I said with a cruel smile.

I didn't believe her act for one minute. Her eyes narrowed just slightly before relaxing. I grabbed the handcuffs I had previously discarded and held them up for her to see.

"Hands behind your back, lovely," I ordered. "If you can get me off with just your mouth in less than five minutes, I'll give you that kiss."

She swallowed thickly before putting her hands in front of her. I shook my head.

"Everything off."

She didn't need to be told twice. She quickly threw her top off, baring her breasts to me. I couldn't help but swoop down and take one of the stiff peaks into my mouth. They had been begging for attention under the thin top and my mouth was watering at the sight of them.

She let out a hiss when I began to suck on one. I looked up to catch her hooded expression before grazing it with my teeth. She arched into my mouth and I took it as a cue to bite down harder.

A stifled moan tumbled out of her lips.

"Harder," she said. "I want it to hurt."

I clamped down on it harder. She threw her head back and let out a loud groan. Her hands moved to fist the sheets under her. I let my tongue swirl the bud before moving on to the next one and giving it the same treatment.

"Fuck," she moaned. "Bite me again. Harder."

Dammit. I had a plan coming in here and with just that one sentence, it had all but been thrown out the window. *A habit of hers*, I realized.

No matter how much I planned ahead, Willow had the ability to make me forget everything as soon as she opened her mouth.

My hand grasped her waist and along with delivering the bite to her nipple, I trailed wet kisses up to her shoulder before sinking my teeth into the flesh there.

She bucked against my hold. With a growl, I wrapped my arm around her waist and used my other to help put a cuff on her wrist. She complied when I grabbed the other and forced them behind her back.

It was difficult from our position, but as soon as it was down, I detangled myself from her and positioned us so we lay flat on the bed with me hovering over her. My bite mark was clear as day against her skin. The act of marking her for all to see was an erotic thought that caused me to almost break the no-kissing rule I had given her.

"I wasn't going to come tonight." The admission falling from my lips shocked me.

"Why not?" she asked breathlessly, and not at all like almost her entire body was bared to me. I wanted to leave bites all over her skin. From her perfect breasts to those beautiful thighs to the delectable cunt that was just begging for me to taste it.

"I can't remember the reason anymore," I murmured and let my hand trail her chest. She arched into my hand when it passed her nipple. I pinched it between my fingertips, enjoying the mewling that came from her lips.

"Would it make me a sick person to say I was waiting for you?"

"Yes," I answered immediately. The smile that spread across her face knocked the breath from my chest.

"I was dreaming of you," she confessed. "Dreaming of this."

It was my turn to stare at her. She was too perfect. I almost didn't believe that she was real.

"You're different," I noticed.

"Maybe the darkness helps," she offered. "Maybe if I pretend that this is still a dream, I can live with myself the next day."

Heat coiled in my belly, and at the same time, a lash of it went to my chest. But the one that caused my heart to constrict was much less pleasant than the one lower down.

I let out a dark laugh.

"We can't have that now, can we?" I asked. "I guess I'll just have to make it as painful as possible so there is no doubting what happened between us tomorrow morning."

Her eyes widened and her nostrils flared at my threat.

I moved my legs to either side of her, straddling her lightly while I took off my hoodie and T-shirt underneath in one motion.

She sat up and looked up at me with those wide eyes that caused my heart to ache. But at the same time, her confession ran painfully through me.

There was no pretending anymore. I wouldn't allow her to.

I grasped her face and leaned closer.

"Safe word."

"Devil."

I pushed her back down on the bed and looked down at her as her eyes widened. I rolled off her and slid off my sweats, all while she watched.

"Come make yourself useful," I muttered and spread my legs for her.

My pussy was already unbearably wet and my clit was swollen. There was something about seeing her like this, cuffed and at my mercy, that turned me on like nothing else.

She crawled between my legs and lowered her mouth to my pussy. I let out a hiss when her lips closed around my clit and gave a hard suck. There was no hesitation in her movements. It wasn't like before and I doubted that she was even as scared as she once was.

I threaded my hand through her hair and forced her closer to me.

"Yes, just like that," I praised as she licked the length of my pussy before coming back up to my clit. She nuzzled my pussy, sending shocks of pleasure through me.

"Harder," I commanded and pulled her hair. She let out a moan before all but biting into my clit. The swollen bud was so sensitive that the act alone caused my pussy to spasm.

But it wasn't enough. It didn't matter that Willow was between my legs and licking up every single drop of my wetness. It didn't matter that she was sucking on my clit so hard my toes were curling.

The words from earlier played through my mind and quickly my pleasure was replaced with the need to dominate her. I needed to see her below me, begging for me to give her some relief. I needed her to need me as much as I needed her.

I was not willing to have her just forget me so easily.

With a growl, I forced her onto her back and straddled her hips. I circled her neck and leaned down to taste myself on her tongue.

Fuck the rules.

Her teeth clawed against mine in a heated battle. I fucking love the way she tried to match my energy. She gave every ounce of herself in that kiss.

I shifted so our legs were between each other's and I ground down on her thigh. I pulled away to circle my hands around her throat, careful to apply pressure on the sides of her neck.

"Don't you fucking move," I grunted out as I rode her thigh.

It was messy and a bit degrading, but the heat that flared through her eyes as she watched me only egged me on further.

She let out a whine that caused my breath to stop.

"You fucking love this, don't you?" I asked with a cruel laugh. "Love when I use your body for my pleasure."

"Yes," she forced out. My hand wasn't cutting off air restriction to her lungs, but I used enough force to stimulate the feeling of choking. "Please. Use me until you come. Use me until you have no use for me anymore. Please. *Please.*"

If I hadn't been close to coming at the sight of her alone before, those fucking words would have been the thing that had done me in. I let out a strangled moan as I came and rode out wave after wave against her thigh. She pushed it up into me harder and forced the breath from my lungs.

Even before the last wave was over, I pulled myself off of her and forced her over onto her stomach. She raised her ass in the air for me and I took great pleasure in peeling her soaking-wet panties down her thighs. Her wet cunt was glistening in the moonlight and I allowed myself to swipe my tongue through her folds to get a taste.

She let out a moan and pushed her hips back into me. I straightened to look at her back, noting the large, jagged scar on her soft skin.

I had seen it a few times in passing, but this was the first time my mind had been clear enough to see it for what it was.

A sick part of me wanted to run a knife along the jagged edges, placing my mark there forever.

"Do you want to come, Willow?" I asked as I traced the scar on her back.

She tilted her face so it lay flat against the bed.

"Please."

"I don't know," I trailed as my fingers ghosted her spine. "If you're just gonna forget about it tomorrow, maybe I can just leave. After all, I've already got my orgasm."

Her high-pitched whine sent a shiver up my spine.

"Please, Avery," she begged. "I didn't mean it."

I clicked my tongue and let my hand trail her hips before coming to knead her ass cheek.

"Don't lie." I trailed my finger down her slit before rubbing soft circles on her clit. When she sighed and pushed back into me, I pulled away.

"Please, I'm sorry," she said quickly. "Please make me come. I won't forget this. I don't want to. I've been waiting for you to come back."

I let out a hum before pushing a single finger into her. I

pumped it in and out lazily and when she tried to control the pace by rocking her hips, I used the other hand to grab her and stop her movements.

"You've been waiting?" I murmured and fit another finger inside of her.

"Yes, *yes,*" she moaned. "I've been waiting to see you again. Waiting for you to find me."

With each sentence she spoke, I slowly began fucking her, letting her words control the pace of my hand. The more she spoke, the faster I fucked her, but as soon as she paused, my thrusts slowed.

"Keep talking."

"I want more," she cried. "I can't get enough of you. I tried to convince myself I didn't want you, but I—"

I cut her off by fitting a third finger into her. She let out a strangled sigh and spread her legs farther for me, trying to help my finger sink deeper into her wet cunt. Her pussy had a vise grip around my fingers.

She was so fucking intoxicating.

"I can't get you out of my mind. I don't care about the cameras—"

I cut her off by bringing my other hand around to circle her clit.

"I want to know you. I want to understand why I'm so addicted to the way you feel. The way you taste."

"God, have you always been this needy?" I teased and pulled my three fingers out before slamming them back in. Her hips met each of my thrusts, the sound of her wet cunt filling the still air.

"Just for you," she moaned.

Her words caused whatever thread that was holding me back to snap. I pulled my hand away from her clit to tangle my hand in her hair and force her head back. I used the leverage to drive my fingers into her, my fist slamming into her cunt with each thrust.

Her strangled moans filled the air, along with her begging.

"Fuck yes. *Please,* Avery. Harder."

She was close. I could feel it in the way she was squeezing my fingers.

"How does it feel to come on the same hand that murdered that grimy professor?" I asked. "Do you get off knowing that his blood was staining this same hand I'm fucking you with?"

Her mouth opened in a silent cry as she came. It was magnificent and a sight I would never get tired of.

"Say it," I growled. "Say you get off on it."

"I do," she moaned as she writhed against me. "I think about you coming to me. Blood smearing your skin. I think of you fucking me while covered in it—"

I pushed her back onto the bed, taking the handcuffs off before turning her over. Her lips were on mine in seconds, along with a hand between my legs.

"I want to hurt you," I confessed against her lips. "I want to mark you so you'll never even have a chance to forget about me."

There was a strange vulnerability to my words and I regretted saying them as soon as they were out of my mouth. Her fingers found my clit and she pinched it hard, the pain mixing deliciously with the jolt of pleasure that followed.

"Bite me," she whispered and pulled away to bare her neck to me. The same place I had bitten previously was still red and already bruising. "So hard it draws blood. So hard the imprint of your teeth will be forever scarred on my skin."

I leaned down with a moan.

"Are you sure?" I asked and laid a kiss on the previous bite. I planned to bite right over it and I knew it would probably make it hurt more, but I couldn't bring myself to care. Though truthfully, I don't think Willow cared either.

"Yes," she breathed and used her free hand to tangle in my hair and force my mouth to her shoulder. "Mark me, Avery."

This time I didn't hesitate to bite down, nor did I try to slowly add pressure. I bit right into her hard enough that it was only a few seconds until the metallic taste of her blood hit my mouth.

She cried so loud I had to cover her mouth with my hand. Her other hand paused its movement on my clit for only a moment before she furiously started rubbing horizontal strokes on my clit.

I paused before biting her harder, praying that it would scar.

When I pulled back, I almost orgasmed right on the spot after seeing the blood ooze from the wound. It wasn't perfect all the way around, with only a few of my teeth that broke the skin, but it was perfect enough that I was sure it would leave some sort of scar.

When she inserted two fingers into me, I let out a hiss.

"I need to tend to your wound," I said and moved to stop her hand, but she sent me a glare.

"One more," she said, almost begging. "I need to feel you come around me."

With a moan, I forced my lips to her and rode out the orgasm she forced from me.

And it wouldn't be the first time Willow Evens had yet again ruined my plans.

WILLOW

"Ouch, fuck," I cursed under my breath as Avery poured disinfectant over my wound.

She quickly pushed the warm damp cloth on the bite. A jolt of pain ran through me but was quickly chased away by the warmth of the cloth and the gentleness of her hands. A gentleness I didn't know she possessed.

We were in my bathroom, and I was sitting on the edge of the tub. The hard surface had already caused my back to ache, but there was no way I would tell her that and risk breaking whatever it was that was going on between us.

She was silent as she worked. It would have been awkward if she wasn't so focused on her task. I was afraid that she may even be able to hear my heart beating rapidly in my chest.

She was kneeling between my legs in nothing but her sweats. And I was in nothing but a flimsy towel that was wrapped around my hips. The only thing left on me was the cold metal locket that sat heavily on my chest. She hadn't asked about it yet, but it was only a matter of time before she questioned why I never removed it. Once again, I was bared to her, but I didn't feel the need to cover myself.

Her actions were like whiplash.

One moment she would force my head between her legs and

sink her teeth into my flesh, and the next, she was helping me to the bathroom and wordlessly cleaning off the wound.

"Human bites carry a lot of bacteria," she said after a long moment of silence, her eyes shifting to look at mine. Her blonde hair had been pushed out of her face and was still damp with sweat. Our time together in the room took a lot out of us both and I wanted nothing more than to fall into a deep sleep, preferably in the bath. But apparently, treating the wound came first.

My body was aching all over from exertion and every time I lifted my arms, they began to shake.

I was completely at her mercy. Something that should have scared me. After all, I knew now exactly what she was capable of and I doubted murder was the most heinous thing she had done.

"Thank you," I whispered. "For... taking care of me."

The smile that spread across her face caused my breath to get caught in my lungs.

I still didn't understand, after everything, why she was still able to pull such a reaction from me.

"It's the least I can do," she said and let her hand come to cup my face. "After all, the last few times, I did leave without warning."

For just a moment, I let myself lean into her touch.

I still couldn't understand how someone like her—someone who murdered people with no remorse—could be so caring and gentle.

"Why did you?" I asked, my voice barely above a whisper.

She pushed her lips together and her eyes trailed back to my wound. She wiped it again, refusing to meet my gaze.

"Because it was the best thing at the time," she said. "You weren't ready for... this."

A sharp burst of anger spread through me, but I was so exhausted that I couldn't do much about it but frown.

*Who was she to decide what **I** wasn't ready for?* I was a grown adult and more than capable of making my own decisions.

Now whether it was smart to get involved with someone like her was a different story, but it would be *my* decision at the end of the day.

"You don't have the liberty to decide that for me," I said with a pout.

She still refused to look at me, and I winced when she put pressure on the wound. I was almost afraid to look at it at that point. The bloody images of the crash that took over my nightmares sometimes held me in a choke hold for days. Who knew what actually seeing the wounds in person would do to me.

"You were hesitant," she pointed out.

I gently cupped the side of her face, forcing her to look at me. I needed to make this clear to her and I couldn't do that with her avoiding my stare.

"I wanted to get to know you," I whispered. "I don't want you hiding in the shadows anymore. No matter how much I like it when you surprise me."

The small smile that spread across her lips caused a sudden warmth to spread across my body.

"Just moments ago, you were saying you were hoping to forget what happened between us. What changed your mind?"

I licked my suddenly dry lips.

"Even through your actions, I have been able to learn about you," I said. "Learn that you aren't trying to hurt me and maybe that, for the first time in a while, I have someone who will do anything for me. But I don't want it to stop there."

She paused for a moment, her eyes lingering on the locket.

"And if you... get to know me, will you accept what's happening between us?"

"When have I denied it?" I asked.

Her eyes shifted to look into mine before narrowing. I sent her a small, sheepish smile. Maybe I hadn't been as open to the idea of us together, but the idea of a relationship—*with her*—was enticing, to say the least. I couldn't remember ever feeling this way for another person before. But that alone caused me to pause.

"I was—*am*—scared," I admitted.

"Of me?" she said with a small pout. Her actions were almost childlike. Something that amused me greatly.

"Of many things," I said. "You kinda murder people."

"Would you rather I let him touch you? Have his way with you?" Her voice turned hard. "I don't want people to touch what's mine."

The claim she staked on me should have annoyed me or scared me... but instead, it caused a feeling in my chest to expand outward and for my head to spin.

"But he's not the first," I said in a hard tone.

"Or last," she said with just as much of a tone.

I swallowed thickly. Maybe this is a battle I wouldn't be able to win just yet.

"How can you..." I didn't say the words. But I knew she understood what I wanted to ask.

"I have never had a problem with it," she admitted and grabbed the large Band-Aid near her feet. "From the time I was young, I did what I needed to do."

I let the words settle inside me. *I did what I needed to do.*

If what she needed to do was kill people, what kind of life had she lived previous to this?

"What happened with your first?" I asked.

I didn't think she would answer at first. She just continued to clean my wound, apply ointment, then place the Band-Aid over the wound. But then, slowly, she looked me in the eye. Her rage-filled stare caused me to pause and I wondered if I should have just left it alone.

"They tried to hurt someone I loved," she admitted. "Though my fath—*they* hired someone incompetent for the job, so I beat them to it."

I let my hand run through her hair. My arm shook lightly, but we both ignored it.

"Yes," I said, my voice barely above a whisper.

She raised a brow at me.

"If I get to know you, I can try to... accept what's happening between us."

Though even as I spoke, I knew that I had already come to terms with it. She was in my dreams, my nightmares as well. I imagined her behind every corner, lurking and waiting for her chance to get her hands on me.

There was no denying us. No denying what I wanted from her.

My rational mind may try to fight it, but inside I knew it would be impossible to fight.

"Not try to," she said and let her hands trail up my bare thighs. "You will. You and I both know it's inevitable."

"It's my compromise," I said. "That and the cameras."

"They stay," she ground out. "Think of it as a way for me to protect you."

"I don't need protection," I said.

Her expression turned grim.

"No fighting on this," she said. "Now tell me what *get to know me* entails."

I couldn't help the smile that spread across my face.

"Normal people stuff," I said and trailed my hand down her face and neck, enjoying the way her skin erupted in goose bumps under my touch.

"So sex," she said, that wicked grin spreading across her lips. "If that's all you wanted, you could have told me."

I rolled my eyes.

"Talking, going out, dating, eating together," I said. "And sharing information about each other."

"A date?" she asked. If I didn't know any better, I would say there was a bit of excitement in her voice.

I nodded.

"I can do that," she said, surprising me. "And then you will stop fighting us?"

"Only if you sweep me off my feet," I said playfully. "If not, maybe I'll need a few more dates."

A wicked glint passed through her eyes.

"Or I can convince you another way," she breathed, pulling the towel off me.

I opened my legs for her, my breath coming out in shaky pants. I threaded my hand through her hair and pushed her closer to my aching pussy.

"I won't say no to that, but it will take a lot more than a few orgasms to sway me."

She looked up at me as she dragged her tongue across my folds.

"A few?" she said in a playful tone. "Don't insult me."

I didn't have time to fight back as she devoured me. All that I knew was that after this, I was royally fucked.

AVERY

Two things.

I only had two things to complete and then I could see Willow again. I was forced to compromise with myself or risk falling further into Willow. It was only a matter of time before I was in so deep that I wouldn't want to find my way out.

Though the list was taking a fucking lifetime. Realistically, I could have knocked one of them off the list with ease, but there wasn't anything fun about that. And if I tackled the easier first, I may have been tempted to not even attempt the second.

I let out a sigh as I came across the hidden tea shop.

It was nestled between two buildings on the outskirts of Manhattan. It had a three-star average, but the pictures on their website made it look like they put a lot of work into their presentation. My guess was it was one of those struggling cafés that wanted to carve out a space for themselves, knowing that many people would just skip them for a much larger chain store. The place was easily overlooked, but I guess that was the point.

I pushed into the shop and was hit with the scent of plants and sweet brewed tea. The shop was two stories with a patio toward the back. Exposed brick covered the walls, giving it more of a cozy feel. Shelves lined the place and were overflowing with all different types of plants. Many had a price tag on them, but by the looks of the wilting leaves, they had been here for longer than the owner expected. There were a few tables scattered throughout and only two customers toward the back of the shop.

The worker behind the counter greeted me, but I ignored them, heading straight to the customers in the back.

The two women paused in their conversation to look up at me as I approached. The one with her back to the wall stiffened, her blue eyes widening as she took me in. Her light-golden hair was pulled up into a bun. She wore a thick sweater that seemed to swallow her whole. Her ears, neck, and fingers were all decked out in gold.

It had been years since I had seen her up close and personal like this and her reaction tracked, unlike the phone call I had received a few weeks before. I should have realized that someone like her would never seek me out. She was content with pretending that she never had me.

"I'm sorry. Can we help you?" her friend asked.

At first, I was ready to ignore her, but then something tipped me off. I'm not sure if it was the lack of brand names covering her body while she was adorned by large Cartier diamond earrings or if it was the way that she looked at my mother like she was about to get scolded.

Her face was red and there was a nervousness about her that didn't fit a casual tea time with Mother.

"Sorry," I said, putting on my most dazzling smile. "I was here to pick up my mother but didn't realize she had a date with a friend." I held out my hand for her. "Avery *Maddox*."

"Maddox...?" she breathed and reached her hand out to grasp mine. I made a point of twisting her hand to look at the expensive rings adorning her fingers.

My mother sent me a look, telling me all that I needed to know.

"Yes. Avery Maddox, nice to meet you."

"Likewise... I'm Cecilia Hampton."

I made a mental note of the name.

"Sorry, she must have forgotten to mention she had a daughter," I said and sent her a smile, pulling my hand away from hers. "I hope she didn't forget to tell you she shares the Maddox name as well, did she?"

By the look on Cecilia's face, my mother had her here on false pretenses.

"Avery," Mother warned.

"We have an appointment to go see some open houses," I said, putting on my best smile. "You didn't forget, did you?"

Cecilia looked like she'd seen a ghost.

Not only was she probably sleeping with Father, but there was no way that the woman in front of her was old enough to have a child my age.

She was but seventeen when she was pregnant with me. A child. Yet to say she didn't know better than when she got with my father would be a bald-faced lie.

My mother had been young, but she wasn't naive.

She fixed a smile on her face.

"Oh, sorry." She let out a giggle. "I must have mixed up the times. So sorry, Cecilia, I did promise her I'd go check out some houses with her."

She awkwardly grabbed her bag and stood. Cecilia quickly fixed her face before turning to me.

"Thank you." Her grateful tone was not lost on me.

"I'll call you," Mother said as she slipped her arm in mine. Her grip was tight on me. A warning to get her the hell out of there before I could cause a bigger scene.

She was silent as I led her out the front and didn't seem to even breathe until we had walked past the shop and around the corner.

"That was reckless," she spat, her eyes narrowing on me.

I shrugged.

"I just saved that poor woman from becoming cannon fodder."

"She deserves it," Mother spat. "Did you see how much money he splurged on her? There's more than what she was wearing. A whole lot more."

Her tone sounded a lot like jealousy, but in reality, Mother was protecting her status with Father. At the moment, she was the only person who had provided Father with a child that he could rope into his business.

Knowing if he had mistresses lined up, then her position would be in jeopardy. This also wasn't the first time she had done this.

"Call your driver," I ordered, not wanting to talk about this any longer. It brought up far too many memories of when I was younger and still believed they were together out of love. It broke my heart to hear Mother talk about him like this. It hurt even more when I started catching Father in the act. "They're not one of Dad's, right?"

She let out a huff and shook her head as she dug out her phone.

"It's still Beckham," she muttered, her long nails clacking on the phone screen as she texted him. When she was done, she shot me a look.

She could at least fucking act like she wanted me here, couldn't she?

Maybe it was because of everything with Willow, but for the first time, I didn't feel like I needed to grovel for her attention. If she wanted to act like a spoiled brat, then she could, but I wouldn't let it hinder my plans.

"Why are you here?"

I sent her a forced smile.

"I wasn't lying about seeing houses," I said. "Plus, is it wrong to want to check in on your mother once in a while?"

Her lips pushed into a thin line and only then did I notice some of the wrinkles on her face. They weren't there the last time I saw her. A pang went through my chest, just like it always did when we met. She was getting older now. Her young life of being pampered with Father's money was slowly crumbling away, and right before her eyes.

"Your father would hang both of us if he knew."

I looked back toward the street we came from. The car was waiting for us and parked illegally on the street.

"Then it would be in both our favors for you to not tell him."

Fresh coat of light-blue paint. New hardwood floors.

The last owners tried their best to dress up the 1970s house, but the age showed on the outside and in the way the house creaked around us. It was perfect for a family. It had a spacious living room and kitchen. The stairs weren't too steep and it would be enough for a single family of three or four.

But even still, it lacked the appeal of the new builds and buyers these days were picky.

The house had been on the market for over twenty days and while today it wasn't technically available for walk-throughs, the lock was easy enough to pick.

The sound of Mother's heels clacking behind me was the only assurance I had that she was still with me. She had refused to talk to me the entire way here. No doubt because I had ruined whatever she planned for Father's mistress.

For both our hides, I hoped she wasn't planning to murder the poor woman.

We were quiet as we explored the inside. I didn't really need to look it over, given its history, along with the pictures on the listing, but I wanted to be safe just in case I needed to do any repairs later.

When I entered the master bedroom, I paused. There was a large bay window with a reading nook that almost made the age of the house worth it.

Willow would love this room to paint in.

The window was unobstructed and bathed the room in sunlight. I could imagine her sitting there. Her long auburn hair up in a ponytail, shining in the sun. She would wear a tank top and shorts to take advantage of the sunshine. The image of her spread out, the tank top rising up her belly, with the sun warming her tanned skin, caused my heart to stop.

"What do you want, Avery?" Mother asked from behind me. I turned to see her leaning against the doorway with her arms crossed. "I know you didn't kidnap me to come look at shitty houses."

It was a shitty house, but hearing her say it like that caused an unnamed emotion to swirl in my chest. *It's been so many years. Must she still be so coarse?*

"Make plans for yourself," I said. I paused for a moment and let the words sink in.

I shouldn't have taken the risk of warning her. She could tell Father, though I desperately hoped she wouldn't.

Her eyes were calculating as they searched my face.

"What are you planning?"

I couldn't stop the smile. It was a bitter smile. One that really hoped that Mother would have changed after all the years apart. But I was hit with the reality that Mother didn't change because she never wanted to.

I was sure all children went through this though. Or at least ones with parents like mine. But all of them, at some point, would have to face the reality that I was coming to.

Our parents never wanted us. To them, we were tools to get what they wanted. Whether that be attention, money, or to satisfy emotional needs they never got from their own parents, it depended on them, but it was all the same.

"Me? Plan?" I joked. "Have you ever heard of such a thing?"

She rolled her eyes.

"That's all?" she asked. "You pulled me from my tea date to *warn* me? Couldn't you have just sent a text or called me?"

I pushed down the disappointment and cleared my throat.

"Father got my last number from you," I noted. "Why on earth would I trust you with my new number?"

She clicked her tongue, her eyes shifting to the floor. *Was that... guilt?*

Though if it was, it was gone as soon as it came and she was back, her eyes finding mine with malice.

"Why must you ignore him?" she asked. "You know you'll have to come back at some point? I was doing you a favor."

I couldn't help the bitter laugh that spilled from my lips.

"A favor. *Right.*"

"Don't make this worse for the both of us," she said with a sigh. "You remember what happened last time you tried to... make plans."

By "*make plans,*" she means setting her up with her boyfriend in another country and away from my father. Before I could even blink, Father had the man killed and I was delivered the family punishment for trying to escape.

Mother, of course, didn't get in trouble. My guess was she blamed it all on me, but I couldn't bear to let my thoughts go down that path again.

"I love you," I said.

She didn't say it back. She never did.

"I love you," I repeated. "But I can't try to protect you anymore. This is my last try. Either you make plans and get out..."

"Or what?" she asked with a raised brow.

I walked past her and out into the hallway. All the nervous energy I had stored inside me deflated and I was left with a sort of hollowness that one could only feel after dealing with an unloving parent.

"I guess you'll see, Mother," I said. "This may be the last time I see you... so take care."

I was halfway down the hallway before her words caused me to pause.

"You can't keep secrets for long, Avery." Her voice was but a whisper, but it traveled easily through the silent house. "Not from him. Not about this and not... not her."

God. There it was.

A single sentence that showed even a hint that she cared and my mind had already latched on to it like it was starving. She was like me in many ways, I realized after digesting her sentence. She was keeping tabs on me. Even when I thought she had abandoned me.

"Be careful," I said, looking back at her with a bitter smile. "Saying something like that may cause me to believe you actually care about your child."

I don't. That was what her blank expression told me.

But the feelings rising inside me didn't register it. All it knew was that my mother cared enough to issue a warning.

I need Willow.

WILLOW

Avery was back.

I don't know what I expected after our night in my room together... but it wasn't this.

Maybe I expected her to give up the student facade and instead try and act normal. Like she had said.

But then again, I was unreasonably excited to see her again, so I didn't much care how or when it happened... just that it did.

At first, I was shocked when I saw her walking into the classroom and coming down to sit in her seat. She had been missing for a few weeks now and for any other student, I would have waited for them to come up and maybe ask about what they missed. But she just sat down with no pen, no paper, no laptop, no backpack and just stared at me as I taught.

Her attention flustered me multiple times throughout my lectures. I tried to focus on the other students, but the heat of her gaze always pulled me to her. The bite had healed over, though it was still sensitive to the touch and was slightly raised. Though when she arrived, it felt like it was on fire. As if her presence alone caused it to start to act up again.

As nerve-racking as it was, I started to almost enjoy having someone there with me in class.

I had gotten used to the teaching since the start of the term, but I was still new and that knowledge, on top of my impostor syndrome, was a hard battle to fight.

"Alright, class," I said in a light tone. "So last week, I taught you how to put together a gallery for the physical art students. This week we're gonna finish off with some more examples of museums like MoMA and The Broad and then next week, we are going to start crafting our own."

And with that, class was dismissed. It was the last class of the day and I stood still as everyone politely got up and left. Some students came to talk to me about what to expect the following week, so I indulged them for a few extra minutes, all while Avery sat patiently in the front row.

When the last of them left, she stood and stretched.

"I don't know why you do it if you don't like it," she said.

I stood straight, annoyance prickled at my skin.

"I like teaching," I insisted.

She let out an unconvinced noise, though this was not something I wanted to delve into yet. She stayed silent like she was waiting for me to take her cue, but instead I ignored it completely.

"So where are you taking me for our date?" I asked.

A smirk spread across her face. I almost thought she would fight me on the change of subject, but she just leaned straight into it.

"Professor Evens," she breathed, scandalized. "Don't you think you should be more discreet about our relationship?"

I can't help but let out a scoff, though if I was being honest, I loved this playful side of her.

"There's no relationship," I said. "Remember, you have to *woo* me."

"Not *yet*," she corrected. Her footsteps were light as she crossed the room. "And I think I gave you a sufficient number of orgasms to sweeten the deal."

My cheeks burned from the memories of us together.

"That was weeks ago," I muttered.

I was leaning against my desk with my arms crossed and she

moved to stand in front of me. She placed her arms on either side of me on the desk and leaned forward.

She was teasing me by leaning close as if to kiss me but didn't.

My heart pounded in my chest and my breathing stalled.

She was so enticing. So sure, so confident. And I knew in a second, the entire situation could flip and her hand could be at my throat again and I would melt into a puddle at her feet.

"So you *did* miss me," she said teasingly.

I rolled my shoulders, trying to look like I was unbothered by her observation.

"It definitely doesn't help your case," I said. "Who knows what you are doing when you're not with me."

She raised her brow at me.

"Someone's feisty today. Jealous? Afraid I went off and found another pussy to keep me company?"

My mouth fell open and I let out an angry huff. *That's what I was to her? Just another pussy? What happened to the "mine" talk?*

But soon, my anger turned into annoyance as she let out a light laugh. I smacked her right shoulder with a pout.

"That's *not* funny."

Her hand shot forward to grab my shirt and force me closer to her.

"There is no one else, Willow," she said, her breath wafting across my lips. "That much I can promise you."

Her eyes shoot to the shoulder she bit. I didn't stop her as she yanked my shirt to the side so that the mark was bared to her. I knew what she saw. The tender flesh was still reddish, but slowly it was fading, just like the time in the room together.

She leaned toward me, passing my lips completely. I jumped when her tongue swiped across it before she opened her mouth to clamp down on it.

Pain skittered up my shoulder and neck and a moan fell from my lips. When she pulled away, she let out a satisfied hum.

"Not as obvious as I would have wanted it, but we have time to make more."

I tugged my shirt back up and sent her a look while putting some space between us.

"We are in public," I hissed.

She rolled her eyes before standing straight.

"We'll go into the city," she said, her eyes trailing the empty classroom. "There is a special gallery opening there that will only be open for the next month or so. Apparently the guy is a big deal." She paused. "Though if I'm being honest, even after looking at your search history, I'm at a loss as to what you would find interesting."

"Of course you looked at my search history," I said as a spike of anxiety and fear rose in me.

I was so vulnerable with her. I was forced to drop any mask I had. She knew everything.

Well, almost, it would seem.

"One day, you won't be surprised anymore," she said with a shrug. "The search history. Your favorite ice cream. Your favorite food. What you do when no one's watching. You'll just accept that I know every part of you, maybe even better than you know yourself."

Her voice was low and hypnotizing. She walked the length of my desk before leaning against it. Her eyes were searching my face as if to find any secrets I may have hidden inside me.

"You're kind of boring."

The bluntness of her words forced a shocked laugh to spill from my lips.

"*Boring*?" I asked

Her smile was a teasing smile that caused my stomach to flutter.

"You only go out when friends invite you," she said. "Now that school has started, you stopped reaching out to art directors and gallery owners for work. You even stopped your afternoon walks. Any new paintings?"

I swallow thickly. As a matter of fact, I had created three new paintings, all of her. Though this time, instead of reusing the same canvas, I bought brand-new ones. Each one of them was harder to let go of than the last, but they all stayed in my closet as if letting them see the light of day would somehow make what was happening to me real.

Leaving them out would tell Avery, and the world, that I was just as obsessed with her as she was with me.

"Don't act like you didn't see them."

God, her smile had such a vise grip on my heart that if she continued to stare at me the way she did. I knew it would be just a few minutes before I was brought to my knees.

"I'm not sure why you hide them," she murmured. "I'm also not sure why you didn't try for a physical art position. You obviously have a passion for it."

That's where she was wrong. It wasn't a passion... it was a compulsion. I *had* to paint and sketch in order to get the images out of my mind. If I allowed them to stay there for even a moment too long, they would take over my entire being.

I learned that the hard way after the accident.

I had locked myself in my room for weeks at a time, painting the scene over and over again. The dead eyes. The blood. The glass.

For every hour I was stuck in that car, I was forced to paint a rendition of it. Forced to paint the emotions that built up inside me, along with my own cries for help.

There was no passion in what I did with the canvas. It was horror. It was trauma.

But then... what did that make Avery?

"I have my reasons," I said and cleared my throat. "And also, don't forget, it's kinda hard for me to go out when I have a stalker after me."

For a moment, it looked like she wouldn't let me get away with my obvious change of subject. Her eyes burrowed into me and there was a type of expectation in her stare.

I could almost feel the words rolling off of her.

So you can get to know me, but I can't get to know you?

Instead, she let an easy smile cross her face.

"A stalker?" she teased. "We're dating."

The tenseness in my shoulders melted right off and I gave her a smile in return.

"In order to date, you need to go on a date," I reminded.

"Are you telling me you don't like my idea for a date?" she asked with a raised brow.

"No, no," I said quickly. "It's not that I *don't* like it. It's just that maybe—I thought..." I paused, trying to find my words. "I want to get to know *you*, Avery. I don't want the date to be focused on *me* or my wants. I want to understand you... It's only fair."

She didn't respond. Her eyebrows pulled together and her smile dropped into a light pout. She looked almost... confused.

"What do you want to do?" I asked. "If Avery could pick a date that she wants to go on. Where would she go?"

All teasing and amusement had left her face and she stood still as a board, her eyes searching for something. I could tell her mind was working overtime, but there was nothing coming out of her mouth.

In that moment, I realized that maybe no one had ever asked Avery what she wanted to do. Just like in the bathroom that night, I was hit with an uncomfortable feeling in my stomach. What type of life had Avery lived until now that caused her to be like this?

That caused her to kill? That pushed everyone so far away from her that she couldn't even pick what she wanted to do?

"Has no one asked you what you wanted to do before?" I asked her. My tone was light, but her expression made me wish I hadn't spoken at all. I didn't want her to think that I pitied her. If anything, it was the opposite. I knew inside she had to be strong... I just wished that it was different. That she hadn't had to have gone through whatever it was that made her like this.

"No," she said, her eyes searching my face until they finally landed on my own. "If I find myself close enough to someone, sometimes I will ask them to accompany me somewhere that I want to go, but usually I'll just go by myself. No one's ever—" she cut herself off.

Feeling bad for my own stalker was just one of the many red

flags that had crowded my mind since meeting Avery, but for some reason, red was turning out to be my favorite color.

I reached out and grabbed her hand. The roughness of her palm was familiar and inviting. I squeezed it and gave her a smile.

"I'm very excited to go wherever you want to go."

She looked shocked and for the first time, I think I truly rendered her speechless.

She pulled her hand away to dig for something in her pocket. Her eyebrows were pushed together and she had a somewhat pained expression on her face.

...did something happen?

I opened my mouth to ask, but her hand snaked around my neck and jerked me forward before I could ground myself. I gripped the desk to steady myself.

Her hand trailed to the side of my neck and pulled away. It wasn't until there was a soft tug at my neck that I realized she had grabbed my locket.

Panic washed through me, but I made no move to yank it out of her hands. I watched her with bated breath, worried about what she would do with it.

The pained expression didn't leave her face even as she popped it open. I didn't need to look down at it to know what she saw, but ever so slightly, her expression relaxed.

Her other hand came up and positioned something on the empty side. My heart pounded in my chest and all but threatened to break through as she carefully placed whatever it was inside.

When she was done, she dropped it and gave me a look, but her expression was unreadable.

"Don't ever forget me, okay?"

I opened my mouth to speak, but no words came out. Instead, I just nodded and stood there as she walked away from me.

It wasn't until the classroom door shut behind her that I had the courage to look at the still-open locket. With shaky hands, I grabbed it and turned it around.

Tears pricked my eyes when I saw the color photo of her in a blue cap and gown on the empty side. From what I could tell, the photo was taken outside and she was looking at the camera as if she didn't want to be there. She was much younger than she was now but still undoubtedly her.

She looked so young, but there was still something behind her eyes that caused my heart to ache.

Don't ever forget about me.

I swallowed thickly and let my eyes trail to the image of my father before the crash. His wide smile caused my heart to twist. It was one of many favorite photos of him. He was holding peach flowers and a dirty white shirt. I took it when he picked me up after work on Valentine's Day. He had been so happy to be my Valentine every year that he would rush to get me after work with flowers and chocolates. It didn't matter if he was sweaty from work or if his golden skin was reddened by the sunburn he got during the day.

He was there, no matter what.

And now, so would Avery.

AVERY

I'm very excited to go wherever you want to go.

There is no shortage of surprises with Willow.

First, in her room, knowing I watched as she got herself off. Then when she admitted that she likes knowing that I watch her. And now for her to ask me where I want to go on a date?

It was something so small, so simple, yet it had rocked my world. I had seen it happen to people in conversations over and over again. I had done it to people myself, but I was shocked that this was the first time it was happening to me.

I had never expected her to be so curious about me to the point where she *actually* wanted to know what I liked and what I wanted to do.

If I'm being honest, it caused me to panic... and I *don't* panic.

My whole life, I had been brought up to be a perfect heir. I went through rigorous schooling among people who now lead the top companies in the world. Some of them even rule countries. I've stolen money, lots of it.

I *kill* people, for fuck's sake.

I don't panic. I have never panicked.

But the thought of bringing Willow to a place that I actually wanted to go to had caused more panic than I had felt in my life.

Shadowed by some of the stuff I had to deal with for Mother, but that was completely different. It didn't help that there was only one place that I could bring her because there was only one place that I wanted to go.

This wouldn't cause Willow to *get to know me*. This would cause her to actually see me. See the thing that kept me floating throughout the years when I had nothing else.

I skipped class on Thursday so that I could be at Willow's house before she came home. After all, this was a date and I had a certain standard for myself. But Willow wasn't just any other date. I had once told her that I would do anything to keep her, and I meant it.

Her keys jingled at the doorway and a burst of excitement ran through me. As soon as she opened the door, she paused.

"Dinner's getting cold," I called. Her footsteps were hurried as she walked into the apartment and peered into the kitchen.

I finished dinner not long ago but had already cleaned the pans and had two plates set aside for us. The dining room table was set with utensils and a glass of white wine for her. I wouldn't be drinking, at least not yet. I had to keep a clear mind for later.

Though the promise of the relaxation the wine offered me was tempting.

I couldn't do much with the appliances she had at her apartment, as most of them were far too old. The apartments were owned by the university and I doubted they cared too much about updating them every few years. So I settled for a risotto and brought some wine to pair it with.

Nothing fancy and not at all like what I thought she deserved, but it would be a nice start.

She looked over the plates still on the kitchen counter and then looked to me. Though for the first time, I couldn't really make out what she was feeling, and all of a sudden, the turtleneck that I chose to wear for tonight seemed too tight.

Was this too much? Was this not what she meant about getting to know me?

I was worried that I had somehow ruined my chances of getting her to fully accept us already.

Then a smile spread across her face. A real one. One that took my breath away.

"Your hair looks cute," she said.

I fucking flushed. I could feel my face heating and I quickly grabbed the plates and walked to her wobbly dining table. The sound of her locking the door caused my heart to skip.

"I'm serious," she said. "I liked the bun."

My hair wasn't long enough for a full bun, but at times I liked to pull it back, especially when I was cooking. I planned to take it out later for our date, but I guess it was staying.

I was so out of my comfort zone that I had no idea what to do or how to react.

"I know you don't like portobello mushrooms," I said, then cleared my throat to hide the slight nervousness in my voice. "So I just used white."

Get your shit together, Avery.

She let out a little laugh and pulled out the chair to sit down.

She went straight to the wine I had set down for her. She took a small sip of it

"This looks really good. Thank you."

It was my turn to let out a forced laugh. I pulled out my chair and sat as well.

"You're not upset that I broke into your apartment?"

"I was scared at first, but when I realized it was you, I calmed down," she admitted, her hand hovering over the utensils I had placed down. "Also, coming home to a cooked meal after a long day at work is nice. Maybe I could get used to this."

Damn. If that's what she truly wanted, I would make sure to be here and cook dinner for her as often as I could. I had seen the low stock in her kitchen and watched her as she went to the school cafeteria multiple times. Willow truly didn't care about the food she put in her body. Some days I had seen her work on caffeine and a single banana for hours until she dragged herself to the cafeteria.

But not anymore. If she wanted me here, then so be it.

I was starting to wonder if she knew how tightly she had me wrapped around that little finger of hers.

I gripped my fork and motioned for her to try the food.

She sent me a small smile before taking a bite. Her eyes widened and she sent me a shocked face.

"Where did you learn to cook like that?" she asked between shoveling bites into her mouth. I didn't care about the lack of manners or etiquette. Willow reacting like *that* to something I made caused pride to swell in my chest.

"A class," I said and took a bite of my own. I noted it could use more cheese.

She took another hearty bite and moaned. It only caused my ego to inflate even more. I wondered what other types of food could cause her to give me a reaction like that.

In moments I had a list in my head of all the other dishes I would make for her.

"I can't imagine *you* seeking out a cooking class," she admitted.

I sent her a smile and reached forward to grab her wineglass. She sent me a look, but I just winked at her before taking a sip. *Fuck staying sober for this.* I needed something if I was going to calm the racing of my heart.

I took another sip before placing it back next to her plate. A tactic to delay my answer. I didn't really want to talk about my past, but I guess I would have no choice. Not if I wanted this to work.

"I went to a private school my entire life," I said. "On top of classes, they also have you take etiquette, cooking, debate, music, etcetera."

"What school?" she asked. I swallowed thickly before responding.

"You probably haven't heard of it," I said quickly.

She gave me a lingering look before turning back to her plate.

"No, probably not," she muttered.

The dinner was tense for another few moments.

She wants to get to know you, Avery. Giving her just a few bits of information wouldn't hurt. She's not like your fucking father.

"Kingswood Prep," I said after a moment.

"Kingswood," she muttered the name. Seconds ticked by as she digested it. "Oh! That's where Prince—oh my god, you're rich *rich.*"

I stiffened and tried to take deep breaths.

Not me, my family.

I wanted to abide by the compromise and let her know everything, but I wasn't ready to divulge about my father just yet. This was as far as I could go, and I hoped she would understand it without me having to say anything.

I truly wanted to make this work.

She let out a loud sigh.

"It all makes sense now. I could tell there was something about you when I met you," she teased. "So *that's* where you get all your arrogance from."

I shot her a look as shock ran through me.

"Arrogance?" I asked with a laugh. She wiggled her fork at me after taking a hefty bite of risotto and washing it down with some wine.

The tension around us melted away and I couldn't help the smile that spread across my face.

Of course, Willow wouldn't care as much, not like the others, at least. There was a certain reaction you got from growing up with the Maddox name. It didn't matter how I was as a person, but as soon as they heard who my father was. People treated me differently.

But given her reaction to the school, I didn't think it would be the same. It caused a painful amount of hope to grow in my chest.

For a moment, I thought maybe it wouldn't be as bad to share these parts of myself with her.

"You know it's true," she said, waving me off. "So where are we going tonight?"

"Someplace important to me," I said. "But first we have to go shopping."

Why was I so goddamn nervous about this?

I had been to the place hundreds of times, and the people there knew me. But I was still so nervous about stepping through those doors.

My heart was pounding in my chest and my palms were sweaty. I hadn't felt this way for a really long time and it was really fucking throwing me off.

I was fine as I shopped with Willow to get her the perfect black dress for tonight. It was only as we got closer to the club that nerves began to overtake me.

But goddamn, did she look beautiful. We had picked an elegant dress that hugged her curves and stopped midcalf. It had a square neckline that showcased her new peach-colored diamond that contrasted beautifully with her skin. And lastly, her deep-red hair was tied up into an elegant updo.

The locket was pulled tight against her neck and clashed with the other necklace, but I couldn't bring myself to ask her to take it off. Not when my photo was so carefully placed next to her father's. That was saying something, me next to the only other person she loved in the world.

It caused my head to spin.

At first, she complained about how much money I was spending on her, but when I reminded her that I had a lot of it, she quieted down and started accepting my gifts. But she did so with such gratitude that it warmed my heart. I wanted nothing more than to spoil her and when she finally allowed me to shower her with the gifts, I was beside myself.

But then, all my excitement crumbled as soon as the hotel came into view. In the basement of a Brooklyn hotel, there was a small place where classical musicians played for only a small group of carefully curated people. It wasn't a well-kept secret, but they didn't allow just anyone in. You had to know someone to get in and then once you were in, you could visit whenever you wanted, but getting in that first time was damn near impossible.

The hotel itself was fancy and probably cost a grand a night at least, depending on the floor you were staying on. There was wait-staff at the entrance that greeted us, but as soon as they saw me, they paused before motioning for us to follow them to the back of the hotel.

At first, the entrance to the place was hidden, but when you got close enough to the back of the hotel, you were met with a grand staircase that went below ground.

I helped Willow down the steps as music flowed out of the open doorway. There was a man in a suit waiting for us. He gave us a smile when I met his gaze.

"So *this* is your crowd," Willow said. Her voice was teasing, but I could sense the nervousness in it. I wasn't sure if it was the way that people were treating us that caused her nervousness or if it was the place itself.

"Ms. Maddox," the doorman greeted. "And guest." He bowed his head to us and waved for us to go in.

"Thank you, Henry," I said, noting his name tag.

As we passed the doorway, I pulled Willow to me. There was a short hallway with dimly lit lamps that led us to the main area.

"You must come here often," she said, leaning into my side.

I let out a small laugh.

"Sometimes," I admitted. "But I have never seen him before."

"Are you, like, famous or something?" she asked. I shook my head.

"No."

I pulled her farther down the hall, following the music. Since it was the basement, it was only lit by small torch-like lamps on the exposed brick walls. Deep mahogany, burgundy, and bits of gold were splashed around us and when we got to the room, I heard Willow's small gasp.

The room wasn't very large, but it was beautiful. There was a quaint bar on the left-hand side and small tables with love seats and couches lining the place. Deep-red carpet lined the floor and the faint scent of a musky cologne filled the room. Toward the end of the room, there was a small stage with lights pointed at the musicians that stood there. They weren't playing fully yet, but just testing their instruments as they waited for people to filter in.

I didn't recognize the man who held the cello, but I did recognize the piano player. I'd seen him here many times, but even before that, rumors of his talent spread across the musical industry. Excitement swelled within me and I pulled Willow to one of the couches closest to the stage.

The majority of the room was dim, but the light from the stage reflected off of Willow's face and gave me a perfect look at her excitement. I wrapped my arm around her, letting my fingers slip into the neckline of her dress and feel the slightly raised bumps of my bite.

It sent a pang of lust and possessiveness through me. I never realized just how turned on marking what was mine made me, but now I wished I had gotten her a strapless dress so everyone here would see that she belonged to me.

When she shivered against me, I had to pull my hand away lest I risk taking this further than what was allowed in this space.

"You see that piano player?" I asked her in a low voice. She nodded. "His name is Austin Barker. He has been playing for over thirty years and has won far too many awards for someone who doesn't give two shits about them. He doesn't play much anymore, so places like this are the only place you can see him."

"What is this place?" Willow asked, her eyes trailing the stage before moving to the rest of the room. She paused when she looked at the older couple to our left.

"A place where people who like this type of music meet," I said. "The musicians kinda just show up and play, and well... the money follows."

She made a noise and looked back toward the musicians. Other people started to fill the seats beside us, but Willow was still deep in thought. She didn't speak even as the waiter came to take our drink order. She was too busy watching them get ready.

I ordered from the waiter and gave her the space to take it all in.

"Have you played here before?" she asked. The piano player took that moment to jump into his first song, almost drowning out her words.

I stilled next to her. She turned to look up at me with a gaze so sharp it felt like she was seeing right through me. Everyone else was pulled to the musicians in front of us, but her focus was entirely on me.

"You thought that long for that to be your question?" I teased, hiding my discomfort.

"It's the first of many," she said. "I was trying to tie you together. I think I got most of it, but I have a few questions."

More panic. The music was getting louder and hiding our voices, but it gave me no reprieve.

"Yes," I said after clearing my throat. "I play here sometimes, though it has been a while."

"Why?" she asked.

I am running from the FBI and because of my father, that was what I should have said, but instead, I said, "Because I am preoccupied with more *important* things."

I sent her a flirty smile, but her gaze did not let up.

"You learned violin in private school?" she asked. I nodded.

Two glasses of white wine were put in front of us and I quickly took mine, happy for a break. How many of my plans was she going to destroy just by asking questions?

She leaned close to me, the warmth of her body seeping through my clothes and into my skin.

"You're acting different," she whispered.

"So are you," I shot back. I wanted so badly to wrap my hand around her throat and force her into submission for making me feel this way, but I needed to keep a low profile. So, I locked the idea away for later.

"I like it," she said with a grin. "If I didn't know any better, I would say you're nervous."

I made a show of tightening my arm around her and grabbing her chin, though I wished it was her throat.

"You'll pay for that later," I warned.

"I'm looking forward to it," she said with a grin.

Heat flashed through me.

The music was getting louder now. Far too loud to speak. Everyone's attention was on the people on stage as the music floated around us.

Except for mine, as much as I wanted to take in every moment of the performance, I'd much rather enjoy watching Willow take it in for the first time.

And *god* was it a sight.

We didn't talk much as the show went on, but I didn't mind. Seeing Willow's reaction was enough for me to understand a part of Willow I had never expected to see.

She was enraptured by the performance. She swayed along with the music. Actually *felt* it as it swirled around us. It was different than when I watched her paint on camera. When she painted, she was so focused the world could be burning around her and she wouldn't even flinch.

But here she was a part of the music. Her entire body had melted against mine. All the tenseness in her muscles was gone and she didn't so much as flinch as I let my fingers trace mindless circles on her skin.

Instead, she leaned into my motions like she craved my touch, and not just in a sexual way.

Warmth and satisfaction hummed in my chest because I had never seen anyone feel the music the way I had.

There were many things I had to do in life to become what I was today, but the first time I heard a classical melody, my life became forever changed. It was the only thing I was able to keep consistent in my life, and many times, it was the only thing I craved like nothing else.

Until her.

Even as we sat there, enjoying the music and drinking our wine, I still couldn't wrap my head around just how rapidly I had fallen for Willow. As I pulled her closer to me, the warmth of her body left me with a feeling of rightness.

I knew, somehow, after our moment in the room, that she would be perfect for me. The nervousness and hesitation I had about her getting to know me were quickly falling by the wayside. She had done nothing groundbreaking yet had single-handedly cracked the wall I had raised up around me.

I didn't expect her attention to turn to me, but when it did, I felt my face flush. I didn't care to hide how much she affected me, but in that moment, I felt like I had been caught with my hand in the cookie jar.

I leaned down, hoping to capture her lips with mine, but she stopped me by leaning back.

"Is there a bathroom?" she asked shyly. *There* was the Willow I had become so accustomed to.

I let out a light laugh and pulled away, motioning behind me.

"Behind the bar," I said and pointed it out to her. She gave me a grateful smile, and slowly, she stood up and slipped out of our bubble.

I watched her leave for a moment, enjoying the way the dress hugged her before turning my attention back to the performers. It was but another minute before I was interrupted again.

"Avery, I heard you were here," a voice from my side called.

It was Justin, one of the floor managers here. I'd heard him come up, the squeak of his shoes giving him away. I turned and sent him an easy smile.

His blond hair was combed back and had so much gel in it that I was sure it was just about fused to his head. He looked like a lot of the people I went to school with and it was easy to tell that even though he was working here, he probably grew up around money.

I had no doubt that he probably waited for Willow to leave in order to approach me. He was trained to sniff out money and could probably tell that Willow was dressed in mine.

"You don't have to seek me out every time I'm here," I said, keeping my voice light though I was a few seconds away from snapping at him.

Not only was I enjoying watching the show and being with my date, but I wanted to attract as little attention to myself as possible and his standing over me with his suit and gold name tag just caused everyone to stare. He didn't come down often to see how everyone was. This place ran pretty much by itself, so he never needed to intervene. He only came down if there was an important client and his talking to me labeled me as such.

When I was performing, I would watch him and his slimy smile as he went from group to group of high-level businessmen and tried his best to weasel himself into a conversation.

"How can I not?" he joked. His voice was far too loud. "I'm surprised you're not playing tonight. I have a violin in—"

"No need," I said quickly, cutting him off and making a show of grabbing my wine and lifting it. "I'm here for the show."

His eyes trailed to the wineglass that was still on the table and then to the empty seat next to me.

"I saw your date," he said. "But I'm at a loss as to her name. I've never seen her before. You *have* to introduce me."

Something like jealousy curled inside me. I didn't understand why though. Willow would never choose someone like him.

Nor would I let her.

Maybe it was just the threat of him taking something from me. It just didn't sit right with me.

"No need." I got up and grabbed my wine. "We're going to leave soon."

I didn't want to, but it would probably be the safest thing to do. Justin didn't seem like a man who would be able to keep his mouth shut and there would no doubt be people here in minutes when they heard Maddox's daughter was here.

His panic was written all over his face. He was going to jump in, probably try and convince me to stay, but I waved him off and turned toward the bar at the back of the club.

Willow was already there, standing against the bar with her arms crossed over her chest and an uncomfortable look on her face. A man in a cheap suit was standing in front of her, and by the looks of it, he was trying to coax something out of her.

My jealousy turned into rage.

WILLOW

"I'm sorry, I think—"

I was cut off by the man leaning closer. He cornered me out of nowhere and it took every fiber of my being to not kick him in the balls.

What was it with strange men cornering me near bathrooms?

"Don't be fooled by it," he said, dropping his voice. "I'm telling you I can get you out of here. You don't need to be scared. You can trust me."

Something about his words caused the violent thoughts about hitting him to pause.

"Trust you?" I scoffed. "I have no idea who you are, nor do I want *anything* to do with you."

His eyes wandered to where Avery was still sitting before darting back to me. *So this was about her.*

What did this man know about her that would cause him to corner me like this?

"They'll find out about the hands sooner or later. You think that that teacher hasn't had complaints upon complaints piling up on him? There are cameras all around the school and—"

"Are you blackmailing me?" I hissed. "Was it your people that were questioning me?" My blood ran cold. Whoever this man was, he already knew far too much. No man cornering a woman outside a bathroom had good intentions, but the man in front of me was dangerous.

He stood straight and let out a sigh while fixing his suit jacket. His eyes had deep bags under them and his brown hair was threaded with gray.

"I'm just trying to help," he said. "You lying to them is only going to get you in trouble."

I swallowed thickly. It had been weeks since then and I hadn't heard anything from them since, but I knew that sooner or later, I would meet them again. Unless Avery had an elaborate plan to get them off her tail, they would continue to pester me until they found the professor's killer.

But that begs the question: *who the fuck is this guy?*

"How do you know this?" I asked.

Jonson tugged at his jacket to show me a badge nestled on the inside.

FBI.

Horror washed through me. *He's one of them.* He knew this because he had figured out what Avery had done. Suddenly, his questioning made all too much sense.

I needed to get out of here with Avery before this turned into a bloodbath.

A new type of fear welled up inside of me. The fear of Avery being taken away or caught. The fear that she wouldn't sit back and just be arrested like that. The fear that this entire room would watch as she murdered their man in front of us.

Leave.

"Just trust me, ok—"

A strong arm wrapped around my shoulders. I swallowed my sigh of relief and leaned into Avery. The constant string of anxious thoughts was silenced as soon as I felt the weight of her arm around me. It was like an anchor, calming my nerves and keeping me grounded to this world.

His eyes widened when he caught sight of her. There was only a small pause before an emotionless mask was firmly placed on his face. He let his jacket fall closed and dug in his pocket for something. Confusion rolled over me as I caught sight of a sleek, black flip phone.

I looked up to Avery, but her mask was stone cold.

So this wasn't going to be an arrest or a bloodbath.

"Sloan sends her well-wishes," he muttered.

A smirk was the thing that cracked her mask.

"Liar," she tutted but still took the phone from him and slipped it in her pocket. "Sloan wouldn't wish anyone well."

Sloan?

At times I was really bad with names and faces, but that name rang a bell...

Lillian's voice flashed through my mind.

I was thinking of asking Sloan to tell me. But I wanted you to tell me and I wouldn't break that confidentiality, no matter how curious I was.

I shouldn't have been surprised since Avery had admitted that she worked at the club our first time together... but for us to have friends or at least know people in the same circle was daunting, to say the least.

"Surprisingly enough, she was worried about you. About your *involvement*," he said, a frown pulling at his lips. "I had some choice words with her about letting you escape, but I'm sure this... *deal* will work out in both our favors."

Avery let out a noncommittal hum. The man's eyes flitted back down to me. I obviously wasn't a part of the deal though I still didn't quite understand why he offered to take me away.

"I don't need to tell you that you should be careful wit—"

"Then don't," Avery clipped.

The tension between us was rising steadily and panic grew inside me.

What went from a nice date with Avery quickly changed into something scary.

This whole time Avery had acted like any other person. The

woman who had cut off the professor's hands and delivered them to me after touching me inappropriately for most of the date was nowhere to be seen.

It allowed me to lower my guard. To treat her like I had in that room.

But she came back in full force and without warning. It was like a reality check in the form of a gut punch.

Her arm was gripping me in a comforting fashion and even though she wasn't squeezing me, it felt like I was rooted to her side.

"His name is Jonson," Avery said after a moment. I looked up at her and our eyes met.

Could she sense what I was feeling inside? The quirk of her lips and the hooding of her eyes told me she knew exactly how I was feeling... and that she liked it.

"*Agent* Jonson," I corrected. The squeeze of her hand on my shoulder set butterflies throughout my stomach. I looked toward the man in question. His eyes were narrowed on me.

"Maybe I misjudged what's happening here," he muttered.

"Or maybe..." she teased. "It's exactly what you think it is. Big Bad Avery Maddox has stolen this young, *innocent* professor and has forced her to come listen to classical music and drink wine. Sounds like a terrible punishment, doesn't it?"

The last part was directed to me. I probably shouldn't have been goading an FBI agent, but a part of me really loved her playfulness. It caused my body to heat and an excited thrill to run through me.

"Oh, it's terrible," I said, copying her tone. "*Please.* Save me. It's the worst punishment I could imagine. And to think what might happen after."

I looked back up at her and my breath caught when I caught sight of her gaze. Her eyes held that playful light to them. But there's nothing playful about the desire on her face.

"I'm not like them," Avery said and looked back to Jonson. "Whatever you do with Ax and Sloan won't work here."

She patted her pocket where she'd slipped the phone.

"I'll contact you when I'm ready."

Jonson looked like he was gonna say something but instead screwed his mouth shut and stepped back, letting us leave.

We were silent as we walked up the stairs. The doorman wished us a good night and asked to call us a taxi, but Avery waved him off.

I didn't ask her where she was going as she circled us around the building and led us down the street. It was late now and the outside was pitch black. There were very few people roaming this part of the city, with only a few cars quietly running up and down the streets. The sounds of the city weaved in and out of the buildings accompanying us, but for the most part, it was just the two of us.

I gasped when she yanked me into an alleyway. The breath was forced out of my lungs as my back slammed against the cold, damp brick.

Avery was in front of me in moments, her hand clasped my neck and forced my chin up. Her lips captured mine in a bruising, hungry kiss. I melted into it. Heat ran through me and my knees threatened to buckle.

She did more than just dominate me through her kiss. She fucking *destroyed* me.

Her tongue slid against mine and when I reciprocated, her teeth bit down on it. I let out a pained moan and the hand from my throat left so she could yank my legs around her.

We were still in public and barely hidden from view, but as she trailed kisses down my neck, she nudged my dress out of the way to lick and suck where she had left her bite. I couldn't help but moan loudly.

She was frenzied. I don't know what it was specifically about our interaction that kicked this off, but I would make sure to do it tenfold the next time, as long as I could meet this Avery again.

Her blunt nails dug into my skin and she pushed her entire way into me, forcing me against the wall.

I could hardly breathe, but honestly, the need to breathe was overcome by my desire for her.

One of my hands tangled in her hair while the other slipped

the dress off my shoulders. She trailed kisses down my neck and chest until I could push down the material and expose my breasts to her.

When she pulled a nipple into her mouth, I let out a strangled moan. I needed more.

"God," I choked out.

She sucked, licked, and then bit my nipple, causing a clash of pain and pleasure to run through me. Her hips bucked against me, creating additional delicious friction between us. From the moment she pushed me against this wall and started kissing me, my pussy started to ache unbearably and sooner than I had the confidence to admit, my underwear had become so slick with my own arousal that it began to stick to me.

She switched to the other nipple and I let out a high-pitched whine.

I needed more.

She kissed back up to the junction between my shoulder and neck to whisper against my heated skin

, "Tighten your legs around me." I did as she asked without question. She removed her hand from my thigh to quickly bunch up my dress and slip her hand into my underwear.

I flinched when her cold fingers found my slit.

"Please. Please. Plea—"

My begging was cut off by her hand clamping down on my mouth.

Without warning, she pushed two fingers into me and her mouth opened wide to bite down on my already sensitive skin. My scream was muffled behind her hand and turned to sobs of pleasure as she used her fingers to fuck me viciously against the wall. I hope to God this time she broke the skin.

It was fast and animalistic as she pounded into me.

I should have been scared about someone finding us. I hadn't even looked really at our surroundings, but honestly, in that moment, I couldn't care at all.

She was creating such a delicious heat between my legs that all I could think about was begging her for more. Begging her to bite me harder.

The heel of her palm was slapping against my clit and causing a zing of pleasure to run through me with each thrust.

Through the sounds of my moans and the city around us, I could still make out the sound of my own wetness.

I writhed against her as I felt the first wisp of heat run through me. My body was tensing. I was so close to an orgasm so fast, but I needed more.

"Do that again," she whispered, lifting her mouth to my ear. "And I'll fuck you right in front of everyone. I don't care who sees." Her voice was husky and her breathing was heavy as she spoke. "I swear to God. I wanted to throw you over that bar and make every single one of those old bastards watch as I made you beg like the whore you are."

I gasped, but my noises were still muffled by her hand. She left heated kisses up my neck and face before biting down on my ear.

"When we get back home," she whispered. "I'm going to make you come so many times you beg me to stop. Then after, I'm gonna ride that pretty little mouth of yours for as long as it takes to choke on my cum and you'll sit there and take every bit of it."

Home. She didn't even give me a moment to register the word or what it meant to the both of us.

Her hand slipped from my mouth back to my neck.

"Yes," I moaned. "I'll take everything you give me."

She was cutting off my air supply with her grip and causing my head to swim, but it only made my cunt tighten around her fingers.

"You're gonna come for me now," she ordered. "Come for me and I want to hear your shout echo through these buildings. I want you to come so hard and scream so loud that people will wonder what wicked things I'm doing to you down here."

I couldn't hold it in as I came around her, nor did I want to. I wanted to please her.

"*Yes,*" she moaned against me.

Wave after wave of my orgasm ran through me. I let out a

scream-like sob as she fucked me through it. Even after the last wave, I was hoping foolishly that she would continue. That she would make me come again and again until I begged for her to stop, but far too quickly, she let me down and fixed my dress.

Her movements were hurried and I was barely keeping up.

She gave me another bruising kiss that left me breathless before she pulled on my hand and rushed me out of the alleyway.

A little time to steady myself as we rushed down the sidewalk.

She sent me a devilish grin as she looked back at me. Her hair was ruffled and her lips were red and puffy, giving away exactly what we had been doing. Even that beautiful face of hers was flushed.

The image of her smiling like that would be burned into my mind forever.

AVERY

I was still running off the high from the date with Willow and I hadn't noticed the slight smell of cologne right near my door.

I was too busy thinking about how Willow looked at me when Jonson was questioning her. The playful flirting had caused my lust for her to move into overdrive, and again, I found myself losing all sense of control around her.

I was head over heels.

It happened so fast and so abruptly that I couldn't have stopped it even if I had tried.

She was perfect in every way and it hurt to leave her. She was mine. It was becoming more and more obvious by the day. The plan I crafted to make her fall in love with me may have been a bust, but at least now we were both intertwined so deeply that there was no way we could be forced apart.

She wouldn't forget me. I would occupy that space in her mind, just like she had with me. Forever.

It was something I had never experienced before. Nothing that I ever let myself dream of.

Until now.

I wished that I could stay in dreamland for the rest of the day, only to be interrupted when Willow was awake again, but all of those thoughts blew up in flames when I placed my hand on the doorknob and turned.

It was unlocked.

A coldness ran through me. Someone was inside. They had to be. The door being unlocked was an exit for them. One of the few ones.

Slowly, I turned the knob and pushed my door open. I had gotten the larger single dorm. The ones with a small living room, bathroom, and bedroom. It would allow me to sneak in without them noticing me.

The dorm was dark, with the only light coming from my room. The blue hue of the computers dimly lit the hallway and if I strained, I could hear the clicking of my keyboard.

I stepped in, shutting and locking the door behind me.

They wouldn't be leaving this place alive.

I grabbed the hidden bat I kept in the living room before peeking into the room.

There was a man hunched over my desk. His hands were flying over the keyboard and he was pulling up financial files I had on my father.

So this is why Father had been so quiet.

My guess was that he wanted to see exactly how much I had stolen from him. Or maybe even how much dirt I had on him, but I wasn't stupid enough to keep something like *that* on a computer. All the files he was looking through had been carefully curated and as soon as they handed them to Father, he would know.

But I wouldn't give him that chance. My hand tightened around the bat.

When he brought up the cameras of Willow's apartment, I froze.

She was still awake even after I left. He enlarged the video and we both watched as she was hunched over, painting a canvas on her dirty kitchen floor.

She was wearing my shirt. The one I had left after sneaking into another apartment with handcuffs.

Pure rage filled me.

I took one step toward him, then two, then three.

By the time he noticed my presence, I had already raised the bat above my head. Then, when he turned, I slammed it right into his disgusting fucking face.

One hit would have been enough. As soon as it connected with his jaw, he was knocked out. But even as his body flopped to the ground, I couldn't stop myself from raising it and bringing it back down onto him.

"You. Don't. Get. To. Fucking. Look. At. Her."

Each word was met with a hit from the bat. Three in his chest. The rest in his legs.

I couldn't kill him yet, but I would make it as fucking painful as I could for when he woke up.

When I stopped, I let the bat fall to the ground and looked up to the ceiling. I counted backward from a hundred and took deep breaths to calm my racing heart.

When I finally had my violent thoughts under control, I looked back at Willow's camera. She paused and leaned back, giving me an unobstructed view of her painting.

My heart soared when I saw it.

It was me, of course. Not finished, but the image was clear. Unlike her other ones, this one was happy. My hair was wild and I was smiling the biggest smile I had ever seen grace my lips.

Yes... this was for her. For this. For us. I would clean this up and betray my family name... if only to save her.

While keeping an eye on her, I pulled out the black flip phone and dialed the single saved number.

"That was fast," Jonson said from the other end. "I hadn't expected—"

"I need to meet you now," I said, not caring about interrupting him. I had made my decision. I wished Quinn would have taken up my offer and just killed Father, but I guess I would have to do things the hard way.

I had planned to wait until I could get Willow and me to a safer place, but if there was already one of his men breaking into my apartment... there was no telling what Father's next step was.

"It's almost four in the mor—"

"Then you better make it quick," I said. "It wouldn't be great if they saw us together in the daylight."

He let out a grunt.

"I'll send you an address. Meet me in thirty."

"I'll be there in ten. Don't keep me waiting."

I didn't give him time to object and slammed the phone closed. For a final measure, I delivered a kick to the unconscious man's side.

Time to get to work.

Showing up to a meeting with an FBI agent in bloody clothes wasn't ideal, but desperate times called for desperate measures.

I pulled on a dark zip-up hoodie to cover my bloody shirt and took only a few things with me from the apartment. I didn't know how long I would get to spend with our FBI agent, but just in case *another* guard showed up at my house, I made sure to grab my drives and whatever computers I could carry.

Many of them were stained with blood still and so was the backpack I housed them in.

I'm not sure if the man would still be alive when I got back. I hoped for information's sake he would be, but I didn't have much hope.

I hog-tied him and shoved him in my closet to be safe. A part of me thought even that had been too lenient.

No one could watch Willow like that except for me.

But I had to get rid of that anger, at least for the time being. I lingered near the corner of the abandoned warehouse and watched the spot where Jonson and I were supposed to meet. There was a park right next to it and the light was a little too bright for me to venture into it.

The sun was threatening to rise in another hour or two, and I was counting my blessings for the darkness, being in such an open area.

The air was chilly that morning and it caused bumps to rise on my skin. I cursed the man still in my dorm. I had to be careful on the way back in case there were more people hiding out. I made a mental note to take a picture of him and send it to Father when I got back.

I hoped it wouldn't make me have to find a new place. I had yet to make a decision on one.

And I quite enjoyed being able to be close to Willow.

Maybe I could convince her to let me move in while I threw Father off my trail.

It was already startling enough that there had been a man smart enough to find my apartment. But hopefully, if he was the only one, then it meant that the rest didn't know where I lived.

I made sure to put his electronics in the microwave to be safe. I didn't set it off because I still wanted to see what information I could glean from it later, but that should be enough to stop anyone from finding me for the moment.

I tensed when I caught sight of the FBI agent. He was wearing casual clothes, a hoodie and sweats, but the bastard forgot to cover his face. With a huff, I tightened my hood and let out a soft yet high-pitched whistle. His head snapped in my direction.

He looked around quickly before walking toward me. When he was a few feet away, he stopped. The annoyance on his face was visible even in the darkness.

"I told you—"

I unzipped the jacket to show him my blood-stained shirt. Even in the darkness, the color leaving his face was visible.

"You can see why I stayed away."

My voice shook him from his stupor and he let out a sigh. He shot a panicked look over his shoulder before walking closer.

"This deal is off if you keep—"

"It was my father's man," I said. "He broke into my apartment. I acted in self-defense."

He pushed his lips together in a tight line. His eyes dropped down to my bloody shirt and back to my face. We both knew it was a lie, but I wondered if he had enough balls to call me on it.

"If you want the security of an informant, you have to play the part," he hissed. "You think just because you are helping us with Russell Maddox that we will let this slide?"

I couldn't help the cruel smile that twisted my lips.

"Not helping, *handing*. I'm practically handing him to you," I corrected. "And if you looked up the information I gave you, you would know it won't take much else to get him."

The information, and the only thing that got this slimy bastard here, was an offshore account that washed money up to the hundreds of millions. This specific account comes from other well-known companies that would no doubt go down with him when it leaked.

But what were they paying my father for?

It's the only thing I didn't tell Jonson. My only leverage.

My father was the middleman to a shit ton of illegal businesses. He used the information he gleaned from drunk business tycoons to connect them to others. Yet somehow, he was careful enough to never get involved in the actual crimes, but there were many times he facilitated them.

This specific account was connected to a scheme that promised a handful of young immigrant girls working visas in exchange for working on a remote island. What they didn't know was that when they got there, they would be forced into human trafficking until they paid off their debt.

Father, of course, never took part, but he was the one that connected them all.

Wanted young girls? He had a connection.

Wanted to use a business to use as a front for laundered money? He had a connection.

Wanted to snort coke off your secretary's tits? He would dig up every bit of information he had to force her into silence.

Hell, that bastard had even helped cover up the reports of toxic water in many of the cities that surrounded powerful manufacturing plants.

"The offshore account with laundered money isn't enough," he said quickly. "You know if he gets a good team of lawyers, and he will, that he'll barely get a slap on the wrist."

"Then you better find out what they are paying him for," I said, the cruel smile getting even bigger.

"If you know, why don't you tell me?" He was exasperated. You could hear it in his voice. For some odd reason, I got the sense that maybe the man in front of me really *did* care.

"I need what I asked for," I said. "Then I will guide you to the answer. Or *answers* in this case."

"How many people are paying him?" he asked.

"This account?" I asked with a raised brow. The color left Jonson's face. "You really think he stopped at one? You're stupider than I thought."

He swallowed thickly but didn't say anything.

I let out a sigh.

"This is a small account," I said and buried my hands in my pockets. "He funnels three main clients into this one."

His eyes widened.

"Three, that's it?"

I gave him a sharp nod. He had a system. From the outside, the clients looked like they had nothing to do with each other. In reality, he paired them together based on whatever business they were involved in. So all three of them had a part in trafficking those young girls.

He looked around before digging out his phone. I took a hurried step back. He brought it to his ear, all while staring at me.

"I'm taking little Bateman in as a bird," he announced to the other person on the line. I couldn't help my visible cringe. He was far too loud for my liking. I looked around to see if anyone was watching, but I couldn't make out if the shadows in the forest surrounding us were actually moving.

They exchanged a few words before he slipped the phone back into his pocket. Not more than a few moments later, a blacked-out SUV stopped at the other side of the park. Its lights flashed in warning.

I should have known he had people standing by.

"I'm nothing like Patrick Bateman," I grumbled and pushed past him. He let out a rare laugh and fell into step with me.

"Gonna give me a hint at what your father is doing with that account?" he asked.

I didn't speak again until I was safely loaded in the car and we were on our way to his place.

"Every year, the CEO and CFO of Cooke Industries plan an overseas trip," I said. "They sunbathe, get drunk off their asses, do insane amounts of drugs, and have more girls than they can handle."

"They were contributing to the account," Jonson said from beside me.

I sent him a smirk.

"They would be a good place to start."

He nodded and leaned back in his seat.

"Do they... hurt people?" he asked softly.

The driver's eyes looked at us in the rearview mirror.

"Have you met a billionaire that didn't?"

He let out a huff but didn't respond. I gave him much more than I should have already. I hoped he had the brains to figure out what to do with it.

WILLOW

Aweek had passed since our first date.

Avery kept her promise and fucked me hard and nonstop for that entire night. She left early in the morning to do God knows what, but since then, she hadn't been in my class and I hadn't been able to talk to her since.

She dropped by my class a few times after that. Sometimes she just lingered toward the back, but it hadn't been hard catching her. And after everything, it made my heart hurt.

So, I was relieved to find a note from her next to my pillow after a straight week of us not speaking. At first, of course, there was a shock of fear that ran through me when I saw it and when I realized that someone had been in my house. But when I opened it to read the message, I knew it had to be her.

I miss you. I'll see you soon.

I folded up the note and slipped it in the back of my phone case. It made me unreasonably happy.

I was tempted to seek her out, but instead, I kept with my plan because I needed to get answers.

Avery seemed willing to supply them to me, but that was when we were together. Maybe her avoidance was also another way to keep me from finding out why the hell an FBI agent was handing her what looked to be a burner phone.

I may have been some random low-level art professor, but I wasn't stupid.

So instead of kicking my feet at the giddiness of getting noticed, about two trains and an hour and a half later, I was in New York again.

I held two coffees in my hand as I walked through the somewhat crowded park. The air was getting chillier by the day and the threat of break was looming over the university.

There was a freshness to the air and each breath that I took burned my nose and lungs. But it also caused a wave of calmness to wash over me.

I tried to enjoy the scenery and act like this was just any other coffee date and push away the nagging feeling that there was something going horribly wrong. The trees had started to turn various shades of red, yellow, and orange. Many of them crunched under my feet as I walked.

Fall was my favorite season. I loved bundling up in the cold and sitting in the darkness of the house. It was a time of quiet. A time when I could be alone with my thoughts without them threatening to overtake me.

I looked over at the people in the park. Some were walking dogs, some were playing with their children. All of their lives seemed so carefree.

I used to be like them.

And most of the time, I still was... until I remembered that there was always someone looming over my shoulder. Someone who was bloodthirsty. Someone who scared me and made my knees weak all at the same time.

But today, somehow, I knew that she wasn't watching me. The familiar prick in the back of my neck wasn't there. My body was somehow attuned to her in such a way that it had to warn me of her presence.

I paused when I caught the familiar sight of dark, curly hair.

Today she wore a red knit beanie with a matching red hoodie. Over it, she had a large leather jacket that looked to be a hand-me-down and ripped jeans with her Docs.

Lillian, always the artist.

I envied her style. All I was able to dress in was the ball cap and hoodie with jeans and my Converse that I hadn't replaced in over five years.

Though I tried not to be too jealous of her. I was happy for her. From what she told me, she had worked hard to get to where she was now. And maybe I was just still stuck in that time period where I needed to work hard to get to where I wanted to be.

But with the arrival of Avery, I had no idea what my end goal was anymore.

"You're early," I said as I came up to the bench she was sitting on and handed her the hot latte.

She smiled and took it from me. I noticed the bit of flush on her tanned skin and immediately felt guilty about making her wait so long.

"Sloan is still sleeping," she said. "I thought that maybe if I left early enough, I could sneak out without her coming to track me down."

I let out a laugh. "Does she do that often?"

I almost hoped that she'd say yes.

"Not really," she said and shot me a slight grin. "But she will blow up my phone."

I shook my head and sat down on the bench next to her. The coldness of the wood seeped into my pants, causing a chill to run through my body.

"How's classes?" she asked. "Busy?"

I shrugged and took a sip of my latte. The bitterness exploded on my tongue and there was a hint of hazelnut in it. The last time I had coffee seemed so long ago. I wanted to enjoy it, but my nerves wouldn't allow me to.

"I wouldn't say it's busy..." I trailed. "I don't assign much work and a lot of it is lecturing. So maybe just tiring."

"Busy enough to keep you from the club."

I bit my tongue to keep from talking.

"Was it really that bad?" she asked, still referencing my time in the club.

"No," I said quickly.

"Come on. Will you tell me who you matched with?" she asked with a whine.

"Avery," I said and took a sip of my latte as I looked over at her, watching her reaction.

Her brows furrowed.

"Avery...?" she trailed with a questioning tone. And then her eyes widened and she let out a gasp.

Her hand came to cover her mouth and she gave me a sort of shocked look. I stood straight. Her sudden reaction alarmed me.

Does she know about everything? The FBI agent mentioned Sloan, so she could have told her something.

Seconds ticked by and my face began to flush.

"Avery?" she asked again. "The one with blonde hair and mastectomy scars?"

I nodded.

"Is that a problem?" I asked carefully.

"*Girl,*" she breathed. "You're so fucking kinky."

Her words caused me to pause before a shocked laugh spilled from my lips. *I wasn't,* but her reaction caused a burst of relief to go through me.

"*That's* what caused you to react like that?" I asked, raising an eyebrow at her.

It was her turn to get a little flustered. She looked at her cup and shifted uncomfortably in her seat.

"I didn't know much about her," she admitted. "Though I was almost matched with her."

Just like that, I was snapped back to reality. Jealousy burned violently through my veins. It was hard to imagine Avery with anyone else, especially with someone as perfect as Lillian.

"Almost?"

She nodded.

"Let's just say Sloan convinced me otherwise... and we've been together ever since."

She snuck a peek back at me.

"She choke you?" she asked quietly.

I should have been embarrassed about her questioning, but instead, I gave her a slight smile.

"Among other things."

"You filthy slut," Lillian said with a laugh.

"It was good," I said sincerely.

Lillian nodded and leaned back with a sigh, "Well, at least now I know why you won't come back."

I raised a brow at her.

"It's because she's not there anymore, right?" she led. "After that, I would understand not being able to pick anyone else."

I chose not to answer her and let her believe that she was right. It was much easier than trying to explain everything.

"Why did she leave anyway?" I prompted and took a sip of my coffee.

Lillian bit her lip and silence spread over us.

"Sloan didn't tell me much," she whispered. "But I think there was some... legal trouble. We don't talk much about her."

I hummed.

"Does Sloan... know any FBI agents?" I asked, trying to keep my voice light.

Lillian's sharp gaze traveled to mine.

"We both do," she said warily. "Are you in trouble, Willow? Do you need help? If you need someone, I can—"

I waved her off quickly and shifted in my seat so I was facing her.

"I'm fine, really. I just..." I let out a sigh and dropped my gaze toward the bench. I wasn't about to go around spilling everything about Avery, but I needed to know about this Jonson guy. And if both Sloan and Lillian knew him... he couldn't be *that* bad, could he?

"I had a run-in with one." I settled on finally. "He said he knew Ax and Sloan, but obviously, I wouldn't trust the guy at face value."

I peeked back up at her to catch her concerned expression.

"Is his name Jonson?" she whispered.

There it is.

I nodded.

"Is he... trustworthy?" I asked.

Lillian gave me a forced smile.

"Not at all," she whispered. "He's dirty, but I think he means well. He... he's helped us all."

But none of them were murderers who had delivered severed hands to their classroom.

"A dirty FBI agent who means well?" I mused. "Sounds perfect."

Lillian gave me an exasperated look.

"There is no better way to describe him," she said. She looked around us quickly, the action making me check our surroundings as well.

There was no one staring at us and it made me relax until I felt that familiar prickling at the back of my neck. I peered behind me, checking the path I came from and the surrounding trees, but no one caught my eye.

"Why would an FBI agent be reaching out to you?" she asked, her voice dropping to a whisper.

I looked back at her with a frown. I didn't want to lie to Lillian, but something told me that telling people about Avery probably wouldn't be the best idea.

"Someone left some severed hands on my desk."

Lillian's jaw dropped open and her hand shot out to squeeze my knee. A comforting gesture I was woefully unprepared for.

"Holy shit, are you okay?" Her voice rose an octave. "What kind of fucked-up person would do that?"

Suddenly, I was glad I didn't tell her I was seeing Avery.

My mind slowed to a stop. *Was I seeing her?* We went on a date, but we haven't talked since then.

We also fucked, but that wouldn't make this a relationship either.

It was almost jarring how open I was to being with a stalking, murdering, stranger.

"I'm fine now," I said. "Though it scared me a bit at first. The FBI is trying to figure out who was responsible and school was closed for a while."

"Do they know why you?" she asked.

I shook my head.

"Nope," I said. "About Avery... what kind of legal—"

The incessant buzzing of her phone interrupted me. She gave me a look before digging it out of her pocket.

"Told you," she said with a smile. She put the phone up to her ear. "I'm with Willow like I told you last night."

Sloan said something that caused her eyes to dart toward me. I took a sip of my coffee to try and calm my nerves.

"Ya, that's fine. We can go get brunch," she said. She pulled the phone away from her face. "Do you want to get food with us? Maybe you can ask Sloan if you have more questions about Jonson?"

"Jonson?" Sloan asked from the other line. It was low and I could barely make it out of my seat. Panic shot through me.

I stood up and made a show of looking at my phone.

"I have to catch the train," I said, sending her a smile. "But next time, we can go get something, okay? I'll text you."

"Wait, Willow, I want to talk more about—"

"Sorry!" I called as I retreated. "I have an appointment after this!"

It was a lie, but it allowed me to hightail it out of there. This was supposed to be a little talk to try and get information. The more people that knew what was going on, the more I was worried about it getting back to both Avery and Jonson.

When I got home, the first thing I noticed was the strong smell of seasoned meat. It made my mouth water and caused my heart to stop in my chest.

There was only *one* person that would let themselves in and start cooking.

As soon as I unlocked my door and closed it behind me, Avery's voice called out from the kitchen.

"Right on time."

I couldn't see her from the entrance, but it was a mere few steps before I saw her again.

Her hair was in a bun again, something I noticed she did when she cooked, but instead of wearing that turtleneck that hugged her body, she wore one of *my* oversized tank tops and jeans.

I couldn't help the smile that spread across my face.

"So not only are you allowing yourself into my apartment, but you're also wearing my clothes now?" I asked and walked toward her.

It had been so long since we'd been so close to each other that excitement zipped up my spine and I wanted nothing more than to reach out to her.

Her eyes trailed down my form before traveling up to my eyes.

"Better for cooking," she said.

I stepped close enough to her that our fronts were barely brushing across each other.

Her scent surrounded me and all I wanted to do was to lean into it.

Her hand came to trail along my neck until she grabbed the side of my face. She leaned down and pulled me into the most gentle kiss she'd ever given me.

When she pulled away just enough so that our lips were still brushing across each other's, I was breathless.

"I missed you too," I breathed, referencing her note. I felt her smile against my lips.

In a flash, her hands were around my waist and pushed me toward the opposite counter and away from the stove. My back hit the hard stone and caused pain to radiate through me, but she quickly leaned down and captured my lips with hers, which chased away all the pain.

Her hands gripped the countertop on either side of me and she put all of her weight on me.

I moaned against her as her tongue invaded my mouth. It was hot and had a slight taste of mint on it.

The kiss turned frenzied and I wrapped my arms around her neck to try and pull her closer, but she pulled away to look down at me with a smirk.

"Did you have a good coffee date?" she asked. I froze against her.

But of course, she would know, but I expected that.

"It was good," I said. "Lillian didn't have much information on Jonson."

"Oh?" she asked with a raised brow. There was a slight quirk to her lips, almost as if she was amused.

"Yeah," I said. "It looks like Sloan has a little bit more information, but I'm guessing you already knew that."

"Why'd you go ask her?" she asked. "Why not just ask me?"

"You've been gone," I said with a frown.

"I've been right here," she countered. I rolled my eyes.

"No, you stayed at a distance."

"I was doing stuff with Jonson," she admitted after a moment and put some space between us but kept her hands on either side of me.

"Doing stuff?" I asked, tilting my head to the side.

She paused, her eyes trailing my face.

"Would you be offended if I told you I didn't want to talk about it?"

"Not offended," I admitted. "...but maybe a little hurt."

She nodded.

"Then I apologize for hurting you." The coldness of her voice only caused it to hurt more.

"You know everything about me," I said. "You watch me constantly and even when you're not here, you still are in some ways... yet I can't know any of this?"

She turned back to the food.

I hadn't noticed that it was already on plates until she grabbed both of them and turned to the side.

"Let's say it's safer if you don't know," she said. "Think of this as me trying to protect you."

She walked to the small dining table without another word and I was forced to follow her. She sat down in one of the chairs and motioned for me to do the same.

Reluctantly, I sat down. The meal was braised lamb, roasted brussels sprouts, and garlic potatoes. It made my mouth water.

How could I stay mad at her when this is how she treated me?

I watched as she took a bite and motioned for me to do the same. I took my fork, stabbing a potato before bringing it up to my mouth, but before eating it, I paused.

"And if I ask Sloan?" I looked toward her to gauge her reaction, but instead, she sent me a smile and looked back at her plate. She stabbed a potato as well, but it was much more forceful, but I wouldn't flinch.

She may be angry, but at this point, I was almost positive she would never hurt me.

"I'd probably die."

My blood froze in my veins. Her smile dropped as she took a bite and she continued eating like she had not dropped the bomb of her own death on me.

"Die?" I said with a forced laugh and shakily reached for my knife. She had spoken offhandedly, but Avery wouldn't be one to joke about death. At least I knew that much about her.

"Mhmm," she hummed while still chewing. When she swallowed, she spoke again. "You probably don't need the knife to cut it all the way. I cooked it for long enough that you can probably tear it with the fork."

I paused and placed the fork on the table while clutching the unused knife in my hand.

"Sloan wouldn't do that." My voice was hard, but I wasn't too sure of my words.

"You going to use that?" she asked, gesturing to my knife with hers. "Didn't know secrets made you so angry."

"Avery," I warned.

"Ohhh, there she is." She placed her hands on the table and leaned forward. "Come on. Place it on my neck."

I looked at her with wide eyes. When I didn't move, her hand shot out to grab the one that held the knife and pushed it against the skin of her neck. Luckily, I hadn't used it to actually cut the meat, but it still wasn't clean enough to be doing *this*. I stood up and tried to pull my hand away from hers, but her grip was tight.

"Do it," she said with a crazed smile. "Take your anger out on me, lovely. I can't wait to see you covered in my blood."

I gritted my teeth and did exactly as she asked.

"Sloan wouldn't kill you," I repeated. The point of the steak knife digging into her skin. A drop of blood balled at the wound and then trailed down her neck. Her grip on my hand lightened.

"No," she whispered. "But if anyone knew that I was here or that Jonson was working with me, there is no telling who would come looking. For both me and him. How much money do you think is on his head, hmm?"

I pulled my hand away from her. My breathing was heavy and my chest began to ache. There was something else going on here.

"This isn't just about killing the professor, is it?" I asked.

She said nothing, but her eyes drilled into mine with such intensity that it caused my entire body to cool.

Swallowing thickly, I leaned forward to the wound at her neck. I paused for a moment, taking in her scent, before licking the path of the droplet that fell.

The metallic taste, combined with the saltiness of her skin, exploded on my tongue. I pulled back to look at her from under my lashes.

She was already watching me. Her breathing had stopped entirely and her face gave no indication as to how she felt about what I just did.

Without another word, I sat down and picked up my fork. I used the still-bloody knife to take apart my meat before putting it into my mouth.

"It would be a shame," I said after I chewed the delicious lamb. "For such a great cook to die so young. I would miss these dinners."

She didn't move from her spot. Her nails dug into the table. I looked back up at her. She was staring at the wall behind me.

"I would also miss the sex," I said between bites. "God, our sex has been the best of my life. I would not be looking forward to going back to dating apps—"

Her hand shot forward and tangled in my hair. I barely had time to swallow my food before her lips crashed into mine. I threw the utensils onto the table and let her pull me out of my seat.

Her mouth was rough against mine, but I couldn't bring myself to care.

She pushed me to the bedroom, but apparently, I was too slow in my movements and she had to let go of my hair in order to lift me up. I let out a gasp when we finally made it to my room and she let us fall to the bed.

She let us break for air only to trail kisses and harsh bites down my throat.

I quickly took off my hoodie and undid my bra so I could give her my unobstructed breast. I moaned when her mouth latched on. But then she bit down—*hard*.

My breath caught in my throat and heat pooled between my legs. She leaned back up to capture my lips and grabbed one of my hands and forced it into her pants while she undid the button with a single one of hers.

"Fuck me," she growled against my lips.

I didn't need to be told twice. I pushed my fingers into her underwear until I reached her swollen clit. I let my fingers slip past it to her entrance. She was already incredibly wet and I gathered some of it to bring back to her clit as I rubbed horizontal strokes against the bundle of nerves.

She let her mouth wander again, this time to the other nipple. I let out a gasp as she brought it into her mouth. I arched into her. The feeling of her tongue flicking back and forth was enough to drive me crazy.

"My nightstand," I gasped. "Grab the one you want."

Without removing herself from my nipple, she reached an arm over to try and riffle through the drawers. She didn't even look at the one she ended up pulling out, but I caught the shiny pink of the Satisfyer and smirked.

I removed my hand to grab it from her.

"Take off your pants."

For the first time, she listened and rolled off of me to take off her pants. I did the same and moved between her legs. She spread her legs wide for me, giving me a perfect look at her glistening cunt. Quickly, and before she complained, I placed the circle head of the toy at her clit.

I could feel her gaze on me as I turned it on. Her huff of breath filled the air.

"Faster," she breathed. "As high as it goes."

Swallowing thickly, I upped it another level. Her hips bucked and her head fell back against the pillows. Wetness was dripping from her and I longed to lick it up.

"Higher."

"There is no—"

"If I don't come right now, I will be rougher with you than I intend," she growled. "Do as I say."

Heat exploded throughout my body and I did what she said

before bringing my hands down to my clit. It was so sensitive and aching that even a few swipes were threatening to send me over the edge.

I had never seen Avery act like this. I pulled the toy away slightly.

"It was the knife thing, wasn't it?" I asked in a teasing tone. "You may not want to admit it, but you like when I'm in control. Like when I fight back." I used the toy to tease circles around her clit.

"Shut up," she growled. I placed it back on her clit and her hips jumped to meet it. When I pulled it away, she let out a whine. A goddamn whine.

"Maybe when I have you like this, I can get out what you're hiding from me," I said and brought the toy down her folds before bringing it back up to her clit.

"I swear to—"

I turned it up to a higher setting and she cut off with a loud groan. Her thighs began shaking and one of her hands trailed up her chest and to her neck. The other flailed toward me. Without thinking, I took the hand that was on my clit and tangled it in hers.

Her eyes shot toward me as her orgasm came over her. She arched her back and let out a strangled cry as the waves enveloped her. Evidence of it started to leak out of her cunt.

She was so goddamn beautiful when she came. She was as unhinged during it as she was in life, but she knew her body well. She knew what it would take to get her there and fast.

I loved how in control she liked to be of the uncontrollable.

I used our tangled hands as leverage to pull myself down and cover her mouth with mine. She kissed me back with vigor and before I knew it, I was flipped on my back and we started again.

WILLOW

I snuggled into Avery's chest and let my fingers trail her mastectomy scars.

For the first time in a while, it was silent between us even though we were both wide awake.

My room was bathed in darkness, the moonlight streaming through my curtains. The steady rhythm of Avery's heartbeat was loud in my ears.

We were both still naked and tangled in each other. The blankets were pooled at our waists, the softness of them brushing against our skin with every movement. Everything was heightened in that moment.

The feeling of her scars under my fingertips. The feeling of her breath against my hair. The feeling of security rose in my chest.

"I'm not usually a cuddler," she mumbled.

I let out a light laugh.

"Would you believe me if I said I wasn't either?" I asked.

Her arm tightened around me and she curled a lock of my hair around her finger.

"Yes, actually," she murmured. "You're lonely, but in all this time, I have yet to see you forge any meaningful relationships. I assume this is rather hard for you."

So there are things she doesn't know.

"I like it," I said quietly. "Seeing this side of you, I mean. The cuddles are nice too though."

There was a pause as I ran my finger across the puckered scar tissue. It was smooth in some places while others were raised and rough, giving me the idea that she may not have taken care of it as well as she should have.

"Phyllodes tumors," she said.

I tried to lift my head to look at her, but she pushed me back down to her chest. I understood the vulnerability it took to look someone in the eyes while sharing these types of stories.

"I don't know what those are," I admitted softly. "Are they cancerous?"

Her other hand came to grab mine and she brought it to the far right side of her chest and up a few inches.

"There was one borderline here." She moved my hand over about three more inches. "This one was malignant. They are fast-growing tumors that aren't always cancerous, but some of mine were."

"I'm sorry," I murmured and spread my hand out across her flat chest. "I have to admit though, the scars make you look kind of cool."

She let out a light laugh that caused my head to bounce on her chest. I couldn't help but smile.

"I know," she said in a light tone. "I never liked my chest, so it was an easy decision to get a double mastectomy. That, and at least I wouldn't have to go to the hospital as often to get them checked."

"Can they grow back?" I asked.

I couldn't see her nod, but I felt it.

"The recommendation is to get it checked out once a year," she said.

"But you don't."

"It... makes me easier to find."

I let my fingers move up to the brand just above her heart.

Oderint dum metuant.

"Let them hate as long as they fear," Avery said.

"I know, I looked it up," I said with a smile. "You must like pain if you branded it on yourself."

She made a noise but didn't say anything.

"Who do you need to fear you?" I asked.

"It's a saying my family lives by," she explained. "Though I don't think fear is always the way to solve things."

"Then why did you get it?" I pushed. "For some reason, I don't think it's because you're loyal to your family."

I had thought often about what kind of parents had raised someone like Avery. While she may have been given an expensive private education, the people that went to that school were all groomed for lives in the spotlight. Many grew up in the royal family or were the children of powerful business people.

I had looked up her father. Or at least who I thought was her father. After hearing about her time at Kingswood Prep, I looked at the list of alumni for someone with the same name.

Russel Maddox shared only a last name with her and the same blond hair, though his was almost all gray. He was much older than I assumed her parents would be, so it caused me some doubt.

His bio said he was married with a single child, but it didn't mention names or have pictures.

Either way, he looked like the type of person that was more focused on his work than his family. Last year he was announced as an angel investor for multiple startups, all of them looking to help orphaned children. It looked good on paper, but my guess is it was mostly for a tax write-off or to help his own image.

"Share about your family and I'll share about mine."

I froze. The locket that I had worn every day for the last seventeen years burned on my chest. But she had already seen inside, so the biggest hurdle was over.

"You know everything already," I murmured.

"I know your father died in a car accident," she said. "With you in it. You survived, but your mom left you mere weeks after."

I closed my eyes and took deep breaths. Even just the mention of them sent images of his death and her betrayal exploded across my mind. It was still so fresh and I had worked so hard to push it down.

"What I don't know is why you went to the same school as your mother or took a teaching position there," she continued. "You don't like it, but I couldn't imagine you doing it for her. You seem like the kind of person that would hate her for leaving you like that."

"You promise to share after I do?" I asked, looking up at her. She nodded. I searched her expression for any indication that she was lying before lowering my head to her chest again.

"I hate her," I whispered. I had never said it aloud before. Even when I was at my lowest. There was something so... solidifying about speaking it aloud. I thought that maybe if I didn't say it that it wouldn't be true, but that was a coward's way of thinking. "Growing up, she hated me as well. She and my dad were always fighting and on the brink of divorce, but she never had enough money to move on without him. And no matter how horrible she was to him, he stayed."

"Probably to give you a sense of family," Avery murmured.

I shrugged.

"Or maybe he just wanted to hold on to her as long as possible," I said. "Father was a construction worker. They met through mutual friends who told me later that they fell in love and got married in a matter of months. But they were young, and Mother wanted nothing more than to study at Princeton. It was all she talked about. Dad even helped her pay for it... he just loved her so much more than she ever did him."

I took a steadying breath.

"On the day he died, he had come home from a job and was taking me home from my art club." I took a shaky breath. "I was sleeping, so I didn't see him swerving, but I felt it when we crashed into another car. I was told later that he had fallen asleep at the wheel. It would be hours before they pulled me out of the ditch."

Her fingers trailed the length of my spine until they met the scar from the accident. It was much smaller, I had invested a lot of money in treatments and scar creams, but there was still a faint line even after all these years that pulsed whenever I was going through a hard time.

But recently, with Avery here, I started paying attention to it less and less. Even as she traced it, not once did I feel the ache.

"Your mother was upset and so she left."

A bitter laugh forced itself from me.

"She stayed until I graduated and then took off. She wasn't upset, Avery. It was her chance to leave."

"I still don't get it."

I shrugged.

"I thought maybe if I could get here that somehow I could prove to her I was worth the attention she refused to give me. I can't stress how much she loved this place. Or how she wore the title like a badge of honor."

Avery let out a hum. I let her digest it for a moment.

"But I'm not smart," I whispered. "I don't understand architecture, I suck at math, I'm horrible at business. Getting into exhibition design was my only chance. And my art... it's not something I'm proud of. I don't have a passion for it, like you said. Sometimes it's the only thing keeping me sane. And honestly, it's not Princeton level."

"I get it now," she said, letting her hand trail my back. "That's why you did community college, then Penn State, then Princeton."

I nodded.

"I was lucky the entire time," I said. "Even luckier that I could use my dad's tragedy and my mother's student status here as an admissions essay. I think they felt bad."

She held me closer.

"I love my mother," she said. The abrupt change in the conversation caused me to look up at her. Her gaze was fixed on the ceiling. "But she only had me to rope my father into marriage. There's not much I can say... but I can tell you the branding wasn't because I was loyal to my family. It was the opposite."

I swallowed thickly.

"In other words..."

"I didn't choose it," she finished for me. Her eyes shifted down to mine. "I know what it feels like to be unwanted too."

Tears pricked my eyes. For the first time, I saw Avery fully... and it was painful. She was insane at times, dangerous, but now I could see past it. She wanted nothing more than to be wanted by someone, so she did all she could to pull me in.

Don't forget me.

She did everything... protected me from people who wished to do me harm, cooked for me, got me presents, and stayed by my side as if she was making sure I'd never leave. Never be able to forget her like everyone else had.

And it made all too much sense as to why I loved every moment of it. It was sickening.

I lifted myself onto my elbows and kept her gaze as I leaned over and sent a kiss to her brand. She sucked in a sharp breath below me.

I paused and looked down at it.

It was raised and the skin was darker than the rest. It looked really painful and it caused my heart to ache.

My eyes landed on the mastectomy scars. I kissed one lightly before looking up at her with a smile and swiping my tongue across it.

Her gaze darkened.

"Why can't you tell me more?" I asked and let my hand brush across the scars. Just like mine they were connected to horrible memories, but I loved them, nonetheless. *Loved he—*

I didn't let myself finish that thought.

I was getting too wrapped up in her and the idea of it scared me.

"For your safety," she said. "The less you know, the better."

But her trying to keep it from me only made me want to know even more.

"Let me guess, it has something to do with the FBI agent?"

Instead of answering, she pulled me up and delivered a burning kiss to my mouth. I let her distract me, but inside, I knew I would have to find out sooner or later.

AVERY

The man let out a gargled scream as I broke another finger.

"Jesus Christ," Jonson muttered from behind me.

The man's screams echoed throughout the empty warehouse, but it was remote enough that we wouldn't need to worry about anyone venturing out to see what all the noise was about.

Turns out you *can* count on the FBI to have random torture houses around the country. Who would have thought?

The man that had broken into my apartment didn't die from the beating. A pity and blessing in disguise all at once. I didn't really want to deal with Father's men more than I had been, but he had gotten too close for comfort. I had held him in my apartment for three days as a test to see if anyone was going to come rescue him. When no one did, I called Jonson to get hold of one of the FBI's properties.

Though he was none too happy about it.

Last week I had spent an obscene amount of time trying to help him piece together all of the illegal shit my father was doing. Or more like helping others do it. Even though I had grown up with him, I had somehow underestimated how well he covered his tracks.

More than a handful of times, Jonson complained that this

work would be better suited for someone lower level than him, but he has yet to stumble upon the human trafficking, falsified reports, or cover-ups. I all but literally spelled it out for him, so I was seriously starting to doubt whatever my old boss saw in him.

I debated giving up this partnership and just killing Father myself. At least then I could get this done faster, but that left myself, Mother, and Willow all at the whims of his business associates. Father would have been dead, but that didn't mean that the secrets he kept were.

To them, we were loose ends. Loose ends that now had all their blood money.

The constant attention from Jonson was annoying at best. As much as he complained about his job, he somehow also really wanted to protect us. Or at least Willow. He was open about how I annoyed him as much as he annoyed me.

It didn't bother me though. This was the safest option for us. Both Willow and I.

Without Jonson at our side, I was concerned about what awaited us. But if he didn't pick up the fucking pace at any time this century, all my work would have been for nothing.

I hadn't wanted to leave Willow again so soon. I had spent a blissful few days sleeping with her in her apartment and enjoying our time together while I let the man in my closet cook. Another part of my plan that went awry.

After I climbed into bed with her, I found myself unable to pull myself out of it. It led to dangerous situations. Like opening up when I didn't mean to.

But was it wrong that a part of me was glad? Even if it meant putting Willow in danger?

Willow took it all in stride, never once looking at me with disgust or pity. Because she, too, knew all too well how fucked-up parents could be. Even if our situations were different from each other, there was still a shared understanding of what it felt like to be unwanted by the people who were supposed to want you the most in this world.

The man's guttural moan pulled me from my racing thoughts.

I had to take a few moments to collect myself before giving him my attention.

I needed to interrogate him, not kill him.

"I'm asking you again," I said and lined up another one of his fingers in the nutcracker. "How many men did he send?"

The man was hog-tied in the middle of the concrete floor and he had long since run out of energy to constantly fight me. Most of the time, he lay there with his head pressed to the ground and his breathing labored. I had to bring out a little pain to get him going, but it looked like my father trained his men well.

"I don't know the total," he huffed. Sweat ran down his face and his bloodshot eyes darted toward the FBI agent behind me. If he still thought there was a chance his pleading could cause Jonson to help him, he had another thing coming.

"How many do you know of?" Jonson asked. The hope draining from the man's face was addicting, but Jonson's interference only fanned the flames of my irritation.

This isn't a team sport, I wanted to bark back, but I kept my mouth shut. He was trying to help, and that was my last hope. If I fucked this up between us, I would be back to square one and neither Willow nor I would have anyone to fall back on.

"Five," he said quickly. "That's all my team."

I clicked my tongue. It was less than I expected from Father. But maybe they were more than the standard guards he sent. After all, this one found me easily.

"Shouldn't have said that," I sang, a crazy bubble of laughter rising from my chest. I had missed the days when I could torture Father's guards. It was always easiest when they were supposed to protect me instead of trying to capture me. "Locations."

"No," he breathed, panic lacing his tone.

The snap of his finger was swallowed by his screams.

"Their locations or I visit that sweet wife and child of yours," I said and lined up the next finger. I only had two left. Next would be toes. "You've left them alone for a long time. I wonder who reminds them to charge the cameras when you're gone."

"Avery," Jonson warned. He and I both knew it was useless for him to try and control me.

I don't know why he even tried.

"Please," the man begged. His eyes widened at the mention of his family. "Please, I don't know how to help you. He keeps us separated and working on different tasks. I don't know—"

"Alright," I said with a sigh and stood. "It's 4-7-3 Cherry Lane, right? It's about time for her to tuck the little one in. She'll be distracted enough."

I turned to leave, but his shout called me back.

"Four are stationed at the Club Pétale locations, two each," he choked out. I was facing away from him, so I let the smile I had been holding back spread across my face, but Jonson caught it all. His flinch caused heat to expand in my chest.

"And the last?" I asked and turned around to face him.

He averted his eyes to the ground and it caused alarm bells to ring in my head.

"He's hard to find," he said. He was trying to buy time.

"But he's alone," I noted. "So he must be good."

His eyes met mine and I cocked my head to the side.

"Or was he with you?"

His averted gaze told me all I needed to know.

He was near the school.

Fury grew inside me and I couldn't stop myself from stalking over to him and sending a hard kick to his side. I grabbed his bindings and forced him to turn over before I closed my hand around his throat. He tried to wiggle his way out of my hold, but it was useless. I had straddled and put all my weight on him.

"He's near the school," I growled. "Give me the address."

He opened his mouth, but no sound came out. Anger whirled inside me so violently I started shaking.

There was still another out there. If they were out there, they were near Willow. This one had found my apartment, seen my cameras. The other? He could find her—

Jonson's hand pulling at my wrist caused the rage to subside for a moment and allowed me to relax my grip on the man. He sputtered and coughed as he tried to fill his lungs with air.

"Ahhh," I said with a sigh. "Apologies."

"He's in the Butler building, 3-1-1-6," he choked out.

Two buildings away from Willow.

I shot up and gave Jonson a look.

"Don't," he whispered. "I'll have someone go—"

"No time," I said and stepped over the moaning man. "Bring a body bag, will ya?"

Jonson reluctantly followed me back to the campus, leaving the man back in the warehouse.

He had tried to talk to me many times on the drive over, but I couldn't think of anything other than getting to room 3116 and killing that bastard.

It consumed my entire being.

Every moment I was away from the university was just another moment where I had horrible visions of Willow getting hurt. The realistic side of my brain knew that in order to get me that they would most likely hold on to her and use her as blackmail, but that side was long buried through my violent thoughts.

Unlike the man before, I was going to have no patience to knock him out, steal his equipment, and dump him on the site. No, I imagined beating him to death for even just entertaining the idea of getting so close to Willow.

He had to have seen her by now. Foolishly I hoped that he wouldn't have seen me with her, but with how much I followed her around, I doubt that they wouldn't have put two and two together.

But how did they even find me so easily? I may have used my real name for my classes, but the dorm was under a stolen one. Even if they found me through the roster, they would still have to comb the campus in order to find me.

I knew it was only a matter of time, given my father's resources and money, but the end of the first semester was still a week and a half away.

I didn't wait for the car to fully stop when we reached the campus. Instead, I darted out and ran to the dorm like my life depended on it.

I didn't care that people were watching or that they were whispering.

I only had one thing on my mind.

I had to break the lock to the back of the dorm to sneak into it, but it was quick work. What took the longest was the rickety elevator that took its sweet-ass time getting me up to the floor.

The stairs would have been fucking faster.

Room 3116 was the last dorm and closest to the emergency exit. Something I should have suspected from a hired mercenary.

The hall was mostly quiet, save for the few open dorm rooms down the hall. A few of the students peeked their heads out to see what was going on, but none of them dared to stop me.

One of them let out a squeak when I kicked the door to room 3116 down. It was dark in the room and looked too clean to be used. The only giveaway that someone was here was the pulled-back blankets on the bed. I darted to the closet to check, but there was nothing but darkness staring back at me.

I almost exploded when my phone started vibrating until I saw it was Jonson calling me.

"The room is empty," I said.

There was a pause on the other line.

"Are you gonna talk, or you just gonna stand there while I do your j—"

"I went to check on Willow first," he said. "I knocked on the door, but there was no answer."

"*Shit*, let me check the cameras."

"The cameras?"

I hung up on him without answering and pulled up the camera feed.

My heart stopped in my chest when I saw no sign of Willow. I went further back in the feed to see that she had left more than thirty minutes ago with her laptop and bag in hand.

Damn it.

WILLOW

Waking up to a note was the highlight of my morning. Every time we were separated, I would wake up to one on my pillow and smile to myself.

Meet me at the library at 7.

A bit late to meet at the library on a Thursday, but I had to prepare for the next semester's class anyway.

Just like that, my first semester of teaching was almost over. There were obviously many setbacks and I really didn't predict Avery becoming a part of my life in the way that she did, but I truly believe I did well in my class.

The physical arts students and their teacher came up to me during our last practice session and told me how fun the students were to work with and that they loved how everything was coming together. It's all I could have asked for, really.

My class wasn't the most highly sought out, so I wasn't looking to make waves, but having other people acknowledge that my students were not only kind but learning well was more than enough for me.

Before break, there was going to be a showing of all this semester's work that students and faculty could walk through and that was where the final designs of my students would be shown. I would go in a few days before and grade and critique them, but honestly, they already showed lots of promise.

Surprisingly, I found myself excited for what the next week held.

I showed up at the library at six thirty just to be safe and found a quiet nook to myself. There were only a few people in the library that late, no doubt trying to get in some last-minute study time before finals, but slowly they left. By the time the clock hit five past seven, I was the last person in the study area.

I expected Avery to be there by then, but even as the minutes ticked by, she was nowhere to be found. There was an eerie silence in the air that caused my skin to prickle. It was the first sign that warned me I wasn't alone.

When I realized how much time had passed, I looked over my shoulder, trying to seek out the eyes I knew were watching me, but I didn't find her. She was here. I knew she had to be. The feeling of being watched was proof enough of that.

But how long did she want to hide?

Then out of the corner of my eye, I caught a shadow.

A playful smile spread across my face when I realized that the shadow was going to a more secluded part of the library.

So this is how Avery wanted to play.

Excitement played at my spine and a thousand different dirty scenarios ran through my mind at once. Fucking her in the Princeton Library was a sure way to get me fired, but the anticipation of what awaited me outweighed any logical thinking.

Trying to be as quiet as possible, I stood from my seat and left my stuff at the table. I tiptoed through the aisles, trying to catch sight of Avery but paused and frowned when I couldn't. Her footsteps were nonexistent. I couldn't even make out her breathing.

But I could make out mine. The hitch of my breath as I walked through the aisles broke through the silence. The pounding of my heart in my ears felt like it was amplified throughout the library.

Slipping through the shelves and drawing Avery to me like a beacon.

Bookshelves were all around me, towering over me and blocking my view. The longer I stayed between them, the higher and sturdier they felt.

I was too preoccupied with my own reactions to hear the click of the gun.

A shot rang out.

It was so loud it caused my ears to ring. My scream was stuck in my throat and terror froze my veins. It just missed the side of my face and embedded into the bookshelf behind me, sending paper scraps flying everywhere.

Time moved in slow motion. My heart was pounding in my chest, but quickly the sounds of the library filtered through the ringing. I could hear the bullet ripping through the books. I could hear the steps of the person who shot at me just a few feet away.

My mind stalled.

I never had a chance to figure out if I was a fight-or-flight type of person. The last time I was in a situation like this, I was strapped into the car, fast asleep. My mind didn't have time to work through the accident, nor would I have been able to do anything.

But this was different.

Move.

My own voice was loud in my head. It was screaming at me.

Move. Run. This is not Avery.

The last thought was what I needed to snap me out of my stupor. That *was not* Avery.

I took my body only a second to understand what my mind was screaming, but then my muscles kicked into gear. Adrenaline rushed through my veins. I sucked in a sharp burst of air and grabbed the shelf, using it to help propel me back down the aisle.

My feet were fast as I ran through the shelves, trying to move farther into the library and closer to the emergency exit. I couldn't hear them behind me anymore, but I couldn't stop. The shot had come from the south, right by the staircase to the lower floors, meaning that exit was blocked and I would be forced to find another.

Another shot rang out and a burning pain exploded across my right calf. I let out a groan as white-hot pain flooded through my system.

I thought adrenaline was supposed to numb the pain?

Each step felt like my entire leg was engulfed in flames, but my mind told me that if I stopped now, I would never make it out of this place. I made a sharp right when I got to the hallway that connected the study area to the conference rooms. I could feel the blood soaking into my pants and prayed to God it wasn't leaving a trail behind me.

I could hear the footsteps now, though they were almost drowned out by the sound of my own frantic thoughts. They weren't running like I was. It was a slow, stalking sort of walk that only made the fear I was feeling that much more intense.

They're in no rush because they knew I wouldn't be able to outrun them.

I tried every door I came across, but they were all locked. It shouldn't have been a surprise since the library was pretty much closed at this time and I was all alone. All the students and faculty had filtered out and whatever librarian had been on duty was probably long gone as soon as she heard the first shot.

I rushed down the hallway, trying to find any open door. My hands were slick with sweat as I tried to pry open the doors. Far too many were locked. Luckily, when I hit the archive room, it was unlocked.

I pulled the door open as quickly as I could but shut it as quietly as possible. Inside was very dim, with a few of the lights flickering overhead, the room smelled of musky books and dust. Something I may find comfort and if it wasn't for the situation.

I blinked rapidly, trying to make out the shapes in the darkness. The room was much larger inside than I expected, with rows upon rows of shelves that looked like they could be toppled at any moment. I ran toward the back corner and put my back flat against one of the shelves so that if they opened the door, I wouldn't be visible.

I took a deep breath and tried to calm my racing heart. My lungs were burning and there was a sheen of sweat across my skin. Tears pricked my eyes, but I tried to hold in all of the emotions, at least until it was safe.

If I was ever going to be safe.

The footsteps outside got louder as they came closer, and I could have sworn they stopped right outside the door, but then I heard their footsteps receding.

I don't know how long I waited there. It was probably only minutes, but it felt like hours.

Looking down at my leg, I flinched when I realized my pant leg was soaked with blood. Even just looking at the wound caused a fresh wave of pain to go through me. I made quick work of tearing off part of my shirt and tying it right above where I guessed the wound was.

Images of the glass everywhere, the heat against my skin and the feeling of smoke burning my lungs hit me like a slap to the face.

No, no, no. Push it down. It was *not* the time to be getting flashbacks from the accident. If I let myself get too pulled back into my own nightmares, I wouldn't be making it out of this one.

By the time I was out of there, I knew that I would be leaving a trail of blood, but at least I could try to stop the bleeding.

Bile threatened to rise in my throat when I pulled the shirt even tighter around my wound. My head swam, and I had to take two shaky breaths in order to rein myself in.

I can't die here.

In all the movies and books I read, when the main character was about to die, they always had some sort of guiding image that helped them get through moments like then. Something to fight for.

But in my mind, all I could think about was that I just needed to survive long enough for Avery to find me. Because as long as she was there, I knew I would be safe.

I wasn't fighting, I was running. Running toward Avery.

When I couldn't hear the footsteps anymore, I started to move from my hiding spot but jumped and slapped my hand over my mouth to stifle the scream when I heard two loud gunshots.

With shaky legs, I tiptoed toward the door and pressed my ear against it.

I could hear some commotion and footsteps, but they seemed far from where I was.

Slowly, I opened the door and peeked outside, looking down the hallway. It was still empty. I tried to listen again, and it sounded like the footsteps were farther into the library and closer to the emergency exit.

So back to the main staircase it is.

With one last deep breath, I exited.

When my shoe squeaked against the floors, I paused, but the footsteps and rustling didn't stop. Quickly, I slipped off my shoes and bent down to grab them before tiptoeing down the hallway.

I held my breath with each step that I took and when I got back to the main study area, I peered in and there was no one to be seen. I didn't even try to go for my stuff. With a racing heart and cautious hope in my heart, I made my way toward the main staircase, walking through the various shelves and pausing every time I heard a sound.

When stairs were in sight, a painful burst of hope exploded in my chest.

I was ready to run for them until a hand grabbed my face in a way that covered my mouth and muffled my screams. My back was pushed against the shelf so hard it knocked the air from my lungs. When I caught the sight of familiar blue eyes and a wild smirk, I thought I might cry on the spot.

Avery's hair was a mess around her head, and it was stained with bright-red blood. So were her face and clothing, I noticed after a moment. I could feel the wet blood that was still on her hand smear over my mouth and face.

I didn't care about the blood though. I was just so relieved to see her.

She came... she came for me!

Her face had never looked more beautiful than in that moment. Yes, the devil was still lurking behind her eyes, but goddamn, was I glad to see it.

I couldn't help the tears that started to drip down my face. She leaned to the side to look down the aisle. Her familiar scent washed over me, loosening the tenseness in my muscles. She let out a small breath before looking back to me.

Her eyes ran down my face and her expression calmed slightly. She brought one finger up to her lips, motioning for me to keep quiet, then pulled me to the side and helped me sit down on the ground, slowly lowering herself with me.

Even when she pulled her hand away from my mouth, I was unable to speak.

Her hand came to grip my throat, but instead of it feeling harsh and demanding, it was soft and her thumb rubbed light strokes on the side of my neck.

She was comforting me, I realized.

She held my gaze for a few more moments and slowly, the beating of my heart started to calm. I hadn't realized how much it hurt to breathe until then. Nor was I paying that much attention to the burning pain in my leg.

"Stay here," she commanded. "I'll take care of this."

Panic seized my chest, and I reached out to hold on to her clothing.

"Don't," I choked out. "They have a gun. Let's leave."

The crazed smile was back, this time growing even wider than before and there was a light in her eyes.

"You don't think I'd let them hurt what's mine and get away with it, do you?" she asked. "Though it warms my heart to know how much you care for my well-being."

With one last smile, she got up and left, back down the aisle and toward the intruder.

In that moment, I knew that something had changed between us. I don't know when it happened, but I couldn't stand watching her walk away. I knew the type of person that she was, but the fear that clawed my throat and chest and threatened to swallow me whole was so overwhelming I was left with no choice but to follow her.

As soon as she disappeared, I shakily stood and tried my best to follow her.

It was an idiotic move. Realistically, I knew that staying in that spot and being as quiet as I could while letting her take care of this was the best possible way to get me out of there alive.

I had absolutely no business following a literal murder, but there was some twisted thought inside me that really believed that if I did not follow her... that may be the last time that I saw her.

It didn't take long for me to catch up to her, even with the pain from my leg. She was silent as she walked, but she was so tall that it was hard to miss her. She led me farther into the main study area, past the tables and back into the shelves. I waited a few moments until I was sure she wouldn't see me before following.

I speed-walked across the open area until I caught sight of her again. I had no idea how she knew where to go since the library was still silent, but she was a girl on a mission. She walked down another aisle and then paused. I quickly retraced my steps and hid behind the nearest shelf.

"Father should know better than to go after her," she said, her voice ringing out. "Especially when we know that you're here for me."

Silence greeted her. My heart was pounding in my chest and I gripped the shelf beside me.

It was another few heartbeats before I heard the rustling of the shooter.

"You're notoriously hard to get a hold of," the shooter said. It was a woman. I peeked around the shelf to catch sight of Avery's back and beyond her, the shooter. She was dressed in a hoodie and jeans with combat boots. She looked like any other college student... except for the gun in her hand.

"There's a reason for that."

The shooter's lips twitched.

"Come home," she said. "If you do that, we'll leave the girl alone."

Avery clicked her tongue and put her hands in her pockets before rocking on her heels. It was such a relaxed, almost lazy action. It was almost like she was goading her on and it only made her even scarier than the shooter. Especially when she raised her gun to point straight at Avery.

"Father wouldn't like it if you damaged his goods," she said. The shooter smiled, then adjusted her aim toward me.

"Shit," I muttered under my breath.

Avery didn't even look back at me and that's when I realized she probably knew all along that I was following her.

"Let's put an end to this," she said. "And don't act unaffected because we've seen how obsessed you are with this girl."

Avery let out a light laugh, then cocked her head to the side.

"I'm just buying time."

The shooter gave her an incredulous look, then two shots rang out. The sound of it caused me to let out a choked scream. The shooter's body flew backward. The image of the bullet embedding into her shoulder and into her leg was probably a sight that would be burned into my mind for all eternity.

She fell against the nearby shelf and to the ground. She tried to frantically grab for her gun, but it slipped right out of her hand. Avery was quick as she walked toward it and stepped on it just before the shooter could grab it. The shooter looked up at her with a snarl.

Avery reached down and grabbed the gun before looking it over, flipping it back and forth between her hands. This was definitely her toying with the woman.

"*Don't.*"

The familiar sound of the FBI agent's voice ringing out through the silent library caused me to jump. *So that's where the shots came from.*

She didn't listen to him. She put her finger on the trigger, aimed right toward the woman's forehead, and pulled.

Avery had moved enough that most of her body was blocking the sight of the girl, but that didn't stop me from seeing her crumble to the ground with a fresh bullet wound to her head. Her vacant stare dug into me as the blood from her wound trickled down her face.

The connection was broken by the FBI agent peeking his head into my aisle. His gaze slid down my form, pausing on the places where I had been nicked by the bullets.

"Let's get you cleaned up," he said and offered his hand to me.

I didn't know how much I was supposed to trust him, but seeing as he just probably saved us, I guessed he was a safe bet.

I took a step forward, ready to take his outstretched hand, but Avery appeared beside him with a gun still in her hand. Seeing her in front of me again, her face and clothes splattered with more blood, was a shock to the system.

I was going to have a mental breakdown after this. I knew it. But in that moment, I allowed myself to admire how *goddamn* good she looked covered in blood.

There was something so powerful and positively feral about her that caused my entire body to stand on edge.

And I liked it.

Avery slapped his hand away before reaching up and grabbing on to me.

"How are you going to lie your way out of this one?" Avery asked with a smile.

He sent her a glare.

"If you hadn't killed her, this would have been easier."

She shrugged and then looked back toward me.

"She deserved worse," she murmured. "I was being merciful."

"If you didn't kill her, we could also get information out of her and get your fath—"

"It's done with," she said, interrupting him but not once looking back. Her eyes were locked on me. "Let's go home."

WILLOW

Home, as it turned out, was *not* my small dorm apartment. Apparently, both Avery and Jonson thought it would be best if I didn't go back there.

"It's compromised," they had said.

I couldn't complain even if I wanted to. The shock and adrenaline wore off faster than I expected and by the time we had left the campus, taken the drive back to Manhattan, and entered the luxurious three-floor penthouse... I broke down before I could even get into the shower.

Avery was in there first, washing off all of the blood that had caked onto her skin while Jonson was downstairs making some calls. I sat on the bed wrapped in a towel as my mind started putting things together. The image of the shooter's vacant stare played through my mind over and over again and it started to remind me too much of my father's when I woke up from the crash to see him next to me, dead.

I vaguely remember Avery and Jonson talking about how this place was under the FBI's "careful watch" and that we should be safe there, but other than that, I didn't retain anything about the conversation that we had on the way. Not about who those people were. Not about how her father was involved. And not even about how I was involved.

They had taken care to clean my wounds. Luckily, the shooter grazed both my calf and the side of my face. My calf was worse off but had been patched up, just narrowly missing the need for stitches. I was woozy from the pain meds, but even those didn't chase away the thoughts.

If anything, they made them worse.

It wasn't long before Avery stepped out of the bathroom, a towel around her hips. She was perfectly clean and her hair was pushed back and out of her face, but I couldn't keep her stare for long. All I could think about was her a few moments ago, with blood everywhere. She may have washed it all off, but I couldn't shake the image.

She was calling me, but I wouldn't look up at her. Even though I knew she was trying to get my attention, I had been zoned out as the images played over and over again in my mind, causing me to stare vacantly at the floor.

Her kneeling down with her hands on my bare knees and looking up at me caused me to snap back into my body. I hadn't noticed that tears were running down my face until she reached out to wipe them away.

Again, she was so gentle with me.

When her lips dipped down into a small frown, I couldn't help the sob that escaped my chest. She didn't move to hug me. She trailed her hands up to my shoulders and gave them a squeeze before running them back down to my hands and squeezing them as well. She repeated the motion a few times until my sobs had lessened enough for me to speak.

"I'm sorry," I choked out. "I don't understand why—"

"Shhh," she whispered, a smile pulling at her lips. "This is normal."

I tried to take a deep breath, but it was cut off by a choked sob. She gripped my shoulders again before taking my hands in hers and bringing them to her lips.

"It's normal to react like this when you've seen someone die," she said against my knuckles. "Not to mention you got shot."

"Grazed," I corrected.

A genuine smile pulled at her lips and her eyes lit up.

"I don't expect you to be like me," she said. The image of her feral smile flashed across my mind.

That wasn't normal. I knew she was a killer, but *that* reaction was far from what I expected from her. She wasn't just killing people, she enjoyed it.

"How did you become like that?" I asked, my voice barely above a whisper.

I pulled my hand from hers to reach it out to trace the branding on her chest.

Inside, I could guess as to how she became exactly like this. With everything she had given me, I could piece it together. Not only had she grown up in a family that branded you if you displeased them, but now her father had sent *assassins* after her.

That didn't really scream a happy and accepting childhood.

"Sometimes it happens to people like me," she said, then quickly corrected. "To people who grow up like me."

My sobs had quieted then and I was able to take a deep striding breath.

"I don't know many fathers who send assassins after their children," I murmured. "It was him, right?"

She gave me a stiff nod. We were reaching dangerous territory again.

"They weren't assassins," she said. "More like... trained guards. They had a mission to bring me back."

"Why?" I asked, my voice barely above a whisper.

Her smile dropped and her brows pushed together. We were getting into territory she didn't want to speak about. That much was obvious, but she had never looked so conflicted before.

Maybe it was because of how this whole situation had affected me. I knew it would be a shitty thing to capitalize on how she was feeling right now, but it was time I got some answers.

"I think it's the least you can do," I said. "They came here for you and I almost—I could have—"

"They wouldn't have killed you because if they killed you, they wouldn't have gotten me," she said. "They timed it perfectly so I would show up there and come to your rescue. But I don't think they realized that I had an FBI agent by my side... surprising since they had seen everything else."

I stayed silent for another long moment. She let out a sigh.

"I'm his child. In his world, fathers have heirs that come in and take over the family business. Or businesses, in my father's case. From the time they are born to adulthood, they groom us to take over one day."

"But that's not what you do."

"*No*," she hissed. "I don't want to have anything to do with him."

"With Russell Maddox," I said, watching her expression carefully. If I didn't know her as well as I did, the cold mask that spread across her face would have scared me. "On paper, he seems like a good man." I paused, looking back down at the branding and the unevenness of her mastectomy scars. "Though something tells me he's not."

She didn't say anything and her hands came to grab my knees. Her long fingers curled in, causing her nails to dig into my skin.

"You avoided the hospitals 'cause he could find you," I continued. "Is that why you left the club as well? Did your father threaten to take them—"

A hand came to cover my mouth.

"No more talking about him," she said in a low voice. "I don't want to think about what he's done. I'm already at my limit today and I don't want to take it out on you."

Her plea caused my stomach to twist. Just how much anger was she holding inside her? Not just from this incident but since her childhood?

The shackles of it must have been excruciating.

I nodded, and she slowly removed her hand.

"You must have had a hard childhood," I said and brought my hand up to cup her cheek. "I feel sorry for the little Avery that had to go through all this to become the person you are today."

She leaned into my hand.

"Do you not like the person I am today?" she asked. The normal playfulness was gone and replaced with something a bit more vulnerable.

I couldn't fight the smile that rose to my lips. Regardless of everything, I could still see the child in her, fighting to be seen. Fighting to be loved.

"There may be some things I don't like or that scare me..." I trailed off and let my other hand comb through her wet hair. "But even still, I think I've come to love the person you are today."

She gave me the softest smile I had ever seen before it disappeared completely. She looked almost... *sad*.

"Let's get you in the shower," she said. "I have a feeling as soon as the hot water hits you, you'll start to feel the fatigue."

I swallowed my disappointment at her reaction and nodded, letting her pull me up with a careful touch.

The way she took me to the shower and helped me wash was almost embarrassing. Or at least it would have been if we hadn't seen each other naked so many times before.

But this time felt different.

Even though she had just washed, she didn't hesitate to jump into the shower with me. We washed my body first, getting rid of all the bloodstains. And even after everything, when her hands brushed my nipples, I couldn't help but let out a sigh.

When her hands traveled south, I froze and tried to grab her hand, but she shot me a look.

"I have done so many things to this pussy, but washing it is what gets you nervous? What happened to the girl who was begging for me to fuck it?"

My face flamed, but I offered no response. I could have sworn she was purposefully teasing my clit, but her touch was gone before I could say anything.

When she was done thoroughly washing my body, she moved to my hair. I tried again to help, but as soon as I tried to reach for my hair, she smacked my hands away. So I was forced to stand there while she did everything for me.

It was vulnerable being taken care of like that and even though we were both standing there naked, and her touch had lingered in places that caused heat to run through me, there was nothing inherently sexual about this.

A small moan slipped from my lips as she worked the shampoo into my scalp and my lips fluttered closed at the sensation. The warm water beating down on my back, combined with her motions, turned me into a puddle.

I didn't realize when I had started to sway or when I started leaning forward until my cheek connected with her chest. I expected her to stop and push me away, but instead, she looped one arm around my back, holding me closer to her, then started shampooing the back of my head.

This was her way of taking care of me.

I don't know why I expected her to still be harsh when I have so obviously experienced so many facets of her... but it would have been easier if she were harsh. Maybe it would have made my chest feel less heavy and would not have caused the tears to well in my eyes again.

"Let's wash it out," she murmured above me. I didn't want to move but nodded anyway. She helped me lean back and wash the shampoo out of my hair. My eyes never left her face. She was so intently focused on her task that it would have been heartwarming if it didn't feel like she was ignoring me.

She didn't meet my eyes until it was done.

"Are you sad?" she asked.

"Are you?" I asked.

Her lips pursed and her gaze flitted to the conditioner. She didn't look me in the eyes as she squeezed a hefty amount into her palms.

She was silent again as she worked it through my hair, still not meeting my eyes.

"I was scared," she admitted. "When I couldn't find you, I thought the worst."

I let myself fall back into her chest, but this time, I wrapped my arms around her waist and pulled her closer to me.

"I don't get scared," she muttered after a moment. I let this one slide. A confession that may have been better if ignored. She was being vulnerable, and I was worried that my calling attention to it would cause this all to blow up in smoke.

When she was done with the conditioner, she paused before wrapping her arms around me as well.

"I shouldn't want to be with you like this," I mumbled against her skin.

"Is that why you're sad?" I shook my head.

"Is it because I'm not the person you wanted me to be?" she asked.

I shook my head again.

"I told you I lo—like the person you are now," I said with a sigh. "It's because I don't remember the last time someone had taken care of me like this just because."

There was silence before she unwound her arms and helped me wash out the conditioner.

Another burst of disappointment and hurt blossomed in me. If she noticed, she didn't say anything.

When we were done, she pulled me out of the shower and wrapped the towel around me. She pushed me toward the sink. The mirror was still fogged because of our shower. She wrapped a new towel around her waist and used a third to help dry my hair.

She was still so gentle when she did it that it caused my heart to twist.

Slowly the fog started to clear, and I was able to watch her as she carefully dried my hair. Her expression was blank, giving nothing away.

"Hand me the silver bottle," she murmured.

I reached forward and grabbed it. It was a leave-in conditioner from the looks of it. I handed it to her and she poured it into her hand. She placed it back on the counter beside us.

The sweet scent of coconut and fruit hit me as she combed it through my hair with her hands.

When she reached for the brush on the counter, I gripped her wrist.

"I can do it," I said, but she grabbed it from me anyway.

Even with brushing, she was gentle. I disliked how silent she was being.

When she was done, she placed it on the counter and leaned forward, pushing her back into me. Both of her palms were on either side of mine and she fit her face into the crook of my neck, placing a kiss on the sensitive flesh. It caused me to shiver.

When she raised her head to meet my gaze in the mirror, my heart stopped.

"You're *mine*," she whispered. "I don't do this *just because.* I do this because you're mine and you deserve to be cared for."

I didn't want to cry, but her words made it too easy.

"What does that mean? Being yours?"

"It means that I'll take care of you," she said. "It means wherever you are, I will be. No matter where you run. You can't hide and if you try, I will always find you."

She inhaled deeply and nuzzled into my neck.

The possessiveness shouldn't have caused a shiver to run through me. Or for heat to pickle where her lips brushed my skin.

"Why?" I breathed.

Her eyes darted back to mine, but this time they were narrowed. Her hand came to grip my chin, forcing me to stare at myself in the mirror. She tugged off my towel, leaving me exposed.

"You're telling me you wouldn't be obsessed with this?" she asked, her other hands trailing down the side of my breast to follow the curve of my hip, then to the tuft of curls between my legs. When her fingers found my clit, I let out a whine. "Or those noises?"

"So sex," I said with a bit more venom than I wanted. Her lips pulled into a feral smile.

"And the attitude," she said, then leaned closer to place a kiss on my temple. "And contrary to what you might think... I like how strong you are."

I opened my mouth to speak but slammed it shut when her fingers ran through my folds.

"I don't particularly like how well you can *see* me or the pity-filled looks you give me... but you're the only person I've met that can understand on a certain level."

I let out a moan when her fingers came to massage my clit.

"Does it make it easier to say this when I can't fight back?" I asked.

Her smile told me it did.

"Yet you still do," she murmured.

When she pulled her hand away, I let out a huff. Her chuckle caused a shiver to run down my spine.

"I was going to give you a break tonight."

I turned around to face her with a smile of my own.

"Maybe I'll just..." I made a show of trailing my hand between my legs.

Her hand was around my throat again, her eyes digging into mine.

"You should rest," she said with a growl. "Tomorrow, if you want, I'll fuck you until you can't remember your name, but tonight we rest."

"Please?" I asked. It was hard to speak with the pressure on my neck, but the control she exhibited caused my entire body to relax into her. "This is taking care of me too."

"Fuck," she breathed. "But tonight, we take it easy. No—"

"No," I choked out. "I need something—"

Her grip tightened.

"Don't say I didn't warn you."

"I swear to God if you don't—"

"Quiet down, or our FBI friend may think I'm abusing you up here," Avery said as she leaned against the far wall. Her face was lit up with moonlight and gave me the perfect view of her shit-eating grin.

I should have realized when she forced clothes onto me and tied my wrist to the bed that I wouldn't be getting fucked tonight.

"You said," I whined with a pout and tugged at the silk rope on my wrist. It was tied to one side of the four-poster bed and gave me more than enough leeway to move around as much as I needed, but I would still be confined to this space.

Hence Avery standing right outside of my reach.

"And I warned you," she said with a shrug and pushed herself off the wall. I sat on the bed, watching her stalk over to me. When she reached the bed and took my face in her hands, I absolutely melted into her.

She gave me a gentle kiss that took my breath away before taking a step back.

"I need to talk to Jonson for a bit," she said. "Stay here and be good, and maybe I'll think about waking you up with a present."

"But—"

"*Rest*," she said and used gentle hands to push me into bed. This time I didn't fight her and watched with a frown as she left the room.

AVERY

Seeing Jonson in the kitchen of my penthouse was one of the few things keeping me sane.

Even after hours had passed since we left the library, I found it hard to think of anything other than how much I wanted to burn my father's entire empire down.

How dare he?

Mother's warning had been in the back of my mind the entire time I had been searching for her.

You can't keep secrets for long, Avery. Not from him. Not about this and not... not her.

She had been right. Of course. She had been dealing with Father for far longer than I had. She could see through the rage he ignited and right into his mind.

I should have fucking listened.

Jonson didn't say anything as I pulled a bottle of rum from my alcohol cart. Nor did he stop me when I grabbed two glasses and placed one in front of him. He was leaning against my island with his arms folded, only moving to grab the cup after I filled some for him.

He shot it back with zero hesitation.

After I poured myself one, I refilled his glass, almost expecting him to ask for more, but he didn't.

I took a hearty swig of my own, though I didn't even register the burn of the alcohol as it slid down my throat.

"It was a woman."

Jonson grunted and took a sip of his whiskey.

"Which means there is another one out there," I continued, anger seeping into my tone. "It's not safe for us to stay here."

"Is any place safe?" Jonson asked with a raised brow. "We can move the both of you. Get some type of detail on you. But... I have a feeling your father will not stop until he gets what he wants."

I slammed my cup down with far too much force on the counter.

I hated when he was being reasonable. I knew he was right. No place would be safe until that bastard was dead.

Over and over again, he would come after me until I was kneeling in front of him.

How far would he go?

He had already gone against the FBI agents and killed them without any mercy. What was next?

The more I thought about it, the heavier my anger got.

"That's why you need to do your job," I hissed. "I have given you everything—"

"Except hard evidence," he shot back. "I cannot wage war against one of the most powerful men in the country without the FBI's backup."

I scoffed and gulped back the rest of my drink.

"Then I will do it myself."

I pushed myself off the counter and passed him.

"Avery, you've already—"

"Don't send anyone after me," I called behind me. "If I'm not back in a few hours, untie Willow from the headboard and move her to someplace safe."

"Listen, I don't want to be in the middle of whatever this lovers' quarrel is, bu—"

"It's not a lovers' quarrel," I snapped, turning to send him a glare. "This may take a few days. Make sure she's cared for."

He didn't fight me this time as I turned to leave.

It had been seven days since I thought Willow was going to die.

It had also been seven days since she let it slip that she loved me... or at least hinted at it.

It was enough for me to understand her meaning.

I thought when we got to this moment I would be overjoyed. And I was to an extent because all I could think about was wanting Willow to be mine in every sense of the word.

If I knew how to love, I would say that what was between Willow and me was it. As twisted and messed up as it was.

But then, why did I feel so bad about it?

Why did my chest ache every time I thought of her? And why couldn't I get the way that she looked at me when I found her in that library out of my head?

I didn't like it. And to some point I didn't understand it.

Jonson was protecting her. Maybe things were even better when I was gone. Father's men were probably carried away with trying to find me instead of going after her.

But the heavy feeling in my chest stayed. And now I knew that there was only one possible reason as to why I felt so awful. As to why I couldn't shake the guilt off.

My father.

And that's why even when Jonson called and begged me to come back, I couldn't. I hadn't done anything like this before. Sometimes I kept tabs on my mother, but most of the time, I wanted to separate myself from my father instead of actively seeking him out.

Maybe that's why it was so easy to find him this time. Because he had never expected anyone to track him down like he was trying to do me. He even had his assistants put everything in his calendar and he followed it perfectly. Never a moment late.

I expected Willow to call me out on my absence, but maybe she was happy for the break. The thought made my mouth sour.

Tonight Father was going to dinner with the CFO of the NFL. But what they didn't put on the invite was that he had been going to dinner with this same woman every last Thursday of the month at the same place, which turned out to be her house.

I didn't know what plans Father had with her or the organization she represented, but he was moving up in the world.

Getting reckless.

Just the thing I needed.

They were discreet in the way that they did it and used a house that she owned outside of the city. One with a sprawling yard that was at least an acre in the back and in a community where there was no one under the age of fifty. It was a community of people who had nothing to fear, so much so that they didn't really invest in street lighting.

It was dark in every corner and perfect for me to hide in.

I watched from behind a tree to the side of her house as my father met the woman outside. He greeted her with a kiss to her cheek and she flushed in his presence. His driver pulled away as soon as he got out and the two were left alone.

They stood outside talking for far too long for people who were having an affair.

After a few minutes, the woman ushered my father into the house. As soon as the door closed, I snuck to the back, letting myself in through the guest room window. It was unlocked.

I heard their laughter down the hall and waited for them to pass the room I was in before sneaking out. I pulled the gun from my backpack and readied it.

As usual, they weren't going to have dinner for another hour. They were already going toward the master bedroom on the second floor. I followed them, making sure that none of her staff saw me. Though she only had two and both of them were preparing dinner.

I didn't have the patience to watch him try and fumble around, nor did I want to. Frankly, it was disgusting. As soon as they entered the room, I went in right behind them and slammed the door.

Both of them jumped and turned to me. I lifted my gun and aimed it directly at the woman. Her scream was caught in her throat, and my dad looked at me with more anger than I had seen on his face in a long time.

I had to admit I liked seeing it. Sent a sort of rush through me. But all the anger from the last few weeks boiled up inside me, overpowering any of the joy I got from this situation.

"Phones. Both of you. Throw them over there," I said and motioned to the far side of the room.

She looked at my father to see if he was going to comply, but he just nodded to her and threw the phone.

She followed suit after a moment's pause. I reached for my backpack with one hand, unzipped part of it and grabbed a rope inside. I threw it to Father.

"Tie her up," I ordered. "Gag her with something."

She looked shocked and hurt.

"Don't worry, I'm not here for you," I said. "No one's dying. If you listen to what I say."

Father did as I asked and helped her to sit on the right side of the bed. Still acting as the caring boyfriend.

"She's probably here for money," he whispered to her. She nodded at him through her tears.

"Hurry up," I barked. "Over to the other side."

He gave me a scathing look as he passed but did what I said.

When he was seated, I quickly walked toward the woman and hit her at the base of the back of her neck with the butt of my gun.

She went out cold and I didn't bother to catch her as she fell forward and off the bed.

"Don't bring her into this," my father said. "If you're mad at me, be mad at *me*. She has nothing to do with this."

"Careful," I warned. "Sounds like you may have a thing for her. You better hope I won't let that slip to Mother, or we'll have *another* incident on our hands."

He cringed. The last time Mother killed a mistress, I was in middle school. The fallout had been insane. I didn't let the newest one she found out about slip, but I knew sooner or later, her name would be smeared across the headlines.

"I mean that she is an important person in my business."

I let out a laugh.

"Which one?" I asked. "The legal one or the money laundering? Maybe blackmail? I'm curious, though as to what dirt you have on the NFL."

He didn't respond to my jab and instead said, "You'll work with her at some point. She's a good woman."

"So that's why you didn't tell her that I was your daughter," I mused, pointing the gun toward him.

I walked around the bed to face him. He wouldn't be stupid enough to try and attack me, but just to make sure, I grabbed a pair of handcuffs from my backpack and threw them to him.

"Put them on."

"Avery, what are you—"

"Put them on," I ordered.

He did with surprisingly steady hands. I squeezed them even tighter around his wrists. He didn't deserve the comfort.

He let out a groan when they started to cut off the blood flow.

"There we go," I sang in a cheerful tone.

I stood back, taking in the sight of my father at my mercy before hitting him with the butt of the gun right across his jaw.

The sound of the teeth cracking in his mouth caused a flare of satisfaction to run through me. He spat out blood on her perfectly pristine white comforter. He sent me an angry glare.

"You think I won't get you for this?"

"I'm just surprised you're so compliant," I said. "But maybe it's a face thing."

I pushed the gun under his chin.

"If you hurt her again, I will bury a bullet in your face. I don't care that Mom relies on you, nor do I care about your company." I forced as much venom as I could into my words. "I'm sure your goons reported back to you when I dumped the bodies of their coworkers at their hideouts. I've been holding myself back, but I swear to you, if you try again, I will show you no mercy."

His eyes widened, and then there was a light that passed through them.

"*Touchy*." He spoke as if he had a revelation of some kind. "Little Avery found someone to care about."

Yes. But like hell would I tell him that.

"Shut it."

"My god, you *have*," he said with a bitter laugh. It grated on my nerves and made me regret the choice of coming here.

"I have not," I spat.

He ignored me.

"It's eating you up inside, isn't it?" he asked. "Here I thought you were like me, but your coming here only proves that you have more of your mother in you."

"This is your warning."

"Just come home," he said. "I have a spot for you and everything. It doesn't have to be this hard."

"I will not take part in your dirty business," I said. "My hands may be stained with blood, but there are some things I'll never do."

He let out a laugh.

"God, I can't believe you." He shook his head and gave me a pitiful smile. "You know it will never work out, right? As long as you refuse me, I will find you, always, and if the way to get you to come is through her, you can bet your ass that she will be at my feet in a matter of hours."

"I should kill you now," I said.

"Probably," he said and shrugged. His nonchalance only pissed me off even more. "But I think there are some things even you can't do. You come here acting all big and strong. Threatening me. But you won't kill me." He paused, the smile spreading even further across his face. "Because you're *weak*."

"I'm not weak," I spat.

"But your girlfriend is," he sang. "And even if it wasn't me coming after her, do you really think you wouldn't hurt her after a while? You're only delaying the inevitable. I know how you get, the obsession will wear off at some point and you'll get fed up with her."

"I'm not you," I growled and pushed the gun to his forehead. All it did was cause him to smile at me.

A smile that looked too much like my own.

The similarities between us hit me right in the face then. He saw it too.

"Aren't you?" he asked. "Right now, you're looking like the spitting image of me."

I stood straight and took a steadying breath.

"As much as I love to hear you speak, I have something to do," I said.

It took tremendous strength not to bash his head in, even if his words rang too true to be comfortable.

Keeping my eyes on him, I backed up until I reached their phones. I leaned down and scooped both up. His eyes widened when he realized what I was doing.

"Oh, scared now?" I said, matching his mock playful tone. I took another step toward him with a wicked smile. "*Good.*"

I made the next hit hurt, the one after was to actually knock him out. Before I left, I dragged the still-knocked-out woman to the bathroom and used the excess rope I had to tie the door to the heaviest item in the room, which happened to be the bed. So that when she woke up, she wouldn't be able to pull it open easily, and give me more time to get as far away as possible.

That, combined with my father's weight, would make it almost impossible to move with her small frame. And if she woke up early to scream for help, maybe the staff would probably assume she and Father were still going at it.

To be safe, I barricaded the door to the master and slipped out through the window.

I threw myself at the tree and stifled my groan as the sharp parts of the bark dug into my skin.

I paused to make sure no one heard me and when the coast was clear, I dropped to the ground with a soft thud. I left the grounds and made quick work of calling Jonson for backup.

Even though I got what I came there for, I left that house with the distinct feeling of failure filling my belly.

"I can't use these," Jonson huffed and threw the bag of cell phones back toward me.

"This is the best chance you have of getting them," I growled. "They are perfectly good pieces of evidence."

Jonson leaned forward and placed his hands on the counter. His wrinkled skin and eye bags were more prominent under Willow's grandmother's dim kitchen lighting. The man had definitely seen better days, but if he thought that would make me go easy on him, he was sorely mistaken.

I hadn't been happy to learn that Jonson moved her here without me knowing, but even through my anger, I realized that it was probably safer than what the penthouse could provide. And closer to the school.

"Illegally obtained evidence, might I remind you."

I slammed my fist down on the counter, the anger finally getting the better of me.

"Everything about this has been illegal! How come all of a sudden you start to care—"

"Hey, we have neighbors, you know."

I froze and stood straight, giving Jonson one last glare before turning to look at Willow. She was standing at the end of the staircase with her arms crossed. It was far too late for her to be up. The fitted tank top and fuzzy sleep pants were evidence that she had literally just rolled out of bed.

I hadn't seen her in days and all the feelings that I had been bottling up inside me came to a head as soon as we locked gazes.

God, I had missed her.

I went to Father to try and get back at him for what he had done to Willow... and I failed. I may have gotten hard evidence for Jonson, but Father would be even angrier than before.

I hadn't thought this through when I left the penthouse that night and now I was regretting it. Especially when Father's words were running through my mind at high speed, each one feeling like a punch to the gut.

Do you really think you wouldn't hurt her after a while?

You're only delaying the inevitable.

The obsession will wear off at some point.

My father was nothing but scum... but he wasn't delusional. He got to where he was through devious and twisted ways, but he was meticulous. Anyone else of his stature would have been brought down by the FBI a long time ago... yet there he still was.

So who was to say he wasn't right about *this*?

I had already felt it as soon as Willow hinted at her feelings for me. The rush of guilt that I blamed on my father... it wasn't because of him, I realized. It was because of me. I was scared.

Willow deserved better than... this. Better than *me*. I was telling the truth when I told her I wanted her to be mine. That I wanted to care for her... but what if that wasn't what was best for her?

I swallowed thickly and turned my attention back to Jonson.

"Please," I whispered and pushed the phones back to him. "This will spell out everything for you. We don't have time to waste anymore."

"Because *you* pissed him off," he shot back.

I bit my tongue. He wasn't wrong, nor was his annoyance unjustified.

"I wanted to send him a message."

Jonson let out a sigh before snatching the phones away from my grip.

"You better hope it sinks in," he growled. "Don't bother me after this. Grant and Chelsea are your contacts from now on. Use them."

I gave him a grin, but it felt forced and unnatural on my face.

"Because of me, you're gonna get the biggest break in your career," I said in a low tone. "I will contact you when I want."

I hadn't heard Willow come to my side, but when I felt her lithe fingers curl around my arm, my body stiffened on its own accord.

"Let the man be, Avery," she murmured. "It's two a.m. already. I'm sure he'll do what he needs to do. He's already come this far. Let's trust him a bit more, ya?"

It's not him I was wary of. It was my father.

I had made a mistake. A horrible one that I didn't realize until this very moment.

Damn it all.

WILLOW

A normal person would be hurt by Avery's disappearance. Maybe even feel a little betrayed.

And that's not to say I wasn't at all affected by what she had done... but there was something much more here than what she was telling me.

But that was okay. Her expression as I pulled her to bed last night gave me all the information I needed to know.

She was hurt. What happened in the library... what had been happening with her father... all of it had wounded her so deeply that she was beginning to fall off the deep end.

Faster than I could catch her.

"I was going to tell you to take a picture because it stays longer, but I've found I quite like it when you look at me like that."

Avery's voice pulled me from my daydream. Only then did I notice that her eyes were open and staring right at me.

I hadn't slept well the night before, so when the sun came up, I found myself watching Avery as she slept.

The dark circles under her eyes told me that she hadn't gotten a wink of sleep in the days we were apart. Or at least if she had, it was shitty. Her pale skin seemed sunken, and I doubted she had had a good meal in days.

I forced a small smile to my face as I propped myself up on one arm and looked down at her.

Her hair was a mess and splayed out on the pillow she lay on. She didn't bother to put a shirt on last night and chose to sleep only in a pair of my pajama shorts. Her branding peeked out over the covers and made my chest feel tight.

After hearing what she said about it, I felt for her. I didn't want Avery to live such a life anymore... but with her father, when would this ever end?

"Now I know why you do it," I said. "There is so much you can learn from someone as they sleep."

She gave me a small smile.

"That and the vulnerability of it all," she said. "For example, if someone sleeps deeply enough, you could get away with installing eleven cameras in their apartment and they would be none the wiser when they woke up."

"Eleven?" I echoed. "I thought you had more in you than that."

A light passed through her eyes that I hadn't seen in a while, but then it was gone.

"My father and I... don't have a good relationship," she said after a moment.

A sarcastic quip was on my tongue, but I bit it to stop myself. I stayed silent, letting her take her time.

"But him bringing you into this... *hurting* you, was unacceptable," she said. "So I paid him a visit, but I am afraid it made it worse."

My hand found hers under the blanket. She squeezed my hand back. Her grip had a slight tremor to it.

She's scared.

"I thought Avery Maddox wasn't afraid of anything?" I raised my brow at her.

It was supposed to be a light joke, but her expression turned stone cold and her hand squeezed mine.

"I'm afraid of one thing," she said. Her eyes bore into mine and for a moment my heart completely stopped. "And he knows it."

I licked my overly dry lips.

"Is that your way of telling me that you love me?" I asked, a sort of shocked smile spread across my face.

She didn't say anything for a long moment before there was just the smallest hint of her chin jerking.

Wait... that was a nod.

She nodded at my question. Meaning she—

Don't panic. Excitement, fear, and giddiness rose up in me. Avery Maddox loved me. *Me* out of all people in the world. We hadn't known each other that long, but she was still willing to go to that level with me.

Her eyebrows furrowed. I hadn't realized how long I let us sit in a tense silence while I digested this information.

"Took you long enough," I said with a relieved smile. "I thought I scared you off."

"You did," she said. Her words were so blunt they pulled a laugh out of me. "I'm serious. I really don't understand how or why you—"

"Love my stalker?" I asked and leaned closer to her. "Love a murderer? Love someone whose father wants me dead?"

She pursed her lips before answering. "All of the above."

"Because you're *you*, Avery Maddox."

I untangled our hands to grip her chin and forced her mouth to mine. As soon as our lips touched, she wrapped her arm around my neck and shifted us so that she could roll me onto my back.

Before the kiss could get too heated, she pulled away from me and looked down at me with hooded eyes.

"You say it first."

Another laugh burst from my lips and I shook my head at her.

"Nuh-uh," I said through my laughs. "I think I deserve for you to say it first. I was shot because of you, after all."

"Grazed," she reminded with a scowl.

I tangled my hand in her hair and forced her face closer to mine.

"Then I guess I'll wait until you're ready," I said. "But until then, I won't say anything."

She let out a growl, causing me to laugh even more. For once, she wouldn't be getting what she wanted out of me.

"If you don't like it that much, then say it."

"Maybe I can force it out of you," she said, that beautifully wicked smile crossing her face.

She swooped down to cover her lips with mine. In seconds, her hands were slipping into my shirt and grasping my breasts. I let out a gasp when her fingers pinched my nipples.

I turned my head to the side in order to catch my breath, but she only used that to her advantage and started kissing down my neck.

"Hey-y, a few kisses won't make me forget about you leaving for as long as you did. I'm still hurt."

She let out a chuckle against my skin before lightly biting into my neck. I couldn't stop the moan that escaped my lips.

"Then I better make it up to you, hmm?" I could hear the smile in her tone.

She yanked my shirt up just enough for her to have access to my nipples. I let out a gasp at the feeling of her hot, wet tongue circling one, then the other. I used the hand tangled in her hair to force her closer.

I arched into her when she pulled one fully into her mouth. It was such a little gesture. One I should have gotten used to by then. But it still caused pleasure to zap through me, and before long, heat was coiling in my belly.

She shifted between my legs and I couldn't stop myself from trying to grind on her in hopes of relieving the tension building in me.

Both her hands gripped my hips before sliding down to the hem of my shorts. In one movement, she pushed them over my ass and to my midthighs. She didn't even bother to remove them all the way before a hand slipped between my legs.

"I missed this pussy," she said with a sigh as her lithe fingers brushed across my clit.

"You're not acting like it," I growled when she trailed her fingers over my entrance. Her movements were so gentle they did nothing to help.

She bit down on my nipple before pushing a single finger into me. I let out a sigh as she pumped it in and out of me. I had waited so long to feel her again that even just this caused my body to go into overdrive, but I needed more.

I opened my mouth to command her to add more, but I was interrupted by a knock at my door.

Avery pulled away, her eyes glancing toward the door and back to me.

"Chelsea," I whispered to her.

A devious grin spread on her face before she forced another finger into me.

Fuck yes. I spread my legs as far as they could go, reveling in the feeling of her sinking into me.

"Go on," she taunted as she began to slowly fuck me. "Answer the FBI agent, Willow."

"Yes?" I called, trying to keep my voice even.

"Just letting you know if we want to get there early for your last class, we will need to leave soon." Chelsea's voice was muffled by the door.

The walls were thin in Grandma's house, so I was worried that once Avery picked up the pace and allowed her palm to slap across my clit, that she could hear it through the walls.

"Oh god," I whispered. My pussy clamped around her fingers.

"Willow," Avery chided. "Don't keep her waiting."

The breath was knocked out of me when she inserted a third finger. A delicious heat swirled inside me, and I closed my eyes against the feeling.

"Just like that," I gasped.

"Willow?" Chelsea called.

"Give me ten more minutes and I'll be down," I called shakily.

I waited until I heard her footsteps walking down the hall before I let out a whine that was building in my throat.

Avery's other hand came to thrum my clit, and my hand reached out to grab hold of her shoulder. I pried my eyes open to catch a glimpse of the expression on her face. She was playing me like an instrument and her face said it all. She knew that I was under her spell and any moment she would—

"Say it," she commanded. "Say it, and I'll let you come."

I shook my head wildly. "This is supposed to be you making up with me, remember?"

She let out a laugh.

"Who said this was what I had planned?"

When she curled her fingers inside of me, I couldn't stop my cry. Since she was gone, I had not once touched myself. I was, in part, too worried and hurt to even think of getting off. But right then, when she was fucking me, and with that look of hers, I realized just how long it had been since I last came.

I wasn't going to have to beg her to let me come. Nor was I going to have to say those words.

She seemed to notice it as well, but it was too late.

Her lips crashed into mine and swallowed my cries as I came around her fingers. Wave after wave, she strummed my clit and fucked me through it all and when it was done, I couldn't stop begging for more.

She pulled away with a smirk.

"I'll find you tonight," she promised. "During your event. I promise."

I frowned at her words.

"You're not coming for your last class?" I asked.

She shook her head, her smile falling.

"I need to check with Jonson about the phones," she said. "But I will be there."

Disappointment welled up inside of me, but I didn't let it dampen this. She would be there and that was good enough.

"You did good," I said as I came to stand next to my student.

Naomi Richardson, a second-year with straight black hair and a sweet smile, looked up at me with a sheepish gaze. Her project this semester was a freestanding wall that was placed in the middle of the room with a single artist who had done two inverse paintings.

"It gets better," she said. "Take a step to your left and look over the piece to the mirror."

I did as she said and my breath caught. Another exhibit just a few feet away was perfectly placed to give us an unobstructed view of the opposite side. I stepped farther back so I could compare the two pieces.

"That wasn't in the guidelines," I murmured. If I remembered correctly, that piece was supposed to be on the opposite wall.

"I got approval from the artists," she said, rolling her shoulders back. Seconds ticked by before I sent her a smile.

"Do you plan to take over your father's gallery when you graduate?" I asked.

Her eyes widened and her gaze dropped to the ground.

"I was hoping no one would make the connection," she whispered.

I walked over and nudged her side, causing her to look up at me. I gave her a soft smile.

"I think it's just me," I admitted. "And only because I had a friend who wouldn't shut up about being shown in his gallery."

Lillian, actually. She called me while Avery was gone and it was just a few Google searches, and after that, I found a picture of my student staring back at me.

She let out a sigh.

"I plan to help out," she said after a while. "I've loved the place since I was a kid. Maybe one day I will be experienced enough to take it over." She looked back at me with a smile. "At least your class helped prepare me for that."

There was a warm emotion that I couldn't name in my chest.

Was this what it felt like to see your students learn something from you?

I wanted nothing more than to meet her again in a few years, but next time as a gallery director.

"I'm glad," I said over the knot in my throat.

She gave me a smile and excused herself. I let myself linger on the art piece a moment longer before moving on. By the time seven o'clock came around, the bodies in the gallery were slowly disappearing.

Most of my students had come and gone and all that was left were random kids that stumbled upon our finals.

It would be another hour and a half before we closed and then I could conclude my first-ever semester. For the first time, I let myself feel proud of what I had done.

I wondered what Mom would think if she saw me now.

Would she be surprised?

I was never very studious, so she never made a point to push me toward Princeton. Not that she would have cared to see me make something of myself anyway.

But I still couldn't help but wonder. Couldn't help but imagine the look on her face when she saw me *here,* of all places, here in her sacred place.

"Willow."

I jumped at the voice and turned to the intruder. Daniel was standing but a few feet away from me. His hair slicked back and greasy. His shirt wrinkled. Overall, the man looked like he had been through hell.

"Daniel," I breathed. "It's been a while. Sorry I haven't reached out. I've been... busy."

He shook his head and sent me a forced smile.

"I should be saying sorry," he said. "I all but abandoned you after..." He swallowed thickly. "Sorry, I just... it's been hard."

I nodded, though there was a heavy feeling in my chest.

"I hadn't realized you and him were so close," I admitted. "I'm sorry for your loss."

He shrugged.

"His death was hard to take. Learning about his hands being delivered to your desk more so." He looked out into the gallery with a far-off expression. "The police thinking we were in some kind of fucked-up love triangle was my breaking point."

I stood straight and swallowed thickly. *That's why he hadn't reached out? Because of that?*

"I tried to tell them—"

"Why *were* they delivered to your desk?" he asked, his gaze narrowing in on me. "Did he... did he hurt you?"

The feeling of his hand gripping my wrist flashed across my mind, along with the feeling of his palm cupping my ass.

"Once upon a time, he tried to take advantage of me," I whispered. "But I do not know why his hands ended up on *my* desk."

He nodded.

"Right, why on *your* desk when there weren't even images of you on his hard drive? Why not in the dorm of the girl he forced into a sexual relationship with him or the one he blackmailed nudes from who ended her life just a month before his death?"

His words stunned me. I hadn't been keeping up with his case and didn't know about what they found at his house.

A hard drive?

Maybe Avery had been right to kill him.

I let the words come together in my head before responding to him.

"You're angry because you didn't know who he was," I said. "You're angry you couldn't stop it when it happened right under your nose. I get it—"

"You *don't* get it," he said. His voice had risen a level. "I was his friend. He helped me through everything, and he—those pictures they showed me—"

His voice cracked, and he was forced to clear his throat. His eyes shimmered in the dim lighting overhead.

"Why didn't you tell me?" he said softly after a moment.

The hurt in his voice caused my chest to twist.

"The only thing I can say is I'm sorry," I whispered. "Sorry for not telling you and sorry for not being there for you, even when you were there for me for everything."

He took in a deep breath and rolled his shoulders.

"But you have been... safe?" he asked.

I nodded. "As safe as I can be. No more visits from the police."

"Or the stalker?"

I swallowed thickly.

"No sign." The lie felt heavy on my tongue.

He let out a noise.

"I just wanted to come see your work, that's all, truly," he said. "Sorry to bring all my baggage. I've missed you, ya know. Maybe after this semester, we can get a coffee again."

I gave him a soft smile, but I knew it would probably be best to distance myself from him going forward.

"Of course, thank you for stopping by," I said. "Take care of yourself... please."

"I'll try."

He gave me an awkward goodbye before stalking out of the gallery hall. When he was gone, I could finally let out the breath I'd been holding.

I had been so busy with Avery that I had forgotten entirely about what had happened with him and the police. At the time, I had been somewhat relieved that they were off of Avery's trail, but now I felt horrible that Daniel had to take the weight of it.

And to be forced to face just how awful his friend was.

The seconds ticked by, and suddenly, the hair rose on the back of my neck and the weight of a stare was on me.

She's here.

Would she be upset this time after seeing me talk to Daniel? I was forced to realize just how shitty of a person I was when the thought of her getting jealous again caused a thrill to go through me. I shook off all the thoughts of the interaction before turning to look for her.

There was nothing I could do to fix this. Nor anything I wanted to do. Professor Lynch had gotten what was coming to him and while it sucked that Daniel had gotten mixed up in it, there was no going back.

So instead, I let the excitement of seeing my stalker overtake my body. I let myself feel the heat that was rising in me. I even let a smile spread across my face.

When I saw her, she would fuck all these awful feelings from me, bringing an end to them for good.

I didn't see anything at first, but then I spotted a small folded-up paper near the back of the gallery, where there was a long, dark hallway leading to the storage area.

My entire body hummed with anticipation.

I looked around to see if anyone noticed, but the only people still there were all so focused on the artwork that none of them even stirred when I crossed to the room and picked up the note.

Come find me.

I spared one last glance behind me before heading straight into the dark hallway. There was only a single door at the end and it was slightly open. A dim light shone through from the crack and was cut off by a shadow moving inside.

My heart lodged in my throat, but still, I walked toward the room.

I gripped the edge of the roller door, slipped in, then shut it behind me.

In front of me were mountains of stacked art and displays, many covered by sheets. A movement caught my eye and then the room was doused in darkness.

There was a window to my right that let in a bit of moonlight and it was the only thing that helped me make out the shape in the far corner.

"I thought you were supposed to be the one finding me?" I asked and started walking toward the figure.

I paused when the sound of a lighter broke through the room. I watched as the shadow lifted it to their face and lit their cigarette, giving me a glance at a strong jaw with... a bit of stubble?

As they inhaled the cigarette, it lit up parts of their face giving me a glimpse of a man I had never seen before.

Panic seized my throat.

My hand found the handle behind me and I tried to slide the door back open, but it was stuck.

No... someone was on the other side of the door, holding it closed. I could feel it in the way they put their weight into keeping it closed.

When the cigarette was fully lit, the man shoved the lighter into his pocket and exhaled with his head positioned toward the ceiling.

I swallowed thickly. *There is no way I'm going to be able to run this time.*

"So, to what do I owe this pleasure?" I asked, lifting my chin. "I'm guessing Mr. Maddox sent you?"

I could just make out his eyes shifting to meet mine. They caused a shiver to go through my body. But against every voice in my head, I stayed my ground.

He stood straight before walking toward me.

He was much taller than me, so he crossed the room in just a few strides. I had to crane my neck to look up at him.

I tried, unsuccessfully, to hold in my cough as he blew the smoke in my face.

"Getting you alone has been a fucking pain," he muttered. "If it's not that freak, it's the FBI agents. How on earth did a pitiful woman like you get so much protection?"

Anger rose through me and before I could even think through my actions, I raised my hand and slapped him across the face. His head snapped to the side, the sound of it echoing throughout the room.

"Don't blow that shit in my face," I growled.

"I've been waiting to do this."

The only warning I had was the door opening behind me. I turned to look at his accomplice, only to come face-to-face with the glint of a metal bat.

My head exploded in pain, then darkness enveloped my vision.

Willow

Dull pain traveled from temple to temple.

My eyes were so heavy it was a struggle to open them, but when I did, I found myself in an unfamiliar room.

It was dark, but I could make out the almost sterile environment from the three large windows that filled the back wall. In front of me was a glass coffee table and just beyond that was a floor-to-ceiling bookshelf. Near the windows was an all-black desk with two monitors on it.

The smell of cleaning products burned my nose and my throat was dry.

I pushed myself up and realized that I was on a leather couch. There was a small blanket draped over my body that pooled in my lap when I sat up.

Air hit my bare bod—*wait.*

I scrambled to grab the blanket when I came to my senses enough to realize that I was completely naked. Even the locket that I hadn't taken off for years was missing.

"Apologies for those rude guards," a male voice came from my right. I jumped, clutching the blanket so hard to my body that my knuckles began to ache.

He had been just out of sight while I had lain down, but across from the desk and right in front of the last window was a large love seat and a small side table that was currently occupied. The man was wearing a suit, which seemed to fit the environment but was so out of place for the current situation.

Salt-and-pepper hair fell around his face in light waves. His blue eyes were focused on the cup of dark liquid in front of him. His facial structure was similar enough that it caused alarm bells to ring through my head even without seeing his picture plastered all over the internet.

"Also, about you waking up naked," he said with a slight laugh in his voice. "Though I couldn't be too careful."

"Mr. Maddox," I breathed and gave him my best forced smile. "I wish we could have met under better circumstances."

He let out a laugh so loud it caused the pain in my head to hit me full force. I wanted to throw up. I wanted to cry. To scream. But I swallowed it all down.

He noticed my wince and tried to quiet his laughter with his hand.

"Yes," he said after regaining his composure. "I wished so as well."

He got up and walked over to lean against his desk. I tried not to make any moves to show him my vulnerability, like clutching the blanket even tighter to me or shifting for him to stay fully in my sight.

I didn't know much about men like the one in front of me, but I knew acting scared and trying to flee at a moment's notice wouldn't work well in my favor.

His goons had already knocked me out with a fucking baseball bat. They obviously didn't care about my well-being. And as much as Avery doesn't want to admit it, I can see the resemblance to him, not just in the face but in mannerisms as well.

His eyes were sharp as they took in my movements, but instead of feeling power flood my system, it was a sliminess. He didn't strip me to be safe.

He did it to make me feel powerless. To remind me that I was not in charge here and that, at a moment's notice, he could do anything he wanted to me. He wanted to take what little dignity and comfort I had left and rip it to shreds.

I leaned back on the couch like I was relaxing into it. The leather stuck to my bare skin.

"So, how can I help you, Mr. Maddox?" I asked. "Or am I supposed to just sit pretty and wait as bait?"

The smile that crossed his face caused a sourness to spread across my tongue.

"Well, I can see why my daughter has become so obsessed with you," he said. "But yes, that's the plan. But I have something else to ask of you."

Shit.

I motioned for him to continue.

"When she comes back and takes over for me—and she will—I need you to stay far away from her. Better yet, move out of this state. Out of this country even. The longer you're around her, the more distracted she will get, and I can't have that with the type of business I run."

Against the raging emotions in my mind, I cocked my head and asked, "Which is what exactly?"

What I wanted was to yell at him. To tell him to fuck off and that there was no way either of us would ever agree to this.

He returned a smile of his own.

"Avery has a bad habit of grasping on to the shiniest toy she can find and playing with it until... well, to put it bluntly, until she tears it to shreds," he said. "If anything, this would be ensuring that you could have a normal, fulfilling life after this."

I ground my teeth together. Comparing me to a toy was one thing, but the way he talked so casually about Avery's... *obsessions* caused all the scary doubts that I had in my head to come up to the forefront.

Has Avery done this before?

I remember her telling me our... relationship was a first for her. Had she lied?

"Oh," he said, letting out a light laugh. He must have read right through me with an ease that terrified me. "You didn't know you were what... I think it's sixth in line now?"

I prided myself on my ability to bullshit, but this man saw through me even better than his daughter.

"If that was true, you wouldn't have bothered to use so many resources to kidnap me in hopes of getting her to come home," I said with more venom than I intended.

That damn smile was back.

"Even better than I thought." His words were supposed to be praise, but they made me feel gross. "Then I have one more thing to sway you."

"Not interested," I said with a sigh and ran my hand through my hair. I regretted it as soon as I came across the dried blood that caused my hair to stick to my scalp.

"Even if I told you that I knew where your mother was?"

I perked up at that.

As much as I wanted to forget about the mother that abandoned me, I had dreamed of finding her for years since she left. Sometimes I would type her name into the search bar and hope to hear *some* type of news about her, even an obituary, but I never did.

"And in exchange, you want me to stay away from Avery?" I asked.

"And act as bait, of course," he said. "Can't forget the reason you are really here."

Even if I promised him, there was no way I would follow through on it. I also had full faith that Avery would be here in a matter of hours and probably end up killing her father.

I acted like I was thinking through his offer and then, after a few moments, I nodded.

He clapped his hands together, the sudden loud sound causing me to jump in my seat.

"Perfect. I knew you would come around."

I opened my mouth to speak, but the door opened and in came the man who had cornered me in the storage room, and behind him was the man that hit me with the bat. Russell didn't move as the men walked toward the couch and started to grab at me.

I slapped their hands away, glaring at Russell, who stood there smiling at me.

One of the men grabbed my hair and yanked it backward. A pained moan spilled from my lips. The blanket was pulled from me and an ice-cold fear crawled up my spine.

"What the fuck do you thin—"

A hand covered my mouth and one of them sat next to me, his hands grasping my bare hip. Another hand laid itself on my shoulder.

"Your mother has been living right under your nose," Russell said, calling my attention to him.

I hated how exposed I was to the men and it caused angry tears to prick my eyes.

"She's living right near the border of New York and New Jersey, with a new family and one—no, *two* girls, which she treats better than she ever did you. Private school, and extracurriculars, she loves them dearly. As much as she loves her husband. Who works for a law firm."

I wanted to curse at him, but I couldn't fight the hands that held on to me.

Russell dug through his pockets and pulled out his phone.

"Say hi to Avery, Willow," Russell ordered.

He's fucking recording me?

Disgust filled my gut. I pushed my knees together and tried to lean forward to cover my body, but the men pushed me back onto the couch.

One of them leaned closer. Their breath was hot on my neck. I shuddered violently when a tongue came to lick the side of my neck.

"You know where to find me," Russell said. "Get here quick before I let them have fun with your newest toy. Don't bring the rats."

He lowered the phone and the hands were off of me in seconds.

I scrambled for the blanket and sent the men glares, but neither of them looked at me as they maneuvered around the couch.

"Apologies," Russell said with a far too cheery tone. "Gotta add a bit of incentive."

I didn't let my guard down this time. Russell Maddox may have looked good on paper, but there was something dangerous lingering under the surface.

"The note..." I trailed.

I looked to Russell for an answer, but it was the man that cornered me that answered.

"Avery is predictable," he said. "She would drop the presents once she had you wrapped around her little finger. It was just a matter of stepping in to keep them up."

My throat went dry.

"How many?" I croaked. I didn't truly want the answer for fear it may have been "all of them," but he answered anyway.

"Three," he answered.

Three?

The note on my pillow said, "*I miss you.*"

Horror washed through me. I remembered how Avery reacted back then. I had told her I missed her, but afterward, she never mentioned the note.

All this time...

"You were in my house," I whispered. "How?"

The man shrugged as if he didn't just admit to breaking and entering.

And the notes? How long had he been watching me? One of them was found on my pillow when I woke up, which meant he was there while I—

I'm going to throw up.

This whole time I thought it was Avery, but he had someone that had slipped under both of our noses.

"Avery is only one person," he said. "And human at that. She can't watch *everything*."

"That's enough," Russell said, his tone turning hard. The two men took their chance and left him and me alone in the room.

My eyes fell to my blanket-covered lap.

Damn it. Why didn't we notice? She had cameras, didn't she?

Russell's hand appeared in my sight, a white scrap of paper in his hand, along with the heart locket. My heart lurched at the sight of it.

A part of me was going to say thank you, but I slammed my mouth shut. He didn't deserve a fucking thank-you. He was using this as another way to bind me to his will. He may not have said it outright, but the threat was there.

"An address," he said and dropped it in my lap. "Remember our deal."

I sat there, numb, as he left the room. First, I opened the locket. The tears finally fell down my face when I realized that he had taken out the picture of Avery, leaving only my dad.

When the door clicked behind him and his footsteps echoed down the hallway, I ripped the paper to shreds.

AVERY

There was a chill in the air as I walked through the campus. There was a light warm buzz going through me and with each step I took closer to the gallery, the more nervous I was to see Willow.

My hand clutched the bouquet of peach roses, but not too hard for fear I would break them in my nervousness. It was surprising how many places around here *didn't* have this specific color of roses, though I blamed myself for not being prepared enough.

This was supposed to be a congratulatory moment for Willow. I had watched her over the first semester as she tried her best to be a good teacher, even though she had no real desire to keep her job.

Inside, though, I knew her being here was important to her. She may not have wanted this *exact* role, but the prestige of entering Princeton was the most important part.

I paused when the gallery came into focus.

I'm scared.

Scared of what Father would do. Scared of admitting to her how much she meant to me.

Father's words may have been hanging over me like a cloud, but I refused to let them control me. I had been so close to letting them. So close to throwing it all away.

But not anymore.

I walked into the gallery, noticing that there were still a few people left. It was going to close in another twenty minutes, making this the perfect time for me to corner Willow.

This would be better if we were alone anyway. Maybe then I wouldn't chicken out.

The gallery wasn't that big, but still, as I walked through it, looking at all the art, I couldn't find Willow. I started to panic when I made my second trip around the place.

I checked both bathrooms and there was no sign of her. I paused when I passed a dark hallway toward the back of the gallery. I had overlooked it before, not thinking much of it. But when I passed that last time, I realized that there was a door at the end of it and it was cracked open.

My heart lodged in my throat, and panic seized my body. I gripped the flowers in my hand, the sound of the stems cracking filling the air. I rushed toward the back room.

I only had one overriding fear that filled my mind. All other worries fell to the wayside as images of a mutilated and broken Willow entered my mind.

Please. Please don't be in that room. Please don't let me find you there, not like that.

As soon as I got to the door, I slammed it open.

The room was shrouded in darkness, save for the moon shining through the far window. I stayed silent. Nothing but my own breathing filled the space. Even my own heart had quieted in anticipation for this moment.

All the tension in my body was released when I realized she wasn't in the room with me. It only lasted a few moments before it came back, rearing its ugly head.

She isn't in the room with me.

My eyes fell to the ground, and everything in me stopped in its tracks. My breathing. My thoughts. Even the blood in my veins felt like it had come to a standstill.

There, on the ground, was just the slightest hint of blood. It was only a few drops, but it was enough to cause me to step in and kneel to touch it.

It's cold but not yet flaking.

I looked back behind me and the horror of seeing blood smeared on the white wall was indescribable.

My phone buzzed in my pocket. I fished it out, numbness filling me.

I didn't even register the number that sent it to me, even though I had it memorized for years.

The video's thumbnail was a naked Willow with two men at her sides. With shaking fingers, I hit play on the video.

"Say hi to Avery, Willow." My father's voice filtered through the phone. It took me a few seconds to realize that she was on the couch in his office.

White-hot rage exploded in my chest as I watched Willow attempting to hide her nakedness, but the men holding her forced her back, exposing her to the person recording.

There was a guy sitting next to her, his hand gripped her hip and the other man sitting behind her gripped her shoulder, his hand slowly moving south. He leaned forward and licked the length of her neck. Her mouth was covered by one of their hands and her eyes were wide with terror.

I wanted to scream. Wanted to yell at them to get off of her.

I had only felt a rage this powerful a few times in my life. It threatened to take over my entire being, whispering to me that the only way to end this would be to kill them both.

And my father.

It was a mistake to let him live. My own weakness was coming to bite me in the ass.

"You know where to find me," he said. "Get here quick before I let them have fun with your newest toy. Don't bring the rats."

The video ended there. I stood, shaking with rage. I let out a guttural scream and threw the bouquet on the floor, causing the flowers to fall apart.

It was my fault. My fault that she was taken. My fault that those fuckers' hands were all over her.

I kicked the flowers. Threw the remnants against the wall. I grabbed the covered objects in the room. They varied from paintings to easels to frames, but all of them were thrown onto the wall or floor. The more they shattered, the better it felt.

When a hand grasped my shoulder, I turned around, glaring at whoever dared.

The familiar face of the woman FBI agent who was assigned to Willow came into my line of sight. But it was already too late for me to stop myself.

I grabbed her hair and forced her head back. I noticed that she was already bleeding from a head wound, but it wasn't enough for me.

"Useless," I spat. "Useless *fucking* scum."

I threw her to the ground. Her pained groan did nothing to sway me as I picked up a chunk of a broken-off wooden frame. It pricked my palm and my thoughts were clear enough for a second for me to curse my weapon of choice.

It would be hard to kill her with this.

"One job," I growled and stood over her. "You had one fucking job."

I dropped down so I was straddling her. I brought the stake over my head, ready to bring it down into her chest.

She flailed her arm out to stop me, but I just slammed my foot into her arm, forcing it to the ground.

"It's your fucking father that did this," she gasped out. "If anything, you're to blame for them taking her."

The red cleared, her words hitting me like she was the one wielding the stake and chose to sink it right into my chest.

My heart was pounding in my ears and I hadn't realized until then that the act of destroying the storage room had caused a sheen of sweat to rise on my skin.

Yes. It was Father.

An eerie calmness flooded my system, chasing away the boring anger that threatened to consume me.

"Ah," I said with a small laugh. I let the stake fall to the ground. I looked down at the FBI agent with a small smile spreading across my face. I patted her right cheek with too much force to not sting but far less than what I would use for a slap. "So you do have something between your ears. Right. *Father*."

I stood and walked toward the door, leaving the stunned agent on the floor.

"Wait, Jonson is on his way with—"

I didn't let her finish. Walked right out of that gallery, making no stops until I got to Father's house.

At least Father wasn't dumb enough to send the men he used in the video to greet me.

If he had, I wouldn't have even made it two steps into the house before murdering them with my bare hands.

"Young Master," a maid younger than me greeted me when she opened the door.

I cringed at the title. Father had a sick fetish that involved being the master of the house, even though he was nothing more than a greedy man with no kingdom behind him. I pushed her back into the house, causing her head to slam against the door, and she let out a pained whine.

"Is Mother here?" I asked, letting my eyes roam over the polished floors and decorative wallpaper.

While my father preferred the more minimalistic approach to decorating, my mother forced him to let her have control over the rest of the house. She had changed the style since the last time I was here.

Greens and beiges turned to whites and golds. It was almost like she used the decorations to force-feed the image of our wealth to everyone who walked through the doors.

Oftentimes, it hurt to think of her, but now I couldn't even feel a dull ache for the woman.

"No," the girl replied meekly behind me. "Just Master." I didn't pause for her to catch up and I beelined for my father's office on the second floor.

The walk, which normally took less than five minutes, seemed to drag on forever. The maid was following me with quick steps, but as soon as I turned down the hall to Father's study, I looked back at her.

"If you stay, I cannot promise I won't kill you," I said.

She blanched at my bluntness and stopped in her tracks. When she didn't follow me, I gave her a smile.

"Go lock yourself in your room," I ordered. "The fewer witnesses, the better."

I didn't wait to see her turn around, not when the sound of Father's office opening broke through the silence of the house.

My head snapped around to look at the intruder. My eyes widened when the face of one of the men from the video appeared.

Kill him. Make it hurt.

Red splashed across my vision. My feet carried me forward at a frenzied pace and before I knew it, I was in front of the man, my hand slamming into his face.

The violent thoughts in my head and my actions became one.

He thought he could touch her. He thought he could get away with it. Away with touching what's mine.

He tried to block my fists as they rained down on him, but it was no use. I forced us to the ground, delivering hit after hit.

I wanted to yell at him. To scream at him. But none of the words could escape my clenched teeth. I couldn't stop myself, even if I wanted to. The need to make this man pay gripped me by my throat, making it impossible to breathe until I had enacted my revenge.

The sickening crunch of his bones under my fists did nothing to calm me and I didn't stop until his face was unrecognizable. Blood was splattered everywhere. I could feel it splatter across my face and body.

He was dead. No doubt about it. He had probably been dead a few punches ago, but it took everything I had to not continue to beat the dead body. I searched for weapons on him, finding only a lighter.

I grabbed it and stood, peering into the semi-open door of the study.

"Come in, Avery."

Father's voice sent another wave of anger through me. He had waited there until I was finished killing one of his men. I wouldn't have been surprised if he specifically sent that man first so that I could get some of my anger out before facing him.

Like a lamb to slaughter.

I kicked the door open, letting the light from the hallway light up the dim room. Father may have done this to protect himself, but he had another thing coming if he thought I would just turn a blind eye.

I had fallen to my own weakness last time. Let whatever shred of love I had for him consume me. But not anymore. He would use it as a way to control me. As a way to hurt Willow.

I won't allow it.

The other man that put his hands on Willow was at the back, behind Father's desk. In front of him was a semi-naked Willow, clutching a blanket to her body. His hand was around her mouth and there was a knife to her neck.

I expected to see her crying. To see her panicked face.

But instead she visibly relaxed when our gazes met.

That's right. I'm here. I will fix this.

I got us into this mess by not killing him when I had the chance. I had no other choice but to kill him. Something I should have done years before this.

Father was leaning against the desk, his arms crossed and he had a smile on his face.

"You all but ruined our NFL contact," he said. He motioned for the guard behind him and in a flash, the blanket was pulled off Willow and handed to Father.

Seeing her bare in front of these two caused me to go still. He threw me the blanket. I caught it with one hand and brought it up to my face, inhaling deeply.

It smelled just like her coconut shampoo.

"You've got a bit of blood on you," Father said with a sly smile.

"I've come here to retrieve Willow," I said, taking a step farther into the room. "If you hand her over now, I'll consider sparing your life."

Father's booming laugh echoed throughout the room. He was laughing like I had just made the world's most hilarious joke as opposed to threatening his life.

"You tried that, remember?" he quipped. "You didn't get very far. Seems like you still have a soft spot for your dad."

I clenched my jaw so hard I could hear the cracks of my own teeth.

"I'm not playing this game with you," I hissed. "Hand her over. You don't need me."

Father clicked his tongue.

"That's not how that works in this business," he said with a sigh. "You'll understand once you take over, but people like us who deal in... the dirty laundry of others. They will not settle for some rando in their business. Now it's time to introduce you and start the process of you taking over."

I shifted on my back leg and gave my father a shit-eating grin. I knew there had been something off about the timing. Father hadn't once tried *this* hard to get me to his side in all the years I left, so why now?

Turns out, the bastard was probably in over his head and *I* was his last choice.

"I get it now," I said wistfully. "They don't trust you anymore, hmm? You need to rope me in now. Let me guess, you already sold out some of my dirty secrets to keep them on retainer?"

For a moment, his eyes glanced to the floor, almost like he was ashamed, but it was gone too quick.

I didn't care what he told them though. All I cared about was the woman that was currently staring at me with a determination that caused my heart to stop. The man behind her had his eyes on me, so he wasn't paying attention to her as her hand came to grab the knife ever so gently.

I let out a loud laugh, causing the men to jump.

"You're fucking pathetic," I said but didn't make a move to get closer to him. Not when the guard was so distracted. "For the last time, I won't do this. The days where you controlled me are *over*."

Father gave me a sad smile. He really thought that he had won here. That I would easily kneel back down at his feet like I once did.

"Pity," he said. "Then I'll just have our friend here sink that knife into Willow's neck."

"If you do, I won't join you," I spat.

He shrugged.

"Or you could join me and stop it from happening altogether," he offered. "I'll give you until the count of ten to figure it out."

I paused, looking toward Willow. She gave me the smallest nod. *She trusts me.* Enough to do what I thought necessary when she had a literal knife to her throat.

"Ten."

I shifted on my feet.

"Nine."

I wanted to be the person she trusted. I wanted to have some big plan to execute to save her... but the threat of losing her was clouding everything.

"Eight—oh fuck it. George? Can you just—"

I threw the blanket straight at Willow and the man. Father's shocked gasp barely had time to leave his lips by the time I was in front of him, my hand wrapping around his throat.

The man holding Willow grunted, and I looked over just in time to see Willow's foot embedded into his junk. She already had his knife in her hand.

Father fought against me, but my grip remained tight.

Do it. Kill him.

My thoughts quieted when I watched Willow grip the blade in her hand and slice the man's throat open with no hesitation. I was enthralled by her actions. Willow, the quiet teacher that had been shaking and crying after I shot someone just days ago, had now somehow killed someone without even a moment of hesitation.

I was in awe.

From the start, I knew she had a darkness in her. I could see it lurking behind her eyes and in her drawings... but *this*... she was... *magnificent.*

And I had never once let myself dream that maybe—just maybe —sweet little Willow had the same darkness in her that I had in me.

When her bloodstained face turned to me, all my breath was stolen from my lungs.

Father used my distraction to swing at me. His hand connected with my jaw hard enough to cause me to see stars. I stumbled back, unable to keep my balance. I didn't see the gun he had hidden in the back of his pants, but I sure as hell saw it when he swung it around to point it at me.

But we were both too slow.

Willow was behind him in a second, her hand snaking around his neck. The blood-covered knife was at his throat.

He paused, a look of pure horror crossing his face.

"For you," Willow said, her voice barely above a whisper. "I will kill for you, Avery. Give me the word."

"You bitch," Father seethed. "I told you you're just another pawn in her game. She doesn't care about you. Whatever nonsense she filled your head with, she's lying just to get you to bend over for—"

"Don't talk to her like that," I growled, clutching my head as a pounding ache made itself known.

Father let out a shaky laugh.

"And you," he hissed. "You know that once this is all said and done, she will leave you. You're too fucking crazy for her, and she will realize it as soo—"

"Shut up!"

The shrill sound of my voice silences even the beating of my own heart. My throat ached, my head swam.

Shit. I couldn't even think.

I didn't hear the cocking of the gun, but I heard the shot.

Pain flashed through the right side of my head and threw me to the ground. Ringing exploded in my ears. I had to pry my eyes open to look back at the two.

Father's mouth had fallen slack while Willow's eyes widened then narrowed. Her brows pushed together, and she bared her teeth.

In one more swift moment, she dragged the knife across his neck. The world stopped. Willow let go of him, and Father rolled off the side of the desk and to the ground, clutching his neck.

I pushed myself up to my knees. Then tried to reach for her.

"Willow—"

"Hands in the air!"

I hadn't heard the pounding of the officers' footsteps through the ringing in my ears, but I was sure as hell aware of them when they swarmed the place.

Willow dropped the knife and held her hands up, not even trying to cover her nudity.

Hands grabbed at my arms, but I fought them off. My body was weakening. All the exhaustion from hunting him and trying to protect Willow hit me all at once.

I needed to get to Willow.

I needed to cover her.

I needed to protect—

Black spots covered my vision. I tried to fight them. Tried to reach for her. But all at once, my body fell into darkness.

WILLOW

Ascratchy blanket covered my form, but it did nothing to protect me from the freezing cold temperatures in the hospital.

One of the young maids from the Maddox estate was kind enough to give me a hoodie and sweats to wear, but I still felt just as exposed as I did in that room with all of the cops' eyes on me.

They picked Avery up without hesitation and ran her to the ambulance while multiple of them forced me to bend over the desk so they could handcuff me. I let my fingers trace the marks they left on my skin.

I shouldn't have been surprised by their treatment. After all, I was caught with the knife in my hand while two men lay bleeding out on the floor. If Jonson hadn't shown up when he did, I'd probably still be getting verbally abused in the small room the feds had taken over on the Maddox estate that was then dubbed "the holding room." I flinched at the thoughts of what happened in there.

I shivered as the men pushed me into the room.

The handcuffs were biting into my skin and cutting off circulation. Not to mention I was still naked and in a room with two cops who looked like they took Maddox's injury personally.

"It's not gonna look good for you if he dies, little lady," one of

them said as they closed the door behind them. "Do you know who you just slashed across the throat?"

"I bet it was a crime of passion," the other officer said, his eyes lingering on my body. "A woman naked in a room with two men? I have a few guesses as to what went on there."

"I want my lawyer," I spat.

They looked at each other before bursting out laughing.

"That's not how it works here, sweetheart. Now, why don't you just relax an—"

The door burst open and never in my life had I been happier to see Jonson's sweat-covered face.

"Hey, who the fuck—"

"FBI," Jonson said with a sharp exhale. I wouldn't doubt that the man literally ran here. "And you have a special witness there that I need to speak to."

The cop closest to me rolled his eyes.

"The FBI has no power here. Now fuck off. We have work to—"

*"You have taken an important witness in the FBI's case against Russell Maddox. Not only that, but I found two policemen **alone** in a room with her. Fully naked, might I add. I will need your badge numbers and names before you leave. You bet your ass we will call on you to discuss this."*

"She's out of surgery," Jonson said with a sigh as he sat down on the uncomfortable plastic chair next to me. I couldn't look up at him and focused my gaze on the floor. My hand snaked up to my throat to hold the locket that was missing her picture. "We can't see her yet, but she seems to be fine. Apparently, some of the shards were embedded in her skull, but they were confident they got most of them out. They will scan her later to be positive."

Images of Avery's head being thrown back as blood splattered all over her flashed across my mind. To me, Avery had always been somewhat invincible, but in that moment, I was hit in the face with the stark reality that she was no more human than I was.

An incredibly flawed, dangerous, and insane human... but human, nonetheless.

I thought I had lost her. And it was that thought that caused me to run the knife across Russell Maddox's neck. I didn't feel as satisfied as I should have after getting revenge for her.

But all I felt was empty. It didn't matter what would have happened to her father if she would leave me as well.

"And Russell?"

He was silent for a moment.

"You cut pretty deep, so they had to use a tracheostomy tube to help with his breathing, but luckily you missed the artery."

I snorted.

"Lucky I missed, huh?"

His hand came to grip mine. I hadn't realized my nails were digging into my leg until he pulled my hand away and threaded his fingers through mine.

Tears pricked my eyes.

No. Stop.

I tried to pull my hand away, but he held strong. I didn't like the warmth of his hand. Nor did I like the way it caused my chest to twist.

"Yes," he said in a low voice. "Lucky you missed so he can rot in jail."

My gaze snapped up to his. He was looking at me with a sad smile.

"You got enough evidence?"

He gave me a stiff nod.

"But it won't be pretty. Avery has been tied to him. Used his money. I can't promise she will come out unscathed."

"But now he can't force her to do anything for him," I said. "And he can't send people after us."

He shook his head.

"He's powerful. He will rot in jail, and hopefully, it'll cause all those close to him to scram, but this case is bigger than I have had before." He let out a sigh. "It's not just him that will be implicated. His business partners will be hurt as well and they won't be happy about it. But we will be there to he—"

"Um, is your name Willow?" A voice squeaked from the entrance to the waiting room. A nurse in blue scrubs with a frightened look on her face.

"Yes," I said and stood. "Is Avery—"

Shouts from down the hall rang out and there was a loud crash that caused us both to jump.

She reached forward, grabbing my wrist with a grip harder than I expected from her tiny body. As soon as we entered the hallway, I looked toward the sound.

There, at the end of the sterile hospital hallway, were Avery and two nurses.

Avery still had the bandages wrapped around her head and was dressed in nothing but a hospital gown. The two nurses, one female and the other male, tried their best to grab hold of Avery as she struggled down the hall.

"If you don't calm down, we are going to sedate you!"

"Doctor!"

"Don't you fucking touch me," Avery growled. "Where is she? If you don't let me see her, I swear I will drive that—"

"Avery!" I called and rushed toward them.

"Ma'am, don't—"

Avery froze, her eyes widening as she took me in. Then, ever so slowly, a relieved smile spread across her face.

Her relief shared by me. I could feel the heat of it in my chest as I approached.

I held my hands out, giving the nurses a sheepish smile.

"Please just let me—"

Avery pulled me into a crushing hug before slumping against me. She let out a loud sigh. The weight of her was almost too much for me to hold, especially with the headache that lingered, but I didn't make my struggles known.

I wrapped my arms around her and rubbed soothing circles on her back.

"I'm glad you're okay," I whispered. "But please don't make the nurses sedate you."

She let out a grunt.

"Just let me... stay here for a minute."

The nurses looked at us with wary expressions but didn't intervene. Whatever Avery had done to them just minutes before must have spooked them enough to cause them to hesitate.

I let her rest for a few seconds before trying to shift her, but she didn't budge.

Then I heard the soft snores coming from her.

She did not just fall asleep on me, did she?

"Um..." I trailed, giving a panicked look to the nurses. "Can someone help me get her back into bed?"

The male nurse stepped up and carefully put her arm over his shoulders. She let us both guide her back to her bed without a fuss. Her eyelids fluttered open as soon as her head hit the bed and her fist swung out, just barely missing the nurse's head.

He pulled his hands back like they'd been burned and put at least ten feet between them.

"She needs to stay in bed," he said, giving me a pointed stare. "If she tries to get up again, press the call button."

Avery mumbled something, but it was unintelligible. I turned to her, unable to stop the amused smile that spread across my face.

"You got out of surgery not long ago and you're already causing problems?" I whispered.

She reached for me, and I let her pull me to her chest. It felt so nice to be with her again. Even after everything, with just a single touch, she was able to cause my worries to disintegrate into thin air.

"You did good," she slurred, her hand coming to rub my hair. "And looked sexy while doing it."

I couldn't even let out the laugh that was bubbling in my throat because, at the same time, it tightened and my eyes filled with hot tears.

"He's still alive."

Avery let out a weak laugh, causing my head to bounce on her chest.

"Doesn't matter," she said. "You still did good."

I swallowed thickly.

"I was so scared," I admitted softly. "Promise me you'll never scare me like that again."

Her hand paused on my head.

"Never," she vowed. Her words were getting softer, and her breath was coming heavier now.

"Sleep," I said. "We can talk about this later."

She let out a noise but didn't fight me. I stayed there a few moments, just listening to her heartbeat.

"I love you."

I jerked my head up to look at her in shock, but her eyes were closed and she made no movement that would have indicated that she was awake. Until a single eye popped open and a sly grin spread across her face.

"There, I said it first."

I couldn't stop the tears. She let out a laugh and pulled me back down to her chest.

"I love you too," I mumbled against her, letting my tears fall to her gown.

She let out another sigh.

"I think I should also apologize for roping you into this shit," she grumbled. "I knew when I was getting close to you, it would only be a matter of time before he found me. And in turn, found you."

My breath caught. *An "I love you" and an "I'm sorry" in one breath? Is this even really Avery?*

"But you didn't know he would do *that*."

She let out an unconvincing noise.

"I should have known," she murmured, her voice getting weaker with each word. "So, I'm sorry. I won't let it happen again."

"He's going to get what's coming to him," I said and nuzzled into her chest. "It's okay. I know you didn't mean it to end this way."

"You're right," she sighed. "He'll get what's coming to him. I promise."

"I hate to interrupt—"

"Bullshit," Avery moaned. "Let me sleep. *Please.*"

Jonson let out a laugh. I turned to look at him as he entered the room. His gaze held a soft warmth that I hadn't seen before. One that painfully reminded me of a father doting on his children.

"I just came to tell you that I'll take care of everything from here," he said. "I'll have guards stationed, but it may be a while before I see you both again, so..."

I sent him a smile.

"Thank you... for everything."

He gave me a hesitant smile back.

"Yes, thank you," Avery groaned and wrapped another arm around me. "I'll send you a present or something later."

Jonson shook his head and turned to leave.

"Please never contact me again," he said, then paused. "Avery, at least. Willow, you're welcome to call me anytime."

He left before he could hear Avery's grumbles.

"I love you, Avery," I said again.

She hugged me tighter, but this time she was fast asleep and unable to respond.

AVERY

My entire body stiffened as Willow walked up to the stand.

If she was nervous, she showed no sign of it. Her shoulders were rolled back, her blouse free of wrinkles, her hair impeccably done, and she had a serious expression on her face.

She needed to play a part. After all, she was going after Russell Maddox.

To the world, he was the perfect, well-groomed man. A selfless investor. Philanthropist. A trustee to many businesses. For years, whenever his name showed up in the papers, it was because of a generous donation or something he did to try and aid in solving world hunger for good.

Until our story broke.

Images of Father being carried out of the house, his neck drenched in blood and his face white as stone were plastered all over every news media and social networking site along with the title "Russell Maddox in the hospital after kidnapping young Princeton professor" the followed up shortly by, "Russell Maddox arrested and in custody for aiding and abetting human traffickers."

After the names of his business partners were released, things started to get out of control.

It seemed like every other week, the FBI was releasing a new crime he had committed. At this point, even after the kidnapping charges, Father would be in and out of trials for years.

Turns out, his business partners weren't as trustworthy as he thought. Especially when all his assets were seized. He couldn't pay them hush money, so they used it as their chance to get reduced sentences.

Though their wrath at Father getting caught didn't stop at him. There were many people that would want both Willow and me dead after this. I had already given my testimony and I didn't blame them when the lawyers tried to get me off the stand as quickly as possible.

I held nothing back. I wasn't trying to be argumentative, but that didn't mean I couldn't spill every last one of his dirty secrets. Our testimony was struck too many times for relevance, but the jurors heard... and most importantly, the media did as well.

It was almost easy to get them to play into my hand, and I had to admit I enjoyed it.

Willow, on the other hand, painted a beautiful picture of the put-together Princeton professor. No one had any reason to doubt her, but they sure as hell would try.

"Hello, Ms. Evens," the prosecutor said as he stood up to the podium.

In an instant, cameras were on them. The courtroom was buzzing, even after multiple warnings from the judge. This was the third courtroom that we had to change due to how many people were trying to get a seat.

When the room would just fill up, someone would call in a bomb threat and we would be evacuated. It was insane. Even after living my entire life in Father's world, I don't think I fully understood what it meant when a man like him was being held accountable.

And that didn't even begin to cover the number of people that were outside, just hoping to get a picture of Father.

My eyes shifted to him. He looked like shit. His hair was greasy, and he had lost so much weight his skin had begun to sag. The cheap suits that he had been wearing for the last seven days of the trial pleased me to no end.

"Hello, Trevor," Willow replied with a small smile. Her acting caused heat to curl in my belly. She did so good, from dragging that knife across his neck to testifying. She was so strong in ways that even she couldn't see.

It only made me fall more in love with her.

Father visibly flinched at her tone and even though I couldn't see his facial expression from where I was seated, I could feel the aura his displeased scowl radiated. And from the looks of the jurors, they could see it as well.

"How did you meet Mr. Maddox, Ms. Evens?"

Her lips twitch.

"After I got knocked out in Princeton's showroom—"

"Objection, relevance."

Both Willow and Trevor looked behind them to Father's lawyer with equally fed-up expressions.

"Overruled," the judge said with a sigh. This has been an ongoing issue with Father's team. They would do almost anything to stop witnesses from testifying. "Continue, Ms. Evens."

"I met him after his men knocked me out in Princeton's show-room. When I woke up, I was in his office, naked, and he was there. That was the first and last time we met."

Trevor nodded. He was giving her a sort of compassionate look that was nothing more than a ruse to make him more favorable to the jurors. Jonson had specially asked for him to do the majority of the speaking and for not just the first time, the guy proved to be right.

Trevor, regardless of how much heat my father's team put on him, would stay calm and collected and never lose his footing.

"And if the person you saw in the room is in this courtroom, can you point him out?"

Willow pointed a perfectly manicured finger straight toward Father. We had specifically gotten them done a nude pink for this trial. His ears burned bright red.

My eyes searched the courtroom, trying to see if Mother had made the visit. I wasn't surprised, though I was a bit disappointed that she couldn't see his fall from fame.

I had warned her this would happen. Maybe for once in her life, she listened to me.

"Let the record show that Ms. Evens identified Mr. Maddox."

This line of questioning went on until it was Father's turn to cross and my pride swelled when she met them with strength and a solid form.

"You said you were knocked out and then woke up *naked* in Mr. Maddox's room. Do you remember why you were naked?"

Willow narrowed her eyes just slightly. They were already trying to paint her in a bad light. There were so many times throughout this trial that I had envisioned cutting out his tongue.

Maybe in a few years, when my hate for him had slipped from the limelight, I would do exactly that.

"I was undressed when I was unconscious." Her voice was curt and I could see the voices in her mind arguing back and forth on whether or not it was worth it to snap at him.

I gritted my teeth and pushed my back into the uncomfortable bench.

"So you don't remember?"

Willow pursed her lips.

"No."

The lawyer nodded as if it was something he had to seriously take note of.

"Do you make it a habit to wake up in random strangers' houses naked?"

Before the prosecution could object, Willow leaned into the microphone.

"No. Neither do I make being *bashed* over the head with a bat and then kidnapped a habit either," she quipped.

There were a few laughs, followed by murmurs at her quick-witted response.

God, I loved that woman. Even if I was only able to give her a sick, twisted version of love, it was love, nonetheless. There was not a day that went by where my obsession with her hadn't deepened.

"Ms. Evens," the judge warned. She gave him a sheepish smile.

Father took that moment to turn his head and make eye contact with me. There were so many angry words flashing across his face, but the most obvious was: *You'll fucking regret that.*

Giddiness burst inside me. He was at the end of his rope. There was no getting out of this. We all knew it. There was even a roundup of all his crimes in the paper and how many life sentences it would end up being. He would rot in jail for the rest of his sad, pathetic life.

Until I killed him of course. I hadn't figured out how I was going to do it yet, but I knew it wasn't going to be *that* hard.

My gaze shifted to Willow, who was already staring at me. She gave me a small smile. I'm sure the camera caught it, but I didn't care. Every moment her eyes were on me was just another moment I was enraptured by her.

And after this, I couldn't wait to give her the present.

Goddamn it.

I shouldn't have been so nervous about this, but that didn't stop my heart from acting a fool in my chest.

Or stop my palms from sweating.

It's not that fucking big of a deal. Breathe in and out, remember? Literally, babies can do it.

It made it even worse when Willow clocked it right away. 'Cause she always did apparently. If there was even a moment where I wasn't acting like myself, she would narrow in on it like a bloodhound and wouldn't let me rest until she knew everything.

"Oh, it must be big," she said as she spread out in the passenger seat of the car. My hands tightened on the wheel, but even through my racing thoughts, I couldn't help the wave of warmth that flashed through me when I snorted at just how calm she was next to me.

Knowing that she was in the passenger seat when her father crashed and the trauma she still carried with her because of it only made her calmness that much more impressive.

It stroked my ego as well if I was being honest.

She was comfortable with me, even when coming face-to-face with her greatest fear.

"I don't know what you're talking about," I muttered under my breath and pulled into an all too familiar street.

I had visited the house no less than ten times before buying. Once with my mother and now finally with Willow. I had decided I was going to buy it from the start, but I kept doubting myself.

I knew Willow. I knew what this place meant to her. I also knew that I should trust my gut.

She straightened as we rode down the street. Even though many of the houses were on the older side, the lawns were carefully trimmed and many of them had fresh coats of paint. But I bet it didn't look too much different from all those years ago.

"Wait, is this...?"

She didn't have time to finish her question as we pulled up into the house's driveway. The grass for this house, too, had been freshly cut. The outside had been painted a fresh powder blue, one of the lightest colors the HOA allowed. And the windows were sparkling.

It was *almost* like it had been when they first bought it.

I was surprised that she hadn't recognized the way faster. Much of the drive here was through town and passing communities that had been here for years.

Maybe it was just another sign of how much Willow wanted to forget the past.

She turned to look at me for an explanation, but I only gave her a smile before getting out of the car. She scrambled out as well. Her eyes were wide as she took in the house. I don't know if it was my mind playing tricks on me, but I swore I also saw a small tremble of her lips.

I took this moment to take her in. The sun was shining down on us, lighting up her brilliant-red hair that cascaded down her back. Her normally tanned skin was even darker after the time we had been spending out and about trying to get away from the trial and media when we could.

There was an air about her that she hadn't had when I first met her.

She was happier now. It showed in the way her eyes lit up and the glow of her skin. I could stare at her for hours, but she finally found her words and pulled me from my thoughts.

"I grew up here," she breathed, her voice barely audible over the space between us.

"I know," I said simply.

I looked back at the house. There was still so much to be done with it. The outside was updated, but the inside still needed serious work.

I jerked my head toward the door and made a move to it. She was so silent that the only indication I had that she was following after me was the small shuffle of her feet. My heart started pounding so loud it drowned out the rest of the world.

I dug in my pocket for the key and held it out to her as soon as we reached the door. I was too much of a coward to look into her eyes, instead, I focused my eyes on the key.

"I was afraid the FBI would seize this as well, but I guess you could say we got lucky. I put it under your name just to be safe."

Her hand slowly came into sight as she grabbed the key.

When she didn't say anything, I looked up, bracing myself for a frown.

Panic washed through me when I saw it marring her face, but I also saw a singular tear running down the side of her cheek.

Oh no. I thought she would like this.

Shit. So all the doubts I had in my head were correct.

"I had to sell it to pay for school after Mother left," she said, her voice turning bitter. "I never thought that I—"

"Well, it's yours now," I said, moving around her to place my hands on her shoulders. "I thought you would like it, but if you don't, you are well within your rights to burn the place down."

She didn't answer me right away.

I leaned forward and placed a kiss on the side of her head.

"I'm sorry," I murmured against her hair. "I realize now that there are probably horrible memories here. I should have thought more."

Willow surprised me by letting out a laugh. I turned to look down at her and she turned to look back up at me. Even through the tears, there was a smile on her face.

"You're so *fucking* stupid."

I bristled at her comment and frowned.

"I didn't realize you would hate it *that* much—"

She turned around and covered my mouth with her hand. Amusement twinkled in her eyes.

"This is the most thoughtful gift anyone has ever given me, Avery," she said, dropping her voice into a whisper. "There may be shitty memories here, but I would never think to burn the house down, as much as I may have wished to when I was younger."

She pulled her hand away.

"So you... like it?" I asked hesitantly. I really couldn't tell and between her crying face and the words coming out of her mouth, I was getting whiplash.

She smiled at me.

"Of course I do, stupid," she said with a laugh.

"We may have to have a little chat about your disrespect," I grumbled, not liking the uncomfortable feeling in my chest.

With a light laugh, she pulled me to the house and opened it quicker than I had time to prepare myself for what was inside.

She didn't see it at first and walked straight into the house, looking at the renovations the previous owner had done. The house opened to the living room on the right and a few steps away, the dining room would be on the left. There was a narrow hallway that led to the kitchen in the back and then to the stairs that led to the second floor. My eyes shot to the various wall decorations. At least the first hurdle was over, but that didn't mean I was in the clear just yet.

Her footsteps echoed in the empty house. I stood by the door. Waiting for her to look at the paintings. She took her time looking over the additions. The flooring, the paneling, and the fresh paint. All things that were covering up bigger problems, but she didn't seem to notice.

"Wow, they really redid the whole thing, huh? It looks so much better—"

She paused when she turned to look toward the far wall in the living room on our right.

There was the first picture she had painted of me, right above the fireplace. A fallen angel turned devil looked almost too perfect in the space as if the fire was burning her feet.

She turned again, looking farther into the house through the hallway that connected us to the kitchen. There was another one, one of the more horrific ones she had painted after the incident with Father. It was a pile of bodies and dark blood pooling underneath them.

Nothing you would expect to be hung in a house like this, but she could paint anything and I would hang it for all the world to see.

"You..."

She turned to me with her mouth agape.

"They deserve to be seen," I said with a shrug. "I originally wanted to use our friend Lillian for help with getting them into a gallery... but I am not sure you would have appreciated that."

Another smile spread across her face before she looked back at the picture.

"Are you sure you want something like this in our house? It won't freak you out?"

I let out a sigh and walked behind her. She let me wrap my arms around her waist and bury my head in the crook of her neck.

I inhaled her scent deeply.

Our house.

After all the moments of watching her, I couldn't have thought that we would come to this. I never thought it possible. I had sought out to make her love me, but somehow she had made me fall even deeper for her.

But now Father was going to be sentenced and we would be able to live a somewhat normal life together.

... or at least as normal as two psychopaths could live.

"I love them. As much as I love you," I whispered against her skin. She shivered in my hold.

"And I love you." She threaded her fingers through mine and sank into my hold.

I wanted to enjoy this moment, enjoy her, but there was a buzz in my pocket and I just knew it was Sloan again, begging me to come back to the club.

"I also must tell you that Sloan has invited us back to Club Pétale," I said after a moment. "Now that everything with Father is done, it should be safe, but do you...?"

She turned in my arms to look up at me.

The playful smile on her face told me she would like nothing more.

Damn. It's decided then.

WILLOW

I should have told her it was my idea to come here.

Maybe then she would have looked less annoyed at Sloan... but the idea of *truly* surprising her was something too rare and too sweet to risk.

There was no surprising Avery, even after the fallout with her father.

It didn't matter that we lived together. Or that we spent almost every waking moment with each other. Avery made sure to know everything.

So when I met Lillian for lunch alone one day... well, one thing led to another and we were back in Club Pétale once more.

Though now, it was much more lively than it had been when I first visited.

The main house was filled with people and the noise from the crowd was enough to light my nerves on fire. Sloan and Lillian came to us as soon as they heard we were checking in, but I hadn't expected Avery to stand still and stare at Sloan as if she had murdered her cat.

Lillian looked between the two of them with a concerned expression while Sloan gave Avery a sheepish smile.

Lillian, this time, was dressed in an all-latex bodysuit that hugged her curves. She wore a purple mask and her curly hair was pulled into two space buns. Sloan didn't wear a mask but opted for an open-chested button-down and slacks. Her silver hair was slicked back, showing off the piercings in her lobes.

"Long time no see," she said with an awkward smile. "I'm guessing since I didn't hear from you that Jonson never gave you my message?"

Avery shifted beside me, and I looked up at her just in time to catch her mask breaking. She, too, had decided to go without a face covering and it gave me an unfiltered look at her emotions. Then a slow, feline smile spread across her lips.

"He told me you said hi, but I didn't believe him."

Sloan shook her head and ran a hand through her hair.

"I don't blame you," she said with a sigh. "Look, about before, I—"

"Water under the bridge," Avery said with a tight smile. The air around us thickened. I shot a glance toward Sloan, and her face hardened but looking closer, the shifting of her eyes told me she was almost... scared?

That couldn't be right, could it?

"Anyway, if you want to come back, Jonson has cleared you for—"

Avery slung her arm around me.

"Seriously, Sloan," she said, interrupting her. "You really don't need to feel bad or try to offer me a position. Without you, I wouldn't have been able to go after Willow as easily."

This time, Avery gave her a softer, more genuine smile. It seemed to relax the two.

"And she's my in-home chef, so I would really appreciate her keeping her job," I said in a teasing tone.

Lillian let out a light laugh.

"Lucky you."

"Well, now that that's settled," Sloan said, a twinkle in her eye. "Let us show you our newest attraction."

We let Sloan and Lillian drag us through the house and into the backyard. Before, the large space with a connected guesthouse was mostly empty save for the flowers lining the edges and a large fountain in the middle., but now there was a huge stage set up toward the back.

I had heard the strum of the music inside the house, but outside, it was much louder.

A three-person band was on the stage, all wearing masks. I could have sworn I recognized the voice of the lead singer when she leaned forward and belted out the lyrics to a popular punk song, but her name slipped my mind.

There were people standing out in the backyard, watching them as they performed. With the number of bodies in the area, it was much warmer than it should have been during that time of year, but the heat radiating off of my skin could have also been because of my nervousness.

Lillian had been sending me conspiratorial glances the entire time. If Avery caught them, which she definitely fucking did, she didn't say anything.

Instead, she held my hand as we looked up at the performers. Then when no one was paying attention, she leaned close to me, her front touching my back, and leaned down to whisper in my ear.

"Was there something special you wanted to try tonight, love?" she asked. "Maybe we can get a room to ourselves so I can carve my name in that plump ass of yours."

I jumped when her hand came to grab my ass.

She was getting so close to what I was planning that I was worried it wasn't a surprise at all.

"Carve?" I asked with a small smile. "That's child's play."

She froze against me.

"Oh?"

I pushed my lips together in a thin line, not trusting myself to answer her. I leaned forward and signaled to Lillian that we were ready. She tugged at Sloan's sleeve and Sloan called for us to follow her behind the stage and toward the guesthouse.

"This is my new space when I'm not performing," she said as we followed behind her. She raised her voice slightly to be heard over the loud music.

My nerves started whirling around in my stomach as Sloan unlocked the door for us.

Inside, it wasn't much larger than a single-bedroom apartment, but the purpose of the room was obvious.

The entire place was dark, save for a few dim lights and neon signs that decorated the walls. There was a large main room with a well-made bed, a trunk no doubt filled with toys, and a few stools.

"There is a separate, more sterile room over there," Sloan said, pointing to a closed-off room to the right. "And over there is a bathroom."

Avery was looking around the room with a light smirk on her lips, but once her gaze fell to the chaise and metal tray to the left of us, her expression fell. Her eyes narrowed in on the tray and I knew the moment she saw the metal "AM" because her eyes widened.

An almost disbelieving type of smile spread across her face.

"Sloan and Lillian have agreed to help me with a sort of... present for you," I said and took a step toward the chaise. Both of them gave me encouraging smiles. "For everything you have done, I wanted to say thank you as well as..."

The words were hard to find.

"As well as *what*, Willow?" Avery asked, her tone dropping low.

I rolled my shoulder back and puffed my chest.

"As well as prove that I am yours," I said. "Collars, rings, and status are not permanent enough for me. I need something stronger. Something more..."

"Painful." She finished for me.

I nodded.

"Something we will both remember," I said. "So you are going to brand me." I pulled at the loose collar of my shirt, showing off my bare chest. "Right here."

"Not the ass?" she teased.

I couldn't stop the smile from spreading across my face.

"I thought that was reserved for carving?"

Lillian sucked in a sharp breath.

"*Damn.* Maybe we should add that to my list," she whispered under her breath.

Avery looked behind her and at the two. I should have been embarrassed that they were here for this, but after Lillian found out about Avery, it was much easier to divulge everything I was into.

And as it turned out, Lillian may be even kinkier than me in some senses.

"You'll help, but I want to be the one to do it."

Sloan nodded, an easy smile spreading across her face. I looked between her and Lillian, only now realizing just how much they complemented each other. Lillian met me with a smile so similar to Sloan's it made warmth spread throughout my chest.

They were here to help. We could trust them.

"We are only here to show you the ropes. Make sure it's safe. We will then leave you to..."

"Celebrate," Lillian finished for her.

Avery nodded and that was Lillian's cue to help lead me to the chaise while Sloan and Avery set up. I watched with bated breath as Sloan went through every piece of equipment and taught her how to attach her initials to the stick-like handle.

Lillian was trying to explain aftercare to me and the importance of washing and keeping hydrated but all of it just sounded jumbled in my head. Especially as I caught sight of Avery's hooded gaze as she listened to Sloan.

The smile on her face told me she was excited. The darkness of her eyes told me she craved this more than anything else.

Sooner than I thought possible, they were both gone, and it was only Avery and me left in the room.

"Strip and lie on your back."

Her command sent a shiver of anticipation through me. I did as she said, wincing as the leather chilled my skin. Instead of gearing up right away, she stalked toward me.

When she got toward the end of the chaise, she used one hand to pry my legs open so she could kneel between them.

"Who would have thought..." Her fingers brushed across my cheek before they trailed down my throat. "You of all people..." She paused at the place where she was going to brand me before continuing downward. She twisted my nipple painfully between her fingers, causing me to cry out. "Would be so willing to be marked as mine, hmm?"

"I told you," I said breathlessly. She used both hands to pluck at my nipples, sending bursts of heat through me. I was already getting so wet by such small motions that I was sure in a few moments, I would be dripping onto the chaise below me. "I love you, and I am yours, in every sense of the word. And I want to prove it to you. To the world... to your father."

She stiffened at the mention of her father, and I knew she was remembering his words from back then. She didn't admit it, but I could tell just how much his words affected her. On more than one occasion, she told me I was hers, but the number of times she believed it was so few, it worried me. Because I was hers, just as much as she was mine.

A bitter smile spread across her lips and she ducked down to take a nipple into her mouth. I let out a moan and threaded my hands through her hair.

This time, she paid extra attention to them. Sucking, biting, and teasing while I writhed under her. She took her time. Using my moans as signals of what to focus on for longer. She was dragging it out.

She then kissed down my stomach and placed my legs on her shoulders. I didn't dare protest, not even when she shifted and pulled my bottom half up with her. I had to grab the back of the chaise for fear that I might fall. She let out a low groan as she trailed her nose and mouth on my inner thigh.

"You look so fucking delicious," she whispered. "All soaked at the idea of getting marked by me. Such a gorgeous sight. And all *mine.*"

I let out a cry as her lips descended on my pussy. She used a hand to keep my thigh wrapped around her while the other held up my hips.

She started at my clit. Pulling the swollen bundle of nerves into her mouth and sucking on it. When I looked down at her, her eyes were already on me, and I saw the smirk spread across her face before I felt her teeth against me.

I arched into her and cried out as the pain of her teeth biting into me swirled with pleasure. Her tongue traveled down my folds and then back up to my clit. She slowly lowered us back down to the chaise so she lay between my legs.

She used her free hand to push two fingers into me.

I let out a breathless moan and spread my legs wider for her.

"That's right, lovely. Show me how much you want this."

"Please," I gasped and tried to spread my legs as wide as they would go. She pumped her fingers in and out of me almost lazily. My reward was her latching back on to my clit.

I was tumbling against her. The anticipation of what was to come and the pulses of pleasure coming from my clit were causing my body to heat unbearably.

I plucked my nipples harshly. Needed the bite of pain to stay focused and not fall into the warm pool of pleasure that was waiting for me.

"I love you," I moaned as she thrust into me. She pushed a third finger inside of me, and all the breath from my lungs left me. The stretch was nice, but I needed more. I wiggled against her fingers. She let out a huff of a laugh and pulled them all out before slamming them back into me.

"You have no shame," she muttered against my wetness. She lifted her face, showing me the mess I was leaving on her face.

"None," I said breathlessly. "Not when it comes to you. You could do anything and I'd thank you afterward."

A dark desire flashed across her face, and in moments, her hand was pinning down my lower stomach while the three fingers that had been lazily pumping into me turned rough.

I opened my mouth, but no sounds came out.

"This is what you wanted?" she asked. The sounds of her hand hitting my skin filled the room, along with the squelch of her fingers moving in and out of my cunt.

It was obscene... but I loved it. I loved the sound of how turned on I was. Of how much I wanted her.

When she fit a fourth finger into me, I thought I was about to explode.

Heat coursed through my veins, causing a sheen of sweat to rise on my skin. Pleasure was gathering low in my belly and my pussy was beginning to clench around her fingers.

"Yes," I managed to force out. "Fuck, I'm gonna come."

A wild smile spread across her lips.

"And when you do, I want you to thank me for your orgasm, understood?"

Her words set off something inside me. I couldn't respond as the first waves of the orgasm gripped me violently. I let out a cry as it raced through my body.

"Yes. *Fuck.* Thank you. Thank you. Thank you—"

My voice was cut off when she used the hand that was pushing down my lower belly to rub hard circles on my clit.

Oh fuck, not again.

I didn't even have time to recover as my second orgasm blurred into the next. I couldn't breathe. Couldn't move. My cunt violently pulsed around her and sent waves of warmth fluttering through my body.

"One more," I gasped. "Please, Avery. One—"

She pushed herself up and captured my lips with hers. This time as she pushed me into my next orgasm, she was gentle. Her tongue danced with mine and the noises of our fucking blurred into the background.

I cared nothing about the outside world or about what waited for us after we were done here. All I could think about was how perfectly we fit together.

When the orgasm finally hit, it was just as gentle as she had been. My moans fell from my mouth like sighs and I had no choice but to relax into the warmth it provided.

"Are you ready?" she asked as she pulled away. For the first time, there was a slight hesitancy in her. For once, I had stunned even Avery.

I nodded, sending her a somewhat sleepy smile. I was more than ready and had been dreaming of it since the idea popped into my head.

"I'll help you clean and—"

"No," she said quickly. "Let me take care of everything. It's the least I could do after you offered yourself up to me so sweetly."

I wanted to protest, but instead, I fell back onto the chaise. I let her clean between my legs and cover me with a warm, fuzzy blanket.

She listened to Sloan's instructions exactly. She was gloved up and cleaning the place where the brand would go with an intense expression.

I had a rubber-like block in my hand that I could use to either bite down on or squeeze if needed. It was necessary to put it in my mouth, but I was debating if it would be the best way to go. The other hand was clutching the chaise below me.

I knew it would hurt. I wasn't afraid.

"I trust you," I said when Avery paused to look at the metal branding. She gave me a hesitant smile.

"Does it scare you that I'm excited to see my name on you like this?" she asked.

I shook my head.

"I wouldn't have planned this if it scared me," I said truthfully.

She nodded and came to my side in order to steal one last kiss from me.

"I love you," she whispered against my lips before pulling away.

"And I love you," I said.

There was a small torch-like device on the tray that she picked up. She paused before turning it on and lowering the metal near the flame. She was silent as she watched it heat up, turning it every few seconds.

"It will hurt," she mumbled.

"Good," I said with a smile. A small smile spread across her face when she was finished heating up the metal.

She stalked over to me.

My heart rate picked up when the brand was placed above my skin. I carefully fit the block into my mouth and looked up at Avery. I nodded to her, signaling to her I was ready.

"Such a good girl," she cooed.

She counted down from three and pushed the hot metal into my skin.

Blinding-hot pain burst from the area. My first instinct was to jerk away from it. To make the pain stop. My groans spilled from my lips and I bit down so hard on the block that I was sure if it wasn't there, I might have cracked a tooth.

Tears spilled from my eyes and the burning pain only intensified the longer it was on me.

Realistically, I knew it wasn't very long until she would pull it off, but each moment felt worse than the last. I had often burned myself on the stove or various hot irons, but this was a deeper, more intense pain than any of those.

When she pulled the iron away, there was just a bit of relief before the burning hit me again. Just because the iron had been taken away didn't mean the skin would stop burning.

I was crying heavily now. Emotions rushed through my body and I was trembling from it. They hurt even worse than the pain and for some reason, even as Avery was helping me clean the wound and apply the salve, I couldn't stop myself. She pulled the block out of my mouth, causing my loud sobs to fill the room.

"I know," she cooed and ran her hand through my hair. "Let it out. It's okay. You're safe."

Her words were my undoing. Everything from the last few months hit me like a tornado. The shootings, the kidnapping, seeing her almost die, the trial. All of it decided to rear its ugly head in that moment.

I wanted to pull Avery down into a hug, but she kept me pushed down on the chaise, probably to protect my wound.

When I could finally breathe again, I pried my eyes open to look at her.

Just like every time, I was taken aback by the rush of emotions I felt for her. It was an unconventional type of love, but it was everything to me.

She was everything to me.

Just like with painful activities during sex before, I used it as a release to let out all of the emotions that had been bubbling inside of me, this being no different. But this time, after I had let it all out, there was a wave of calmness that went through me.

"Thank you," I croaked and lifted my hand to cup her face. "I didn't mean to..."

She gave me a smile.

"It's what you needed. I see that now," she murmured. Her eyes trailed down to the branding. "I love it."

Her words sent heat flashing through me. She let me pull her down this time and deliver a light kiss to her lips.

"You're what I needed," I said. "Forever if you're willing."

Her eyes widened before she swooped down and deepened the kiss. There was still a burning pain from the branding, but her kiss, along with the grip she had on my hips, caused my body to flare to life.

"You can't get rid of me that easily," she said when she pulled away. "Wherever you go, I go. Forever."

I couldn't help the smile that spread across my face.

Yes. Forever.

It may not be what works for everyone, but it works for us, and that's all that matters.

EPILOGUE

"Hey, Dad," I mumbled as I brushed the fallen leaves off his headstone.

It had been years since I visited him. Sometimes work got in the way, but other times it was simpler than that. There was a part of me that, at times, felt too ashamed to show my face around him. As if maybe he would see right through me and realize how much I had been hurting myself to try and get over what happened.

But things were different now.

The cemetery was mostly quiet, save for a few families visiting their loved ones. I tried not to let my eyes linger on them for too long and allow them their privacy. The air was chilly, and the leaves had begun to turn various shades of red and orange. I pulled at my cardigan, wishing I had brought something heavier. But I hadn't expected to stay so long.

I was silent for a long time before I uttered my hello and then I couldn't think of anything to say after.

What do people even say when they visit a grave?

"I'm sorry I didn't come sooner," I whispered. "But I'm better now. I've started to work through... the guilt of everything."

I don't know why the words came easier after that, but it's like they were spilling out from me.

"I haven't seen Mom in years, but that's okay because now I have someone else who loves me... someone who I love as well. I don't know if I ever thought this day would come, but now all I can think about is how sad it will be when you're not here to see everything."

I imagined him at my wedding. He would have had a full head of gray hair and smile lines. I couldn't help but smile at imagining how deep the crinkle lines near his eyes would get. He always had them and in his older age, they would be more prominent.

I wished I could have seen him grow old. But sometimes even that carries a painful reminder that your parents were growing old as well and they too had only a set time on this earth.

My eyes trailed to the headstone. The fresh white roses I had brought him lay near it in a cheap vase that would no doubt get thrown away in a few days when the cleaners showed up.

"I miss you," I said after a moment. "But I want you to know I'm doing better. That I'm happy now."

I let the silence fall over me. There wasn't anything more to say. The crunching of leaves behind me told me that Avery finally decided to venture forward.

She was allowing me time with him, something I appreciated but ultimately wasn't needed.

"You can come," I called behind me and turned to smile at her. "It's not like I have anything to say that you don't know about."

She gave me a smile and shifted on her feet. Her hands were in the pocket of her hoodie and today, she had her hair back in the bun I loved so much.

She was nervous about something. I could tell from this morning when she shakily handed me my breakfast.

"He's dead," I reminded. "He's not gonna bite you."

She let out a huff before coming toward me and sitting on the ground next to me.

"Did you pick this plot?" she asked, her gaze looking around the cemetery. I nodded.

"Mother wasn't much help, but I wanted to make sure he had a good view," I said and motioned to the tree not too far from us. "I imagined him being able to sit under the tree and watch people as they came."

"You believe in ghosts?" she asked.

I shrugged. It wasn't so much that I didn't believe in ghosts, just that I didn't believe in much of anything. God, heaven, hell, the imagery was what stuck with me, but the actual beliefs surrounding them evaded me. Though it was a nice thought. Comforting sometimes.

"Not sure, but one can't be too careful, hmm?"

I sent her a smile, but it was not returned. She had that nervous look again.

She straightened her shoulders and looked down at the gravestone.

"Right," she said, then cleared her throat. "In that case. Mr. Evens, I have come to ask you if I can have your daughter's hand in marriage."

My mouth fell open, and a shocked laugh fell from my lips.

Really? This is how she was going to do this?

She gave me a glare, but it lost all its effect when I realized she wasn't joking in the slightest.

"I am very serious about this, Willow," she grumbled. "Don't interrupt me."

I slapped my hand across my mouth in hopes of keeping in the laughter.

She cleared her throat again.

"I may not be the ideal partner you would have imagined for Willow, but I can tell you I am the best." I couldn't stop the eye roll. "I will love her. Take care of her. And more importantly, I will accept her for everything that she is. I will not try to change her, nor ever hurt her. So please, with your blessing, I would like to marry your daughter."

I let her sit in silence for a few moments before placing my hand on her shoulder. Her head whipped around, and her eyes narrowed when she caught the amused smile on my lips.

"You think he's gonna answer anytime this century?"

Her lips twitched.

"Well, I haven't been shot down by lightning yet," she said, letting a playful smile spread across her lips. "What do you say, Willow? Do you think your dad would approve?"

No. He probably wouldn't have, but not because she was her or because she was a woman. Mostly because he would want her to work harder to prove she deserved me.

He was the type of father that thought none of my little partners would be worth my time. He had always been overprotective, and I bet he would have changed for her.

But... maybe he would see just how protective she was with me as well and change his mind. Though murder was hard to excuse.

"Not at all," I said truthfully and gave her a smile. "But I do. So if you're asking for my hand in marriage, you better have a ring or..."

My voice trailed off when she pulled out a black box from her pocket. The triumphant smile on her face only widened when she saw my reaction.

She opened it with a shaking hand, giving me a view of the diamond-encrusted band on the inside. It was beautiful. More simple than I would have expected from her, but beautiful. Or at least that's what I thought until she pulled it out to show me that her initials were on the inside and slightly raised so that whenever I took it off, her initials would leave a light indent on my finger.

She's crazy possessive... but I fucking love it.

I looked up at her with a smile. I didn't miss the extra shake in her hands or how her triumphant smile turned into a nervous one. Just like at the house, she hadn't expected this reaction from me.

"I see," I said. "The brand faded, so you needed something like this?"

When she frowned, I let out a small laugh.

I gave her my left hand. She slid it on my ring finger. It fit perfectly. But of course it did.

"Are you gonna ask me?" I asked with a raised brow, enjoying the way it flustered her.

She swallowed thickly. The tips of her ears turned the cutest shade of pink.

"Will you marry me, Ms. Evens?" She said after a moment, all her nervous thoughts written across her face,

I leaned forward with a smile, putting both my hands on the side of her face.

"Yes," I whispered. "Though it'll be Mrs. Maddox soon."

She caught me off guard by tackling me to the ground and peppered me with kisses. I let out a surprised laugh before pulling her lips to mine. She groaned into my mouth and held me tight against her.

There was an excitement to her kiss that I wholeheartedly returned.

The sound of a throat clearing caused us to pause and remember... that we were making out in a fucking graveyard.

We broke apart to see Lillian and Sloan peek their heads out from behind the tree. Lillian had a camera in her hand and an excited smile on her face.

"Congrats!" she yelled across the space.

I looked at Avery, shocked.

"You invited them?" I asked. "What if I said no?"

She gave me an incredulous look.

"You wouldn't have."

There was so much confidence in her voice that it should've annoyed me, but it didn't.

She was right. From the moment I met her, I was obsessed. She had controlled my every thought, dream, and hope since then. In my mind, there was no life without her... and I didn't want there to be one.

And now, I had friends to celebrate with as well. It may not have been the life I chose for myself in the first place, but this was my life now and I wouldn't let the darkness take it from me ever again.

THE END

It's been years since my first kill. I have my process down to a science.

And maybe sometimes I even allow myself to **enjoy it**.

But when I'm asked to infiltrate Club Pétale to get close to a target, I never expected how my entire life would shift.

Blake. An easy target.

Or at least she was supposed to be.

I've never felt love, but when her green eyes looked at me with such warmth, I'd like to believe it felt something like that.

But a job is a job, and no matter what, *I would see the end to this.*

CONTINUE ON FOR A BONUS EPILOGUE

Bonus Epilogue

How the fuck did I get roped into this?

    I blamed my younger self for being such a fucking idiot.

Though Avery Maddox, heir to the Maddox empire, wasn't a person to mess with. Getting noticed by her was more of a curse than a blessing. She would make my life harder than it had to be. And with the added complication of my little secret service agent, I didn't need any more of her shit piling up.

Last I heard, even though her father was in jail for the rest of his life, there had been multiple attempts on his life by none other than his own child. I had to hand it to her though. Her level of dedication to killing the man was impressive.

Maybe if I lived another life, we could be friends.

Though the reasons for killing people may have been different, it was a bond we shared and for the first time since I got into this career, I found myself wanting to foster that bond.

That's why even though I told her I wouldn't listen to her demands, I found myself in FBI Agent Jonson's house while his wife and child slept peacefully upstairs. It wasn't even about the blackmail she had on me anymore. I realized very quickly that if she used it, she would be losing an ally she couldn't afford to.

And even though I was shit at reading others' emotions, I could sense that she, too, was interested in what I had become after all these years apart.

Before when I slipped a note into his car on her request, I hadn't known that Special Agent Jonson had an almost fully grown child and wife. I assumed, like all slimy agents, that he preferred to be unbound. They seemed happy, even if his work took up the majority of their lives.

I had been staking the place on and off for a few days in-between my work with Tiffany and not once had I seen any indication that the family was anything but happy.

It was stupid of him to keep them here. I had found the place and broken in just as easily. It's like he hadn't had the forethought to realize how dangerous his work would be for his family.

Not that I cared, but it put into perspective just how careless he had been.

I relaxed a bit when the sound of his front door opening broke the silence. *Finally, I could get this shit over with.*

He shut the door behind him and locked it, but he had been doing this long enough that he had already sensed my presence before putting his bag down. Avery complained about his inability to do his job but even at his age, his instincts were still sharp.

He ran into the kitchen, his eyes wide and searching for me. I wondered what tipped him off. Maybe it was the way I turned his welcome mat slightly askew. Or how I moved the bowl he stashed his keys in slightly to the left.

I raised my hands in the air and sent him a smile, though I knew he couldn't see it through the mask that covered my face.

To him, all he saw was a woman in tactical gear, gloves, and a zip-up hoodie. Though he could see my eyes, and by the look on his face, it only scared him more.

Some people got off on that fear, but I didn't. If anything, the fear was so predictable now it was boring.

Though, his eyes... his eyes showed me everything he hoped to have kept inside. They showed me how wary he was of me while also letting me know how much he was beating himself up. Eyes were such expressive little things and a few of the only things that I allowed myself to obsess over.

His were particularly telling.

"What is the Sapphire Demon doing here?"

Ew. I cringed at the nickname.

After being in my world for so long and killing the people I did, there was obviously going to be some sort of nickname. Though I just wished that people could get a bit more creative with it. And it just sounded *so* nerdy.

I was almost surprised he knew who I was when Sloan and Ax clearly didn't.

"A favor," I said, keeping my voice low. "And to deliver a present."

I motioned to the brilliant green emerald in the middle of his island. I wasn't surprised he didn't notice it until that very moment, and suddenly, everything that little psychopath was complaining about made sense.

He looked it over for a second before reaching out as if to grab it.

"Stop." He shot me a look, and I held out my gloved hands for him to look at. "This diamond was recently stolen from a traveling art dealer. It would be a pity if your prints were left on it."

He let out a sigh and ran a hand through his graying hair.

"Just spit it out. What do you want me to do with it?"

I shrugged. This was a *present* for him to do what he pleased with. At least that's what Avery said, but that didn't mean I wouldn't try to push him in the right direction.

"I heard there will be a raid on Senator Bennett's house in the coming week," I murmured.

His eyebrows shot to his hairline.

"What do *you* want with a senator?"

"I don't."

I didn't want him. More importantly, I wanted him gone. It was hard to move around Tiffany when he was in the spotlight. Especially after he had announced he was running for president. If Jonson could make this stick, maybe there would be a chance for Tiffany to get off his detail and for me to finally make my move.

He looked at me for an answer.

"I don't need to spell it out for you, do I?" I asked. "This is your present from the crazy one. Do with it what you wish, but my recommendation is Senator Bennett. Russell Maddox will be going through trial after trial and there's no telling when the FBI will promote you. Use this to speed things up."

I pushed off the counter and headed toward the door that led out to his backyard. Past the tree line awaited my car and if I was quick enough, I would be back at the club and in front of her in twenty minutes.

My entire body was on edge just thinking about seeing her tonight. It was different than with the other targets. She was my forty-second target. I had gotten this down to a science. But somehow, she had outshined all the rest.

"Wait, that's it?" His voice rose an octave at my sudden movement.

"Yep. Try and find me, and I kill you."

I couldn't make it out fully, but I could have sworn he muttered, "*Thank God.*"

The club was the same as it always had been. Packed with people. Their light conversations filled the halls, mingling with the low vibrations of the music that filtered through the speakers.

The music varied from room to room and I weaved through the space with no plan. I knew I would come across her at some point anyway. It had been years since I had been able to get out of my cave and be around people so often. It was almost refreshing. It helped that Tiffany had a schedule, something I loved about her.

The inside of the club was stifling. The button shirt I had on stuck to my chest uncomfortably, and the slacks were itchy. I missed my normal gear, but it would look out of place here. I would have shown up in a hoodie if it wasn't against the rules they sent out.

The sleek black mask sat comfortably on my face, though I still felt far too exposed. People looked as I walked by as if sensing that I wasn't supposed to be there. Rolf, my handler, had told me to draw as little attention as possible, but by my third time there, I had given up on it.

They could look. But only if she did as well.

I walked into the voyeurism hall. It was only a few shallow rooms that lined the space. Couples, or even sometimes more than that, would rent out the room to live out their fantasies while people walked by.

The two on the right had a one-way mirror in place, while the one on the left only had clear glass. The first glass one drew my attention because a very familiar brunette was on the bed in the middle, facing the small crowd that had gathered.

Her moans filtered through the halls and sent a burst of heat right through me.

I turned to her room and positioned myself right in front. Just like always, she took my breath away.

Her head was thrown back, her mouth open, allowing her moans to spill out, her hair was damp and sticking to the sides of her black mask. Her skin was flushed and her green eyes were wide as she took in the crowd.

God, those eyes. Even behind the mask, they were so expressive. They told me everything her file left out. Her need to be cared for. Her need to be used. Her need to be degraded and humiliated.

And even her pain. She hid it well, but I saw it all.

She didn't even bother to look at the two people fucking her.

One was underneath her, they lay on the bed while driving an impossibly large strap deep into her pussy. Another was behind, taking her ass. There was a collar on her throat that the one in the back had the leash to. They yanked on it, forcing her head back.

The one below her used this chance to pull her erect nipple into her mouth.

Tiffany Yates. A longtime performer at Club Pétale. She could pull anyone in with the bat of her eyelashes and keep them frozen with just a single sigh from her mouth.

She was perfect in every way... and my target. In just a matter of months or weeks, if I did my job right, the person who put a hit out on her would wire me money on the delivery of her head to him.

I doubted he knew about what she did here. Or how she had changed her whole identity to fit in.

Here she didn't go by that highly unflattering name.

Here, she went by Blake.

WANT EXCLUSIVE NSFW ART?

For NSFW DFM art (and other series) join my Patreon!

I also update my novellas on there every other week and they are the FIRST to get ARCS of all my newest releases!

Check it out here or go to https://www.patreon.com/ellemaebooks

Acknowledgments

Thank you to everyone who continues to support me on this journey! We are officially twos years past since I published my first book and because of you it's looking more and more like I have shot at this thing.

Also to Bex (who you may know as Ashley pines) for constantly supporting me. Even when I can't answer simple questions like, "What's the conflict?"

And of course to my lovely wife for not judging me for these books!

About the Author

Eden Emory is a contemporary spicy pen name for Elle Mae. This pen name will mostly focus on spicy dark wlw romance that pushes the boundaries and incorporates troupes normally seen in f/m romance.

Eden Emory was born out of a want for more. More spice, more wlw, and even more smutty vibes with little to no plot.

Loved this book? Please leave a review!

For more behind the scene content, sign up for my newsletter at https://view.flodesk.com/pages/61722d0874d564fa09f4021b

 twitter.com/mae_books

 instagram.com/edenrosebooks

 goodreads.com/ellemae

Made in United States
North Haven, CT
10 October 2023

42586407R00187